The Lives Before Us

'Superb storytelling! *The Lives Before Us* chronicles the courage and endurance of two women in wartime Shanghai, separated, then reunited, in a dangerous and desperate place. Strongly drawn characters quickly demand attention, and empathy, and their compelling story charts a little-known aspect of the Second World War, and of a persecution felt far beyond Europe. Very well written and well researched. Thoroughly recommended!'
— SARAH MAINE, author of *The House Between Tides*

'Juliet Conlin vividly recreates the lost world of wartime Shanghai's Jewish ghetto – a place of hope and despair in equal measure; a city of temporary refuge, yet continuing daily struggle. I was absorbed.'
— PAUL FRENCH, author of *Midnight in Peking*

'Opens up a captivating new world in a war I thought I knew about, a raucous Casablanca transposed to the East, filled with the intrigues of outcasts and determined survivors.'
— ALEX CHRISTOFI, author of *Let Us Be True*

'Brings wartime Shanghai so vividly to life with a wealth of fascinating detail.'
— SARA SHERIDAN, author of the Mirabelle Bevan series

'Mesmerising and compelling, A beautifully written novel, telling a little-known story from World War Two. Once you start reading this, you'll have to finish.'
— EI ___ ___ ___ *saw*

'I recommend this book with my heart and soul. It's life changing!'
— LOVE BOOKS GROUP

'The book really drives home how one single moment – one chance meeting, can have such a profound effect . . . It's unique, gripping and beautifully written.'
— BIBLIOPHILE CHRONICLES

'A mesmerising, empathetic, gripping story, quite often heart-wrenching too . . . I loved every minute of it! This is a book that you will take into your heart and never let it go. Alfred's story needs to be heard, and you need to hear it.'
— WHISPERING STORIES

'A book which made me feel profound sadness for Alfred at times, but also great joy. Juliet Conlin is a natural storyteller and it almost felt as though Alfred was talking directly to me . . . It is a memorable tale of hope and shows that being a little bit different isn't always a bad thing.'
— PORTOBELLO BOOK BLOG

'There is an endearing, insightful and captivating experience listening to an elderly person reflect on the events and experiences they witnessed during their life. When those events include world wars or other major historical moments, then be prepared to sit up all night long listening or reading. When the writing is as good as Juliet Conlin's, you will be immersed in the life of Alfred Warner. It is a very sentimental and poignant story of reflection, loss, love, and a family secret Alfred must pass on.'
— THE READING DESK BLOG

SISTERS
of
BERLIN

SISTERS *of* BERLIN

JULIET CONLIN

BLACK & WHITE PUBLISHING

First published 2020
by Black & White Publishing Ltd
Nautical House, 104 Commercial Street
Edinburgh, EH6 6NF

1 3 5 7 9 10 8 6 4 2   20 21 22 23

ISBN: 978 1 78530 288 6

A CIP catalogue record for this book is available from the British Library.

Typeset by Iolaire Typesetting, Newtonmore
Printed and bound by CPI Group (UK) Ltd, Croydon, CR0 4YY

To Jenny Brown

July, 2019

The sun had set over an hour ago, but the sky was still tinged with a pink blush, the air thick and warm as a blanket. They were sitting on Marie's ornate but crumbling balcony, between them a small table with a citronella candle and the oily remnants of the tapas that had taken an hour to prepare and only minutes to demolish.

Marie topped up their wine glasses, almost to the brim. Her short hair, as dark as Nina's was light, curled up damply at her neck.

'Here, eat,' she said, pushing the plate with the last few toothpick-skewered chorizo slices towards Nina. Nina reached out to take one, savouring the spicy, garlicky meat on her tongue.

'So, how's it going?' Marie continued.

Nina swallowed. 'How's what going?'

'The practice.'

'Well, lots of mums are away in the summer holidays, so it's normal for things to be quiet.' She glanced out across the street. From here, on the second floor, she could see into the little grassy square on Boxhagener Platz. Wisps of smoke from illegal barbeques drifted into the sky, and the happy drunken laughs and shouts coming from the park fit the mellow summer mood perfectly. The yellow flame of the candle was perfectly still.

Marie had been living here for two years, in this small grubby flat in the district of Friedrichshain, the longest she had ever lived in one place since she'd left their parents' home. Nina wondered if she was starting to put down roots, and felt an unexpected tug of sadness that the burden of adult life might finally have caught up with her vivacious, carefree little sister. But it was for the best, wasn't it? Everyone had to grow up sooner or later.

Marie put her head to one side. 'So you're worried about the practice?'

Nina shrugged.

'Hey. It's me you're talking to.'

'I know, sorry,' Nina said. 'Yes, I'm worried about how few patients I have, but I tell myself I just need to give it time. And I do love being my own boss.'

'Me too,' Marie said, smiling.

'Not quite the same thing.' Nina exhaled loudly. 'It's so much responsibility. I lie awake at night fretting. But I really want it to work.'

'You'll be fine,' Marie said and placed a hand on Nina's, squeezing gently. 'It's early days. And I've been recommending you left, right and centre.' She sat back and lit a cigarette. 'Besides,' she continued, 'it's easy for you. Everything you touch turns to gold.'

Nina cocked an eyebrow and gave her sister a side glance. 'Listen, if you need a bit of money, I can give you a hundred, max. I'm not exactly flush –'

For a moment, Marie didn't speak, just stared at the glowing tip of her cigarette. She shook her head. 'No, I don't need any money.'

Nina laughed. 'What? I never thought I'd see the day! D'you win the lottery or something?'

Marie blew a neat column of smoke circles. 'No, I've been careful with my spending, that's all.' She reached over to pluck a birch seed from Nina's hair. She opened her mouth to speak, then her eyes slipped away from Nina's. 'I spoke to Bekka the other day. She wants to sleep over, while the school holidays are still on.'

'Have you two been making secret plans or something?' Nina boxed her sister playfully on the arm. Despite Sebastian's misgivings, she was pleased that Bekka and Marie got along so well. The relationship brought out the best in both of them, she thought.

Marie grinned. Her lips were stained bluish from the Beaujolais. 'Everyone's entitled to a secret or two.'

Nina boxed her again. 'Ha! Not on my watch.'

1

Kommissar Franzen is younger than he sounds on the telephone. Mid-thirties, perhaps, with short dark hair and mild eyes. He doesn't look like a police detective, Nina thinks, before she realises the only detectives she knows are those in films and on TV. But still, he looks like someone better suited to a caring profession than investigating violent crime – a social worker. Or a teacher.

'I hope my visit isn't inconvenient,' he says and shakes her hand with a smile that is unexpectedly disarming.

'No.' Nina offers him a seat and sits down behind her desk. 'I do get male visitors here now and again,' she says, 'but they're usually accompanied by their pregnant partners.'

He laughs gently, and she realises he's interpreted her words as a joke. She notices the warmth in his eyes and for a snatch of a moment, the reason for his visit seems forgotten. Then something in her stomach twists and hardens. She skipped breakfast this morning, couldn't face even half a slice of toast after Franzen called to arrange the meeting. She takes a deep breath to dispel the queasiness.

Franzen takes a TicTac box out of his shirt pocket. 'Would you like one?' he asks.

She shakes her head. He taps out two mints and pops them in his mouth.

'My allergy pills give me a dry mouth,' he says, as if in apology. Then he chews the mints, swallows, and clears his throat.

'Dr Bergmann, I'd like to ask you some questions about your sister.' He pauses.

She has been expecting his words, and yet they hit her with force, like the unanticipated shock of bumping painfully into the corner of a chair in the dark.

'When was the last time you saw Marie?' he asks. 'Before the attack.'

Nina takes a breath. Her throat is hot and tight and it's an effort to push out the words. 'Last week. Wednesday. She came for dinner.'

'To your house?'

'Yes.'

'Then you'll know that she was pregnant.'

Nina is not prepared for this. She stares at him, wordless, can think of nothing to say.

'Approximately ten weeks,' he continues after a pause, his eyes resting on her. He seems to be expecting a reaction. He waits for a moment, then clarifies: 'You didn't know?'

She shakes her head.

'So you're not close?' he asks. Then, 'What's the age difference between you and your sister – five years?'

'Ten.' And, then to correct his initial assumption, she says, 'We *are* close.' She pauses. 'Very. I thought we were. I –'

Franzen puts his hands on his lap. 'I'm sorry,' he says, his face flushed, 'I didn't mean to – I thought, because of what you do, professionally I mean, your sister is bound to have told you.'

'Marie and I are very close,' Nina repeats. She keeps her face blank while her brain struggles to process what he's just told her. 'Perhaps . . . perhaps she wanted to wait before she told me. For another couple of weeks. Just to be sure, you know? After twelve weeks, the risk of miscarriage drops significantly.' She pauses, hears the words echo inside her head. This is what she recently told a patient when she confirmed an early pregnancy. The woman had been trying for years to become pregnant and was desperately afraid of disappointing her partner. For her, a miscarriage would have constituted a personal failure, and nothing Nina said managed to convince her otherwise. But Marie? Surely she would have known she could count on Nina's support and understanding?

But then Franzen nods. 'Yes, that's probably it.'

Something in his voice, something soothing, gives her the feeling that he's right. That must be it. There would be no other reason for Marie to keep it a secret. When Nina found out she was pregnant with Kai seven years ago, she hadn't waited an hour to tell Marie. But by then, it would have been too late to do anything about it anyway.

'*Was*,' she says quietly.

'Sorry?'

'You said she *was* pregnant. Not *is*.'

Franzen nods slowly. 'She lost the baby as a result of the assault. I'm sorry.'

It's not your fault, Nina wants to say, but stays silent. Her mind is curdling. She feels seasick. Her sister was found yesterday in her flat by her elderly next-door neighbour, beaten, bleeding and unconscious. She hasn't yet recovered consciousness, is lying in intensive care, wired up to machines. Before Nina can stop it, she sees in her mind the swollen, purple eyes, the bandaged head, the tube coming out of Marie's mouth, pulling the corners of her mouth downwards so that it looks as if she's on the verge of crying.

'Dr Bergmann?'

Nina blinks. The image fades, leaving behind a sick, hollow desperation. 'Yes. What did you say?'

He frowns. 'Please forgive me if this question sounds clichéd, but did you notice anything different, anything out of the ordinary, about your sister when you saw her on Wednesday? Was she quieter than usual, or livelier? Did she mention anything unusual?'

'No,' Nina says immediately and only then stops to think about the last time she saw Marie, whether something, however trivial, has stuck in her memory that might be considered odd in retrospect. But nothing comes to mind. Marie arrived just in time for dinner on Wednesday evening, at around seven, unannounced. But this is something she does regularly, at least twice a month. Sebastian wasn't happy about it, though that wasn't exactly a surprise, either. He considers it rude to drop in on other people's mealtimes.

'Your sister was in a relationship with a –' Franzen hesitates, evidently retrieving a name from memory, 'a certain Robert Kran until two or three months ago, is that right?'

'Yes. How do you know?'

'I visited your parents yesterday evening,' he says, 'and asked them similar questions.'

'Oh.'

'Did Marie mention a new boyfriend? Or that she got back together with Herr Kran?'

'No. She definitely doesn't have a new boyfriend,' Nina says, then adds, 'She would have told me.' Trying to sound convincing, to herself and to Franzen.

'And Herr Kran?'

'No. Robert moved to Leipzig two months ago. They're still in touch, they're still friends, but as far as I know, he has a new girlfriend.'

'Well, it sounds like you're in the know,' Franzen says, but she can still hear doubt in his voice.

'I certainly am,' she says, coolly. 'As I said, we don't have secrets from each other.'

Franzen leans forward, his eyes kind. 'Dr Bergmann, I appreciate how difficult this is for you. If you'd prefer, I could come back another time, to your house, if that's more convenient.'

'No, it's fine,' she assures him. 'At home – well, the children don't know the details of what happened to Marie yet. I'm not sure how they'd cope.'

This morning at breakfast, Kai and Rebekka wanted to know when they could visit Aunty Marie in hospital. Nina and Sebastian have decided not to tell the children about the attack; not yet, anyway. As far as Kai and Rebekka are concerned, their aunt is in hospital recovering from an accident.

'I understand,' Franzen says. 'But they'll have to be told sooner or later. I might need to talk to them.'

Nina looks down and runs her finger along the edge of the desk. She straightens a patient file that is lying askew. 'We'll see.'

'So,' he continues. 'Marie was – is – still in contact with Herr Kran. I'm sorry, would you mind if I took some notes?'

'Please, go ahead,' she says and wonders vaguely why he asked. Surely he doesn't need her permission.

He takes a spiral notepad and pen from his jacket pocket. She almost smiles. Suddenly he seems just like the police detectives on TV.

'Do you have any idea who might have attacked her?' she asks him as he doodles on his notepad until the pen releases its ink. He isn't wearing a wedding ring, she notices.

'That's exactly what I wanted to ask you,' he says, then adds: 'Great minds.'

That smile again. It throws her off balance.

'You assume Marie knows her attacker?' she asks.

'I'm not assuming anything yet, Dr Bergmann. But statistically speaking, it's most likely that she knows him. Or her.'

The desk phone rings. It's the internal line. Franzen nods his approval, although she didn't ask for it. She feels a strong surge of irritation towards him as she reaches for the phone, and forces herself to take a deep breath. It isn't his fault. It occurs to her that she has been in a position similar to his, having to inform a desperate patient she is unlikely ever to become a mother, feeling the sickening shape of a tell-tale lump in a middle-aged woman's breast, seeing the dread in another's eyes when she has to inform her that her smear test results are 'abnormal'. Those are the times she wants to discard her professional distance and wrap the women in her arms, promising them everything will be okay – knowing it is a lie.

She picks up the phone. 'Yes?'

Her receptionist, Anita, tells her that Frau Scholz had now been waiting for half an hour and was getting restless.

'Okay, Anita,' she says, 'I'll only be five more minutes. Thanks.'

She puts the phone down and looks up at Franzen. He's staring out of the window, lost in thought.

'Kommissar Franzen.' She gets to her feet. Too quickly. The blood drains from her head. 'My patients are waiting. If there's nothing else . . .'

Her speech is slow and stupid, her head feels like it's full of ash. This meeting has exhausted her and she still has a long day left at the surgery.

'Of course,' Franzen says, but he sounds disappointed. 'Thank you for your time. I'll be in touch, of course, but if you think of anything, or if you have any questions –'

He pulls a card out of his pocket and hands it to her.

'Thank you,' she says and lays the square of white card on her desk.

'One last thing.' He frowns, as if the thought has just occurred to him. 'Your husband, Sebastian. How does he get on with Marie?'

She doesn't like his tone. 'They get on fine,' she says tersely. 'They're not best friends, or enemies. They get on like brother- and sister-in-law.'

Franzen nods. 'Thank you, Dr Bergmann,' he says and goes, leaving her oddly bereft and regretting the sharpness of her last words.

2

Nina doesn't actually need the toilet, so instead, she stands at the sink and assesses her reflection in the mirror, waiting an appropriate amount of time before until she can re-join Sebastian and her parents at the table. She's utterly spent. No, more than that – she's numb and on edge at the same time, and it's almost more than she can bear.

But she'll have to bear it. She'll have to bear it until the moment Marie recovers, when she finally wakes from the barbiturate-induced coma, when they know there will be no lasting brain damage, when Nina can hold her beautiful, vibrant, glorious sister in her arms and they can joke about the faint, jagged scar that remains just above her left eye, dream up wild stories about a bar fight, or a shark attack, or a secret double-agent operation gone wrong. The kind of adventure stories Marie made up when she was younger. People assumed they stemmed from her overactive imagination; Nina has often wondered whether Marie had, in fact, simply been writing herself into roles she found easier to inhabit.

Now Nina finds herself gripping the edge of the sink so tightly her fingers are beginning to ache. The longing for Marie to recover, and the dread she might not, leave a hot, shocked tightness in her chest. She takes a deep breath and traces the shape of her face with her hands, runs them over her cheekbones and then pulls a face, making fine wrinkles appear around her eyes. She relaxes again and waits for the wrinkles to fade.

Kommissar Franzen hasn't been in touch since his visit to the practice. That was four days ago and there has been no change in Marie's condition. She is stable, they say, but because of the barb coma, they can't tell if her vital functions are actually improving, or whether her survival is entirely dependent on the machines her body is wired up to.

Every evening Nina goes to the hospital, where she sits in Marie's small, sterile room with her parents. These evenings are intolerable: hours that drag on, filled with tense, silent waiting. They don't talk much – what is there to say? – yet Nina can read the unspoken reproaches in her mother's eyes, can barely endure her father's wordless stoicism, while they wait for Marie to wake up or die. It was Sebastian's suggestion that they all go for a meal after the hospital visit today, and Nina didn't know how to refuse.

She pulls her mobile out of her pocket and checks the time. Eleven minutes past eight. She should have checked the time as soon as she left the table, but she reckons that a little over ten minutes has passed. She leaves the Ladies' and walks up the staircase from the toilets, where their faint stench melds unpleasantly with the smells – olive oil, garlic, rosemary – from the restaurant kitchen. From across the room she can see that Sebastian is in animated conversation with her parents. She sits down beside him.

'You were gone for a while,' he says, as Nina assesses the

remains of the mixed appetiser plate: a pale, tired pile of *vitello tonnato*, a stuffed pepper and two greasy slices of baked aubergine.

The sight of it makes her feel ill. Marie hated aubergine when she was a child, family dinners would erupt into arguments when she refused to finish what was on her plate. *I will never make my own children eat food they hate*, Nina thinks, flicking through her memory to see if she has in fact done this, with mushrooms perhaps, or asparagus soup, and then notices Sebastian looking at her as though expecting an answer.

'I'm sorry, what did you say?'

'I was wondering if you're okay, baby. You were gone for ages.'

'I'm fine.' She takes her starched napkin and unfolds it on her lap.

'We haven't left you much, I'm afraid,' he says with a sweeping gesture.

'Well, that's what happens if you spend half the evening on the toilet,' her mother says bluntly. She's sitting opposite, her face softly illuminated by the candles on the table. The setting feels inappropriately romantic.

'It's fine,' Nina says. 'I'm not that hungry, anyway.'

'But you've hardly eaten all day,' Sebastian says, 'and you barely touched your dinner last night.'

'Perhaps that's because my sister has suffered a brutal attack in her own home!' Nina says, surprised at the loudness of her voice. 'Perhaps you'll concede the fact that she's lying in intensive care and fighting for her life is reason enough to ruin my appetite.'

Sebastian lays his hand on her arm. 'Hey, baby, take it easy,' he murmurs. 'Nobody wants you to eat if you don't feel like it.'

She breathes out shakily. She's not herself. No one can expect her to act normally; not under these circumstances.

Their waiter comes to the table. '*Va bene?*' he asks, his head tilted to one side.

'*Si*,' Sebastian replies.

The waiter clears the table and no one speaks. When he walks off with his arms full of plates, her mother tells her, 'You're behaving like a child.'

'Please,' her father says, 'we're all just very tired.'

Nina glances up at her mother. She returns the look, maintains eye contact. *If you hadn't got her that awful flat in Friedrichshain,* Nina can read in her eyes, *living next door to squatters and anarchists, filth and graffiti everywhere, if you hadn't encouraged her to drop out of university, if you hadn't sat by idly, watching as she ruined her life for the sake of 'artistic creativity', if you hadn't, if you hadn't . . .*

She feels, for a moment, exactly as she had when she was younger, when Marie had done something naughty, or something stupid, and for some reason, in the eyes of their parents, Nina was to blame. She was the one cornered into taking responsibility. Except this time, Marie hasn't done anything at all. Someone else has done something terrible to Marie, and this fact changes the rules of the game fundamentally.

'I know you think it's my fault,' Nina says calmly.

'Don't be ridiculous,' her mother snaps. 'This is not about you, for once.'

Nina flinches, gut-punched. She is back at the dining room table of her youth, being reproached for letting a teacher's praise go to her head, or for humming too loudly when her mother had one of her 'migraines'.

'Of course it's not your fault,' Sebastian says. 'Hans is right, we're all just very tired.'

It's true. She feels drained, more tired than she has in ages. It is a deep emotional and physical exhaustion, the kind that requires more than a good night's sleep to shake off. She recognises that parched sense of hollowness: the last time she felt this way was in the weeks after Kai was born.

Her father breaks the silence. 'Sebastian was telling us that the doctor suggests reading to Marie while she's in the coma. Or playing her favourite music.'

'When did he suggest that?' Nina asks, confused. She had been at Marie's bedside the whole time, like always, and can't remember hearing the doctor mention reading, or music.

'Yesterday,' her mother says.

'You went to the hospital yesterday?' Nina asks Sebastian. 'You never told me.'

He shrugs. 'What's to tell? I was seeing a client a couple of streets away and thought I'd pop in during lunch.'

'But –'

'I think that was very thoughtful of him, Nina,' her mother says. 'And it's not as though you make the effort to visit your sister during the day.'

'You know very well I can't leave the surgery whenever I feel like it,' she replies, defensive and snappy, hating herself for reacting like this, like a child.

'Yes, well –', her mother begins, but Sebastian interrupts her gently.

'She's doing her best, Antonia, I'm sure. And Nina's got so much on her plate right now, am I right, darling?' He cups the nape of her neck and squeezes.

Nina wants to scream and lash out at his touch, imagines herself jumping up and running to the hospital, shaking Marie out of her coma. A wild rushing in her ears, black and deafening, ends abruptly as the waiter arrives and places a plate of ravioli in gorgonzola sauce in front of her. She stares at the steaming pasta and is seized by an appetite so overwhelming she cannot wait until the others have their plates in front of them. Instead, she starts eating, her hunger uncontrollable. The ravioli are hot, she scalds her tongue, but she doesn't stop until her plate is empty. Finally, without looking up, she takes one – no, two – slices of soft white bread from the basket beside her and wipes the thick, creamy sauce from the plate.

'Well, you certainly seem to be hungry all of a sudden,' Sebastian says, smiling indulgently at her.

Nina doesn't answer. She's hardly eaten for two days and it's as though her stomach has shrunk as a result. Now her jeans are cutting into her waist and she's finding it hard to breathe; she's afraid that if she moves, she will throw up.

It takes almost twenty minutes until the others have finally, politely cleared their plates and the waiter returns.

'Would you care for a grappa on the house?' he asks.

'I'd like to go home now,' Nina says, before anyone can consider the offer.

Sebastian hesitates, but she adds quickly that Rebekka

is babysitting Kai and will be in a bolshy teenage mood if they get home too late.

*

Rebekka is sitting in the dark watching TV when they get home. Nina gives her a goodnight kiss before sending her upstairs, and asks Sebastian to check on Kai, offering to do a quick tidy up and make sure the back door is locked. She waits until he has climbed the stairs and goes into the downstairs toilet, locking herself in.

She turns to face the wall, rests her forehead on the cool, white tiles and takes several shallow breaths. A surge of self-hatred stronger than she's felt for years washes over her. Her mother was right, she is a selfish, over-sensitive bitch. That's probably why Marie didn't tell her about the baby. That tiny cluster of cells in which her sister's DNA was hidden, now dead. She lets herself slide to the floor until she's kneeling in front of the toilet bowl. Her waist-band digs into her belly making her feel sick. Serves her right for eating such a disgusting amount of pasta. She takes a deep breath and holds it, knows what she has to do. Losing control now isn't going to help anyone.

Ten minutes later, at the sink, she rinses her mouth out with water several times, not daring to look in the mirror. Then, she summons all her courage and looks up at her reflection.

'I swear,' she says, not quite out loud. 'Just this once.'

3

On the day Marie dies, two weeks after the attack, the summer returns forcefully and unexpectedly. It's late September and the warm weather has turned the city inside out. On every pavement, every street corner, people sit in sunglasses or baseball caps, faces turned greedily towards the sun, ashtrays and *Eiskaffees* and frothy-topped beers on the tables beside them. Public parks abound with naked toddlers and overexcited dogs and Nordic walkers and multi-generation Turkish families cooking over aluminium barbecues – all desperate to relish as much outdoor life as they can before the cold, dark winter sweeps into Berlin.

Nina drives past all of this to the hospital as fast as she can without risking an accident, or rather, as fast as traffic will permit. The air-conditioning is on the blink, and before long, she's sitting in a moving sauna. Her skirt slid up as she got into the car, and now her thighs are sticking uncomfortably to the imitation leather seat. The sweetish smell of a half-eaten, half-rotten apple, which is lying next to Kai's booster seat at the back, spreads through the thick air. She cranks open the window. Traffic has slowed to a crawl. She's caught in a frustrating sequence of accelerating and braking, accelerating and braking, while her heart is beating so hard she can feel it in her mouth.

When she arrives at the hospital, she double parks and dashes across the car park. Her clothes are sticking to her damp skin as if she'd stood under a tepid shower in them, but she hardly notices as she runs up the stairs toward the ICU. Sebastian, pale and tired, is waiting there on the other side of the automatic doors. The door opens as Nina approaches, and she shivers as the air-conditioned chill comes into contact with her skin. The tart smell of disinfectant catches in her throat. Sebastian opens his arms for her; she lets him embrace her and feels his heat.

'How long have you been here?' she whispers.

'I only just got here. Your mother called me.'

He gestures to the right with his head. Nina's parents are locked in a desolate embrace on the landing in front of Marie's cubicle. She can hear them weeping, and with a sudden swoop of guilt, she resents their grief.

'She didn't say it was urgent,' she says.

'Who?'

'My mother. She rang work and left a message with Anita that I should ring the hospital when it was convenient. *Convenient.* I was in a meeting with a pharma sales rep, and when I came out, Anita told me about the call. I only found out half an hour ago that – oh god – they told me she'd … she'd died.'

She presses her hand to her mouth. Sebastian goes to put his arms around her again, but she pushes him away.

Oh god. Marie is dead. She's struggling to breathe and hears herself sobbing; making noises that sound alien and hoarse, as though it weren't her making them, but instead some wounded animal.

Sebastian breaks her resistance and takes her tightly in his arms. 'Shhh, baby,' he says, 'shhh.'

'I want to see her,' Nina says, when her breathing has levelled itself out a little.

'Not right now,' he says. 'They're –'

'I don't care, I want to see her.' She frees herself from his arms, walks past her parents, into Marie's cubicle, where a nurse is in the process of removing the ventilation tube from Marie's mouth. It makes a small sucking noise on its way out. Marie doesn't look much different than on the previous visits; she's lying on the bed, washed-out and sad. Just from the absolute silence, the absence of the hissing and pulsing of the machines, Nina knows this is the last time she will ever see her sister.

The nurse looks up. 'Give me ten minutes,' she says gently. 'Then you can say goodbye.'

When Nina doesn't respond, the nurse comes and places her hand tenderly on her arm. 'Come on,' she says, and guides Nina out of the room. 'Dr Krüger will want to speak to you,' she adds. 'With you and your parents. To talk you through the next steps and –' She hesitates. 'And about whether your sister had a donor card.'

Marie's organs failed her, Nina wants to say, but can't find the strength to speak. In the corridor, she lets herself be handed over into Sebastian's arms.

4

'You look great,' Sebastian whispers into Nina's ear.

She looks at herself in the bedroom mirror and is ashamed to feel pleased that the black dress fits her again.

'Black is slimming,' she says.

'It's not the dress,' he replies. 'It's you.'

Nina looks away. 'Please don't, Basti. Not now.'

Sebastian straightens his tie in the mirror. The height difference between them is large enough for him to be able to do so over her head. Then he presses his body against hers, leans forward and kisses her on the neck.

'Please, just . . . don't,' she says again.

'What? Don't what?'

'You know what. This isn't a good time.'

He takes a step to the side and looks straight at her. 'What are you implying?' His tone is irritable, challenging.

'I'm not implying anything,' she replies. She fixes a loose strand of blond hair into a clip and then picks up a packet of tissues from the bedside table.

'You know,' says Sebastian, as she heads out of the bedroom, 'this sort of thing brings some families closer together.'

She pauses at the door. She can feel her eyes starting

to well up. She searches for the words to explain how it's impossible to be touched, to feel the comfort of another body, to *know* you are alive – as though it were nothing. 'I'm sorry,' is all she can manage.

In the kitchen, Rebekka and Kai are squabbling. They fall silent as soon as Nina enters. She briefly considers asking what the fight is about, but is too numb to care.

'Will there be anything to eat at the funeral?' Kai asks.

'No,' Nina says. 'You'd better eat now if you're hungry.'

'But what if I get hungry later?'

She sighs. 'Then you'll have to wait until we get home.'

'That's typical,' says Rebekka.

Nina turns to look at her. 'What is?'

Rebekka shrugs huffily. 'You get to wear something nice, and I have to make do with this.' She nods at the dark blue blouse and black trousers she's wearing. 'Black and dark blue – it doesn't even match. And this blouse is too small for me. I haven't worn it since last Christmas. It makes me look fat.'

'I'll just pretend you didn't say that,' Nina says. It's costing her a huge effort to stay calm. 'Now go and get your shoes on. We don't want to be late.'

Kai tugs at her waistband. 'Can we take some of those muesli bars?'

'For god's sake!' she shouts, then softens her tone. It isn't his fault. 'All right.'

She opens the cupboard above the sink. 'Here,' she says, handing him a bar.

'Can we take four? So there's one for everyone?'

His childish sense of fairness touches her. She reaches

24

into the cupboard and takes out another three bars, presses them into his soft hands.

They've decided on a small, private funeral; something Nina and her parents instantly agreed on. She's grateful for this – the weight of others' condolences and commiserations, the well-meant words that wouldn't have made the slightest dent in her pain, would've been more than she could bear.

In the car on the way to the cemetery, Nina turns in her seat to look at the children. They're both wearing headphones, cut off from the outside world. Rebekka is nodding her head to music, Kai is listening to his favourite audio book on Sebastian's iPod. He looks small and frail in his dark shirt and trousers. Children should never wear black, she thinks, and turns back around to Sebastian.

'Marie was pregnant,' she says.

Sebastian says nothing, keeps his eyes on the road ahead.

'You're not answering.'

'You didn't ask me anything,' he replies. He turns his head briefly to look at her and then fixes his gaze back on the road. 'Did you read that in the autopsy report?'

'No. I haven't read the report,' she says. 'Kommissar Franzen told me.'

Franzen had, in fact, asked if she wanted a copy of the report, but she was too frightened, too cowardly to say yes. There are things she doesn't want to know, thoughts she doesn't allow herself to think. Did Marie suffer? Was she knocked unconscious quickly, or was she fully, agonisingly aware of every blow to her face, her head, her torso? No, Nina doesn't need answers to these questions. She flinches, then folds her hands in her lap, tightly. She breathes in and out until her heart unclenches. She might not be brave, but she is good like this, she is able to parcel off and compartmentalise; she is efficient, rational, in control.

An old silver Mercedes suddenly undercuts them from the right and Sebastian has to hit the brakes.

'Wanker,' he hisses.

'So whoever attacked her is responsible for two deaths, really,' Nina continues.

'What?'

'Whoever attacked Marie. He has two deaths on his conscience.'

'But you don't even know whether she wanted to keep the baby,' says Sebastian. 'Maybe she was planning to get an abortion.'

'And that is relevant, how?' She snaps her head around to stare at him. 'What makes you say that?'

'I'm just saying, we know what Marie was like –'

'What's that supposed to mean? And why do you assume I would only find out about the pregnancy from the autopsy report? That she didn't tell me herself?'

The light ahead of them turns red. Sebastian slows down, puts the gear in neutral and then places a hand on her leg.

'Why is this upsetting you so much?' he asks softly. 'Look, we only saw her a couple of days before she was attacked. And she was smoking, right?' He gives his head a small shake. 'Besides, if she'd told you about it, you would have mentioned it to me, wouldn't you?' The look he gives her is conciliatory. 'Am I right?'

She sighs and shakes her head. 'Yes, you're right. I – I'm sorry. I didn't mean to snap at you. I'm just –'

'It's okay. It's okay to be confused. You have every right to feel the way you do.' He smiles. She tries to smile back. Then the light changes and they drive on.

They turn into the road that leads to the cemetery and Nina keeps her eye out for a free parking space. On a nearby public lawn, a handful of nudists are enjoying the afternoon sun. It is a perfect late summer; the light is warm and rich, the sky an extravagant and unbroken blue. Nina watches the people on the grass. They are young, healthy, beautiful, carefree. She twists her head around as far as she can until they're out of sight and catches herself thinking that perhaps one of *them* could have died in Marie's place, so that she and her family would not be on their way to a funeral, but instead on some family outing, a picnic bag in the back of the car and her children dressed in patterns of reds and blues and greens. Not in a uniform of black. She senses the lump in her throat and the prickling of tears behind her eyes, her hummingbird heart, by now familiar, constant companions.

'Here, on the left.' She gestures towards a free parking space.

'We'd better try a little further on,' Sebastian says, 'or Bekka will be moaning all the way there. And back.'

Sebastian continues driving slowly, his right indicator on. 'Do you know who the father is?' he asks suddenly.

Nina frowns. It takes her a minute to understand what he's asking. 'No, not yet,' she says. 'They'll probably do a DNA test, or something.'

'D'you think they'll go to that much effort? It's probably Robert's.'

'Perhaps. I've got an appointment to see Kommissar Franzen tomorrow. I'll ask him.'

'What does he want?'

'I have no idea.' She shakes her head. 'More questions about Marie, I suppose.'

She spots a parking space some ten metres from the entrance to the cemetery.

'Quick, take that one,' she tells him.

5

She's there, constantly, and most acutely in the memory of the last time Nina saw her. It was nothing out of the ordinary, that Wednesday night, a run-of-the-mill evening meal that Marie happened to drop by for. Yet it won't leave Nina alone, and she spends hours trying to extract some meaning out of it. Marie arrived just as they sat down to dinner, casually getting herself a plate from the kitchen and helping herself to the lasagne Nina had cooked.

She and Bekka had chatted about a film that had just come out – some horror movie that Bekka was far too young to watch – while Sebastian ate in the kind of silence that screamed his disapproval at Marie's presence.

After dinner, Marie went outside for a smoke, while Sebastian and Nina cleared the table. He was still in a mood, she could tell, but she wasn't going to rise to it. He'd snap out of it soon enough.

Outside the kitchen window, Marie stood leaning against a birch tree, chatting into her phone, her lovely lean back illuminated by the light from the house.

Nina rinsed the plates and Sebastian stacked them in the dishwasher. 'She needs to watch her language,' he said. 'And she shouldn't be smoking in front of the kids.'

'It's nothing the kids don't hear every day in school,' Nina replied as she dried her hands on a tea towel. 'And she's just being herself. But I'll talk to her about the smoking.'

But Sebastian hadn't finished. 'And I don't like her just dropping in like this. It's presumptuous and inconsiderate.'

'Oh come on. She's my sister. That's what family does.'

He opened his mouth to contradict her, but then apparently thought better of it and brushed past her.

She turned back to see Marie crushing her cigarette butt under her foot, then bending over to pick it up. As she straightened up, she caught Nina's eye. *Sorry*, she mouthed at her through the glass, then blew her a silly kiss.

Nina thinks about this as she sits at her desk, filling in a twelve-page form the accountant has sent her for occupational disability insurance, one of many insurances he considers essential. Marie can't have known she was pregnant. She wouldn't have been smoking if she'd known, would she? Or perhaps she just didn't care. But if she knew about the baby, why hadn't she told Nina?

Nina puts down the pen. Her hand is shaking. How long will it be like this? How long will everything always come back to Marie? To her and Marie and the tangle of shared memories. Will Nina have to relive her grief all over again, every time she thinks of her sister? And if not, if the pain really does get better over time, that would mean that from now on, every experience, every memory, will be Nina's alone. It's a desolate thought.

Anita buzzes the intercom twice to let her know that the next patient is on her way in. Nina gathers herself and rises from the chair as a young woman enters.

'Please, have a seat,' she says and gestures towards the chair facing her across the desk. 'How are you today?'

Frau Thiel – Nina's eyes flick down to the open patient file; she's thirty-two, the same age as Marie – is dressed in a denim skirt and a blue silk top that is cut to expose a neat circular tattoo and a sun-tanned left shoulder. She smiles a greeting and hesitates briefly but then sits down slowly, using the arm rest as if to alleviate the pressure of her weight. This action reminds Nina of the new mothers who come in for their first postnatal check-up and have difficulty sitting down due to the stitches and soreness. But on the form Frau Thiel was required to fill in on arrival, she has written *N/A* next to the question of pregnancies and live births.

Nina smiles at her and give her a moment to speak first. But she just smiles back uncertainly and flicks a loose curl of bleached, almost white hair that has fallen forward into her face, back over her shoulder. She reminds Nina of the youngest of her patients, teenage girls coming for the first time to get the pill, or because of heavy, painful periods, or just because they have questions or anxieties about their youthful, developing bodies. Their embarrassment and acute vulnerability showing in their body language, letting Nina know they would rather be anywhere but here.

Her job involves the most intimate of contact, and she's profoundly aware of the responsibility this entails. In fact, this was one of the reasons she left behind the busy, noisy, rigidly structured Ob-Gyn department at the Virchow Clinic to set up her own practice. She has since come to realise that this is a job she does well. She draws an emotional strength from her patients' trust, which she repays by affording them the time and individual attention they need. Frau Thiel, she thinks, needs some gentle coaxing, to let her know she's in safe, kind hands.

'You've a lovely tan there,' she says with a smile. 'Have you been on holiday?'

Frau Thiel shrugs. 'Tanning studio,' she says, almost apologetically, then falls back into silence.

Nina picks up the file on her desk. 'You're overdue a smear test,' she tries, encouragingly.

'Oh.'

'But that's not why you're here?' Nina suggests gently.

Frau Thiel lets out a nervous laugh. 'No.' Then her face turns serious. 'But I guess we could – you could, now that I'm here?'

'Well, you wrote here that it's been three years since you last had a test done, Frau Thiel, so I'd say it's probably a good idea.' Nina puts down the file. 'So, what else can I do for you?'

Frau Thiel rolls her eyes and lets out another tight laugh. 'It's a bit embarrassing,' she says. 'And you can call me Jessica.'

'Don't be embarrassed, Jessica, please,' Nina replies. Her initial guess – from the young woman's nervousness and the way she lowered herself onto the chair – is that she has inserted something she can't remove herself. It doesn't happen frequently, but more often than people might think.

When Jessica doesn't speak, Nina says: 'Why don't you let me have a look?'

Jessica looks down at her hands and her expression collapses, but then she forces a smile and eases herself out of her chair.

'Just remove your skirt and pants behind the screen,' Nina says, adopting a gentle but assured tone she hopes Jessica will respond to, 'and then you can lie down over there.' She points to the examination table under a frosted-glass window. 'Or, if you'd rather, you can put on one of the paper gowns,' she adds, as Jessica disappears behind the screen. 'They're on the shelf.'

Jessica busies herself getting undressed, and Nina slips on a pair of latex gloves. Anita accidentally ordered a dozen packs of gloves in the wrong size – L –, and the pair she's wearing wrinkle horribly and impractically around her fingers, making her hands look like those belonging to some nuclear disaster victim. She knows she has to be extremely careful with her budget, but wearing gloves she can hardly work in seems a ridiculous way to avoid any additional expenditure.

As she makes a mental note to tell Anita to re-order smaller gloves, Jessica comes out from behind the screen. She has opted for the patient gown, something the younger patients normally don't. She climbs onto the table and lies down. Before Nina can speak, she says: 'I cut myself shaving. I think it must have got infected or something.'

'You poor thing,' Nina replies. 'Well, just part your legs, knees up, and I'll take a look. I'll be gentle, I promise.'

Jessica raises her knees and opens her legs. Nina almost flinches at the sight. The entire genital area is a raw, purplish mess. Just by looking – she is reluctant to touch at first – she can see that the left labium majus is infected and swollen. She looks up at Jessica through her knees, but she has placed her forearm over her eyes. Nina uses her fingers to pull the labia minora to either side, gently, gently, and hears her gasp.

'I'm sorry,' Nina says. 'I'll be as gentle as I can.'

Pus has begun to form on a cut, or tear, of the perineum. The pubic hair has begun to grow back; there is about a week's worth of black stubble, but it can't hide the nature of Jessica's injury. There is a pattern of small, semi-circular teeth marks on her labium majus. A bite mark.

The sight stuns her and she's momentarily paralysed. She clears her throat to try and dispel the feeling of horror. 'When did this happen?' Her voice is thick.

Jessica lifts her head off the table a fraction. She has tears in her eyes and her face is taut with misery. 'About a week ago,' she says in a small voice. 'I was shaving my, well, down there, and I slipped in the shower and cut myself.'

'A week ago,' Nina echoes. She wants to ask why Jessica waited so long before coming to see a doctor, but instead, she says, 'I'll have to clean the wound for you. It looks infected.'

She walks over to the cabinet where she keeps the gauze pads and disinfectant. Jessica lies completely still on the table.

'This will be a bit uncomfortable, Jessica,' she says as she squirts some antiseptic fluid onto a gauze pad. Her hands are shaking slightly. 'If it's too painful, please let me know and perhaps I can give you a local anaesthetic.'

'Okay.' She squeezes her eyes shut, her hands clenched against the sides of the table.

Nina is as gentle as possible as she cleans the wound. Jessica doesn't complain, just takes a few sharp breaths every now and then.

'Okay,' Nina says when she's done. 'You can get dressed again. There are some sanitary towels on the shelf, next to the gowns.'

As Jessica disappears behind the screen, Nina asks, 'Have you had a raised temperature at all?'

'Um, I don't know,' Jessica says from behind the screen. 'I was feeling a little hot yesterday, but that might have been the weather.'

'I'll prescribe an antibiotic, just to be on the safe side. The infection should clear up within a couple of days. If it isn't any better by Thursday, I'd like you to come back and see me. Or go to the emergency room if you like.'

Jessica reappears, dressed again, and sits down gingerly. 'Will I need stitches?' she asks.

'No. The cut should heal on its own. I'll give you some antiseptic to take home.' Nina begins to write out a prescription. 'You need to apply it three times a day. No baths for a week please, only showers. Keep it nice and clean and you should be fine.'

She hands Jessica the prescription, waits a moment and then finally asks, 'Do you want to tell me how this happened?'

Jessica looks down at her lap. 'I cut myself shaving.'

Nina doesn't reply straight away. Years ago, when she was completing a four-month residency at A&E, a heavily pregnant woman presented with severe bruising to her arms and legs, implausibly claiming an accident on the stairs. The senior physician bullied her into pressing charges against her partner – the patient was found dead in her flat two days later with thirty-seven stab wounds, of which twenty were to her abdomen. Nina's mind still lurches at the memory.

She opens a drawer, takes out a card and hands it to Jessica. 'Here. This is the number of a counselling centre. For women. They have a twenty-four-hour hotline.'

Jessica sits there, looking down, unmoving.

Nina takes a pen and scribbles her mobile number on the card. She slides it across the desk. 'Please,' she says, then adds force to her voice. 'Take it. My number's on the back.'

Jessica swallows and reaches out for the card. She doesn't look up. Then she gets to her feet and swings her bag over her shoulder.

Nina also rises from her chair. 'Come back next week,' she says. 'Just to make sure the cut is healing properly. Anita will give you the prescription.'

Jessica nods and leaves. Nina remains standing, motionless, her emotions a sickening swirl of horror and despair, anger and shock. Despair wins. She sinks to the floor, curls into herself and bursts into tears.

6

The door of Franzen's office is slightly ajar, but still Nina knocks before she enters. Franzen is sitting behind his desk. On the other side of the office, next to an identical desk, is a man – fat, red-haired – retrieving some papers from a filing cabinet. The office smells musty, as though it hasn't been aired in days, with a faint trace of something vinegary.

'Yes, hello, Dr Bergmann, do come in,' Franzen says. He gets up and wipes his hands on a paper napkin before holding his hand out.

'You're on your lunch break,' Nina says. 'Shall I come back later?'

'No, no. Come in.'

He offers her a chair and she sits down.

'Do you mind if I finish my sandwich?' he asks and points to the half-eaten sandwich on his desk, forlorn among the clutter of telephone, files, keyboard and piles of papers.

A long-forgotten, sleepy mechanism is reactivated in Nina's brain. She's a little out of practice, but after several seconds she calculates that the sandwich is made up of a total of 382 calories.

'I didn't manage to get out for lunch earlier,' Franzen continues.

'No, please eat,' she says.

He takes a bite of his sandwich, chews, swallows, takes another bite and chews it quickly. Nina feels guilty to be depriving him of his enjoyment. He swallows, and says: 'First of all, my condolences, Dr Bergmann.' A pause, then: 'Thank you for coming. I hope this isn't an inconvenient time for you?'

'Thank you,' she replies quietly. 'And no, it's not inconvenient. I close early on Wednesdays and I'd rather do this here.'

'I understand,' he says, wiping his hands on the napkin again. 'Oh, and this is my colleague, Hauptkommissar Maslowski.' He nods in the direction of the red-haired man.

'Hello,' Maslowski says. It isn't a particularly friendly greeting.

'Hello,' Nina replies, uncomfortable at the thought of discussing Marie in front of a stranger.

As if he can read her thoughts, Franzen says: 'Just so you know – Kommissar Maslowski and I are both working on Marie's case. So, we can talk openly.'

She glances at Maslowski again, then turns to Franzen and nods. 'All right,' she says finally. 'How can I help you?'

Franzen puts the last piece of bread in his mouth and is still chewing as he opens a file.

He swallows. 'Actually, I wanted to keep you up-to-date on the status of our investigation. And ask you a couple of questions about Marie.'

He sits there for a moment, silently, as though sorting his thoughts. 'Your parents,' he says, and his voice is slow and calm, 'are very shaken about the death of Marie. Of course. But I must say – and forgive me for being frank – they don't seem to know much about her. About how she lived.'

'Be as frank as you like,' Nina says. 'In fact, I'd prefer it.'

He smiles. 'That's good to know, Dr Bergmann.'

He places both hands on the open file. His nails are pinkish-white, with a mother-of-pearl shine, and perfectly shaped.

He continues. 'There is no indication that anyone broke into your sister's flat. By that I mean there were no obvious signs of forced entry. So either your sister knew her attacker, or she opened the door to a stranger. The door to the main building as well as to her flat.'

He looks at her.

'So?' she asks quietly. He appears blissfully ignorant of the pain his remarks are causing her.

'Well – I'd like to know whether your sister was in the habit of opening the door to strangers.'

'Oh.' She tries to think about it, but finds it difficult. She does nothing *but* think of Marie, but these thoughts make her bite her lip to keep the tears back. It's not just the tears she's stopping, it's the thoughts she doesn't allow herself to think, excruciating, dark thoughts about the attack. So she closes her eyes and imagines Marie in her messy, thrift-store flat, reading or listening to music, playing with a curl of hair, lost in thought, the doorbell rings, she jumps up, eagerly, impatiently, full of life and runs to the door –

Then she remembers something.

'Yes, I mean, no, Marie wouldn't have opened the door just like that. There's an intercom system in the building, it was broken for a while, and I remember she was annoyed because it took so long for the landlord to fix it. She was on the phone to him dozens of times before he did anything about it, we talked about that.'

'I see.' Franzen writes something down in his notebook. 'And how long ago was this?' he asks without looking up.

'What, the broken intercom? Oh, a year ago, at least. There was a series of arson attacks in her street at the time, she had quite a few Turkish neighbours, so they assumed the attackers were likely to be neo-Nazis. So, anyway, everyone in her building was very careful about keeping the main door locked, checking first to see who they let in. Especially because a few people there have kids, and keep their buggies downstairs in the front hall. Apparently, buggies are good for starting fires.'

She stops when she realises she's blabbering. It must be nerves. She wonders why she's nervous at all. She feels slightly dizzy, as well. She hasn't eaten anything today and her concentration is dwindling. Where was she? Oh, right, she was blabbering about intercoms and arson attacks.

'But that's irrelevant,' she says quietly.

'No, no, carry on,' Franzen says. 'It's all helpful.'

Behind her, Maslowski clears his throat and sniffs. Nina wants this conversation to come to an end. She feels wrong-footed by Franzen, and she can't quite figure out why.

'There isn't much more to say,' she adds.

'Well then,' Franzen says and looks down at the file. 'Yes, that's pretty much in line with our assumptions.'

'Assumptions?'

'That Marie knew her attacker. As far as we can tell, nothing of value was taken from her flat – there was some cash on the kitchen counter and a laptop and a stereo in the living room. The only thing missing, really, was the TV.'

'Marie didn't own a TV,' Nina tells him. 'She said it took up too much valuable time.'

What she doesn't tell him is that Marie was terrified of the ordinary, the mundane, of being sucked into mediocrity and disappearing without a trace. She didn't watch TV, she didn't do small talk, she dropped in for dinner, uninvited. She completed a couple of semesters of a Cultural Sciences degree, but left without any qualifications. Her parents were horrified when they realised she'd quit university, and spelled out to her in a long, bitter, emotionally laden letter that if she chose to throw away such opportunities, they had no choice but to cut her off financially. Nina happily stepped in, tore up the letter and encouraged her sister to focus on something she felt a vocation for, something artistic, something creative. And leave her parents to stew in their disapproval.

It shames her now to realise that perhaps she was perpetuating the drama by rescuing her sister again and again. That she could only stand up to her parents in an act of rebellion by proxy. But what was she to do? It was the only kind of rebellion open to her; it was never quite articulated, but the threat was always there, that if she went against her parents on anything, however trivial, she'd cause unimaginable harm to everyone.

Marie, by contrast, took their parents' disapproval in her stride. She thrived on acts of defiance, on challenge, hurtling headlong towards god-knows-what as long as she could feel herself moving, anything not to stop and stagnate. This is why she loved Berlin, a city that changes itself constantly, at vertiginous, anarchic speed; a place that's always becoming, and never being. Maybe, Nina thinks now, maybe this city had been toxic for Marie. That what she needed was security, stability and a rootedness. Perhaps she needed to settle and to *be*.

But this is impossible to explain to Franzen. 'Marie didn't watch much television,' she says vaguely. 'She always said she could spend her time doing other things. Such as writing. She liked to write, you know.'

Franzen put up his hands in agreement. 'You don't need to explain that to me, Dr Bergmann. I don't have a TV at home, either.'

He smiles. Maslowski sniffs again and mumbles something Nina can't quite make out.

'My colleague here on the other hand,' Franzen waves his hand in Maslowski's direction, 'would be stuck without his daily fix. Am I right, Mika?'

'Yeah, yeah,' Maslowski grumbles into his paperwork.

Nina's dizziness increases, intensifying the stupor she's feeling, and adding to the surreal quality this conversation has taken on. Her vision is accosted by numerous small black dots and she has to concentrate hard to follow what Franzen is saying. She will have to join Sebastian and the kids for supper tonight; yesterday, she claimed she wasn't feeling well. Maybe she should make ratatouille, then it won't be so obvious that she's just eating vegetables.

'Are you okay?' she hears Franzen ask.

'What? Yes, I'm fine.' She takes a deep breath. 'It's just – I'm still feeling a little shaken.'

'That's completely understandable,' he says softly. 'Would you like to come back another time?'

Nina shakes her head.

'Perhaps you already know this,' he says, 'but the initial stages of an enquiry are crucial. Anything we miss out on now, well, there's always the chance that it'll get lost altogether. So, if you're up to it, I'd be very grateful for anything you could tell me about your sister.' He pauses, as though to check she's okay to continue answering his questions, then asks: 'Did Marie have any friends?'

She tells him what she knows, the names of a few friends Marie knew from university.

Franzen is scribbling away furiously. When Nina pauses, he looks up. 'Good, go on, anyone else?'

She opens her mouth and closes it again. Behind her, Maslowski slams a file drawer shut. She jumps. She's finding it impossible to concentrate. Finally, she says, 'She was part of a writing circle with five or six other writers. They met up regularly.'

'Would you happen to have their names?'

'No, sorry. Marie was ... guarded about her writing. It was very personal for her, so she didn't talk about it much. I just know that she and these other writers met up. But they had a name for the group. *Wortspiel.*'

'*Wortspiel*,' he repeats. 'Wordplay.' He writes it down.

'Not very original, for a group of writers,' Nina says. 'Marie hates it. I mean, hated it.' Her hands are trembling in her lap. She interlocks her fingers and squeezes them tight. She will never get used to referring to her sister in the past tense.

Franzen puts down his pen. 'We found several writing journals in your sister's flat. Did she ever show them to you, Dr Bergmann?'

'No. I mean, I've read some her stories, but –'

'No matter. I read the journals. It appears she liked to familiarise herself with the topics she was writing about. Her research was really quite in-depth.'

'Yes, that sounds right.'

'There were a few stories, and copious notes, about political extremists. The far left as well as the far right.' He pauses, then adds in a pensive tone: 'She was a talented writer.'

Nina almost thanks him, but stops herself in time.

'Well, you've been very helpful, Dr Bergmann. I guess that's all from me right now. Unless you have any questions you'd like to ask us?'

'Did she fight back?' Her voice is hardly more than a whisper.

'I'm sorry?'

'Marie. Did she – her attacker . . .'

'Oh. I see. Yes. There was most definitely a struggle.' He clears his throat. 'I'm sorry, I'm not sure how much detail I should go into. We've no DNA evidence. Apart from the baby.'

The baby. The thought of the baby – the sudden image of a perfect shell-like curl of a foetus – shocks Nina so much she forgets how to breathe for a moment.

'Dr Bergmann,' Franzen says, concerned. 'Can I get you a glass of water?'

She shakes her head, although her mouth is dry and sticky. She gets to her feet slowly. Then another question occurs to her. 'Have you spoken to Robert Kran yet?'

'I'm driving to Leipzig tomorrow,' Franzen says. 'Our initial focus is on people who knew Marie. And –' he gets to his feet, 'we will be speaking with your husband, as well.'

Nina stands up straight, the black dots fizzing and then settling behind her eyes. 'My husband was with a client on the morning Marie was attacked,' she says calmly, her cheeks burning. 'It shouldn't be too difficult to confirm that. He's a lawyer.'

'Don't worry, Dr Bergmann,' says Franzen. 'We will. As you said, it won't be difficult to confirm.'

Her stomach growls audibly as she opens the door to leave.

'You obviously didn't get around to having lunch, either.' He smiles.

Nina swallows and bites her lip.

'There's a Bratwurst stand on the corner,' he says. 'They've got by far the best Currywurst in town. Home-made tomato sauce. Secret recipe, I'm told.' He smiles. 'You should try it.'

'Yes, I'll do that,' she says.

Stepping outside into the grey Berlin air, she turns and

looks up at the imposing police building, tips her head back at the fourth floor and tries to locate Franzen's office. The building, with its grand sandstone columns and barred windows, seems to tilt towards her and for a split second, she has the terrifying sensation it might fall and crush her. She steps backwards, into the path of a man shoving a Currywurst into his mouth, and she apologises hastily, nearly heaving at the smell of the spicy ketchupy sauce.

7

It's ten o'clock. They ate at seven thirty, and Nina was able to take a brisk walk around the neighbourhood after the meal, with the excuse that they were out of milk for tomorrow's breakfast. The children are upstairs – Kai asleep, Rebekka pretending to be, no doubt, while listening to music under the covers – and Nina and Sebastian are sitting on the sofa, watching the evening news.

The living room is dark, apart from the blue light from the set that never quite seems to penetrate the corners of the room. The contrast between the flickering light of the TV and the room's darkness always makes her eyes hurt after a while. This constitutes one of those never-resolved minor conflicts in their marriage – whether or not to watch TV in the dark. Sebastian likes the dark, for the 'feel'; Nina is often left with a headache. This evening, he got there first while she was putting Kai to bed. To switch the light back on now would be an act of unspoken confrontation, however mild.

Beside her, Sebastian yawns.

'I went to see Kommissar Franzen today,' she says. 'He thinks that Marie is likely to have known her attacker.'

Sebastian doesn't take his eyes of the TV. 'Any leads? Do they know who the father is yet?'

'No,' she replies. 'But he's driving down to Leipzig tomorrow to speak to Robert.'

'Right.'

'And he also mentioned that he wants to speak with you.'

'Yes, I know,' he says flatly. 'There's been a bit of a mix-up. That client I saw the day Marie was attacked, Grünblatt? He got his dates wrong.' He shifts position on the couch. 'I have to take the idiot out to lunch, sort it out. Anyway, Franzen had a chat with my secretary, and then left a message asking me to call the police station "at my convenience". Not exactly discreet.'

'What's there to be discreet about?' Nina hears herself demanding. 'There's nothing shameful about what happened to Marie. There's nothing shameful about being the victim of violent crime.'

'Don't put words in my mouth, Nina. I just don't feel comfortable with my family's business laid out for all to see, that's all.'

'I see.'

He turns to face her. 'And what's that supposed to mean?'

'All of a sudden, it's *your* family. As if you were best friends with Marie when she . . .'

Then, unexpectedly, Sebastian reaches across and pulls her towards him.

'Oh, baby,' he says. 'I'm so sorry about what happened.' He strokes her cheek. 'It's going to take a while for us to

48

get through this. We just need to take care of each other in the meantime, right?'

She nods. Her throat is tight. She gets up and goes to the kitchen for a glass of water. When she comes back, Sebastian is refocused on the TV: a documentary on the days leading up to the fall of the Berlin Wall, one of many such programmes dominating the media in anticipation of November's thirtieth anniversary celebrations.

She sits down and watches without taking anything in. The images are so engrained in every Berliner's mind – the masses gathering on Alexanderplatz; hundreds of revellers standing on the Wall, shouting and singing; a huge slab of concrete toppling over to the cheers of onlookers – as to hardly feel meaningful anymore.

Like most Berliners, Nina was asleep in bed when the Wall fell, and missed history happening on her doorstep. She was twelve at the time; old enough to remember the almost provincial cosiness of life in West Berlin – a small, vulnerable half-city living under the threat of Soviet attack, protected by its overbearing Western bodyguards – but young enough to navigate the upheaval of the *Wende* and move forward freely, unencumbered by the past. Perhaps this is the problem, she thinks for the second time today, perhaps the city is always changing too fast, adding layer upon layer, not one washed clean before another is placed on top, leaving the lower layers to rot and ferment, unmarked by memory.

Sebastian changes the channel and she blinks. A quiz show flashes up on the screen, the contestant a young blonde woman perched uncomfortably on a stool.

'I saw a patient this morning,' Nina finds herself saying. 'Young. Attractive, a bit shy. She had bite marks on her vulva.' She glances over at Sebastian to gauge his reaction. 'Some twisted *fuck* had bitten her.'

'Jesus,' he says, finally shifting his gaze from the TV.

'She said she'd cut herself shaving. I didn't know what to do.'

'What *can* you do?'

'I don't know,' she says, aware that her voice has taken on a confrontational tone. 'Call the police? Insist she press charges? Not just sit there and let her walk out, probably to go home and have him abuse her further?'

She breathes in and out deeply to stop herself from crying.

'You can't make her get help,' he says. 'If she says she cut herself, then you have to take her word for it.'

'But she had bite marks! Her entire genital area was one infected, broken mess. I could clearly see that she'd been bitten.'

He lets out a deep sigh. 'I wasn't questioning your professional judgement.' He sounds tired, as if she's deliberately bringing more unnecessary drama into their lives. 'I was just saying that you can't help those who don't want to be helped. And besides –'

'Besides what?' She hates the fact that they're having this conversation now, that the conversation has taken on this edge, but she doesn't know how to make it stop.

He sighs again. 'I don't think it would be wise to frighten off your patients at this stage,' he says. 'You know yourself that it's going to take a year or so until you're financially stable.'

'So it's best I let the woman suffer,' she says quietly, 'while I make sure my business is up and running.'

He lets himself fall back and closes his eyes. 'I'm sorry,' he says. 'I'm sorry to be talking like this.' He opens his eyes and looks at her. 'You're obviously too stressed out to have a normal conversation. And I get it, I do. So why don't we leave it for tonight?'

She holds his gaze for a moment and then looks away. She misses Marie so acutely, she can't bear it. She misses not having her to talk to about this. Marie would have known what to say. At the very least, she would have listened. Nina suddenly feels herself lose the ability to breathe, knowing that she will never, *ever*, be able to talk to her sister again.

'Mama?' It's Kai, crumpled in his tiger pyjamas, from the top of the stairs.

Nina snatches a breath and looks at Sebastian. 'Maybe he should sleep with us tonight,' she says.

He shakes his head a fraction, blows out a thin stream of air. 'I don't think infantilising him is going to solve anything.'

'There's nothing wrong with wanting to be physically close after something like this has happened,' Nina says, getting to her feet.

He looks up at her.

'When you're a child,' she adds, and leaves the room to go upstairs and comfort her son.

*

June, 2004

Nina spotted her through the hot crush of people. She was sitting slumped against a grimy wall, knees up, head resting on them. From inside the club behind her, strobe lighting and deafening music, a violent, hypnotic beat. Not a metre away, a young man suddenly doubled over and vomited against the wall. A cheer rose up from his friends – out on a stag night, it looked like – and the young man, reeling slightly, fist-pumped the air with a grin. Marie didn't move.

It was a warm night, or rather, morning. It would be dawn soon. The sharp-sour stench of the man's vomit crept up Nina's nose and she had to overcome the urge to gag. She had rarely been out all night clubbing or partying, even when she was younger, and sometimes wondered what she'd missed out on. Didn't seem she'd missed out on much. She shouldered her way through the clubbers and crouched down in front of her sister.

'Marie, are you all right?'

Marie looked up through sweat-damp curls that had fallen into her face. Her eye makeup was smudged, and it seemed to take her a minute to recognise Nina. She managed a lopsided smile. 'Hi. You're here.'

'Course I am. I was worried. Come on, up you get.'

She took Marie's elbow to help her to her feet and her arm came into contact with the brick wall. The wall – graffitied from top to bottom – was coated in a slimy, unrecognisable substance. She pulled away, fast, and Marie slid out of her grip, stumbling and narrowly missing the puddle of vomit.

'Fuck's sake, Nina,' she snapped, 'don't rush me.'

Nina's earlier worry, after receiving the incoherent, panicky phone call from Marie half an hour ago, telling her someone had stolen her purse and she didn't know how to get home, was replaced by a surge of anger. 'I've every bloody right to rush you. It's half past four in the morning, I've got a baby at home, ready to wake up for a feed in an hour, and I'm standing in a stinking, filthy alley with an eighteen-year-old, smashed out of her head, who should know better.'

Marie lowered her head. 'I'm sorry,' she muttered, though the noise from the club was so loud, Nina could only lip-read the words. Then Marie started to cry, the way drunk people cry, with her face screwed up and spit and snot coming out of her nose and mouth. 'I got my results today,' she said, her words hopelessly slurred.

Her school leaving exams. Of course. Nina had forgotten. 'Oh.'

'You know what Papa said?' she continued, her sobbing angry now. 'He said my "efforts" weren't worth the paper they were written on ... that I was a failure ... that he'd never expected much from me,' she gulped and choked on her words, 'but that I'd managed to fall short even of that. But I passed, Nina! I passed the exams.'

A spray of saliva hit Nina's cheek. She put her arms around her sister and held her tight. 'It's okay,' she said, although it wasn't okay. It was far from okay. 'C'mon, time to get you home.'

8

'Bekka, darling!' Nina's mother throws her arms around Rebekka and acknowledges her daughter's presence with a nod.

'Hi, Omi,' Rebekka says, smiling.

'Sorry we're late,' Nina says, coming up the steps that lead from the driveway to the front door. Her parents' house isn't quite large enough to be considered 'grand', but it's nonetheless listed as a villa at the land registry. Located in the lush district of Zehlendorf – the closest the walled-in city of West Berlin ever came to having a proper suburb – the house nestles in neatly among other, similar turn-of-the-20th-century houses. The streets are hushed and leafy, rubbish bins tucked away behind the houses, the mature front gardens enclosed by wrought-iron fencing. The area exudes a sense of affluence and privacy that makes the accidental visitor feel distinctly unwelcome.

Antonia clears her throat. 'Hmm,' she says, looking at her watch.

Nina ignores her tone. 'Sebastian wanted to take Kai to the zoo this morning, and my car wouldn't start, so we decided I'd drop the two of them off at the zoo with Basti's car and pick them up later.'

'Oh?' Antonia's face crumples momentarily. 'Kai's not with you?' Then she shrugs. 'Oh well, never mind. You'd better come in. It looks as though it's about to rain.'

They go inside, Nina's heels clacking noisily on the tiled floor. She likes people to remove their shoes in her own house, but her mother considers it vulgar to walk around in stockinged feet.

'Hannah's just made some coffee,' Antonia says now, slipping her arm through Rebekka's and pulling her closer. 'And I had her buy some Coke for you.' She smiles indulgently at her.

They sit down; Antonia and Rebekka take a seat on the sofa, and Nina sits on the armchair next to the large bay window. She notices that the sofa has been re-upholstered in a dark green fabric. It's an antique, like much of the furniture in the house, and even with its new covering, smells stale.

Hannah, the Bergmanns' domestic help, comes in with a tray of coffee. She smiles at Nina and says a small 'Hello'.

'Don't forget the Coca-Cola,' Antonia tells her. 'It's in the fridge.'

Hannah nods and leaves the room.

'It's such a shame that Kai didn't come along,' Antonia continues, pouring two cups of coffee.

'He's into reptiles at the moment,' Rebekka says, pulling a face. 'He's so gross.'

Antonia laughs. 'Well, it's very sweet of Sebastian to give up his Saturday morning to spend time with his son.'

Nina lets out a puff of air. 'I don't think he views it as a sacrifice to take Kai to the zoo.'

Antonia puts down the coffee pot. 'Don't twist my words, Nina,' she says without looking up. 'You know exactly what I mean.'

Yes, Nina does know exactly what she means, but she doesn't want to get into an argument in front of Rebekka. The smell of her mother's perfume, a heavy, musky scent she has worn as long as Nina can remember, cloys the air.

'Hand me my bag there, would you?' Antonia says brightly to Rebekka, indicating the handbag sitting on a side table. Rebekka obliges, and she snaps the bag open and retrieves her purse.

'Here,' she says, pulling out a twenty-euro note and handing it to Rebekka. 'Because you're such a good girl.'

'Mama!' Nina says. 'You're spoiling her.'

'A grandmother is entitled to spoil her only grand-daughter.' Antonia winks at Rebekka. 'Especially when she's such a good girl.'

Nina takes a sip of coffee, ignoring the angry look Rebekka shoots her. She should be happy that Bekka and her mother have such a playful, uncomplicated relation-ship, free from weighty expectations, in which Bekka can accept her grandmother's generosity knowing it doesn't put her in any emotional debt, a relationship in which she is safe to express herself without fear of reproach. And Nina knows should be happy about that, but she can't help recalling what it was like for her growing up, where the honest expression of feelings was forbidden and everything she received – pocket money, praise, affection – came at a price. It puzzles her to think about how life might have been, had her relationship with her mother been different.

'You know,' Antonia says, dropping two sugar cubes into her own coffee, 'you really ought to think about getting a new car. Yours seems so unreliable.'

'I can't afford a new car at the moment.'

Antonia sniffs. 'Surely Sebastian can buy you one?'

'I'm not going to take money from my husband when I have a job of my own,' Nina replies. 'You of all people should understand that.'

'It was different then,' Antonia says crisply. 'The women of my generation were at their husband's mercy if they didn't have their own income. Why you younger women can't gratefully accept all that has been done for you, I don't know. It doesn't have to be fight, fight, fight all the time.'

'Whatever,' Nina says, as if she were an indifferent teenager again.

They'd had a similar argument when Nina and Sebastian got married: Nina had decided to keep her own name, much to her mother's displeasure, who felt that for Nina not to take Sebastian's surname – Lanz – was an act of disrespect to him.

'I just prefer to be financially independent, that's all,' Nina adds.

'In that case –' Her mother places her cup on the saucer, almost triumphantly. 'I don't understand why you gave up that position at the hospital. It was perfect for you. And you were sure of a steady income.'

It is a blatant attempt to fuel Nina's creeping self-doubts about the folly of setting up her own practice. She's not playing that game. She leans back in her chair. 'Let's please drop it, all right?'

Her mother looks poised to argue, but evidently thinks better of it. She straightens her posture. 'Very well.'

They sit in silence. The light is suddenly sucked out of the room as it begins to pour with rain outside. Antonia switches on a small Tiffany table lamp and a muted, multi-coloured glow fills the room. Nina glances over at Bekka, who is wired to her phone, nodding her head up and down to music. Her two thumbs tap the screen at high speed.

'Where's Papa?' Nina asks finally, to break the silence.

'He's at the Ministry,' her mother replies. She sighs. 'I don't know. Ever since he agreed to sit on that stupid anniversary committee, he's been so busy. It's as though he never retired.'

Nina's father retired as a judge from the Ministry of Justice nine years ago, and seemed to age ten years overnight. She strongly suspects that his involvement in the anniversary celebrations for the fall of the Wall is a welcome opportunity to do something worthwhile – even if it is only temporary. For a brief moment, she feels sorry for her mother, sitting in this pristine house, waiting, thinking, with nothing to distract her.

'Well, give him my love when you see him,' she says. 'And tell him not to work too hard.'

'From your mouth to God's ear,' Antonia replies. Then she says: 'Have you heard anything from Kommissar Franzen?'

Nina places her cup down and looks over at Rebekka, who is still lost in her own world. 'He spoke to Sebastian on Thursday,' she says in a hushed voice. 'He just asked some questions about Marie – not that Basti knows anything I haven't already told them.' She doesn't mention that Sebastian was asked to give a saliva sample.

'Nothing new, then?'

She shakes her head.

'I don't understand it.' Antonia throws up her hands. 'They must have *some* lead, something to give them an idea who might have done it. What about her neighbours? Surely one of them must have seen someone leaving her flat, after – you know.' Her voice trembles and drops to a whisper.

'It's a big city, Mama. People only see what they want to see.' But still she makes a mental note to ring Franzen on Monday. She wants to know what came of his meeting with Robert. Or maybe she should call Robert. Yes, she'll do that. As soon as she gets home.

'It's just so frustrating,' her mother says as she dabs at her eyes with a tissue, careful not to smudge her makeup.

'Are you okay, Omi?' Rebekka asks suddenly. She looks at Nina. 'Oh. Are you talking about –?'

'Never mind, sweetheart,' Nina says, seeing the anxiety blossom on her daughter's face.

But Rebekka's attention is drawn back almost immediately to a *pling* coming from her phone. She pulls one earplug out. 'Mama?'

'Yes?'

'Emilia wants to know if I can come round for an hour or so. She only lives ten minutes away. We've got this project together at school and –'

'But you've only just arrived!' Antonia exclaims. 'And you were late getting here in the first place.'

Rebekka tilts her head to one side. 'Sorry, Omi. You're right. I wasn't thinking. I'll text her back and –'

'Nonsense,' Antonia says abruptly. 'You go out and enjoy yourself. I insist. Just promise me you'll visit during the week.'

Rebekka jumps up. 'Thanks, Omi.' She kisses her grandmother's cheek. Antonia closes her eyes and smiles as if being blessed.

'You're to be home at eight o'clock at the latest,' Nina calls out as Rebekka makes her escape, wishing she could jump up and leave with such ease, then turns back to her mother. 'Sorry, Mama. She just does as she likes these days.'

'She's fourteen, a young woman,' Antonia says and pours herself another cup of coffee. They sit in more uncomfortable silence. Outside, it's still pouring, and there is a far-off rumble of thunder. Nina stares down into her cup. Perhaps she should claim a forgotten appointment. They will both know it's a lie, but Antonia will accept it as truth.

Nina opens her mouth just as the doorbell rings. Hannah walks through from the kitchen, throwing Antonia a questioning look as she heads towards the front door.

'Tell whoever it is that I already donate plenty of money to charities of my choice,' Antonia tells her. 'And don't let them in!' she adds, in a louder voice.

Nina places her hands on her lap and looks down at them, waiting for Hannah to send away whoever has rung the doorbell, so she can finally make her excuses and leave. Her mother cranes her neck towards the door.

Nina hears Hannah say, 'I'm not sure. I'll see if she's in,' and then she comes to stand in the doorway.

'It's Herr and Frau Klopp,' she says to Antonia. 'Herr Klopp has some papers for your husband. I told them I'd see if you're available.'

Antonia stands up. 'Don't just leave them waiting on the front step,' she says. 'Invite them in. And fetch some more cups. They can join us for coffee.'

Hannah does as she is asked. A moment later, a man and a woman enter. The woman is dark-haired, in her early sixties perhaps, dressed with understated elegance. Her husband's suit looks bespoke, and despite the wrinkles around his eyes and the receding hairline, he carries an awareness of his own attractiveness. They both do.

'Antonia,' the woman says, walking towards her and miming a kiss on the left and right side of her face in which their faces don't actually touch. 'I'm so sorry for your loss,' she says in a low voice.

Antonia squeezes her eyes shut briefly, mouths 'Thank you', and then turns to Nina.

'Gloria, this is my daughter Nina. Nina, this is Gloria Klopp. Her husband, Bernhard, is a former colleague of your father's.'

'And a good friend,' Gloria Klopp adds. Her Saxon accent is audible, though only vaguely. Like many middle-class Saxons, she has presumably worked hard to rid her speech of the squashed, centralised vowels that West Germans still associate, unpleasantly, with former communist party leaders.

'Very nice to meet you,' Nina says, getting up to shake each hand in turn.

'Please, take a seat, Gloria, Bernhard,' Antonia says.

'Will you join us for coffee? Hannah's making a fresh pot.'

Herr Klopp hesitates briefly. 'We don't want to disturb you,' he says. 'We were just driving past and I remembered I have these papers in the car.' He gestures at the blue folder he's carrying.

'You're not disturbing us at all,' Antonia says. 'You must stay until the rain has eased off a little, at least. Hannah will take your coats. Hannah?'

Hannah enters the room with a tray. She places two cups and a fresh coffee pot on the table, then helps the Klopps out of their wet coats.

'Anything else?' she asks.

'Thank you,' Antonia says. 'That'll be all.'

Gloria Klopp sits down on the sofa next to Antonia, her husband takes a seat opposite Nina.

'Bernhard did ask me to drop them off for Hans a couple of days ago,' Frau Klopp says, 'but, goodness, I've been so busy with one thing or another. I completely forgot.'

'I hope the delay hasn't caused any problems,' Herr Klopp says, holding out the folder.

Antonia takes it and places it on a side table without giving it a second look. 'I can't imagine so,' she says, as she leans forward to pour the coffee. 'It's probably to do with this speech he's giving at the anniversary celebrations.'

'How is poor Hans?' Frau Klopp asks. 'Bernhard says he sounds fine, but . . . it must have been such a . . . such a . . . shock. I can't imagine . . .'

'He's distracting himself, that's what he's doing,' Antonia says, and Nina can hear an edge of reproach in her voice.

Frau Klopp doesn't appear to notice. 'Well, that's

probably the only thing you *can* do, under the circumstances. When I heard, I couldn't believe it. Such a beautiful, spirited young woman . . .' she trails off, as if genuinely overcome.

'You knew Marie?' Nina finds herself asking.

Frau Klopp looks at her as though suddenly surprised at her presence. The woman's eyebrows have been plucked a little too severely, and when she raises them a fraction, it gives her face a sharp, artificial look.

'Yes, indeed.' She picks up her cup and saucer. 'We both knew her.' She nods at her husband. 'Bernhard and I met her, what, only a few months before she . . . before . . .' She takes a nervous sip of coffee. It appears to calm her. She continues, her voice now perfectly composed, almost matter-of-fact.

'Marie won a poetry competition, you know, in June, and I was one of the judges. We had a few – shall we say – *turbulent* discussions about her poem.' She smiles, more to herself than to anyone else in the room. 'A couple of the other judges thought it too dark, too . . . dislocated, a little Kafkaesque, but in the end, we decided that the quality of her writing was simply streets ahead of the other entries.' She pauses and looks into her coffee cup. 'It was remarkable, really, when I finally met her at the awards ceremony. She was . . . *dazzling*. Bright, and sunny. So unlike her writing. We had a lovely chat with her, Bernhard and I.'

This information is unexpected, disquieting almost. It has never occurred to Nina – Marie certainly never mentioned it – that her sister would know any of their parents' friends. Marie was openly disdainful about their social group, their "caste", as she put it, to a point where Nina was sometimes forced into defending them. And now Marie was being spoken about in such glowing terms by an archetype member of this caste. Nina can't pinpoint quite why, but it unsettles her.

Bernhard Klopp leans forward. His cologne is pleasant, and undoubtedly expensive. 'I was so sorry to hear about what happened,' he says. 'To be honest, my wife makes out that we were well acquainted, whereas in fact, we hardly exchanged a word with Marie. But regardless –' He looks down at the floor. 'She was so young. Such a tragedy.'

Nina glances across at her mother. She sits straight-backed, unmoving, a sculpted smile on her face, as though she's listening to a neighbour talking about her prize-winning roses. This is her mother's public face, practised and honed over a lifetime of acting the perfect wife of an increasingly eminent judge. But Nina can also tell, from the ache in her eyes, that the mask is only being held together by a herculean force of will. She can't bear the sight and looks away, feeling a hot lump of grief in her own throat, panicked by this awful, piercing connection between them.

'I'm sorry,' she says, 'but I'm afraid I have to go. My husband and son, they . . .' She stands up, barely nods her goodbyes, and hurries out.

*

Outside, the rain has eased into a fine drizzle. The downpour has brought out a dark, earthy smell from the

64

surrounding gardens and nearby forest, beneath it a subtle, unpleasant tinge of sewage. As Nina fastens her coat, negotiating the water that has pooled on the driveway, she looks up and sees that the Klopps' car, a sleek black Audi, has parked her in. She turns back to the house just as the front door opens.

'Sorry,' Bernhard Klopp says, stepping out and closing the door behind him. 'It occurred to me the second you left. I'll let you right out.'

He takes a step forward and places his hand on her arm. 'Again, I'm so sorry about your sister. I hardly knew her, but I have some, some understanding of what you, your parents, must be going through.' He pauses. 'We lost a daughter, Gloria and I. Sophie. She was eight years old.'

His handsome face suddenly looks much older, wretched.

'I'm so sorry,' Nina says with feeling.

He gestures, as if to brush her concern away. 'It was a long time ago. She was riding her bike and got hit by a car. The driver didn't stop and we never found out who he was.'

Nina doesn't know what to say. 'That's terrible,' she manages finally. 'I can't imagine –'

'Forgive me,' he says. He gives her arm a quick squeeze and removes his hand. 'I didn't mean to upset you, Nina. May I call you Nina? But I want you to know that if there's anything, *anything* I can do.'

'Thank you, Herr Klopp, but –'

'Bernhard, please.' He reaches into his jacket pocket. 'I don't normally do this sort of thing, but my position at the

Ministry does grant me certain perks. Like knowing who to call to make sure the officers in charge are doing their job properly.' He holds out a business card. 'Please call me if you need any help, any assistance.'

'That is kind of you,' Nina hesitates, discomfited. 'But I don't think –'

'Please. I insist,' he continues, pressing the card into her fingers. Her hand is freezing, his is warm and soft. 'In fact, promise me you'll call and let me know how the investigation is going. The police, well, I know from experience that they can quickly lose their enthusiasm in the absence of leads or suspects.'

She looks briefly at the card before putting it in her pocket, touched now by his concern.

As she waits for him to move his car, she looks back at the house and glimpses the twitch of a curtain. Antonia is standing at the window, watching. Nina raises her hand in a wave. Her mother doesn't wave back.

9

It is almost dark by the time they get home. It's only three o'clock – they stopped at McDonald's for lunch on Kai's insistence – but the sky is black with fresh rain clouds. In this light, the house looks sad and old, nothing like the dream home they fell in love with ten years ago. It stands in one of those residential pockets of the inner city that is rarely featured in magazines and travel guides: full of history yet too low-key to attract many sightseers. Nina likes it this way, away from the wheelie-case-dragging Airbnb tourists and all-night-partygoers, but with newsagents and cafés and playgrounds within easy walking distance. The house was a lucky find: built in the 1930s, it resembles a set of small brick cubes set atop each other – the "Lego house", Kai calls it – appearing streamlined and compact on the outside, while being deceptively spacious inside. Nina has no idea who designed the house originally, but its pleasing architectural feel, together with the mature enclosed garden at the back, means she has never regretted their decision to buy it. With her recent drop in income, however, there's been little left at the end of the month for maintenance after the mortgage has been paid.

When they arrive, she switches on the outside light and

Sebastian puts his key in the lock. He looks up. A part of the drainpipe on the porch roof is hanging loose.

'This house is falling down,' he says.

'The sky is falling down,' Nina murmurs. Kai looks up at her and laughs.

When they get inside, Kai shoots upstairs to play with his Scalextric set, while Sebastian retreats to the study to finish some work that can't wait until Monday. He wasn't particularly enthusiastic when Nina told him about Klopp's offer of help on the way home.

'The Ministry of Justice has bugger all to do with the local police,' he said. 'And the homicide division certainly won't like being told what to do by some jumped-up civil servant still steeped in the ways of the past, believe me.'

Alone in the kitchen, Nina sits down at the kitchen table and takes out her phone. She has a message from Sara, asking her to call whenever she feels up to it. Sara is her oldest friend; they've known each other since school. For the past three years or so, they've made a habit of meeting for brunch once a month at the *Café Bilderbuch*, a picturesque old café with book-lined walls and moth-eaten sofas.

She hesitates briefly, then deletes the message. She can't face Sara, not yet. She's afraid she'll fall to pieces in front of her best friend, and right now, she isn't sure she'd ever manage to put herself back together. No, Sara will have to wait.

Next, she scrolls down the list of numbers in the address book and hits 'Call' when Robert's number appears. He picks up almost immediately.

'Hi, Robert. It's Nina.'

'Nina! Hi.'

He sounds pleased to hear from her. She is relieved.

'I'm so sorry I didn't call you,' he says, and his voice takes on an unhappy note. 'I – I just didn't know what to say.'

'That's okay.'

'I'm sorry, about ...'

'Thanks.'

There is a brief silence. 'How's the new job?' Nina asks.

'Fine. The apes are on their best behaviour.'

Nina can't help but smile. Robert has the best job. He works as a research scientist at the Max Planck Institute for Evolutionary Anthropology, focusing on the reproductive strategies of chimpanzees.

'Great.' She hears the click-hiss of a cigarette lighter on the other end of the line. 'Still haven't kicked the habit?' she asks.

'What?'

'Oh, I just heard your lighter. Look, Robert,' she says quickly. 'I'm sorry. I don't want to make this awkward. The reason I rang is that the police officer in charge of Marie's case, Franzen, told me he was going to Leipzig to talk to you. I was just wondering if there's anything, you know, anything you can add to the investigation.'

'No.' His tone is cool.

'It's all I've got,' she says, hearing the desperation in her own voice and willing herself not to crack.

He doesn't speak for a moment. Then: 'Franzen wanted to know when I last saw Marie. I told him it was a couple of weeks before she was – before she died.'

'Did he mention she was pregnant?'

Robert breathes out heavily. 'Yes. And no – I'm not the father. We broke up three months ago and, well, let's just say that our sex life wasn't as active as it could've been. I gave Franzen a swab.'

'I'm sorry, Robert. I'm sorry to get so personal. It's just –'

'It's okay. I guess I'd feel the same way in your position. But it's not like she wasn't interested in other guys, even when things were still . . . happening between us,' he says.

'What do you mean?' Nina asks. She gave up smoking fifteen years ago when she was pregnant with Rebekka and has never felt the desire to smoke since. But the urge that hits her now is shocking.

'Nina,' he says, 'I really don't want to speak ill of Marie. Not now. But – you know what she was like.'

'There were other men?' she asks quietly.

'Yes,' he says. 'I'm surprised you didn't know. It's not like she made any effort to hide it.' He pauses. 'And it's not as though I was happy about it,' he continues after a moment, 'but, to be honest, I loved her. I thought she needed to get it out of her system. It sounds stupid, I know.'

'No. That doesn't sound stupid at all.'

'That's why we split up. I tried to handle it, be cool, but it just got too much for me. We didn't argue much – it was a clean break-up. That's what I told Franzen, too. We –' he clears his throat, 'we wanted to stay friends.'

Nina realises she's out of words.

'I'm surprised she didn't tell you,' Robert continues.

'There was no shame involved for her and she always said how close you were, how she loved having this older, level-headed sister who did everything right but never judged her for sometimes doing things wrong.'

'Oh, Robert.' His words break her heart and she starts sobbing. She gulps down large bubbles of air, but still she can't breathe for anguish. 'I don't know what to do. I can't deal with knowing I'll never see her again. I can't – I can't *do* this. Do you understand? I can't *do* this!'

'Hey, shhh, hey, hey. Nina.' He murmurs comforting words down the phone and she wishes he were actually in the kitchen with her. 'Listen. Have you talked to someone about this? I don't mean Sebastian. I mean –'

Nina manages to calm down slightly. 'You mean a therapist.'

'Yes. There are people who are specialised in coping with grief. Look, please go and talk to someone. It might help. Just to get over the next few weeks. Please, will you do that?'

'I'll try.' She nods, though she knows she's lying. 'But, Robert ... Did you know any of these ... these men that Marie –'

'No.' He lets out a deep sigh. 'I wish I did. I wish I'd – well, there's a lot I wish I'd done differently.'

Nina hears the study door opening. 'Thanks, Robert. Thanks for telling me this.'

'No problem,' he says. 'And if you ever feel the need to talk again, please call me.'

She hangs up just as Sebastian comes into the kitchen.

10

Nina's first visit to a therapist was a disaster. She was twenty years old and had collapsed the day after her first-year medical exams at university. She had refused to speak to the on-call psychiatrist at the clinic, and had only been released from hospital on condition that she regularly visit the therapist her parents had arranged for her to see.

Professor Doktor Werner was an old man, well past retirement age, and had an unkempt moustache and enormous red hands that he would wring victoriously whenever he reduced Nina to tears. Which was often. She's still convinced it was the personal goal of liberating herself from the psychiatric clutches of this sadistic old man that constituted her ultimate recovery – six kilos in nine months – rather than any psychoanalytic insights he claimed to have provided her with. Her recovery was her triumph over him. Still, whenever she hears the name Werner – common enough – it never fails to induce a sting of discomfort.

Thus, Nina immediately discards Robert's suggestion, however kind. Instead, she focuses on getting through the days under her own steam. She does what is necessary, running on auto-pilot. She keeps her focus narrow and tight, rarely pausing from the moment she wakes until the moment she drops, exhausted and hollow, into bed at night. If she dares to stand still, her mind springs to life like a wound-up toy, allowing grief and panic and anger to take on shape and slip out of her control.

And she recognises the demons: the constant counting of calories has returned, like a computer in her head that refuses to be switched off – she has allowed herself eight hundred a day; sit-ups in the office and endless fidgeting to keep up her metabolic rate; the need to walk up *just one* more flight of stairs, do *just one* more squat, walk *just one* more kilometre, to give herself permission to eat. She recognises the demons and she invites them in, lets them settle themselves around her, because she knows that if only she can get down to fifty kilos, the weight she was before she had Rebekka, then she'll be okay. Fifty kilos. Not much to ask. It's nothing like the eating disorder she suffered from twenty years ago. She's worked through that; she's recovered.

On a Tuesday, three weeks since Marie was attacked, the office phone rings. The next patient is due in half an hour and Nina is forcing herself to deal with the fresh batch of paperwork sent by her accountant, paperwork that seems to increase, rather than decrease, the more she works through it.

It's the outside line. She picks up the phone.

'Hello?'

'Hello, Nina. It's your father.' As though she's not able to recognise his voice.

'Hello, Papa. How are you?'

'I'm fine. A little busy, so I'll come right to the point. I've just had a telephone call from Kommissar Maslowski.'

'What?' Her heart skips. It's an unpleasant sensation. 'Have they –?'

'No,' he interrupts. 'They don't have a suspect yet. I spoke to Chief of Police Lampwitz last week, on your mother's insistence, and he told me that Franzen and Maslowski were competent detectives and that it would be best to leave them to do their job. The DNA analyses have come back negative, so far. Not the most agreeable conversation I've ever had, but it made Mama feel better. Anyway, the reason I'm calling is that Maslowski is releasing Marie's possessions. And as her heirs –' He pauses. Nina can tell he's having trouble keeping a handle on his voice. He clears his throat, then continues in a low tone. 'As her heirs, your mother and I are required to sign for receipt of them.'

'I see.' She can't think of anything else to say.

'The thing is,' he continues, 'Maslowski tells me that Marie had over fifteen thousand euros in her bank account. Do you know anything about that? Mama and I know that you gave her money from time to time, but this seems rather a lot. But if it was from you, we would return it, naturally.'

Nina frowns, recoiling slightly in surprise. 'No,' she says. 'I gave her two hundred when she came round for dinner, the last time before –', she steadies her breath, 'before she died. I don't know –' A light on the telephone dashboard blinks, indicating a call waiting. 'I'm sorry, Papa. I don't know anything about that.'

74

'Hmm. Well, I'll see to it that the two hundred euros are transferred to your account. I have your bank details somewhere.'

The formality of his tone causes her almost physical pain. She cannot bear it. 'I have to go now, Papa,' she says. 'I have a call on the other line. I'm sorry. Say hello to Mama from me.'

Nina pushes the button that is blinking insistently.

'Hello? Dr Bergmann speaking.'

'Dr Bergmann. This is Kommissar Franzen. Do you think it would be possible to come to my office sometime today? There are a few things I'd like to discuss with you.'

*

September, 2015

Marie placed the bunch of flowers on the table in the corner. They looked like they'd been plucked from someone's front garden, but it was the thought that counted.

'How are you feeling?' she asked Nina.

'Woozy. Sore. Glad it's over.'

'You poor thing. Here, d'you mind if I –?' Marie gestured towards the bed.

Nina eased to the side a little, carefully, to make some room. The local anaesthetic around the stitches hadn't worn off yet, but in a couple of hours, the pain would be red raw. Two floors down, in the ob-gyn department of this same hospital, she'd collapsed with a burst appendix earlier that afternoon. Her proximity to the operating theatre had saved her life.

Marie lay down gently beside her. She smiled. 'You look knackered,' she said, reaching out to smooth Nina's hair from her face.

'Thanks. It's my best post-op styling.'

'You look beautiful, too.' Her face was now so close Nina could feel her warm breath on her cheek. It smelled cinnamony. She felt a dull throbbing in her lower belly. Maybe she should ask the nurse to bring her some pain medication as a precaution, in case it got bad during the night.

'What's wrong, Nina? Are you in pain? Should I get a doctor or something?'

Nina shook her head, nodded, took in a gulp of air. 'I'm tired,' she said.

The door opened with a squeak and Sebastian came in, carrying a briefcase clamped under his arm and a coffee cup in his other hand. Strands of his hair stood up rakishly, and his t-shirt had circular sweat stains beneath his armpits. He looked drained.

His smile turned into a frown. 'Do you think that's wise?' he asked, sharply.

Nina swallowed. Her mouth was dry and numb. 'What?'

He gestured with his chin towards Marie. 'That's a single bed. Nina, you can't possibly be comfortable like that.'

'I did ask if it was okay, Sebastian,' Marie said. The way she said his name – it couldn't have sounded more petulant if she'd tried. Nina wished they'd get along, or at least pretend to, if only for an hour or two. She turned towards

Marie. A tiny shake of her head said, Be nice. Marie gave a small apologetic smile.

'It's fine, Basti,' Nina said. 'There's plenty of room.'

'Hmm,' he muttered in response and put down his briefcase.

'How are Kai and Bekka?' she asked.

'They're at your parents'. They're fine, they were . . . upset and worried. But they're asleep now. It was shock for all of us.'

Nina felt an ache in her throat. 'Will they be staying there? Until I get home?'

Sebastian frowned. 'Well, I've got to be in court tomorrow, and I have some meetings lined up that would be hell to reschedule, so . . .'

'I'll help out,' Marie said brightly and sat up. The movement caused the throbbing in Nina's abdomen to turn into a sharp needling pain.

Sebastian shook his head 'No, I don't think that'll be necessary, you –'

'But it's no problem, really. I can pick them up from school and kindergarten, make their tea, play with them, whatever. Nina?'

Nina shrugged. 'Fine with me,' she said breathily. The anaesthetic was wearing off, fast. 'Basti? Let her help out, okay? It'll make the kids happy, and I'll be out of here in no time.'

Sebastian let out a long breath. 'Fine.' He walked to the other side of the bed and kissed her on the forehead. 'But get well soon. We all need you at home.'

11

Shortly after five that afternoon, Anita comes in.

'Frau Müller was the last for today,' she says. 'I've left the forms for you to sign on the front desk. I'll be off then.'

'Okay, thanks, Anita,' Nina says. Then she adds, 'By the way, did Frau Thiel make another appointment?'

Anita shakes her head. 'No.' She has short hair that undergoes a monthly colour cycle: blue, pink, blonde. This month, her hair is bright red, although Nina can see the natural chestnut growing back at the roots. Nina senses the disapproval of some of her more conservative patients, but she likes it. It's fresh and playful. Anita has been with her since she opened the practice and hasn't taken a single sick day. Nina knows how lucky she is to have her.

'Right,' she says, making a mental note to get Anita something special – a wellness gift card, perhaps – to go with her Christmas bonus. 'So, before you go, could you get her home phone number – or mobile number, if you have one – and write it down for me?'

'Sure. I'll pop it on the desk. Well, bye, then.'

'See you tomorrow, Anita.'

Nina tidies her desk, then puts on her coat and scarf. On her way out, she signs the forms Anita has left out and picks up the piece of paper with Jessica Thiel's number, stuffing it into her handbag. It's half past five, and she has agreed to meet Franzen at six. Traffic is unusually light, and she's ten minutes early as she turns into the street that leads to the police station on Keithstraße. It's lined with a mix of residential and commercial buildings in a mismatch of architectural styles – grey, unimaginative buildings containing open-plan offices, and grand high-ceilinged flats in nineteenth-century tenements – lending the street an awkward, shabby feel.

Nina is familiar with the area – it's close to the hospital she used to work at – and she knows that the only available parking spaces at this time of day are to be found behind the Turkish cash & carry on the corner. She pulls onto the gravelled lot, negotiating the deep potholes, and has to wait, engine idling, while a couple of men finish loading a van with drums of cooking oil. Her stomach growls and squelches. The children have asked to have schnitzel for supper, and Nina's planning not to batter hers and to steer clear of the mayonnaise dressing the others insist on drowning their salads in. That way, she should be fine.

When she arrives at the imposing grey police station, she ignores the lift and takes the stairs to Franzen's office on the fourth floor. Eighty in total. The door is wide open and he spots her straight away.

'Dr Bergmann,' he says, holding his hand out for Nina to shake. 'Thanks for coming.'

She takes his hand, noticing how clammy hers feels against his warm, smooth skin. Maslowski isn't in, she is pleased to note.

'Please, sit down,' he says. 'I'll take your coat, if you like.'

'Thanks,' she says. The effort of climbing the stairs has left her breathing shallow.

She takes a seat opposite and waits for him to speak. Spread out on the desk in front of him are photocopies of bank account statements and what looks like a telephone bill.

'Kommissar Maslowski has already spoken to your father,' he says.

'I know. He mentioned Marie's bank account.'

'Oh.' His eyes widen. 'News travels fast.'

'I don't know why that should surprise you,' she says. 'He is my father, after all.' She waits a moment, but when he doesn't speak, she adds: 'Is this going to take long? It's just … my children are waiting for me at home.' She crosses her legs. The right leg crosses comfortably over the left. She must have lost weight on her thighs, a thought at which her irritation subsides somewhat.

'Of course, of course,' Franzen says. 'Yes. The money. Fifteen thousand isn't a huge amount, but your sister was claiming unemployment benefits, wasn't she?'

'Yes.'

'And she didn't get it from your parents,' he continues.

'And not from me, either.'

'Which means,' he says, 'it's something we ought to follow up. Do you know where Marie might have got the money from?'

'No,' Nina says. 'I'd have thought it says on the bank statements where it was transferred from.'

80

'That's a good thought,' he says, and she can't tell from his expression if he's being sarcastic. 'Yes, we checked that, but Marie paid the money in herself, in cash. On the –', he looks down at the statements in front of him, 'on the fifteenth of August.'

'In one lump sum?'

'Indeed.'

Nina shrugs. 'I'm afraid I can't help you. Marie – well, she never had much money, so I helped her out every now and then. But fifteen thousand . . .' She trails off.

Franzen is staring out of the window, as if entirely untroubled and unhurried.

'Is there anything else I can help you with?' she asks, irritable again. Why couldn't they have done this on the phone?

'Yes, in fact there is. It's why I needed you to come in,' he says, again giving her the strange feeling that he can read her thoughts.

He picks up the telephone bill. About twenty calls are listed, and one has been marked with a yellow highlighter. But instead of showing it to her, he lays it to the side and picks up a photograph. 'Do you know a Jakob Fraunhofer?' he asks.

'No.'

'I'd like you to take a look at this and tell me if you recognise anyone.' He places the photo in front of her. She picks it up and feels him watching her, gauging her reaction. The corners of the photograph have curled slightly, and it shows a group of people holding up glasses towards the camera in a toast. The picture was taken in a bar, or a pub. It is underexposed, dark and grainy, but there in the centre of the group is Marie, eyes bright and her mouth wide open in a grin. The context is unfamiliar, but Nina's heart thumps to see her sister so radiant, so alive. And it hits her now why a violent death, unlike a death by illness or old age, can have such an aftermath: the brutal knowledge that anyone, at any time, can be ripped out of life.

'What is this?' she asks.

'Marie's writing group. I wonder if you recognise anyone,' he says, adding unnecessarily, 'apart from your sister.'

The other members of the group are all men, all around Marie's age. Nina has never seen any of them before. 'No,' she says.

'She's the only woman in the group,' he says. 'Which is unusual, for a writing group. Or so I've heard.'

'My sister was unusual.'

He holds his hand out and she passes him the picture. 'We've contacted them all, except for this individual here.' He points at a man with glasses and a slender face. The only one not looking into the camera, but at Marie. 'Jakob Fraunhofer,' he says. 'He's out of the country at the moment, at a conference, so we haven't been able to speak to him.'

Nina swallows. 'It might be a lead?'

Franzen nods. 'Yes, it might be.' He doesn't offer any more information.

'Is there anything else?'

'No. Not at the moment.'

He gets to his feet and unhooks her coat from the stand behind the door. He offers to help her into it, but she takes it and puts it on herself.

'We're doing our best,' he says. 'And I'm sorry if it seems as though this is taking forever, but –' He sighs. 'Unpicking someone's life like this, forensically. It requires patience.'

Nina doesn't reply. Instead, she asks, 'When will we get Marie's stuff?'

'Everything that isn't relevant to the investigation has been replaced,' he replies. 'And we've removed the seal to her flat. So you and your parents are free to enter. But I'm afraid –' He pauses.

'What?'

'The flat hasn't been cleaned,' he says quietly. 'I would recommend you send in a cleaner before you go in. It can be ... traumatic. There are special cleaning services for these types of situations. But Kommissar Maslowski has already informed your father of this.' He sighs heavily. 'I'm sorry.'

*

When Nina gets home, there are no lights on downstairs. She can hear Kai laughing, and, after hanging up her coat and removing her shoes, she climbs the stairs quietly. Rebekka's bedroom is the first on the left. Nina knocks on the door softly and enters. Bekka is sitting at her desk, a circle of light illuminating what appears to be homework. She looks up, her forehead creased in a frown.

'Everything okay?' Nina asks.

'Yeah.' Bekka glances down at her books and shrugs.

'You busy with homework?' She steps closer, her hip grazing Bekka's shoulder.

'Kind of. It's a history assignment. For the end of term.'

'What's it about?'

Bekka shrugs again. 'Collective amnesia in recent German history, you know, when people told themselves they never knew about the Nazi concentration camps, or that *all* East Germans were victims of the system, that the helpers and the spies were always the others.'

'Sounds fascinating.'

'I guess. We're supposed to find instances in books and films and newspaper articles. I've been working on this for ages.'

'Well, if you need any help . . .'

'Yeah, okay, thanks,' Rebekka says and tucks a strand of hair behind her ear. 'It's kind of intense.' She's quiet for a moment before adding, in a small, tight voice, 'Mama?'

'Yes?'

'Auntie Marie was going to help me with the assignment.'

'Marie?' she asks, genuinely surprised. 'I didn't know she'd been talking to you about your schoolwork.'

'Yes. She said she's got lots of – what did she call it – *source material* on the topic, and . . .' She bites down on her lip, hard, but then starts to cry.

Nina swoops down and puts her arm around her. 'Oh, Bekka, it's okay. It's okay to cry.' She holds her tight, knowing these moments were always bound to come but wishing all the same that she protect her daughter from the pain of grief. 'Do you want to talk?'

84

Rebekka sniffs and shakes her head. 'No, I . . . I mean, I'm okay. I just –'

'I know, my love, I know.' Nina keeps her arm around her daughter, feels her warmth and softness. Her hair smells of the strawberry shampoo she's used since she was little. Children, even fourteen-year-olds, can be surprisingly resilient or frighteningly fragile; you just never know until they're put to the test. For a fleeting moment, Nina is full of rage with Marie for meeting such a violent, shocking death. She takes a shaky breath, squeezes her daughter a little too hard.

'We'll get through this, sweetie. I promise. I'm here. And if there's anything I can do, you just tell me, promise?'

Rebekka nods her head and lets out a soft puff of air. She smiles shyly. 'Actually, Mama, I'm a bit hungry.'

Nina gives her a kiss on the cheek. 'We're having schnitzel for dinner. In about half an hour.'

Nina closes the door and walks towards Kai's bedroom at the end of the hall. The door is slightly ajar, and from where she's standing, she can see Sebastian and Kai sitting on the floor, putting together Kai's train set. They haven't noticed her, so she stops and watches silently. Kai is facing in her direction, and if he looked up, he would see her. But he's concentrating hard on his father's instructions, eyebrows pulled together in a wrinkle-less frown and his tongue poking out of the side of his mouth.

Kai's hair is darkening, she notices, as Sebastian places his head right next to his son's in order to show him how to fix one piece of track onto another. She thinks, indulgently, how he'll probably have the same hair colour as Sebastian when he's older – but then her mind is involuntarily jerked back to an embrace in a Zurich hotel room seven years ago. An embrace with a kind, beautiful man whose name she has long since buried, the taste of cheese *rösti* and *Klosterbräu* from the conference centre dinner still in her mouth – and his – to a joyful, coordinated dance of limbs and pelvises. And the next day's feeling of bewilderment that she should feel so exhilarated rather than ashamed at her escape into physical abandonment, as she stood looking out of the hotel window onto the pretty, snow-covered roofs of the city's buildings. The bewilderment and bliss that morphed into numb panic three months later, in a grubby toilet cubicle at a café on her way to work, when the pregnancy test she held in a trembling hand revealed two faint strips where – in a perfect world – there should have been only one.

Kai snaps a track into place and Sebastian leans across and places a big, fond kiss on his cheek. *But it shouldn't matter*, she tells herself, fighting down the guilt that now catches and burns in her throat. Kai is the sweetest, kindest boy she could imagine – what does it matter how he came into existence?

Kai looks up and grins. 'Mama, look!' he says, pointing proudly at his newly constructed railway line. She gives him a proper smile.

Sebastian turns around. 'How did it go?'

'Fine. I'll tell you later,' Nina says. 'I'd better get supper on. I promised the kids schnitzel.'

'Yeah! Schnitzel!' Kai shouts and starts running around in a circle, joyful arms flung out to either side.

'Let's get this cleaned up first, Tarzan.' Sebastian smiles up at him, and Nina leaves them to tidy up while she goes downstairs.

Later, Sebastian slips his T-shirt over his head and climbs into bed.

'Bekka was a sweetheart tonight,' he says. 'I can't remember the last time she cleared the table without an argument. And without being asked.'

Nina smiles in the dark beside him. They had a lovely family evening; she even managed to persuade the kids to play a game of Scrabble. Nina was set to win, but ultimately let Sebastian pip her to the post right at the end. He's an epically sore loser, and she didn't want something as silly as a triple word score to sour the mood.

'Yes,' she says. 'When Bekka's like that, you almost forget how insufferable she can be sometimes.'

'Hormones,' he replies. 'By the way, Sara rang while you were out.'

'Oh. Yes, she's been trying to get in touch about brunch, but –'

'But you're not up to it yet.'

She gives her head a little shake.

Sebastian turns and props himself up on one elbow. She can smell his toothpaste. 'I don't blame you,' he says. 'You'd think she'd understand that you need a bit of space right now. But I'm not surprised, to be honest. I've always found Sara a bit . . .'

'A bit what?'

'You know.' He pulls a face. 'A bit . . . vacuous.'

'Vacuous?' she asks, astounded. 'You do know she has a PhD in macroeconomics?'

'Sure. But aren't you the one who said that any dummy can get a doctorate?'

She bites her lower lip. Yes, she has said this. She does think it – and, as a student, she thought it about lots of her peers – but never about Sara. Sara is smart, and Sebastian knows it. But she doesn't pursue it. Secretly, she thinks her doctorate is a sore subject for him, or rather, the fact that she has one and she doesn't. She smiles to herself. It's petty, of course, but we all have our weaknesses.

'Anyway,' he continues, 'I said you'd call her back when you were up to it.'

'You weren't rude to her, though, were you?'

He exhales noisily. 'Of course not. I know to behave in front of your friends.'

Nina closes her eyes. Another messy conversation. Lately, she's somehow always managing to strike the wrong, contrary tone, leading their exchanges down a path that leaves her feeling tired and bruised and mean.

Sebastian lets himself fall onto his back and lifts his hands behind him on the pillow, releasing a sickly hint of his tuberose scented deodorant. 'So, what's the news from Franzen?'

'A couple of leads. Maybe nothing. He doesn't give much away.'

'But what did he actually say?'

'There's an unexplained amount of money in Marie's account. Fifteen thousand euros.' She turns her head, wanting to see Sebastian's reaction.

He lets out a small snort. 'Where did she get her hands on that kind of money?'

'Nobody seems to know,' she says. 'And there's a man from her writing group they've yet to speak with. Jakob Fraunhofer.'

'Who's he?'

'No idea,' Nina replies. 'You don't like him, do you?'

'Franzen?' He reaches across and gently pushes a loose strand of hair behind her ear. 'It's nothing personal,' he says. 'Him, and that fat guy Maslowski – I don't know. I don't like their style. But anyway,' he continues, leaning back and pulling her onto him. 'That's enough about them.'

She lets him wrap his legs around hers. She feels his erection on her stomach and tries – but fails – to conjure up erotic images that might put her in the mood. The smell of his deodorant isn't helping.

'Did I tell you?' he says, teasing her earlobe with his teeth. 'You're looking hot. Have you lost weight?'

'A little.'

'It suits you,' he says and rolls her deftly over onto her back.

She simply closes her eyes as he enters her, trying to push her mind into a place that isn't grief and pain and darkness.

12

On Gärtnerstraße, Nina parks the car in front of a dumpster. The sign behind her says that parking is not permitted between nine in the morning and six in the evening, but it's the only free spot on the street, and it's still a good few hundred metres from Marie's flat. Despite the drizzle she walks slowly along the shabby cobbles, careful to avoid the dog shit that smears the pavement, only semi-consciously noting the sprawls of graffiti and flaking paint on the buildings she passes. In summer, the street is glorious, with long lines of lime trees that provide verdant, sun-dappled shade, and the sun bleaches the dirty plaster façades so they appear almost clean. But now, with the low, grey autumn sky and naked trees, there is nowhere for the ugliness to hide.

Further up along the road, past a small playground and beyond the next junction, Gärtnerstraße is fresh, clean, revamped; the Wilhelmian architecture as grand – perhaps even grander, who knows? – than its period of origin, bulky BMWs fighting for space next to Mercedes, SUVs and brand-new Mini Coopers. Marie's building is only some fifty metres away from the gentrification sweeping this part of Friedrichshain. In Berlin, the divide is no longer east versus west, but rich versus poor.

Nina reaches number 31 and fishes a set of keys out of her pocket. The door is plastered with tattered posters advertising demos and weekend-long parties. Nobody has bothered to remove the outdated ones, just stuck more recent ones on top. Nina fumbles with the keys, looking for the one that fits the main door. When she finds it, she places it in the lock and pauses. It is the first time she's been back here since a month before the attack on Marie. Her father phoned this morning to tell her that a professional cleaning team had been in, following Franzen's suggestion, and would she please now go to the flat and sort through Marie's belongings. He didn't give her the option to refuse.

A street sweeper comes noisily along the pavement in her direction, forcing her to open the door and step inside. The light in the stairwell is dim, but she climbs the stairs to the second floor without switching on the light. Marie's flat is on the left, opposite that of Frau Lehmholz, the old woman who found her and called the ambulance. Nina can see traces of the adhesive tape from the police seal still sticking to either side of the door frame. She looks at the keys in her hand, then changes her mind. She turns and rings the doorbell to Frau Lehmholz's flat.

It takes a long minute before she hears footsteps coming towards the door.

'Hello? Who is it?' The voice is husky and frail.

'It's Nina Bergmann,' Nina says. 'Marie's sister. Marie, from next door.'

'Who?'

She raises her voice. 'Nina Bergmann. Marie's sister. I was wondering if I could come in and talk to you.'

'Oh,' Frau Lehmholz says. Nina hears the sound of the chain being released from its socket. The door opens a crack.

'Marie was my sister,' Nina says, astonished by how small Frau Lehmholz is; she barely reaches her shoulders. Her head, wizened and brown, reminds Nina of a walnut. The old woman's scalp sprouts whispery strands of white hair. 'I've come to sort through her things, and I – I thought I might come and have a chat.'

Frau Lehmholz smiles and opens the door wider. 'Of course, come in. But you'll have to speak up. The batteries are low.' She pats a small plastic box that is fastened to her belt, presumably the battery pack for her hearing aid, which is attached to the box by means of a wire. Nina almost laughs to see such a device exist outside of a museum.

'They're a special type,' Frau Lehmholz says as she leads her down a dark narrow hall into the living room. She leans heavily on a cane to walk, with a lop-sided, awkward gait. There is a vague odour of stale smoke, as though the place was once inhabited by a smoker.

'A special type?'

'The batteries,' Frau Lehmholz says. 'They're a special type. Can't just use ordinary ones, or I would've taken them out of the remote-control ages ago. Marie knew where to get them.' She lets herself drop into an armchair and props her cane between her knees.

The room is crammed with personal possessions: a glass cabinet contains figurines, crockery and candlesticks; one section of the wall next to the window is covered in framed postcards from Cuba, Yugoslavia and Hungary; an

92

enormous bookshelf – at least twice the height of Frau Lehmholz – covers the entire back wall, more books are piled on an ancient velvet sofa.

On a large teak armoire, Nina spots a faded colour photograph of a much younger Frau Lehmholz. She's smiling into the camera, her arm around the shoulders of a boy Rebekka's age, who is wearing the blue uniform of the *Freie Deutsche Jugend*, the former East German youth association. In contrast to Frau Lehmholz, the boy appears rather cross, his head cocked to one side, eyes squinting at the sun.

'My son, Günther,' Frau Lehmholz says, with a definite trace of pride in her voice. 'At his initiation, his *Jugendweihe*. He doesn't live in Berlin any more, so I don't get to see him as often as I'd like.'

'He doesn't look too happy,' Nina says.

'Oh, it's a difficult age, fourteen,' Frau Lehmholz replies. 'But he was a lovely boy, back then.' Then she adds, with a sudden fierceness in her voice, 'I know what you're thinking. But let me tell you, it wasn't all bad. It was a corrupt, fascist state – I would be the last to deny that – but the ends were honourable. Do you understand? It wasn't comparable to Hitler's fanaticism. The means were rotten and inhumane, but many of us held such high *ideals*, ideals of a just world.'

Nina is taken aback by this sudden outburst. 'I don't doubt that, Frau Lehmholz,' she says, turning to face her, while thinking of her father's "Nothing good to be found in evil" view of the GDR.

'People don't understand,' the old woman continues. 'It

killed my husband. It killed Manfred that people were so quick to accuse him of things he had no choice about. He didn't want to do any harm, he really didn't. He was far too gentle for that.'

She points, with a pronounced tremor, at a framed photograph hanging on the wall behind Nina. Out of politeness, Nina turns and takes a closer look. A youngish man in bathing shorts, tanned and powerfully athletic, grins a little self-consciously into the camera, displaying a small gap between his otherwise perfectly straight teeth.

'That was our honeymoon in Split,' Frau Lehmholz tells her. 'We got married in 'fifty-five but couldn't afford a holiday until four years later. By that time, our son was on his way and I was sick all the time.' She shrugs and lets out a small sigh. 'Manfred was a champion wrestler. So muscular, so strong.'

She pauses, and Nina stops herself from turning around to look at the old woman, afraid she might intrude on some intimate recollection and embarrass both of them. After a moment, Frau Lehmholz goes on with her story.

'But he injured his shoulder badly about a year after that picture was taken. And so he had to retire from wrestling and trained as a physiotherapist instead. He had such lovely hands. Gentle but firm.'

Now Nina turns around. She's feeling somewhat wrong-footed, stuck in this one-way conversation, and for a moment, she wishes she hadn't rung the woman's doorbell. But then, Frau Lehmholz leans forward on her cane and looks straight at her. There is a flash of something – anger, grief – in her eyes.

'He was at the 'sixty-eight Olympics,' she says, 'as part of the medical team. Günther and I weren't allowed to go with him to Mexico, of course. Risk of defection, you know. When Manfred got there, he was taken aside by an official and told it was his patriotic socialist duty to keep an eye on the athletes, and to "observe and report" any contact with the enemy. Western athletes, that is. He was to compile a report on anything he found suspicious, no matter how harmless it appeared. He was told that every member of the Olympic team was doing the same, so they would know if he was withholding any information.' She looks down at the floor.

'So what happened?' Nina asks quietly. She is familiar with patients, not just the older women, who live very lonely lives and are desperate for even five minutes of conversation, of shared memories or troubles. She's always happy to indulge them; it's the least she can do.

'A member of the rowing team, a very young man, nineteen or thereabouts, took part in a friendly table-tennis tournament some of the Americans had organised, and was seen drinking with them later that night. Seen not only by Manfred, but by several others, too. He had no choice but to report it.' Her voice is low, an old person's rattle, now.

'He said it was the most shameful thing he'd ever done. But he had no choice, you see?' Her head quivers. 'If he'd been the only one not to report it, that would have made him just as guilty. What would that have meant for me? For Günther?

'Then, when everything was finally over, when they got

rid of the Wall, it was all dragged out into the open: the Stasi files, the secret documents numbered and filed away. Everything. Well, nearly everything. There are probably some they've yet to pull out of the woodwork, don't you think? People still hiding, people who did really *wicked* things.' She opens and closes her mouth, making her dentures click. 'And there, of course, was Manfred's report from Mexico. They made him out to be a monster, a sneak and coward! As though he alone was responsible for all the suffering.' She slumps in her chair, shaking at the memory. 'He died of shame. You wouldn't think it possible, but Manfred actually died of shame nine months later. My sweet, dear husband.'

'I'm sorry,' Nina says, not finding better words of comfort.

Frau Lehmholz wipes her eyes, gathers herself. 'No, I'm sorry, dear. Ah, my poor Manfred. It would've been our sixty-fourth anniversary next week.' She sighs, then turns to Nina with a smile. 'But I hope I haven't made you feel uncomfortable. Do please sit down and chat with me for a while.'

Nina hesitates, unsure. Frau Lehmholz points to the sofa.

'Just put the books on the floor,' she says. Then she leans back in her chair, cane between her knees, and closes her eyes. She lets out a low sigh. 'Such a shame,' she says. 'Such a shame.'

When she opens her eyes again, they're filled with tears. 'If only they'd knocked at my door, instead of hers,' she says quietly, and Nina realises she is talking about Marie now. 'There's nothing much here of value, of course, but they could have taken it all. And Marie would still be –' She pauses and swallows. 'Nobody wants to die, not really, but I've had my time. Now I'm waiting, passing the days the best I can. And Marie – Marie was so young.'

'The police seem to think that it was someone who knew Marie,' Nina says, not wanting to explicitly agree with the old woman. 'It wasn't a robbery, so . . .'

'Oh, what do they know?' Frau Lehmholz says, waving her hand across her face in a gesture of annoyance. 'Who would want to hurt Marie?'

'I don't know,' Nina says quietly. Then she adds, 'Would you like me to make some coffee?'

'Oh no, I can't drink coffee,' Frau Lehmholz says. 'But I wouldn't say no to a cup of tea. The kitchen's across the hall.' She smiles at Nina. 'You're as sweet as your sister.'

When Nina returns with two cups of tea, Frau Lehmholz is sitting in her chair with her eyes closed. She looks like she's fallen asleep, so Nina places the cups down gently on a side table.

But then Frau Lehmholz speaks: 'I heard the knocking, you know. On Marie's door, the day she was attacked. I thought it was those damn Russians upstairs – they're a rowdy lot, believe me – so I didn't bother going to look.'

'You heard knocking?'

'Yes.' She frowns, pulls her mouth into an *o*. 'At least, I think it was knocking. Though maybe it was the pipes. This building, it's old, it has a life of its own. The pipes in the walls, they make the most awful noise.' She shakes her head. 'They used to keep me awake at night, until I got used to it. And now . . . now it's the thought of Marie that keeps me from sleeping.'

Nina catches her breath. Perhaps this is the first opportunity the old woman has had to talk about Marie. She passes her the cup of tea before sitting down again.

'I didn't realise you and Marie were so close,' Nina says.

'Oh yes! She was such a good neighbour, an extraordinary young woman. I'm – what – more than fifty years older than her, and yet she talked to me like I was as young as her. Oh, the things she used to tell me!' She giggles and places a wrinkled hand over her eyes. Her false teeth appear too big for her mouth; Nina thinks perhaps her jaw has shrunk since she first had the teeth fitted.

This makes Nina smile too; she's unexpectedly touched and delighted to have found someone who knew Marie from a very different perspective. 'Like what?' she asks, detecting a tone of urgency in her own voice.

'Oh, you know, about her boyfriend.' Frau Lehmholz lowers her voice to a whisper. 'What he was like *in bed* – and out of bed too for that matter.'

'Goodness.' Alarmed at the prospect of talking about her sister's sex life now that she's gone, Nina wonders if Marie ever told Frau Lehmholz what she does for a living. All she can think to do is raise a hand to her mouth in faux-shock.

'I'm talking about Robert, now, of course. A bit too *steady* for Marie he was. She didn't talk much about the last one.'

'The last one?' Nina notices that she has tightened her

grip on the handle of the cup. She places it down on the saucer. 'Did you meet him?'

Frau Lehmholz shakes her head. 'Only once. It wasn't really a meeting, certainly not a formal introduction. I went over to ask Marie if she would buy me some milk when she was out shopping, and he was standing in her living room.'

'Did Marie mention his name?' Nina's mind is racing; she's working hard to control herself, not to scare the old lady off. 'Was he called Jakob Fraunhofer, by any chance?'

'Like the institute?'

It takes a second to click into place. The Fraunhofer Research Institute. 'Yes, I suppose so.'

'No. No, that wasn't it. I'm sorry, dear, my memory's not what it used to be. It was something short, that I know. But I can't think what.'

'Of course,' Nina reassures her. 'But do you remember what he looked like? Was he tall, or fat, or . . . what about his hair?'

She tuts. 'I'm sorry, dear, but my eyesight is almost as bad as my hearing. I think he was tall.'

Nina frowns, exasperated but trying not to show it. She doesn't understand why Franzen didn't tell her about this man. Then something occurs to her. 'Frau Lehmholz, when the police first spoke to you, after –'

The old woman groans. 'She was lying there, on the floor . . . and there was so much . . . so much *blood*. I didn't dare touch her, I was frightened. I haven't seen a dead body since I was a child. In the war . . . I thought those times were gone.' Her hands are trembling. Nina reaches over and steadies them with her own.

'I'm so sorry, I didn't want to upset you.'

Frau Lehmholz shakes her head and continues in a shaky voice, her hands resting in Nina's. 'The first police officers that came, the uniformed *Schupos*, they asked if I knew what had happened, but no. I had no idea. And I was so upset, so shocked. I couldn't tell them anything. Apart from the knocking. But that might have been the Russians. Or the pipes. It's a very old building, you know.'

Nina waits a moment, and gently lifts her hands from Frau Lehmholz's. The shaking has subsided. 'But nobody came to talk to you afterwards? No detective?'

'Let me think.' She shrugs, dismissively. 'There was this one fellow, Kommissar something, who came to the door. He asked if I'd perhaps seen something through my peephole. Like I was an old busybody, who watches the world through a hole in the door.' She pulls down the corners of her mouth.

Nina is surprised that Franzen would show such a lack of sensibility. But then again, she's never met anyone so impossible to read.

But Frau Lehmholz hasn't finished. 'A rude man, he was. Fat. And even with my eyesight I couldn't miss that hair. Urgh, I've never been one for red-heads.'

'Ah.' That would explain it. 'I think it's important that the police know about this man you saw in Marie's flat,' Nina says. 'If you like, I can phone them. The officer I've been dealing with, Kommissar Franzen, is really very nice. I think you'd like him.'

'Well, if you think it might help,' Frau Lehmholz says and sighs.

'I do,' Nina tells her and, after a pause, 'So, Marie didn't chat with you about this new boyfriend, then?'

'No. But I don't think they had been seeing each other for long. Such a shame about Robert. He was a very polite, thoughtful young man.' She takes a sip of tea. 'This new one, he seemed older than she was. I mean, not as old as me.' She laughs softly. 'But far too old for Marie. She was such a young spirit.'

'I can't imagine why she didn't tell me,' Nina says quietly, more to herself than to Frau Lehmholz.

The old woman reaches over and pats her thigh. 'Don't look so glum, dear. It was probably nothing serious. And besides,' she winks at her, 'everyone's entitled to a secret or two.'

'Of course,' Nina replies, with an unintentional edge to her voice. Of course her sister would've had secrets, it would be naïve to think otherwise, but this? What else had Marie kept from her?

She gets up, rattled. 'It's been lovely to meet you, Frau Lehmholz,' she says, 'but I'd better be off now. I still need to –' She glances towards the door. 'I need to see about sorting out Marie's things.'

Frau Lehmholz nods. 'Of course. And do come and visit me again. And bring the children! Yes, Marie told me all about your children. And your handsome husband.'

'I would love to come and see you again,' Nina says, truthfully. She bends down to place her cup on the table.

Frau Lehmholz has closed her eyes. 'I'll see myself out,' she adds in a whisper.

In the stairwell, she crosses the hall and lets herself into Marie's flat before she can change her mind again. The air is stale – a tang of disinfectant lingers in the air – and the light is drowsy. The first thing she does is pull back the curtains in the living room and open the windows wide. The air outside is cool, but fresh with rain, and she takes several deep breaths before turning around to look at the room properly.

In the middle of the room, cardboard boxes have been piled on the floor, Marie's laptop placed on top. These are the things the police have examined and returned. A fine layer of dust has already settled on top of them. Nina lifts the flaps on one of the boxes. It contains Marie's letters, journals, photo albums. She shudders and quickly closes the box and goes into the bedroom. It is a small space, but simply furnished with modern furniture, none of the heavy dark wood of their parents' home. The room is tidy, too tidy. The cleaners must have worked hard – Marie's capacity for chaos was spectacular. Nina opens the wardrobe, thinking she might begin here, sorting her sister's clothes into what can be discarded and what might be given away. Her eye is first caught by a green sequined dress that was always Rebekka's favourite; she called it Marie's mermaid dress. Then a tailored suit Nina doesn't recognise. Black jeans. Blue jeans. A red hippie-style skirt with layers of fringes that Marie brought back from a trip to India. A wicker basket full of bras, socks, underpants.

As she reaches out to stroke the shimmering sequins of the dress, sadness rushes up and hits her like a short, sharp punch to the stomach. She can't take it. She needs to get out. She pushes the wardrobe door shut, breathing hard. On her way to the front door, she passes the living room again and hesitates. Then, holding her breath, she forces herself to walk back into the room. She opens one of the boxes and snatches out two leather-bound journals, a photo album and a handful of letters. She has to start somewhere.

*

February, 2017

Marie worked the key into the lock. There was a small grinding sound, then a click, and the door opened. They stepped inside. It was dark in the hallway, the air musty. Marie slid her hand along the wall and switched on the light. Nina suppressed the urge to sneeze.

'What do you think?' Marie asked.

Nina blinked in the glare of the naked bulb. She took in the scuffed skirting boards and grimy wallpaper.

'It's . . .' She arranged her face into a smile, a little too late.

Marie caught the look, but pretended to ignore it. She grabbed Nina's hand and led her further inside. 'I'll show you around. It's even got a balcony!'

It took less than ten minutes to view the flat – probably closer to five. A living room with a tall tiled stove in the corner, a small dark bedroom, a windowless bathroom and a tiny kitchen. Marie kept up her chatter, trying, Nina thought, to distract from the draught at their ankles and the smell – a combination of stale cigarette smoke, mildew and old cooking fat, whose source it was impossible to pinpoint – by describing where she would put what: the sofa here, her writing desk there, just beside the window.

Then she gushed about the vibrancy and debauchery of the local area: clubs, pubs, flea markets, indie book shops; where a veggie döner only cost two euros fifty and a Berliner Kindl two euros; and that she, Marie, would be living in the east of the city, and Nina in the west, and how that would make them proper Berlin sisters.

Then, when she had almost run out of steam, she turned serious for a moment. 'Listen, there's something I've been meaning to ask. A favour.'

Nina laughed. 'Another favour? You'll be owing me free babysitting for years at this rate.'

'It's important. It's . . . my writing.'

'I can hardly help you with that,' Nina said, frowning.

'No, I mean, I've thought about it, a lot, and I want you to burn my stuff if I die.'

'What?' Nina let out an incredulous laugh. 'Don't be daft. I'm older than you, I'll be gone first.'

'No, but seriously, Nina. You have to promise. I can't stand the thought of being up for grabs just because I'm dead.'

'But you're not dead. And –'

'Promise?'

Nina breathed out a long sigh. 'Yes, okay, I promise. But only if we stop talking about it.' She looked around the room again. 'The deposit's three months' rent?'

Marie gave a small nod. Then she turned away and began to chew on a thumbnail.

Nina took her sister's hand, drawing it from her mouth, and smiled. 'That's fine. I'll transfer it to your account as soon as I get home.'

Marie hugged her. 'I knew you'd love it,' she said.

'I do,' Nina replied with a smile. 'But it doesn't really matter what I think. As long as you like it. I just want you to be happy and safe.'

Marie gave her a soft kiss on the cheek. 'Same here.'

'What, you want you to be happy, too? Or d'you want me to be happy, too?'

Marie grinned. 'You're my big sister. You're already happy.'

13

The house is quiet when Nina gets home. For a moment, she wonders where everyone is, before remembering it's Monday afternoon, so Sebastian will have taken Kai to football practice, and Rebekka is at her piano lesson.

She heads straight for the study. She closes the door behind her and takes a seat at the desk. It's covered in Sebastian's papers, coffee cups, and an ancient Dictaphone and spare batteries. Nina picks up the telephone and dials Franzen's number from memory. She counts as it rings five times.

'Yes?' It isn't Franzen.

'Hello. Is Kommissar Franzen available?'

'He isn't at his desk right now. Can I help?'

'Kommissar Maslowski?'

'Yes.'

'This is Nina Bergmann, Marie Bergmann's sister.'

'I know who you are,' he says. 'What can I do for you?'

'Um –' She hesitates. She hadn't planned on speaking to Maslowski. 'I, um, I just wanted . . . Are you expecting him back any time soon?'

'Not today.' He sniffs. 'He'll be in the office tomorrow from nine.'

'Could you take a message please? Can you ask him to call me back? Either on my mobile or at the surgery.'

There's no response, as if he's simply nodding to dismiss her.

'Goodbye,' she says and presses the red button on the handset to terminate the call. Then she goes into the hall, plucks her coat off the hook and slides her hand into the pocket. The card is still there. She wonders if he'll be in his office as she dials the number.

'Klopp?'

'Yes, hi. Um, Herr Klopp? It's me, Nina. Nina Bergmann. We met a couple of weeks ago at –'

'Nina!' He sounds pleased to hear from her. 'Actually, I thought you might've called sooner.'

'Oh. I'm sorry, I – I've been rather busy.'

'Don't apologise,' he says. 'So, how are you?'

'Bearing up, as they say. I'm sorry not to have been in touch.'

'Nothing to be sorry about,' he says. 'I don't want you to worry that I've been sitting here waiting for you to call. To be honest, our meeting only crossed my mind again last night, as it happens.' He pauses. 'Yesterday was the anniversary of Sophie's death.'

Her insides fold. 'I'm sorry,' she murmurs.

'So I thought of you and realised you hadn't called. And it occurred to me that you might have thought my offer was . . . I don't know, insincere, or made in haste.'

He has a deep, soothing voice. Nina closes her eyes for a moment and tries to picture his office. She imagines an expanse of oak desk, a hefty leather chair, an exquisite

Persian rug, and the underlying smell of Bernhard's scent in the air. Him sitting on his chair, phone in hand, perhaps glancing out of the window. She wonders if he ever contemplates the momentous history of his workplace, the former GDR press office from where, famously, Günter Schabowski announced freedom of movement for East German citizens on that fateful November night. Or perhaps not – perhaps that event, like so much else in Berlin's turbulent history, has had to make way for new histories.

She hears him take a breath. She's grateful to have someone to talk to, someone who understands how she feels. With a tiny stirring in her heart, she wonders how things might have turned out if her own father had been a bit more like this man. 'I didn't think your offer was insincere in the slightest, Bernhard,' she says. 'It was very generous of you.'

'And?'

'And what?'

'Are you going to take me up on my offer?'

It takes her a second to understand. 'Oh.' She laughs gently. 'I just –' She stops abruptly, feels silly all of a sudden. What should she say? Please put pressure on the police? Tell them to investigate more thoroughly? It sounds childish, needy and unrealistic. Like Sebastian said, Franzen would hardly thank her for it, and besides, her father has already tried.

'Nina, my dear? Are you still there?'

'Yes. I um, this is more of a courtesy call, really.' Now, embarrassed by her earlier hopefulness, she wants to wrap up the conversation as quickly as possible. 'To thank you for your support.'

'Oh.' There's a hint of disappointment in his voice. 'If there's really nothing I can do . . .' He clears his throat. 'So, I take it the police are on top of things?'

'Well, it's early days, yet. That's what they tell me, anyway.' She shouldn't have called him. 'But if I ever get the feeling they're stalling, I'll be sure to call again.'

'You do that, Nina.'

Her face is burning as she puts down the phone, and she tries to erase the conversation from her mind. But then she remembers another uncomfortable call she needs to make. Might as well get it over with now. She rummages through her handbag, pulls out a slip of paper and dials the number. A man answers and Nina can hear the TV on in the background.

'Hello?'

'Yes, hello. This is Dr Nina Bergmann. I was wondering if I could speak to Frau Thiel, please?'

'No, she's out,' the man says.

'Oh. In that case,' she says, 'could you ask her to call my office when she gets the chance? I have –' Her professional instinct tells her to lie. 'I have some test results for her.' Nina pauses, then: 'Is that Herr Thiel?'

'Yeah. Why?'

'Just –' she hesitates. 'Anyway, if you'd let your wife know I called, that would be great.'

She replaces the phone on its base, praying that Frau Thiel will call her back, then realises she has got through the whole afternoon without thinking of food once.

There is a soft tap on the door. She looks up and sees Rebekka standing in the doorway. She's wearing her favourite Diesel jeans – the cause of a recent major argument between her and Nina, which ended in an unsuspecting Sebastian forking out 120 euros for the trousers – and a faded green sweatshirt. Her hair is pulled up into a ponytail and Nina can't decide if she looks ten or eighteen.

'Hi Mama,' she says.

'How was your lesson?'

She pulls a face. 'Still on the Chopin. I can't seem to get the hang of the second movement.'

'Keep at it, sweetheart.' Nina smiles. 'It sounds lovely whenever I hear you play.'

Rebekka leans her head against the door frame. 'Mama,' she says in a tight voice, 'did you go to Aunt Marie's flat today?'

'I did,' Nina says slowly. 'I … I had to start sorting through her things.'

Rebekka comes into the room and stuffs her hands into her pockets. 'Was it really – terrible?' she asks quietly. 'Being there, I mean.'

'Oh sweetie.' Nina gets up to hug her. She holds her in her arms and strokes her back. 'Yes,' she says, 'yes, it was terrible. But grieving is a process, you know?' She takes a step back and looks at her daughter. 'It's like a path you have to go down, and the first steps are very, very painful, but over time, each step gets a little easier.'

Rebekka wipes her eyes on the soft cuff of her sweatshirt. 'I can't stop thinking about her.'

'Neither can I. But d'you know what? That's a good

thing. That's how we keep her alive.' Her words sound hollow, but they're the best she has. She's suddenly afraid she won't have enough emotional resources to see them all through this. And then what? Her heartbeat slows and she fights back her own tears.

Rebekka leans in again, burrows her face in Nina's shoulder. 'Mama?' she says, her voice muffled. 'Will the police find who did this?'

'I hope so, Bekka. I . . . I'm afraid I don't really know how these things work. But I'm sure they're doing their best.'

There is a painful catch of Bekka's breath. 'Will I . . . will I have to talk to them?'

'No! No, of course not. You don't have speak to anyone you don't want to. I've already told them that.' She doesn't know if she can promise this, but she knows it's what Bekka needs to hear.

Rebekka stays in her arms for a while; Nina hears the long, shaky whisper of her daughter's breath in her ear. Slowly, slowly, she feels Rebekka's muscles relax. Then she thinks of something and releases Bekka from her arms.

'Sweetie, I found a dress in Marie's wardrobe. The green one, you know? The mermaid one with the sequins. Do you think you might like it?'

Rebekka looks at her, as if terrified, and screws up her face. 'I –' She starts crying. Nina takes her in her arms again, unsure of how to take her daughter's pain away. 'How could anyone do that to her?'

'I don't know, Bekka. I honestly don't know.'

14

Nina heaves the shopping bags onto the kitchen counter and goes back into the hall to pick up the post she stepped over coming in. At the bottom of the stairs, Kai is annoying his sister by hooking his fingers through the loops on her waistband and trying to pull her backwards.

'Stop it!' Rebekka says. When he doesn't let go, she lowers her face to his. 'Leave me *alone*!' she hisses.

Nina flicks through the letters in her hand. Nothing important. 'Kai, that's enough,' she says. Then, to Rebekka, 'He has to sit still in school all day. He gets overexcited, that's all.'

'I know,' Rebekka says. 'But why can't he – I dunno – run around outside for half an hour?'

'I know you're talking about me,' Kai says, all self-important.

Nina cups his chin gently with one hand. 'Now you leave your sister alone, all right? And I'll let you have ice cream for pudding.' She pulls his face towards hers and gives him a kiss.

Kai sticks his tongue out at Rebekka and runs up the stairs. She rolls her eyes. 'I'm trying,' she says in a low, tired voice.

'I know,' Nina replies. Then she leans towards Rebekka and kisses her on the cheek, too.

As Rebekka heads up the stairs, Sebastian arrives home.

'You're early,' Nina says.

He sweeps past. 'A client didn't show,' he says, hanging his coat up and slipping off his shoes. 'Bloody idiots. Think I haven't got anything better to do with my time than sit around waiting.'

'Was it Grünblatt?'

'What?'

'The client. The one that didn't show.'

She follows Sebastian into the living room where he flops onto an armchair and leans his head dramatically against the backrest.

'Sorry. You were saying?'

'Your client. Wasn't Grünblatt the one who had to corroborate your alibi?'

He frowns. 'No, the guy who stood me up today was someone else.' He waves his hand in front of his face. 'I sorted out the dates with Grünblatt ages ago. He found it kind of funny, having to provide his legal counsel with an alibi.' He glances up at her. 'Get me a Coke, would you? I'm knackered.'

'A "please" would be nice,' she murmurs, annoyed at his tone, but not wanting to start another argument. He's on a short fuse, she can tell by the tense hunch of his spine.

'Oh, and some rum and a bit of ice,' he says. 'Pleee-ase.'

In the kitchen, she puts the shopping away, sliding the biscuits and crisps onto the top shelf. She has to stretch to reach and comes away feeling dizzy. This morning, she weighed 52 kilos. She pours two glasses of Diet Coke, adding rum and ice to one of them, and takes them into the living room.

'Here,' she says to Sebastian and hands him the drink.

He takes a large sip. 'Thanks.' He holds his hand in front of his mouth and burps quietly. 'Kids?'

'Upstairs.'

'You were asleep last night when I got in,' he says. 'I didn't ask you about going to Marie's. And –' he pauses. 'I didn't like to mention it in front of the kids this morning.'

'Bekka knows. She knows it wasn't an accident.'

He sits up. 'How did she find out?'

'The internet, social media, people talking at school. Who knows? I'm not sure it matters how she found out. She's hurting.'

He rubs the side of his face. 'She's young, let's not forget that. I'm sure she'll cope.'

Nina pauses, thinking of her promises to Bekka, of her child's tears. 'I'm glad you're so confident about that.'

'Anyway, is there lots to do?' he continues after a moment. 'In Marie's flat, I mean.'

Nina shrugs and takes a sip of Coke. 'I – I didn't get much done. It was difficult enough just getting inside, you know? I'll have to go back.'

But she's not at all sure that he knows. Another pause, broken by a thump on the ceiling. They both look up.

'Kai seems a little hyperactive,' Nina says. 'I hope it isn't him reacting badly to this.'

'Let's not start looking for problems where there aren't any,' Sebastian says. 'We don't need any more drama. He's a normal six-year old boy. They get fidgety. God, I can only imagine what I was like at that age.' He smiles to himself.

She has to stop herself scowling at him. Then she says, 'I spent some time with Marie's neighbour, Frau Lehmholz. Yesterday.' She raises the glass to her lips. 'She mentioned a man, a boyfriend of Marie's. Since she split up with Robert.'

'Oh?'

'Yes. And it seems the police couldn't care less.'

More thumping from above. Kai must be jumping from his bed onto the floor and back again.

'I'll go and have a word with him,' Sebastian says. 'Just let me finish this.' He gulps down his drink. Then he looks at Nina. 'You were saying?'

'I was just saying that the police – Maslowski – spoke with Frau Lehmholz in passing, almost. She didn't feel that he was taking her seriously. I mean –' She sits up straight. 'This is a murder enquiry, not a squabble over a parking space!' She suddenly feels like crying.

'Listen, baby,' Sebastian says. 'They know what they're doing. Surely it's best if we just let them get on with it. If they don't think that this Frau . . .' He looks at her quizzically.

'Lehmholz.'

'That this Frau Lehmholz has anything important to contribute, well, then that's their call. I doubt this is the first murder they're investigating. Besides, it's not as though we can tell them how to do their job.'

Nina feels the onset of a headache behind her temples.

Perhaps she should go back and ask Bernhard Klopp for help after all. Didn't Franzen himself say that the early stage of an investigation is crucial? Anything they overlook, they might lose for good . . .

As if on cue, the telephone rings.

'I'll get it,' Nina says, jumping up. Perhaps it is Franzen, returning her call.

'Nina?' her mother asks. 'It's me. I've had a call from the police. They've brought in Jakob Fraunhofer for questioning.'

'What?' Nina's breath catches in her throat. 'Are you sure?'

'Of course I'm sure,' her mother replies. 'Kommissar Franzen just called and said they've brought Fraunhofer in to assist with their enquiries and that he doesn't have an alibi. That's what Herr Franzen said, anyway. Who is this man? Do you know him?'

'No. No idea.'

Sebastian has come to stand next to her. He looks at her questioningly. She waves her hand at him and turns away.

'Franzen mentioned him to me, too. But I'd never heard the name before,' she says to her mother. Sebastian comes around to face her and mouths *Who is it?*, but she ignores him.

'Well,' her mother continues, 'I thought I'd let you know. I can't quite believe they might have the man who – who *did* this to Marie.'

'Thanks for telling me, Mama,' she says quietly. She hears the sound of Kai bouncing down the stairs. 'I have to go now. Please call if you hear anything else.'

'I will. Goodbye. And love to the children,' she says and hangs up.

Nina is shaking as she puts down the phone. She turns to Sebastian just as Kai comes in.

'What's happened?' Sebastian asks.

'Papa!' Kai shouts and runs towards his father.

Sebastian scoops him up and twirls him about. 'Hi Tarzan,' he says. 'How's my best boy?' He looks at Nina over Kai's shoulder.

'That was my mother,' she says. 'The police have brought a man in for questioning. Jakob Fraunhofer. The one in the writers' group that Franzen mentioned the other day.'

'There's a boy in my class called Jakob,' Kai says brightly. 'He used to be my best friend, but now he's not anymore.'

'I know, Tarzan,' Sebastian says. 'I met him at your birthday party, remember?' He lifts Kai's jumper up and blows a noisy kiss on his stomach as Kai laughs. Then he says to Nina, 'We'll talk later, all right?'

She nods and takes herself to the kitchen to start preparing dinner.

*

Later that evening, Sebastian goes to the study to work and Nina heads upstairs with a bottle of Diet Coke. The bubbles give her heartburn, but the caffeine curbs her appetite. She kneels on the floor and pulls out the journals, letters and photo album she slipped under the bed when she returned from Marie's. She feels a bit silly hiding them, but she doesn't want anyone else to look through them.

The thought that the police have read Marie's private letters is repellent enough.

She starts with the photo album, which feels like it might be fairly harmless. It is a large album, covered in a soft green fabric – Marie's favourite colour – which Nina put together in the days before digital photography. It was her gift to Marie when she, Nina, moved out of their parents' house.

*

June, 1999

'You're really going, then,' Marie said. Her voice wobbled although Nina could tell she was trying to keep it steady. They were standing outside in the pouring rain waiting for Nina's friend to come with a VW campervan and collect her boxes.

'Yes, but you'll come and visit me,' Nina said, wishing Marie, whose short dark hair clung damply to her face like a feathered frame, would go back inside and not make this so hard. 'You can sleep over sometime. It'll be fun.' She tried to hide her relief as the VW drove slowly up the gravel path to the house. 'I'm only twenty minutes away on the U-Bahn.'

'You're leaving me!' Marie screamed and ran inside. 'I hate you!'

A week after Nina moved out, she brought Marie the photo album as a peace offering. She hasn't seen it since then; in fact, she'd forgotten all about it. She flicks through the first few pages – pictures of Marie as a baby, of Nina holding her awkwardly in her arms, Marie's first day at kindergarten – but the gently faded images aren't as harmless as she thought. It's a sisterly past that makes her want to sob, and so she closes the album and puts it down beside her on the bed. She wipes her nose with the back of her hand and takes a sip of Coke from the bottle. The letters are in a folder on top of the journals. The first letter is from Robert. Nina doesn't open it. She decides to return it to him as soon as she can.

The other letters, five of them, addressed to Marie in untidy handwriting, are from an American pen pal from her teenage years. Nina finds herself smiling. She's unexpectedly touched that her sister kept them. Marie was loath to hoarding, to keeping 'stuff' from the past that she felt only weighed her down. So why did she keep these letters? Was she planning to get back in touch at some point? For a suffocating moment, Nina feels the weight of responsibility of tying up all the loose ends Marie couldn't help but leave behind. Her thoughts drift to a painful place and it costs her effort to rein them back in.

Next, she turns to the journals. The first contains Marie's notes on short stories she had written, some poems, and what appear to be shopping lists. The second journal looks fairly new; only the first thirty pages or so have been written on. Chunks of prose, scribbles in the margins, words crossed out, corrected, and then crossed out again.

It's hard to decipher in places, but Nina is fairly sure that it's the beginning of a novel. The story is entitled simply, "*Working Title*", with the claim to authorship by 'Dora Diamant'. This makes Nina smile. Dora Diamant was Franz Kafka's lover, and as a teenager, Marie declared this to be her future *nom de plume*. She dumped it later, of course, going on to publish stories under her real name, in small literary magazines and online anthologies, but obviously the name remained a private fancy. Nina reads on; it takes her a while to find her way in, but the prose is dark and beautiful and powerful, and she soon becomes engrossed in what seems to be a story about the son of an unofficial Stasi collaborator, who suspects his father of betraying his mother. Nina is so absorbed that for a moment, she's in another place – a gloomy world of mistrust and anguished passion – entirely. And then the writing comes to an abrupt end, and she's filled with a pointed new sadness, the terrible realisation that this story will forever remain unfinished.

She squeezes her eyes shut, but can't close her ears to the rush of blood racing to her head. The sleeve of grief she has been wrapped up in tightens even further. *It's over.* A deep ache soaks through her and she knows she didn't tell Bekka the truth when she promised it gets easier. It doesn't.

She hears Sebastian's footsteps on the stairs and closes the journal. Quickly, she shoves Marie's stuff under the bed, switches off the bedside lamp and slips under the covers. When Sebastian puts his head around the door a moment later, Nina's eyes are closed and her breathing is deep and regular.

15

Jakob Fraunhofer works for Siemens as an electrical engineer and lives alone in a one-bedroom flat in the district of Prenzlauer Berg. He writes plays for the screen and for theatre, but has yet to find someone willing to produce his work.

'How old is he?' is Nina's first question when Franzen tells her this information. They're sitting in her living room, facing each other across the coffee table. Nina is wearing yoga pants and a chunky woollen jumper and has covered her knees with a blanket. This morning, she felt so light-headed and breathless getting out of bed – her heart felt as though it were crawling – that she decided to call Anita and close the practice for the day. The four patients she was due to see (a worryingly small number, but all the easier to reschedule) would have to come later in the week. Franzen hadn't seemed to mind coming to her house when she suggested it on the phone.

'He's twenty-nine,' Franzen replies. 'Why do you ask?'
Nina shrugs. 'I thought he might be older.'
Franzen is leaning forward with his forearms on his knees. 'Why would you think that?' he asks. He keeps his eyes on her face. When he arrived earlier, he didn't let his eyes travel around the room, like a normal visitor might do, but instead

looked only at her, or at the coffee cup she handed him, or at the armchair before sitting down, as though focusing his attention on what was important. And yet, he gives the impression that he doesn't miss a thing. Nina doesn't doubt, if he were required to close his eyes and describe the room, he would get every detail right, from the collection of antique encyclopaedias on the bookcase, the Bauhaus floor lamp in the corner, to the photo of her and Marie on a beach in Greece ten years ago that hangs behind the door.

Her heart races for a moment, stops and then picks up its sluggish pace. She feels queasy. She shivers, aware that he can see the tremor of her body.

'Are you feeling all right?' Franzen asks.

'Yes,' she says. 'I'm fine.'

'Why would you think Herr Fraunhofer is older?' he asks again.

Nina looks at him for a moment, holds his gaze. It should feel awkward, this wordless eye contact, but it doesn't. The way he looks back at her makes her feel safe. She decides to tell him. 'I went to visit Frau Lehmholz. Marie's next-door neighbour.'

Franzen nods.

'She told me she'd seen Marie with a man, a tall man, who appeared to be her boyfriend. And he was older than her, Frau Lehmholz said. To be honest, I was wondering why this man hasn't figured in your enquires.'

Franzen continues to look at her. He doesn't blink. The way he's leaning forward, taking her in, is unsettling and calming at the same time.

He says, 'I'm glad you told me. I'll go and speak with

Frau Lehmholz. Kommissar Maslowski has already visited her, but he said she seemed – how should I put it – slightly confused. She wasn't sure what day of the week it was. And witnesses, even younger ones, can often be unreliable.' He smiles; a warm, kind smile. Nina feels a sudden longing to trust him. 'But I will certainly go and speak with her,' he continues. 'Did she tell you anything else?'

'No.' She thinks for a moment, then shakes her head. 'Not really. Is Fraunhofer the main suspect, then?'

'He is assisting us with our enquiries.'

She waits for him to go on. When he doesn't, she feels oddly deceived. She's just told him all she knows, after all. 'Is that all you're going to tell me?' She speaks louder than she means to. 'Why Fraunhofer? Have you got any evidence linking him to the attack? Fingerprints, DNA or something?'

She's staring at him now. He holds her gaze and then blinks slowly, disarming her, and she feels something inside her dissolve.

'We did find his fingerprints in Marie's flat,' he says, 'but we know the writing group met there once in a while, so that's not surprising. We're still waiting for the results of the DNA marker testing. It should take a couple of days until we know if he was the father of Marie's baby. Listen, Dr Bergmann –'

'It sounds so formal when you say that,' she interrupts. 'Can you call me Nina, please?'

He breathes out. 'I'm sorry, I'll have to insist on the formality,' he says softly. 'I think it's best, under the circumstances.'

She turns away, embarrassed. She can't look at him, wants to pull the blanket over her head and hide.

'Let me make you a cup of tea,' he says, getting up. 'Camomile? Or peppermint?'

'Camomile, please,' she says in a small voice.

He goes into the kitchen. Nina listens as he fills the kettle, opens one, two, three cupboards looking for where she keeps the tea, then two cups being placed on the counter. The kettle is old and full of limescale, and it makes a dreadful noise while boiling. She reaches out for a box of tissues beside her on the sofa and realises Franzen is standing right behind her. She didn't hear him come in and she tenses.

'I didn't mean to startle you,' he says. 'I've left the tea to brew.' He comes around the sofa and crouches down in front of her, so that his face is almost level with hers. It reminds her of something she does with Kai. They've never been this physically close before.

'I hope I didn't make you feel uncomfortable,' he says.

'No,' she says, taking in how he smells faintly of apples and peppermint. 'It's all right. I don't know what I was thinking. I'm just –'

'A lot of emotions can surface when something like this happens,' he continues, speaking very softly. 'I just don't want you getting more hurt than you already are.'

She looks down at her hands. The wedding band is loose on her ring finger. 'I'm the one who should apologise,' she says and gives him a weak smile.

'Jakob Fraunhofer,' he says, 'claims to have been in love with Marie. Apparently, they spent the night together some months ago and he has been dedicating his work to her ever since, in the hope that she might eventually reciprocate his feelings. That's how he put it. As far as we're concerned, he had an unhealthy interest in her. He denies having attacked her, but he has no alibi and appears to have a motive. We released him after questioning and advised him to be in contact with a lawyer, and he remains the focus of our investigation. And that's all I can tell you at the moment.'

He stops talking. Nina has to resist the impulse to lean her body into his. 'Thank you,' she says.

*

As soon as Kommissar Franzen has left, Nina goes upstairs with the overbrewed tea he made her. She gets into bed, leans over the side and pulls out the folders from underneath. She knows what she's looking for and finds it immediately. Carefully, she teases the letter out of the envelope. The postmark is dated the third of August.

Hi Marie,

Feels strange, putting pen to paper – for me at least. I'm sure it's normal for you, haha. I was going to email, but thought hey, why not write a proper letter! Gives me a chance to put my thoughts in order.

So, the reason I'm writing: Hi, how are you doing? How is the writing going? Finally tackling that novel — I admire you, I really do. I hope it works out.

No. That's not really why I'm writing (as you've probably guessed). I miss you, Marie. And I know we're still friends and all that, and I know you'll say that we can always meet up, or speak on the phone, but if I'm honest, that's not enough. You've left a void inside me. And it can't be filled with a coffee date or a late-night phone call.

I know I said I was all right about the break, and part of me is. Part of me knows, rationally (I guess that would be the scientist-me), that it's better like this, that we want different things and that — like you said — we'd only end up an unhappy couple, rather than happy friends. But another part of me (the human part) thinks this is bullshit. We made a pretty good (happy) couple for over two years, and just because we hit a few bumps recently doesn't mean we can't make it work. Or at least give it a proper try, which (I now realise) we didn't. We never even tried. We took the easy way out (or perhaps it was you who took the easy way out). You said you felt like you were trapped on a hamster wheel, but if you're honest, that has more to do with not having any structure to your life, rather than too much. Sounds patronising, I know. I don't mean it like that.

Come to Leipzig. It's full of energy and light. Berlin is sucking the life out of you.

So. My thoughts and feelings in proper order.
(And far too many parentheses.)
Love you still, love you always
Robert

It takes her a moment to realise she is crying. She wipes her face with the duvet cover. Then she shivers, as if the void in Robert's letter is inside her too, and she pulls the heavy duvet over her head. Within minutes, still shivery and tearful, she escapes into sleep.

*

It is past four and starting to get dark when Nina wakes up. She showers, pulls on her tracksuit bottoms and a jumper and goes downstairs to the study. She doesn't bother switching the light on. The computer is on standby; Sebastian must have forgotten to shut it down last night. She logs on to her email account. There are five new emails; two spams, one from Anita with the updated appointment schedule, a reminder from the accountant regarding the insurance form, and one from Sara. The subject line says: "Long time no hear". Nina clicks this one open.

"Dearest Nina," it reads, "haven't heard from you for so long. Getting worried. I am so gutted to hear about Marie. It's hard to know what to say, but I hope you are bearing up. I'm off to NY for three months in mid-November, so I want to see you before I go. Saturday, same place, same time. If I don't hear from you, I'll come and get you myself. Please call and save me the trouble. Love and kisses, S."

Nina sighs and hits 'reply'. She writes: "Dear Sara, sorry, I've been busy and sad. No need to come round. I'll see you on Saturday. Love, Nina."

She hears, or feels, a movement behind her. She turns and sees Sebastian standing in the doorway.

'Shit, Basti, you frightened me,' she says.

He flicks the light switch on. The sudden brightness is painful.

'Kai's school phoned me,' he says coldly. 'They've been trying to reach you all afternoon.'

Nina lurches up out of the chair. Her heart skips out of rhythm again.

'He's here now. I brought him home. You forgot to pick him up from school.' He hits the door frame, hard, with his palm. 'Jesus *Christ*, Nina! What the hell is the matter with you?'

The sound makes her flinch. She lifts her hands to her head. It's Wednesday today, of course. 'I'm – I'm sorry, Basti,' she says. 'I didn't go into work today, I wasn't feeling well. I must have got my days mixed up.'

'Don't say sorry to me. Go and apologise to your son. He was in a right state when I got there.'

He turns and goes into the hall. Nina follows him.

'Where is he?' she asks.

'In his room. I bought him an ice cream on the way home. I've managed to calm him down now.'

She goes upstairs. Kai is doing a puzzle on the floor of his room. She sits down beside him and kisses him on the head.

'I'm sorry,' she says, trying not to burst into tears, trying not to smother him in her own guilt.

Kai looks up at her, and then turns back to his puzzle. 'You forgot me,' he says in a matter-of-fact tone.

'No, my love, I didn't forget you,' she says in a thin voice. 'I wasn't feeling well, so I went to bed and then I fell asleep. I'm so sorry, Kai.'

He slots two pieces together. 'It's okay, Mama,' he says chirpily. 'Papa bought me ice cream.'

'That's nice.' For a while, Nina sits and watches him. When she is sure he's okay, that he has no interest in reproaching her, she gets up, kisses the top of his head and goes back downstairs. Sebastian is in the kitchen at the fridge.

'You haven't been shopping,' he says.

'I told you, I wasn't feeling well,' she says. 'I had to reschedule today's patients.'

He swings the fridge door shut. He doesn't look at her. 'In that case, I'll take the kids out for a Chinese when Bekka gets home. You can join us, if you feel up to it, or you can stay here. Up to you.'

Nina wants to ask him why he's being so mean to her, so cold, but her guilt over forgetting Kai still lingers. She's lost her claim to any moral high ground. So instead, she says, 'I think I'll stay in, have an early night. And –' She turns her head and adds, 'It's probably best if I sleep in the spare room tonight. In case it's anything catching.'

Sebastian brushes past her on his way out of the kitchen. 'You do that.'

They don't exchange another word until he leaves the house with Bekka and Kai.

16

Nina is in a hurry. Her car won't start and Sebastian has already left to take the children to visit her parents. She lets herself back into the house to get her gloves. The sun is out, and warm on her skin, but she feels a chill that seems to come from deep inside. She's wearing thick tights under her jeans, and a vest and T-shirt under her woolly red jumper. The wool makes her arms itch, but the jumper gives her frame a little bulk.

She fetches her gloves and has her hand on the door handle when the phone rings. She hesitates, but then decides to take the call. It's her mother.

'They're on their way,' Nina says impatiently. 'They should be there any moment.'

'Did Bekka bring her dress?' Antonia asks.

'What dress?' Nina checks the time. It is ten to eleven; she's meeting Sara at eleven and now she'll be at least twenty minutes late.

'For the dinner party,' her mother says. 'I told Bekka I'd like to see the dress.'

Nina hates being late. She sighs. 'What are you talking about?'

Antonia doesn't answer straight away, and Nina can sense the disapproving shake of her head.

'I asked Bekka if she'd like to help Hannah at the dinner party,' her mother says in a measured voice. 'I promised her fifty euros. But I wanted to make sure she wears something suitable, something to match Hannah's uniform. Bekka said she has a black dress, and I asked her to bring it around so I could see it. So I'm asking you, did Bekka remember to take the dress with her?'

'Mama, I'm meeting a friend, and I'm already late.' Nina doesn't mention the car not starting. 'I don't really know what you're talking about, but if it isn't an emergency, I'd appreciate it if we could discuss this later.'

'Pardon me for taking up your valuable time, Nina. I had hoped you would understand how important this occasion is.'

'*What* occasion, Mama?'

'On the ninth. Your father and I are hosting a dinner for the Secretary of State. We talked about this. I was sending out official invitations and asked if you and Sebastian wanted one.' She pauses. 'Why are you being so difficult?'

'The ninth of November?'

'Unless I and the rest of the country have got our historical dates wrong, then, yes, the ninth of November.'

Nina squeezes the bridge of her nose with a finger and thumb. Another headache is edging its way in. 'You didn't tell me anything about this, Mama,' she says wearily.

'Of course I did. Don't be so silly.'

'Don't talk to me like that,' she snaps. Then, in a calmer tone, 'It was probably Sebastian you told.'

'No,' Antonia says, 'I know I spoke to you. But –'

Nina really has to get going now. The only way out of this tangle is to placate her, tell her what she wants to hear. 'All right, Mama. I probably forgot. I've got a lot on my mind. But I don't know if Bekka took the dress with her, sorry. If she hasn't, I can bring it around later, okay?'

'Nina?'

'Yes?'

'Is everything all right?' Her tone is softer.

'Yes, Mama. Everything's fine. I'm just in a hurry. I didn't mean – I've just got a lot on my mind, that's all,' Nina says again.

'Did Kommissar Franzen speak with you?'

'Yes. He called yesterday. Fraunhofer isn't the father.'

'I know. He spoke to your father last night. But they're still viewing him as a suspect.' Her voice is so low, Nina can barely hear her.

'I'll be in touch, Mama,' she says. 'Have fun with the children.'

'I always do,' her mother replies. 'Goodbye.'

Nina puts the phone down and walks slowly into the hall. She opens her handbag and takes out her mobile, sends Sara a message letting her know she's running late, and heads out of the door.

Sitting in the U-Bahn, she avoids eye contact with the other underground passengers and focuses on the upcoming meeting with Sara. She's genuinely looking forward to seeing her, but it will be the first time in ages since she's eaten in front of someone else. Apart from Sebastian and the children, that is, and she's developed methods for that – putting her fork down between bites; spreading the food over her plate so it appears she's eaten more than she actually has; claiming she's eaten a big lunch. Sebastian always has an enormous appetite and concentrates on his own food at mealtimes. And the children wouldn't have noticed anything, either. But today, she will have to watch exactly what lands on her plate. Sara is no fool.

The train slows, brakes screeching, and pulls into a station. Blissestraße. Three stops to go. Fruit is okay; they're bound to have a fruit salad at the buffet. A slice of crispbread would be good, then she could crumble most of it over her plate. She feels an unfamiliar spike of energy. She's almost looking forward to the challenge.

At Eisenacher Straße, Nina gets off the train and hurries to the café. It's quarter to twelve by the time she arrives. A bell above the door tinkles as she enters. The smell of old books, dusty radiators and freshly roasted coffee blends into a musty and slightly bitter scent. It is oddly inviting, the sort of place you could comfortably spend hours in without noticing the time passing. This morning, the café is so crowded it takes a few moments before Nina spots Sara, sitting on a brown corduroy sofa at the back wall. Sara raises both arms and waves. She is, as always, impeccably dressed. Even from across the room, Nina can tell that her outfit – the charcoal-hued scarf draped casually around her shoulders, the slim silver bangles on her wrist, the dusky pink blouse that suits her complexion perfectly – probably cost more than Nina took in from patients last month.

'I'm so sorry,' she says when she gets to the table.

'No problem. I was glad to get your message. I over-slept and only got here ten minutes ago.' Sara laughs. 'I've already ordered a coffee, but I wanted to wait for you before I start pigging out. I've had a quick peek –' She nods her head in the direction of the buffet, which is spread out on three long wooden tables beneath a set of arched windows. 'It looks great.'

Nina forces a smile.

'Oh, god, I'm sorry,' Sara says suddenly. 'God, Nina, I'm so sorry about Marie. I – I don't know what to say.'

'Please don't worry,' Nina says quietly. 'I'd rather not talk about it, anyway.'

Sara lays a hand on hers and gives it a gentle squeeze. Then she raises her arm to attract the waitress's attention, making her bangles tinkle brightly. 'What'll you have?' she asks Nina.

'A black tea with lemon.'

She places Nina's order and turns back to face her. 'If you don't want to talk about it now, that's fine,' she says affectionately. 'But anytime – I mean *anytime* – you feel like talking, you know where I am.'

'Thanks.'

But then Sara pulls the corners of her mouth down. 'Except for the next three months. Unless you want to call me in New York. Which you're welcome to, of course.'

Nina laughs softly. 'Propping up global finances?' she asks.

Sara raises her hands. 'Let's not even go there,' she says with a tone of mock horror. 'Corporate management consultant or not, I'll be glad to still be in a job this time next year. Speaking of which, how's the practice coming along?'

'Slowly. I'm not quite in the black, yet. It's –' Nina swallows and looks away.

'Okay, next topic,' Sara says. 'The kids. How are they? Kai started school this term, didn't he? And Rebekka, how are those teenage mood swings?' She gives Nina a wide smile, which turns into a frown almost instantaneously. 'Shit, I keep putting my foot in it. They must be devastated. Oh, Nina, it all comes back to Marie, doesn't it? How on earth are you coping?'

'Not very well, to be honest.'

The waitress brings the tea. Nina takes a sip and scalds her tongue. She puts the cup back down too quickly, so that the tea sloshes onto the saucer.

'I went to her flat the other day,' she continues, 'to sort through her stuff. And it was unbearable.' She looks up at Sara and has to blink to clear her vision. 'Her life was so – unfinished. And I can't get rid of this urge to finish it for her. Does that make any sense?'

Sara pulls her forehead into a frown and stares down at her coffee. There is something – pain? grief? – behind her eyes, too. 'I remember having to empty my parents' house when they died. It was so unbelievably painful. It took me weeks and weeks to throw anything away.' She lets out a strained laugh. 'Even the actual rubbish bags.' She reaches out and lifts Nina's chin gently with her hand. 'Listen, let me come and help you. Before I go to New York. You can't do this on your own. We'll go there together and get it over with. Okay?'

Nina nods and wipes her eyes. She opens her mouth to tell Sara how grateful she is, but nothing comes out. The air in the café is dry and stuffy with the heat of dozens of bodies.

'And how are things with Sebastian?' Sara asks. 'Is he, like, there for you?'

'Yes,' she replies, a little too quickly. 'He's, he's ... been great. He's – well, you know.' She feels Sara's gaze on her, intense, making her want to squirm.

Sara lays a hand on hers and squeezes. 'I'm here, okay? Anytime you need to talk.' Then she pushes herself up. 'Now, come on, let's go and get something to eat. Before you make me put this waterproof mascara to the test.'

Nina follows her meekly to the buffet. Even from a distance, she can tell that there is very, very little here that is safe to eat. The sight of so much food is overwhelming, and it takes Nina a while before she can pick up a spoon and scoop some fresh berries into a bowl.

When she gets back to the table, Sara has already eaten half of what was on her plate. She looks at Nina, and then at her bowl.

'Not much of an appetite?' she asks.

Nina shakes her head and sits down.

'Never mind,' Sara says. 'But it's important to keep up your strength. Especially when you're feeling low. And, god, look at this tiramisu. I've heard it's delicious. You have to try it.'

'I'll eat later,' Nina says firmly. 'With Sebastian and the kids.'

She lifts a spoonful of berries to her mouth and catches

sight of a couple, sitting three tables away. She immediately recognises the man as Franzen, and the woman he's with is unmistakeably, irresistibly attractive – petite, with dark bobbed hair and perfect, soft brown skin. They sit close together, and the woman must have said something funny, because Franzen laughs. Nina has never seen him laugh like that before. She doesn't look away quickly enough and he catches her eye. He looks at her kindly, smiles, and raises his glass in Nina's direction. She smiles back, nervously, and reaches out to lift her teacup, so she can return the toast. But her hand collides with the cup and she knocks it over. Sara jumps out of the way before the tea can drip onto her lap.

'You okay?' she asks, mopping up the tea with her napkin.

'Sorry,' Nina says. 'I'm all thumbs, lately.' She looks back at Franzen, but he is by now in deep conversation with the woman and doesn't look over again.

Nina exhales sharply. 'You know what?' she tells Sara, 'I've changed my mind. Sebastian and the kids can get a takeaway later.'

Sara gives her a quizzical look, but Nina mumbles something about the food here being too good to waste. She gets to her feet before she can change her mind and tries not to hurry to the buffet. Grabbing the largest plate on offer, she piles on as much food as will fit. She daren't peer over to Franzen's table, but the thought that he might be watching her makes her heart race. She doesn't want to question why seeing him makes her feel like this. All she knows is that something has burst inside, something so aching and immense it can only be staunched by stuffing food into herself.

Her plate is heaped with food; she balances it on the edge of the buffet table and takes a glass bowl, fills this to the brim with tiramisu. With both hands full, she returns to Sara.

'Wow,' Sara says as Nina sits down.

But she doesn't pay her friend any attention because she's eating. The tastes and textures set off little explosions in her mouth – spices melding with fat, salt with sour. With sweet, sweet, sweet. She scrapes the spoon around the sides of the tiramisu bowl with a trembling hand and licks it. Sara is staring at her.

'I haven't had much of an appetite lately,' she says apologetically. 'I thought I'd better eat while I had a chance.' She feels full to bursting, and giddy.

'Great,' Sara says. 'I didn't like to mention it earlier, but you are looking a little – peaky.' She smiles. 'I'm happy to see it's nothing to worry about.'

Nina shakes her head too fast. 'No,' she says, 'nothing to worry about.'

'You have to make sure you're being kind to yourself. Not just to other people.'

*

Later, they hug goodbye outside the café. Sara promises to call when she has a couple of hours free, to go with Nina to Marie's flat.

'The sooner, the better,' she says. 'You don't want it hanging over you.'

'Oh, Sara, what would I do without you?'

'Look, can I give you a lift?' she asks, pointing to a shiny blue BMW parked right in front of the café in a no-parking zone.

'Thanks, but no.' The sun is still out in force. 'I'll take the underground. Give me a chance to clear my head before I get home.'

Sara pulls a face at the mention of public transport, then de-activates her car's central locking. 'I'll call you tomorrow, or Monday at the latest. Stay strong.' And she drives off with a smile.

Nina doesn't hesitate. She walks down Akazienstraße in the opposite direction of the U-Bahn station, picking up her pace so that she's moving with a kind of half-walking, half-running skip. There is a supermarket at the end of the street, on the other side of the junction. She estimates that she has around one thousand calories churning inside her, but still there's room for more. The pavement is crowded; people are taking advantage of the break from the rainy weather they've had for days. Couples, dog-walkers, joggers, shoppers – the entire city seems to be out and about, and Nina is forced to stop, swerve, pick up her pace again, slow down. She's in a hurry now, and wishes she'd eaten the tiramisu first, to line her stomach.

She steps aside to let an elderly man with a Zimmer frame pass only to collide with a pram. She mutters her apologies to the angry mother and finally makes it to the supermarket. She wishes she had her car. She doesn't know how much she'll be able to carry. She has the list ready in her mind: ice cream, crisps, salami, potato salad, wine gums, bottles of full-sugar coke, pastries. She tosses everything into the trolley and when she gets to the till, she is astonished at the cost. But it doesn't matter. Her pulse is pounding high in her throat. She hands her debit card to the cashier and punches in her PIN. She doesn't wait for the receipt.

Outside, she calculates the quickest way to get to Wilmersdorf. Going home is not an option – Sebastian and the children could be there, or might arrive while she's still eating. The urgent sense of anticipation, the surging greed and diesel fumes from the main road are making her nauseous. She takes shallow breaths and moves along the pavement, eyes down. The shopping bags are heavy, the handles are cutting into her hands, painfully.

In an attempt to escape the stinking high street, she turns onto Pallasstraße, a grey, wide road, lined by blocks of high flats and dilapidated shops – a barber's, a *späti*, vaping shops, a couple of arcades. It's a withered area, neglected for decades, left behind when the breathless, heady days of reunification saw public spending pumped into the shiny new city centre, giving everything just east of the former Wall a fresh, gilded face. This here is not a part of Berlin tourists come to see. It's not shabby chic, like Kreuzberg and Prenzlauer Berg. It's just shabby. Nina looks around for a taxi rank, her whole body buzzing, then – a hand on her arm is forcing her to a stop. She almost loses her grip on the carrier bag.

'Dr Bergmann!'

Nina looks up at the woman who just stopped her. Mid-forties, short brown hair, a hefty body. It takes a moment to place her. It's one of her patients, Frau Schüssler.

'Fancy meeting you here! Lovely weather, isn't it? Out shopping, are you?'

The woman eyes the shopping bags and Nina is seized by a panicky shame.

'I'm so sorry, I'm in a terrible hurry,' she says, avoiding the woman's eye. A taxi stops at a red light in front of her and Nina hops in, leaving Frau Schüssler standing there, open-mouthed.

'Rüdesheimer Platz, please,' she says to the driver. He nods and accelerates as the light turns green. She doesn't look back.

When they arrive ten minutes later, she leans forward and hands the driver a twenty-euro note. 'Keep the change,' she says and struggles out of the car with her bags.

It is an upmarket area; Sebastian encouraged her to set up somewhere she could get as many private patients as possible. ('If you're going to do this, then think big.') But she can barely cover the rent. She puts the shopping bags down too quickly at the front door, and the one with the coke bottle topples over and spills its contents over the pavement. She curses and retrieves a set of keys from her pocket, then bends down and stuffs the food back into the bag. She shoves the bottle under her arm and enters.

It's beautifully quiet inside. She goes straight into the examination room, sits down on the floor and carefully spreads the food out in front of her, in the order she will eat it. The white blinds are drawn, diffusing the sunlight in the room. She closes her eyes for a moment, breathes in and out slowly, internalising the calmness of the space, the situation, the moment. Then she begins.

*

May, 1993

'I tried, but –'

Her father cut her off. 'It's not a matter of trying, Nina. It's a matter of doing. Do you think anybody's ever going to ask you hard you tried? No. They're going to look at the facts.' He stabbed his finger at the report card. 'And you're quite capable of getting the grades for medical school. You just have to want it enough.'

Her mother spoke without looking up from her plate. 'Perhaps less time spent with ... what's his name, Markus?'

Nina counted the runner beans on her plate. Nine. With her fork, she separated them into two piles and scraped the gravy off the smaller pile. She felt Marie tugging at her shoelaces. She kicked out and heard a muffled 'Ow!'

'For crying out loud! What's the child doing under the table?' Her father directed this at her mother.

'I couldn't say.' Antonia gave a weary sigh. 'She's been there all afternoon.'

'She's playing,' Nina said. 'That's all.'

'Behaving like a dog,' her father replied, wiping the corners of his mouth with a linen napkin and getting to his feet. 'I'll be in my study.'

17

At home, the children are upstairs in bed and Sebastian is sitting in the living room, in the dark, watching TV. Nina heads for the kitchen and gets a glass of water. Her throat is still raw. With the glass in hand, she goes into the living room and sits down next to Sebastian. He doesn't ask where she's been. The smell of something greasy, meaty, hangs in the air. Sebastian must have got a takeaway in for supper.

They sit in silence for a moment, then Sebastian picks up the remote control and turns off the TV. Nina doesn't reach over to switch on the light. She knows instinctively, even before he speaks, that this is going to be one of those conversations better held in the dark.

'We have to talk,' he says and turns to face her.

She swallows and winces. 'It's –' she begins, but Sebastian holds up his hand to stop her.

'I'll start, if that's okay,' he says. 'I've been thinking about things for a while now, and I want you to hear what I've got to say.' He takes a deep breath. 'To be honest, Nina, it can't go on like this. I know you're still grieving, but I believe it's time you –' He looks towards the blank

TV screen and then back at her. 'It's time we got back to normal, as a family and as a couple. I don't know how to bring this up in a nice way. I understand, I do, that this has been very, very traumatic for you. But we can't go on like this. Everything I say, every little thing, you jump down my throat. I don't feel I can touch you even.' He puts his hand on the nape of her neck and she flinches. 'You see!' he says, pulling his hand back. 'Am I really that repellent to you?'

He gets up and takes three paces across the room. The orange light from the streetlamp outside gives the room an alien, claustrophobic feel.

He turns and sits back down, resting his forearms on his thighs. He lets his head hang down between his shoulders. 'I don't think you realise how much this is affecting us,' he says quietly.

Nina gazes down at the glass of water in her hand. Its surface is perfectly still.

'Bekka wants to give up piano lessons,' he continues. 'She said, what's the point? And Kai keeps asking me why Mama is so sad.'

Her face crumples. *It's so unfair*, she wants to say, *bringing the kids into this*, but instead she says, 'I'm sorry.' Her voice is cracked and she feels herself gasping.

'Yes,' he says. 'So am I.' He sighs, and she wonders at his need to be so melodramatic. 'But I'm not willing to give our lives up, Nina. Not you, not the kids.'

Sebastian takes the glass of water from her hand and places it on the coffee table. A car outside starts its engine, revs noisily and speeds off.

'We need to talk to each other,' he says, and puts his arms around her. 'We need to connect.' For a while, they remain in this limp embrace, silently.

Nina wonders what he can possibly connect with – she has no strength, she is empty.

'I've been thinking,' he says finally, 'and I know how it's going to sound, but hear me out.' He takes a deep breath. 'I've been thinking we should maybe have another baby. While we still can.'

He guides her chin upwards with his finger, so that he's looking directly into her face. 'Hmm?'

Nina starts to laugh. She laughs and laughs until she realises she's not laughing at all. She's crying and crying. Sebastian embraces her again.

'Shhh,' he says. 'It's okay. I'm sorry. I didn't mean to freak you out. I've been playing this over in my mind. Remember when we found out that you were pregnant with Kai? We were so happy, so relieved. Remember? That magical moment when you realise you can forget all the hurt and fighting, that you can put it behind you because all that matters is that this beautiful, exquisite little human being is going to come into your life. I want us to feel like that again, Nina.'

Nina slips out of his arms. She clears her throat, painfully. 'I – I don't know what to say.'

'Say yes! Don't you remember how great it was?' He looks at her, searching her face. '*I* do, I remember how nice it was to come home to you and the kids, and everything would fall off me, the whole work stress, the annoying clients, the rush-hour traffic. It was just us, together, in our home.' He smiles wistfully. 'I'd like that again, I really would.'

His expression is hopeful and vulnerable at the same time. She feels a lick of fear that he's actually serious about it. 'I'm forty-two, Basti.'

'Then it's now or never.'

'And the practice –'

And the morning sickness, and the back aches, and the swollen ankles, the weight gain, the excruciating labour pains, the torn perineum, stiches, mastitis, nappies, exhaustion.

And the practice.

'I've given that some thought, too.' He interlocks his fingers in front of him. 'I think the sensible thing to do might be to cut your losses.'

She looks at him. His hair shines copper in the glow of the streetlamp.

'Regardless of whether or not we have a baby,' he continues. 'It's too much effort for too little reward. It was a great idea at the time, but it's been over a year now, and, if you're honest with yourself . . .' he pauses. 'At least you tried.'

'And failed,' she adds in a small, broken voice.

He shakes his head. 'No. No, you haven't failed. That's not how you should look at it. This happens to people all the time. Good people, smart people. And –'

'You've certainly been giving this a lot of thought.' She gets up off the sofa in a surge of something like anger. What is he thinking? That she relinquish her career, her independence, her body – for his dream of a new baby?

Sebastian looks up at her, his initial look of vulnerability now replaced by self-assurance. 'Yes, I have,' he says. 'And it's never too late to start again.'

'I'm tired, Basti. I have to go to bed.'

'I understand,' he says. 'We don't have to talk about it now. But promise me you'll give it some proper thought.'

'I will.' She leaves the room, walks up the stairs and shuts the door to the spare room behind her.

18

September, 2009

'Do you never, you know, dream of escaping?' Marie was lying on her back, wearing a very tiny red bikini; her skin, after only three days of Greek sunshine, a deep golden tan.

'What do you think I'm doing right now?' Nina answered, dipping her right foot into the pool and watching the water travel outwards in ripples and dissolve into itself. She looked down at Marie, who was lying beside her with her forearm covering her eyes. 'Did you cheat and go to a tanning studio before we came?' she asked.

'I don't mean this,' Marie said, ignoring Nina's question. She propped herself up on her elbows and squinted in Nina's direction. 'This is just a break. What I mean is, have you never thought of escaping, from everything?'

'Actually, no.'

'Never? Never ever ever? Not for one single nanosecond?'

Three young men whom Nina recognised from the night before – they belonged to a loud, drunken group of lads on a stag do – slopped past them in flip flops and long multi-coloured surf shorts. Nina pulled her stomach in instinctively. Four years after Rebekka's birth, her body had more or less regained its pre-pregnancy shape, except for the slight flabbiness of the skin covering her abdomen. For her, her bikini days were over, and she'd bought a painfully expensive black swimming costume for this holiday, which, she thought, made her look rather elegant. But not young. And not hot, either.

'So this is it for you?' Marie continued, sitting up and reaching into Nina's beach bag for the sunscreen. 'Mummy, Daddy, baby, steady job –'

'A steady job that's paying for your holiday,' Nina said, trying to keep the bite out of her voice. She watched as her sister covered her arms and legs with the lotion, then took the bottle from her and began rubbing some onto her shoulders. In the corner of her vision, she could see the young men watching. For the briefest of moments, she had an urge to protect her sister – her gorgeous twenty-two-year old sister – from these looks by covering her with a beach towel.

'And besides, any time I feel like "escaping",' she said, spreading the remains of the sticky lotion on her own forearms, 'I have Sebastian to look after Bekka. He's good like that.'

'Yeah, right,' Marie said, letting out a little snort.

Nina turned and frowned at her. 'What's that supposed to mean?'

'Nothing.'

'No, come on, I want to hear it.'

Marie licked her lower lip but said nothing.

Nina pushed her sunglasses up onto her head. 'What

exactly is your problem with Sebastian?' she said in a low voice, mindful of the other holidaymakers around the pool.

Marie pulled the corners of her mouth down and shook her head slightly. 'You know when guys say they like "strong independent women"?' The last words in air quotes.

'Yes?'

'They don't, more often than not. They just like the idea of strong independent women. They like the idea that they deserve some kind of prize for being a modern man. I mean, he calls you "baby", for fuck's sake!'

'Yes, well.' Nina shoved her sunglasses back on. 'You don't know what you're talking about.' A pause. 'More often than not.'

Marie turned to look at her, then let her eyes slide away. They sat in silence for a moment.

'I'm sorry,' Marie said in a small voice. She leaned in and rested her head against Nina's. 'You know I can't keep my big mouth shut. Please, let's not fight.'

Nina felt her anger fizzle out and die.

Marie got to her feet. 'Where's the camera?' she asked, switching her attention. 'I'll get those guys to take a photo of us.'

*

Nina opens the door to the practice. As always, Anita is there before her. She gives Nina a broad smile from behind the reception counter as she enters.

'Here,' Anita says, standing up and pushing a stack of files towards Nina. 'Lots to do today.'

'Wow,' Nina says.

'Eight regulars, five new patients. I've rescheduled two of last Thursday's patients for this afternoon. I hope that's okay?'

It's meant to be Nina's afternoon off, but she doesn't care. 'That's fine. Thank you, Anita.'

Anita smiles again. 'No problem.'

'I know, but truly, thanks for everything.'

Anita puts her head to one side, looking like a young girl all of a sudden. 'I think you're very brave,' she says quietly.

Nina smiles and picks up the files. As she walks towards the examination room, Anita calls out in an urgent whisper, 'I forgot to say. That police officer, Kommissar Frank, is waiting for you. In there.' She points to the examination room. 'He was here first thing, outside the door when I got here. He asked if he could wait somewhere quiet, so I told him to go in.' She pulls up her shoulders. 'Hope that isn't a problem.'

'Not at all.'

'Dr Bergmann?' she says. 'I should have mentioned this sooner, but –'

'What is it, Anita?'

She plucks at her sleeve. 'The very first time he came, Kommissar Frank, just after your sister ... he asked if I could confirm that you were here all morning on the day she was –' She inhales sharply. 'Of course you were, I told him. I can't believe he might've thought that you – well, I felt awkward mentioning it to you, that's all.' She stops.

'It's okay, Anita,' Nina says. 'He was just doing his job.'

Which she knows is true, but she hadn't considered it before and it makes her feel tainted, somehow. She heads towards the examination room.

'Sorry, Dr Bergmann, one more thing,' Anita says. Nina turns around.

'Were you in here over the weekend, by any chance?'

Nina clears her throat. 'Yes. I was catching up on some paperwork. Why do you ask?'

'Thank goodness,' Anita says. 'All the doors were open in here when I came in this morning – the exam room, the toilet – and I thought maybe someone had broken in. I was glad Herr Frank came in with me. Just in case someone was still lurking.'

'No, that was me,' Nina says. She hesitates briefly, waiting to see if Anita will mention finding any evidence of Saturday's binge.

But all Anita says is, 'Okay, good.'

'And it's Kommissar Franzen, not Frank,' Nina adds quietly, and then opens the door to the examination room.

He is sitting in a chair close to the window, looking out. He must have moved the chair over there. He turns his head quickly as she enters.

'You startled me,' he says, although he doesn't look startled.

Nina places the files on her desk. 'I'm sorry,' she says. 'I didn't mean to.'

He turns away to look out of the window again. 'I have a feeling it'll be a harsh winter, this year,' he says. Nina waits for him to elaborate, but he doesn't.

'Herr Franzen, I'm very busy today,' she says finally. 'What can I do for you?'

He turns, gets up from his chair and carries it back to its original spot in front of the desk. He gestures for her to take a seat behind the desk, and then sits down himself. Nina bends and switches on the computer.

'I went to see Frau Lehmholz on Friday,' he says.

Nina sits up. 'Oh? What did she say? Did she tell you about the man she saw at Marie's flat?'

'Frau Lehmholz thought Kommissar Maslowski was Russian,' Franzen says, ignoring her questions. 'It appears she isn't too fond of Russians.'

'She was here at the end of the war. A lot of German women of her generation aren't too fond of Russians, particularly the men.'

'His parents are from Poland, actually. Poznań, I believe.'

Nina sighs. 'Herr Franzen, I do wish you'd come to the point.' She gestures at the pile of patient files.

'I'm sorry,' he says and gives her a shy smile. 'My mind is a little slow this morning.'

Perhaps he was up late last night with that woman. She feels sure he's dissembling, but still it annoys her that this thought stings.

'I spoke to Frau Lehmholz,' he continues. 'She confirmed what you told me and gave me a description – albeit a rather hazy one – of the man she saw with Marie. We're following it up.'

'Good. So what happens now? What about Fraunhofer?'

Franzen takes his TicTacs out of his pocket and puts two in his mouth. He doesn't offer her any. 'The investigation is ongoing,' he says. 'I'm afraid I can't divulge any more details, other than to say that we will be interviewing him again.'

'But he's not the father.'

'No.'

Nina looks at the clock in the corner of the computer screen. 'I'm sorry, Herr Franzen, I really have to get to work now.' She stands up.

'Of course,' he says. 'Thank you for your time. I'll be in touch as soon as I have something more concrete to tell you.'

Nina accompanies him to the door. 'Do you go there often?' The words tumble out before she can stop them.

'Go where?'

'To *Café Bilderbuch*. Last Saturday, I saw you there.'

'Oh, so you did. No.' He shrugs. 'It was my first visit. Nice place, isn't it? Great food.'

'Yes.' She realises she's waiting for him to mention who the woman was. A few seconds pass, and she knows he isn't going to. 'Well, goodbye.'

'Goodbye, Dr Bergmann. I'll be in touch.' He opens the door.

'One more thing,' she says.

He stops. 'Yes?'

'I'm just curious why you came by in person. You could have told me this on the phone.'

Franzen smiles as if pleasantly surprised. 'I was in the neighbourhood.'

*

During the course of the morning, Nina confirms three pregnancies – a record number in one day. Two of the women are close to forty, both of them expecting for the first time and who came prepared with a catalogue of questions regarding exercise, diet, vitamins and nuchal scans. Their efforts to appear knowledgeable and on a par with Nina's professional expertise only served to make them seem a little desperate and over-anxious; a stark contrast to the younger mum-to-be, a twenty-five-year-old who beamed as she told Nina she was looking forward to holding the baby in her arms.

Nina is not immune to the irony. But she hasn't yet decided whether Sebastian's outrageous suggestion was sincere, or a bizarre clutching at straws. And she doesn't want to analyse it further.

As Frau Bader, her final patient for the morning, climbs out of the examination chair, it occurs to Nina that it's over two years since she had a smear test herself. At the same time, she wonders if she cares. Frau Bader crosses the room towards the changing screen, and Nina takes a seat behind the desk.

The quiet calm of the clinic is abruptly broken by sudden shouting coming from the waiting room outside. A man's voice, harsh and angry. Then Anita's. The sound of a scuffle and the word 'police' stands out, then the door swings open and a man rushes in. He's young, scruffily dressed, and looks as though he's either drunk, high or hasn't slept for a while. He stares wildly around the room.

'You!' he shouts, pointing at Nina.

Anita runs in behind him, grabs his shoulder but he

jolts her away. 'Get out! Now!' she shouts. And to Nina: 'I'm sorry. I couldn't stop him.'

Nina jumps up, dizzied by this unexpected turn of events. 'Call the police,' she instructs as calmly as she can. Anita nods and backs out of the room. Nina looks over towards the changing area. Through the gap between the screen and the floor she can see Frau Bader pulling on her jeans in a hurry. The man follows her gaze. Before she can act, he steps towards the screen and pulls it down. Frau Bader lets out a short shriek.

'Get out, bitch,' he barks at her.

Frau Bader, one arm now inside her jumper, the other still out, throws a horrified, hesitant glance at Nina.

'You should leave,' Nina tells her, trying to sound both reassuring and more confident than she feels.

Frau Bader grabs her handbag from the floor and runs out. The man turns to face Nina.

'You,' he says again. He takes a few steps towards her. He isn't too steady on his feet.

Nina remains standing behind the relative safety of the desk. Her heart is thumping. 'This is an examination room,' she says, trying to keep her voice steady. 'I would like you to leave.'

'I bet you would, you bitch,' he says, taking another step forward, so that he's right across the desk from her. 'Poking around in other women's cunts. *Examining* them. D'you get off on that?' He jabs the air with his finger. 'Do you? Eh? You're fucking sick!'

Nina retreats instinctively and bumps into the wall behind. Feeling trapped, she forces herself to take a step forward. 'Please leave,' she says, aware that her voice is shaking now. 'My receptionist has called the police.'

With surprising speed, the man steps around the desk and grabs her right arm. He twists it behind her back, painfully. Nina cries out. He's standing so close that his belly and groin are touching her, and beyond him, she can see several women – her clients – peering in from the waiting room.

'You talked to my wife,' he snarls. 'I want to know where that whore is.'

He jerks her arm up a fraction, pulling down on her wrist at the same time. She's afraid it might snap.

'Yes, it's me,' he says. His face is very close to hers, his breath rank.

'Herr Thiel,' Nina says, her voice strangely high-pitched, but determined not to cede control. 'I don't know where your wife is. Please let me go. You're hurting me.'

'That's the plan, bitch.' He smiles nastily. 'I'll ask you again. Where's my fucking wife?'

'I don't know,' she repeats.

At that moment, she hears Anita's voice. 'I've called the police,' she says, and Nina can tell she's trying to sound confident, authoritative. 'They'll be here any minute. Let her go.'

Thiel twists Nina's arm a little further, making her gasp. Then he lets go. 'I'm going to find that whore,' he spits, his face so close now that his nose touches hers. 'And see how she likes her examination then.' He turns, knocking his shoulder hard against Anita's on his way out. Nina's legs start to shake uncontrollably and she slides to the floor.

Anita rushes towards her and crouches down. 'Oh Nina,' she says, her eyes full of tears. 'I'm so sorry. I couldn't stop him. I threatened to call the police, but he completely ignored me.'

'You did far more than you needed to.' Nina rubs her shoulder, then her wrist. She finds she can't control the shaking. 'Could you get me a glass of water, please?' she asks, wiping her face with her sleeve. 'Thank you.'

Anita nods. As she gets up, she says, 'I've sent the other patients away. I didn't think you'd –'

'Yes. That was the right thing to do.' Nina hears a police siren on the street outside. 'Could you let them in, please? Give me a minute to get myself together.'

'Okay,' Anita murmurs, and leaves.

*

Sebastian brings Nina a mug of vegetable broth. He hands it to her, with a warning that it's hot, and props up the pillow behind her back, like a nurse with a sick patient.

'I spoke to Lea's mum,' he says. 'She said she's happy to have Bekka overnight.'

'On a school night?'

He sits down on the edge of the bed. 'I'm sure Frau Heitlinger will get them into bed at a decent hour. Kai's fast asleep. He was out like a light even before I left his room.'

Nina smiles. 'I'm glad.' She blows on the broth, takes a sip. The trembling she's felt since the attack has subsided, and she's thankful the day is over. She gave a statement to the police in her office, informing them of Jessica's injuries and the threat Thiel made against her, and confirming that, yes, she wants to press charges against him. They, in turn, promised to contact her as soon as they have any information as to his or his wife's whereabouts.

Sebastian looks at his watch. 'I'd better walk Bekka round before it gets too late,' he says.

Nina sits up. 'I'll just pop down and say goodbye, then. Let her know I'll be fine and not to worry.'

Sebastian shakes his head. 'Do you think that's wise? Not to be harsh, baby, but you look a bit of a fright.' He reaches across and squeezes her shoulder. 'Best if you rest up for tonight. Things'll feel different in the morning, once you've had a good sleep and a shower.'

Nina's hand goes up to her unwashed hair. 'Bekka won't mind how I look.'

'I know, I didn't mean it like that. But you're still totally shaken up. Kids can be very sensitive to that sort of thing and Bekka's less likely to worry if she knows you're recovering.' He laughs gently. 'I guess it's true, doctors really do make the worst patients.'

'I suppose.' He's right. The trembling she's felt since the attack has receded, but it's left her weak and jangled. 'Tell her I love her, then.'

Sebastian leans down and gives her a peck on the cheek, then tiptoes out the room.

The clock on the bedside table says 8:20. She's exhausted, but horribly still full of adrenaline and her mind is racing. The phone rings. Her heart falls into a pocket of air, making her momentarily nauseous.

'Hello?'

'Good evening, Dr Bergmann. This is Alex Franzen.'

It's the first time she's heard him say his first name. Alex.

'I hope I'm not disturbing you,' he says. 'Colleagues told me about today's incident at your practice, and wanted to make sure everything was okay. Have you seen a doctor?'

'That wasn't necessary,' Nina replies. 'I – he didn't really hurt me. I mean, he hurt me, but there's no lasting damage. A twisted shoulder.'

'Perhaps you should see a doctor, anyway,' he says, sounding genuinely concerned. 'To be on the safe side.'

'Well, I am a doctor.'

There is a pause.

'I was very frightened,' she admits, her voice no more than a whisper.

'I can imagine. I'm so sorry this has happened to you. Listen –' He pauses again.

'Yes?'

'If there's anything I can do, please let me know.'

'They said they'd call me as soon as they know more.' She can hear the desperation in her voice.

'So I've heard,' he says. 'I've spoken to my colleagues. They have an ID, his address and car registration. I'm sure it's just a matter of hours before they find him. And if you have any questions, about the status of the enquiry – anything – please call me.'

'That's very kind of you. Thanks.'

'Well, I'd better let you get an early night, then,' he says.

'Yes. Thank you, Herr Franzen.' She wants to call him Alex, but doesn't dare. 'Goodbye.'

She switches off her phone and the bedside light and yawns. She's feeling tired enough to sleep now, and she doesn't want to risk waking herself up again by going to brush her teeth. She stares up at the darkened ceiling and hears a car pull up outside. Sebastian must have decided to drive Bekka round to Lea's. She turns onto her side and closes her eyes. The doorbell rings. Once, twice.

19

By the time Nina reaches the bottom of the stairs, the ringing has turned to insistent hammering on the front door.

'Who's there?' she half-calls, half-hisses, torn between yelling as loudly as she can, and hoping the noise won't have woken Kai. 'I've called the police.'

The voice from the other side is muffled, but she recognises it immediately. 'Don't be ridiculous! It's us.'

Nina opens the door. Her mother rushes in and takes her hands in her own. They're freezing cold. Behind her, Nina's father, Hans, has his mobile phone out.

'I was just about to call the police,' he tells her sternly.

'Oh dear god, Nina,' Antonia says. 'Why on earth didn't you phone us?'

Nina stares at her, uncomprehending.

'Why didn't you tell us what happened? If Hans hadn't rung Sebastian –' Her mother's face falls in alarm. 'First Marie, then this.'

Nina reaches out to give her hands a squeeze. 'Shh, Mama, it's all right. I'm fine, look.' She attempts a smile, but it's too much effort. 'No need to worry. He gave me a scare, that's all.'

'You should've alerted us, Nina,' Hans says. He walks past them into the hall and takes off his coat. 'We have a right to know.'

Antonia holds out her coat for Nina. She hangs it up and follows them into the living room.

'I rang Sebastian earlier,' her father says. 'To ask him if he'd have a look over my speech.' He pulls several sheets of paper out of his briefcase. 'And he told me what happened at the practice. We came straight away.'

Antonia looks around. 'Isn't he here?'

Nina is still standing at the door. 'No. He should be back any minute. Why don't you, um, take a seat.' She doesn't really want them to stay, but Sebastian can deal with them when he gets back.

'I'll have a whisky, if you will,' her father announces, ignoring a look from his wife. 'The Laphroaig. I'm sure Sebastian won't mind.'

'No, and I'm sure he won't mind fixing your drink when he comes,' she snaps, longing only for the dark and peace of bed.

Antonia rolls her eyes. 'I can see you're upset, Nina, but there's no need to be uncivil.' She crosses to the drinks cabinet and pours a small measure of whisky for her husband.

Nina, deflated by her outburst, sits down heavily on the sofa.

'I don't know what's becoming of this country,' her mother says quietly. 'Such brutality.' She looks at Nina. 'You're very vulnerable, you know, alone in that practice.'

'There's more violence in a hospital,' Nina says sharply.

She's tired and annoyed that she's being put on the defensive.

'In the casualty department, perhaps,' Hans says. 'Certainly not on the labour ward.'

'And they have security staff in hospitals,' her mother adds. She looks at Hans, then back at Nina. 'Perhaps you should see about employing a security guard, Nina.'

'That's not going to happen, Mama,' she says, adding, 'I couldn't afford it anyway.'

Antonia sits up straight. 'Well, that shouldn't be an issue. Papa and I would be only too glad to pay for someone, if –'

Nina slaps the armrest, angry to have walked straight into her mother's trap. 'Enough, Mama! I don't want to discuss this now.'

Antonia presses her lips together, her face closes down, but she doesn't respond.

They sit in bristling silence for some minutes. Hans takes a sip of whisky and moves the topic on. 'Your mother and I have been thinking about what to do with Marie's money,' he says. 'The fifteen thousand euros.'

Antonia nods, a haughty lift to her features. 'We'd like to give it to the children. Seven and a half thousand each. For their savings accounts.'

'We don't need it,' Hans says, 'and I've discussed it with Sebastian. He agrees it would be for the best, under the circumstances.'

Nina shrugs. 'It seems you've already decided,' she says coolly. 'What I think hardly seems to matter much.'

Her mother leans forward. 'It's for the best.' She stretches out her hand, but doesn't quite touch Nina. 'After all, Kai and Bekka are the closest Marie came to having children of her own.' Then her face crumples.

Slightly appalled, Nina doesn't want to argue. She isn't used to such emotion from her mother and it makes her uncomfortable. Besides, they're probably right. What else to do with the money? Wherever it came from.

There is the sound of a key in the lock and Sebastian enters the room a moment later.

'I'm sorry for taking so long,' he says, before looking around at Nina's parents. 'Antonia, Hans, how good to see you.'

Antonia gives him a small smile and Hans nods a greeting.

'I just popped into the office after I dropped Bekka off,' Sebastian continues. 'I haven't got any appointments tomorrow, so I thought I'd bring some files home. Then I can keep you company.' He smiles at Nina.

'But I have work tomorrow,' she says, frowning, although she hadn't really thought about it until now.

Sebastian looks across to her parents, then at Nina. 'You're not serious? There's no way I'm letting you go in tomorrow. You need a rest. Look at you! You're exhausted.'

'But I have patients scheduled! They rely on me.' She thinks of Jessica and her heart thumps.

Sebastian crosses the room and crouches in front of her. 'Be sensible. Please. Anita can reschedule your patients. And I'm sure they can cope without you for one day.'

Nina looks down at her hands. The skin is dry and chapped, uncared for.

'Sebastian's right,' her father says. 'Spend the day recuperating in bed. It's no good pretending that nothing happened. That won't solve anything.'

They've defeated her. 'Okay,' she whispers.

Sebastian puts his hands on his thighs and pushes himself up. 'Great,' he says. 'Good girl. That's settled then.' He looks at Hans. 'Did you bring your speech?'

Hans nods and gets to his feet. 'We'll only be half an hour or so,' he says to his wife, and then turns to Sebastian. 'Lead the way.'

The two men head out to the study. Antonia follows them with her gaze.

'That stupid speech,' she mutters. 'He's been working on it day and night. He's obsessed. And this dinner party – I wanted a simple reception, but he obviously feels he has something to prove. It's . . . exhausting.'

Nina tilts her head to one side, surprised – her mother never complains about such things. She feels a sudden jolt of sympathy for her; perhaps it is all getting a little too much. She catches her mother's face as it settles and notices how old she looks. Antonia has always made a great effort with her appearance – perfectly fitting clothes, expensive moisturisers, regular appointments with her stylist – but she hasn't managed to halt the passing of time. She will turn seventy in a few months.

She senses Nina looking at her. 'Nina,' she says, 'I'm going to ask you something, now, and I want you to be truthful.'

Nina holds her look.

'Are you –' She pauses and clears her throat. 'Are you looking after yourself?'

Nina nods her head very slightly. 'Yes.'

'I'm asking because you look as though you've lost weight.'

'I haven't had much of an appetite, lately. It's –' She wrings her hands, aware that's she's covering her untruths with melodrama. 'It's not much, a few pounds. It probably looks more than that because I'm tired.'

'You're not starving yourself, are you?'

'No,' she says quickly. 'No. I'm fine. I'll be fine. It's been so – so hard, Mama.'

'I know.'

'But –' She swallows and attempts a smile. 'I suppose it's getting better. Every day that passes is better.' The lie sucks any remaining strength from her.

'I see,' Antonia says, so quietly Nina has to strain to hear her. 'It's just – the thought of losing you as well . . .' She doesn't finish her sentence.

'I think I'll have a cup of tea,' Nina says into the space. She needs a moment alone. 'Would you like one?'

Antonia nods. Nina passes the study and hears the low murmur of her father's and Sebastian's voices from within. She goes into the kitchen and makes two peppermint teas, adding a spoonful of honey to her mother's cup. When she returns, Antonia is leaning back on the sofa with her eyes closed. The sight reminds Nina for a moment of Frau Lehmholz.

'Here, Mama,' she says, placing the cups on the table.

Her mother opens her eyes. 'Forgive me, I'm tired,' she says. She smooths her hair down with one hand, then leans forward and picks up her tea. 'Did I tell you, I had Bernhard Klopp on the phone the other day?'

'Oh?'

'Yes. He asked me to pass on a message to Papa – apparently, I'm your father's personal secretary.' She raises her eyebrows. 'But anyway. Yes. Bernhard mentioned you'd called him. He asked how you were doing.'

Nina sips her tea. 'That's nice of him.'

A motorcycle speeds past the house outside, the harsh rasp of its illegally modified engine slicing through the quiet.

Antonia twists her head towards the window at the sound, but it fades into a distant buzzing. She turns back. 'I don't want you to be bothering him, Nina. He's a very busy man.'

'I'm not bothering him, Mama. In fact, he gave me his card and told me to call if I needed any assistance.'

'What kind of assistance?'

'I don't know.' Nina lets out an impatient sigh. 'With the police investigation I think.'

Her mother straightens her posture, erasing all trace of her earlier vulnerability. 'You needn't be bothering Herr Klopp with that. He was probably just being polite, giving you his card. Besides, Papa has already spoken with the Chief of Police. The investigation has been given top priority.'

So. He told her exactly what she wanted to hear. It's the way their marriage works. Antonia lets her posture relax again, having, it appears, settled the matter.

'Mama?' Nina says after a moment.

'Yes?'

'You remember that time when you and Papa separated for a while?'

Antonia recoils as though she's been slapped across the face. '*Separated?* What are you talking about?'

'I was eight, Mama. I remember it well. Papa moved out, to a hotel, I think, and you told me he'd be back to visit as often as he could. He stayed away for a couple of weeks, maybe a month.'

'Oh.' She takes a sip of tea, puts her cup down. 'That was a long time ago, Nina.'

'Yes. I know.'

Nina watches her, can see her reliving the memory. 'Mama?' she says again, choosing her words carefully, daringly. 'Was there ever a time that you regretted him coming back?'

Her mother fixes a tired strand of white hair back into her chignon and sighs. 'No, never,' she says. 'It was a little dip, a low point in our marriage. These things happen. I can't imagine why you'd want to mention it. Aren't we feeling miserable enough tonight?' Then she lets out a gasp, her hand moving to her mouth and her face stricken. 'It's not – you and Sebastian, is it?'

'No. I'm sorry. I mean – no.'

'Nina.' She leans forward. 'This is a difficult time for everyone. It takes enough effort just to get through the day sometimes. Of course it's going to have an effect on things, relationships, work. Look at your father!' She waves her hand in the direction of the study. 'He's – goodness knows what he'll do on the tenth of November, when these wretched celebrations are over.' She lets her shoulders droop. 'It's difficult,' she repeats in a frayed voice. 'So you have to hold on, wait for time to pass. And –', she straightens up a little, 'it passes. You and Sebastian have been through this before, haven't you?'

Nina gives her a tired nod.

'Before Kai was born, remember? And you got through it. You just have to be strong, work together as a team. If only for the children and –'

At that moment, Hans comes in.

'Come on, darling,' he says to his wife, giving her a kiss on the forehead. 'We'd best get home. You look tired.'

Antonia gets to her feet. 'Just give it time,' she tells Nina. 'And give the children a big kiss from their Omi.'

Nina stays in her chair as Sebastian accompanies her parents to the door. He waits at the front door until they've driven off, then comes in and slumps down on the sofa.

'God, what a day,' he says.

'Yes,' Nina says, as she starts to cry so quietly it takes a while before he notices. Then, for the first time since they were newly-weds, he picks her up and carries her tenderly, sweetly to bed.

20

The next morning, Nina showers, get dressed and is about to leave for the practice when her resolve suddenly fails. Just the thought of driving through rush-hour traffic sets off the beginnings of a dull ache behind her eyes. She picks up her phone – a residual tremble in her hands – and calls Anita.

'I won't be coming in today,' she says, fighting back the headache. 'I wouldn't be much use to anyone.'

'That's fine, I totally understand.' Anita's voice is warm.

'Would you mind rescheduling today's patients? I think it'll –'

Anita interrupts her. 'Oh, but your husband already rang to say you'll be staying home today.'

'He did?'

'Yes, about half an hour ago. He's awfully sweet, isn't he? He's really concerned about you.'

'Yes, I suppose he is.'

'So don't worry about things here. Just look after yourself and get better.'

Nina ends the call, changes out of her work clothes and crawls back into bed. She's vaguely annoyed that Sebastian called Anita; but then again, she thinks as she pulls the duvet over her and rubs her arms to warm them, she did agree last night that it would be best to take a day off. He was only being thoughtful. And yet.

At lunchtime, Sebastian brings her a plate of shop-bought macaroni cheese, which she flushes down the toilet. At shortly after four o'clock, she hears the children arrive downstairs. She ignores a sharp pain in her stomach, gets out of bed and pulls her tracksuit bottoms over a pair of leggings. Downstairs, Kai runs into her arms, still wearing his school satchel.

'Mama!' he shouts.

She hugs him and his bulky satchel. 'Hi sweetie,' she says. 'How was school?'

'Awesome,' he says, grinning. 'I beat Max in sports, in the race, and Frau Jungmeier said she'd give me top marks cos I was the first to finish in maths. Plus I got every sum right!'

'That sounds wonderful, sweetie.' She hugs him again, marvelling at the unadulterated pleasure of holding her triumphant, happy son.

Kai frees himself from her arms. His expression turns serious. 'Are you still poorly, Mama?'

Nina smiles. 'No. I'm feeling much better. D'you know, I spent all day in bed!'

'All day?' he says, laughing. 'But it's still day, and you're not in bed.'

She straightens up and ruffles his hair. Rebekka comes in and dumps her rucksack on the floor.

'How are you, Bekka?' Nina asks.

'I didn't win a race, and I didn't get top marks in maths,'

she says. Nina can't tell from her tone if she's friend or enemy today. Or lost in grief, she considers with a stab to her heart.

'You look tired,' she says. 'Late night, was it?'

Rebekka rolls her eyes and heads for the kitchen. 'No, actually,' she calls back over her shoulder. 'Lea's mum so strict, like, you wouldn't believe.'

Nina takes Kai's hand and they follow her. Rebekka is smearing a thick layer of peanut butter on a piece of bread.

'Like, she made us switch the light out at nine thirty,' she says without looking up. 'Nine thirty! Unbelievable.'

Kai goes and stands next to his sister. 'Can I have one?' he asks.

Without hesitating, Rebekka takes a second slice of bread and spreads it with peanut butter. 'Here,' she says, handing it to him. She looks up at Nina and smiles. Nina smiles back, relieved. Friend.

'Oh, by the way,' Rebekka continues, licking peanut butter off her finger. 'There's an evening of "celebration and contemplation" at school on Friday night.' She says it in a mock posh voice with compulsory finger quotes. 'In case you want to go.'

'That's pretty short notice,' Nina says. Noticing Kai has peanut butter on his chin, she picks up the kitchen roll and tears off a square.

Rebekka shrugs. 'I know. I forgot to tell you sooner. Sorry.'

'What are you talking about?' Kai asks, letting Nina wipe his face without a fuss.

'It's this thing we're doing in school,' Rebekka tells him,

and Nina can't help but see how grown up she is, leaning against the sink, one ankle crossed over the other. Her daughter has a waist, and hips, and breasts. 'You know, once upon a time –' Rebekka recites, looking over at Nina and winking, 'before you and I were even born, there was this huge wall all around Berlin.'

Kai stares at her. His eyes are large and round.

'And there were some very nasty men,' Rebekka continues, 'who were in charge of the wall, who didn't let anyone out. In fact, they shot anyone who tried to climb over it. And they had big gangs of spies to tell tales on people who were planning to escape.'

Kai pouts and looks at Nina. 'Is she making this up, Mama?'

Nina shakes her head.

'And then,' Rebekka continues, obviously enjoying herself, 'after many, many years, all the people who lived behind the wall got together and went to where the nasty men lived, and told them to tear the wall down. And the nasty men got scared, because there were millions and millions of people shouting and yelling, and then they finally tore the wall down. All that concrete, with loads of hammers, like human-sized woodpeckers.' She folds her arms across her chest. 'And that's what we're celebrating at school.'

Kai frowns. 'Oh, you mean the Berlin Wall.' Then he takes a bite of his peanut butter sandwich and leaves the kitchen.

'I suppose that's one version of the history,' Nina says to Rebekka. 'So, anyway, what does this evening of "celebration and contemplation" entail?'

'Some kids'll be reading out poems, there's a twenty-minute play Herr Walther wrote – which is pure *crap*, by the way – and a kind of dance routine with a PowerPoint display in the background. You don't have to go,' she adds.

'Are you in it?'

Rebekka pulls the corners of her mouth down and shakes her head.

'Then we'll have to see,' Nina tells her. Rebekka hasn't exactly made it an inviting prospect. 'I'll speak to Papa.'

'Speak to Papa about what?'

Nina spins around. Sebastian is standing at the door, leaning against the frame.

'Is he watching TV again?' Nina asks, nodding in the direction of the living room.

Sebastian shrugs. 'His favourite programme.'

'They're all his favourite,' she says doubtfully.

Sebastian shrugs again. 'So, what did you want to talk to me about?'

'Bekka's school is putting on some kind of show on Friday. Tell him, Bekka.'

'Yeah, well, for the anniversary celebrations,' she says. 'It'll probably be really boring, like, but I need you to sign a slip saying whether you'll come.'

Sebastian rubs his face and sighs. 'They're really doing this thing to death, aren't they?'

Nina brushes some crumbs from the table with the edge of her hand. 'Okay, Bekka, just leave the slip on the fridge. We'll decide later.'

Bekka pushes herself out of her leaning position on the counter. 'Fine by me,' she says, and heads upstairs.

'Spaghetti tonight, I thought,' Nina says to Sebastian.

'Do you really feel like cooking?' He takes a step towards her. 'I could get some sushi. We haven't had that in ages.'

'That's because the kids hate sushi.'

'Okay, then I'll drop by McDonald's as well.'

He comes right up to her and puts his hands around her waist. 'Do you remember the first time we had sushi? On that weekend trip to London? I absolutely hated it and you said it was the most delicious thing you'd ever tasted.' He bends down slightly and rests his forehead on the top of her head. 'And I said that was probably because the only alternative was English food.'

She remembers. She visualises a tray of sushi and reckons she can handle it. If she scrapes off the rice and has a napkin handy, then she'll just have to eat a bit of raw fish and cucumber.

'Deal.' She nods. 'Sushi sounds great.'

*

Nina puts Kai to bed. He is tired, and wants her to help him put on his pyjamas. She slips the top over his head and lets him step into the trousers. Then she pulls his bedcovers back and he slips in.

'Story?' she asks.

He nods and snuggles down.

She sits up next to him in bed and reads him "A Big Day for Hedgehog Latte", but notices that his eyes are heavy and so she skips a couple of pages before she gets to the end. He doesn't complain. She closes the book and reaches over to switch off his bedside lamp.

'Mama?' he says.

'Yes?'

'They're building a wall around Jakob's house.' His voice is thick with tiredness.

'Are they?' she replies, before she understands what he's talking about. 'Oh, no, sweetie,' she says and laughs. 'That's just a little wall to stop naughty dogs coming in and doing a poo on the lawn.' She strokes his cheek with her finger. He giggles sleepily. She leans over and gives him a kiss, delighting in how warm his skin is and his innocent smell of soap and toothpaste.

'Mama?' he says again. 'If they ever built a wall around our house, I'd blow it to pieces.' And he claps his hands together and makes the kind of exploding noise only excitable six-year-olds can make.

'That's good to know,' she says. 'Now, close your eyes and go to sleep. Sweet dreams.'

'Night, Mama,' he says as she crosses the room. Then: 'I dream of Auntie Marie sometimes.'

It is enough to make her legs buckle slightly. She turns, and Kai is looking straight at her, his face illuminated by the light from the hall.

'She's in heaven, I think. She's happy. In my dreams.'

She goes back and perches on the side of his bed. 'Do you miss her terribly?' she asks.

He smiles. 'Sometimes, not always. But don't cry, Mama. I think Auntie Marie's having a nice time in heaven.' He reaches up and wipes a tear from her cheek.

'You're my very best boy,' she whispers. 'You're the best thing that's ever happened to me.'

'And Bekka?'

'Bekka too, of course. My two very best things to happen to me, how about that?'

He snuggles into his pillow and yawns. 'I love you, Mama.'

'Love you too, always.' She strokes the hair from his face. 'Nightie-night, then. Sleep tight.'

She leaves the door slightly ajar and goes downstairs.

Rebekka and Sebastian are watching TV in the dark. It's the last few minutes of the news. Sebastian is on the sofa, and Rebekka is curled up in the armchair with her legs tucked underneath her. The remnants of the meal – hamburger wrappers, a couple of pale, cold French fries, small plastic pots of soy sauce and wasabi – are strewn across the coffee table. Rebekka catches Nina looking.

'I'll tidy up later,' she says, 'promise, Mama.'

'Sure,' Nina says and sits down beside Sebastian. For the first time in ages, she feels the need to be close to him. She hitches up her legs and leans into him, appreciating his warmth. He puts his arm around her shoulder and gently twines his fingers in a strand of her hair. Her edges soften. It wasn't a lie; they'll get through this. Everything will be okay. A quiet, barely discernible thought begins to form in her mind, lazily at first, unthreatening. The thought that it's wonderful to be vulnerable sometimes, to just let go, relinquish control. And Sebastian is so kind, so sweet when she's feeling low and bruised. But then the thought ripens and twists. He is kind when she is weak. Is this the price she has to pay to make this marriage work? Is this how he wants her to be all the time? She slaps the thought down, panicked. Sebastian is not like that. He isn't.

The news ends with the weather forecast, and an indication that the subsequent programme will be replaced by a special broadcast on the day's breaking news. They're told how a senior civil servant has just been arrested on suspicion of spying for the former GDR.

Sebastian grunts. 'God, they've just played this out in detail on the news. What more can they squeeze out of it?'

On the screen, a man, his face obscured by a raincoat thrown over his head, is being led by police officers through a crowd of reporters.

'I wonder if my father knows him,' Nina says and immediately thinks of what Frau Lehmholz said about these men being pulled out of the woodwork.

'Probably,' Sebastian says, but is interrupted by Rebekka.

'Um, Mama, Papa? Would it be okay if I went round to Emily's for a bit?'

Nina glances out of the window. It's pitch-black outside. 'It's a bit late for that, isn't it?'

'Just for an hour. And she only lives ten minutes away.'

'I know, but it's dark. And you'll see her tomorrow at school, hmm?'

Rebekka lets out a sigh of dismay. 'Oh, go on, Mama, please!'

'I'm sorry, sweetheart. It's a school night, and I don't like the thought of you out and about at this hour.'

'Papa?'

Sebastian lifts his shoulders, utterly indifferent.

'Basti,' Nina says. 'I need your support on this one.'

'Papa!'

Sebastian looks pained for a moment, then he says, 'I'm staying out of this one, girls. You'll have to sort it out yourselves.'

Rebekka jumps out of her chair. 'I don't believe it! I *never* get to go out! It's so unfair! Like I'm a baby or something. *All* the kids at school get to hang out. Except me. Why is that?'

'Bekka,' Nina says. She throws Sebastian a look, annoyed that he isn't backing her up.

Rebekka pulls a face. 'What am I supposed to do? Sit in my room? Listen to music? I always do my homework, I study for my tests, I even practise the piano – all without being asked. It's not like I'm taking drugs or sharing tit pics on Snapchat. It's so unfair!'

Sebastian gets up. 'Come on, Bekka, it's not the end of the world.' He holds his arms out, but she wraps her arms around herself instead.

'I think about her all the time,' she says, all her fire extinguished. 'When I'm on the bus, at school, especially when I'm on my own in my room.' She looks up, and has tears in her eyes. 'And you never talk about her. It's like she never even existed.'

Nina jumps up and rushes forward. 'Oh, Bekka! No, it's not like that. I think about her all the time, too. And I talk about her with you, don't I, sweetie?' She puts her hands on her daughter's shoulders and tries to pull her into a hug. But Rebekka tenses her body, then turns and dashes out of the room.

Nina turns to Sebastian. 'God, I feel so guilty,' she

whispers as they both listen to Bekka running upstairs, sobbing loudly.

'She's not really coping, is she?' Sebastian says.

'No, she isn't. But what do you think we should do?'

He half-turns away from her. 'It might help if you ease up a little. Back off, let her live a little and get it out of her system.'

Nina takes a step back. 'What? So this is all my fault?'

'I didn't say that.'

'You implied it.'

Sebastian picks up the remote control. 'I don't want to talk to you if you're in this kind of mood.'

A high-pitched laugh escapes her mouth. 'Mood? You think I'm in a mood?'

'Leave it, Nina. I'm not talking to you until you calm down.'

'Calm like you, you mean?' Her cheeks are flushed and her heart is galloping. 'My sister's been murdered, and my kids are completely *fucking* traumatised about it, and I've just been attacked at work by some *psychopath* who bites his wife's *vulva* – and you want me to stay calm? I wouldn't call that calm, I'd call it cold.'

She pauses for breath and Sebastian spins around to face her. The sight of his tight-set mouth and clenched jaw sets her on edge and she tenses. A perverse thrill runs through her. *Bring it on!* she thinks, recklessly.

But then his face goes slack, his eyes widen. 'Is that what you think? That I'm cold?'

His reaction is not what she expected at all. She opens her mouth but no words come out.

He drops heavily onto the sofa. 'You have no idea how much that hurts,' he says, his voice neutral. 'I feel –' he pauses and rubs his face. 'I sometimes feel like I'm out there,' he gestures around the room, 'while everyone in here is falling to pieces. And there's nothing I can do to stop it.' He looks up at her. She's afraid he might start to cry. 'And when you say things like that, you make feel like some kind of monster. Like I don't care, like I have no real emotions. But I do, believe me.' He looks down, his chin trembling, and blots his eyes with his sleeve.

Nina's breathing sharpens. 'Oh god, Basti. I'm sorry, I'm so sorry.' She stumbles forward and kneels down in front of him. How could she be so cruel? He's not cold, he's a compassionate, caring husband and father. He's suffering as much as she is.

'I'm so sorry, Basti,' she repeats softly. She cups his face with her hands, draws him close. She can smell whisky on his breath. 'But we'll be okay. I'm sure we'll be okay.'

21

It's a cool grey day as Nina turns onto Schönhauser Allee. A long, arterial road that cuts through the district of Prenzlauer Berg, it is always, always busy, with everyone improvising their own traffic rules as they go along. As usual, parking is a nightmare. Nina has to weave from lane to lane – looking out for parking on the right, veering left again to avoid double-parked delivery vans. Every third shop is a bar or restaurant, needing their daily replenishment of goods. Honking car horns, the loud rush and rattle of the overhead U-Bahn, cyclists darting out from side streets at speeds that suggest they have some sort of death wish.

Nina grips the steering wheel and tries to block it all out. But then she's lucky; she spots a free space about ten metres from the entrance to number 83. She flicks the indicator on and almost collides with a passing cyclist in her rush to turn into the space. The tattooed young woman in short dungarees turns to shout an expletive at her, but doesn't stop, and as Nina looks up, she sees a sign on the pavement. Loading bay only. No wonder the space was unoccupied. She puts the gear into reverse, hesitates, then pulls the handbrake and switches off the engine. She has no intention of staying long; she probably won't even get out of the car.

It took her less than five minutes at lunchtime to find out the address. She only had one patient this morning – Anita informed her ruefully when she arrived that eighteen patients scheduled for the next few days had rung to cancel their appointments, of which Anita was able to persuade only four to postpone instead. Herr Thiel's thuggery, coupled with Nina's unplanned days off, has had the worst possible effect: her patients are fleeing in droves. So, she spent her unexpected free time tackling paperwork, but after barely an hour, gave up trying to concentrate. And here now is something she's been meaning to do ever since Franzen gave her the man's name.

There are only two numbers for a J. Fraunhofer listed in the online telephone directory, one in Spandau, the other here in Prenzlauer Berg. Nina was slightly disappointed at first that he doesn't have a website – at least, if he does, it isn't easy to find. Regardless of the search terms she used, she couldn't seem to get past sites for the Fraunhofer Institute. Then, riding on a brainwave, she googled images of Jakob Fraunhofer, and sure enough, found three pictures of a young man. The photos were all taken on different occasions – an engineering conference, the Siemens' homepage, some writers' event – but it's the same face as on the photo Franzen showed her: gaunt, a close-cropped beard, round spectacles, short dark hair. She noted down the address and told Anita to go home early.

This area of town was once populated by workers, then squatters and now students and artists with healthy incomes. Nina recalls reading how it's become such a popular area that rental properties are fiercely fought over. Even so, the dark green door to number 83 is covered in scrawled tags. Nina looks up at the building; it's tall and imposing, with wrought iron balconies and a slightly grubby sandstone façade. She sits in the car and waits. The pavement outside is full of life. It's a young area of town – even those who aren't interested in demographics couldn't help but notice the large proportion of toddlers and pregnant women. As if to prove a point, two women – one heavily pregnant, the other pushing a pram – stop to chat in front of Nina's car, blocking her view of the front door to the building. The pregnant woman is wearing a woollen hat and a purple-and-brown checked poncho. The other has on khaki cargo pants, lace-up boots and a slightly worn black jacket. But the apparent scruffiness of the clothes worn by adults and their children in Prenzlauer Berg is, Nina knows, a shabby chic.

She doesn't have a plan. And she has only two hours to kill until she meets Sara at Marie's flat. Franzen hasn't been in touch, and Nina won't call him, because she can't bear the thought of being told yet again that the investigation is 'ongoing'. So she sits in her car and waits. Fraunhofer is probably at work on a Thursday afternoon, and really, Nina just wants to see where he lives. How he lives. One of those Berlin hipsters who may or may not have killed her sister.

She reaches over to the passenger seat to get a bottle of Diet Coke from her bag. As she tips the bottle to her lips, she spots a traffic warden in the rear-view mirror, on the opposite side of the street. Nina takes a sip, replaces the bottle and goes to start the engine. Then the green door to number 83 opens and a man comes out.

He stands for a few moments facing in Nina's direction, as though, in some weird way, presenting himself to her for identification. Then he looks up at the darkening sky and sets off in the opposite direction. Nina doesn't think twice. She scrambles out, glancing over her shoulder, just long enough to notice the traffic warden making a beeline for her car. She locks the car hurriedly and rushes off.

Fraunhofer is wearing a knee-length black coat that flaps about his body like wings, and a bright red scarf that makes it easy enough for Nina to keep track of him as she threads her way through prams and pedestrians and bicycles. He doesn't stop, keeps walking purposefully ahead. He has a laptop bag slung around his body that bounces off his back with every step. Then he crosses the road, not bothering to wait for the green light, dodging traffic, under the green U-Bahn bridge and into a side street. There is a sudden rush of traffic and Nina is forced to wait on her side of the street, until she spots a gap, runs across and barely misses being hit. The Doppler sound of the car's horn rings in her ears until she reaches the side street Fraunhofer turned into moments earlier.

At first, she's afraid she might have lost him and doesn't stop to consider what she might do, or say, if she does catch up with him. She just wants to see him, look at him, take him in – the way Marie did. She draws a deep breath, but the stench of diesel makes her gag. The street she's on is largely residential, but she soon sees a bookshop up ahead on the left, with three or four rummage bins outside. As she crosses the road, she notices a café a little further on from that. Bookshop or café, that's where he must be, and at that moment, he materialises from behind one of the rummage bins. Nina almost runs right into him, but manages to stop a metre in front of him and pretend that her mobile has just gone off. She reaches into her pocket for the phone and self-consciously begins a phoney conversation, feeling like a character in a bad Cold War spy novel.

But Fraunhofer pays her no attention. He turns and heads in the direction of the café. Nina tracks him along the empty pavement, feeling spectacularly conspicuous. Despite the building's elegant 19th-century architecture, the café inside turns out to be a Starbucks. Nina follows him in, smiling her thanks awkwardly as he stops to hold the door open for her. He heads for the counter. Nina hesitates, not sure what to do, but is promptly addressed by a uniformed *barista*, who leans over the counter and waves to attract her attention.

'Hi there, what can I get you?' he says.

'Um, a coffee, please,' Nina says quietly, although she feels foolish now, keeping her voice down to prevent Fraunhofer noticing her. She registers an unpleasant taste in her mouth and the beginnings of a headache.

The *barista* reels off a list of coffee bean varieties – Maragogype, Ethiopian Harar, Ethiopian Sidano, Arusha, Mayagüez – that mean nothing to her.

'Just a black coffee,' she says. 'No sugar.'

The *barista* frowns, then smiles. 'Our weekly special, then. Mayagüez.'

'Please.' Nina takes some coins out of her purse, trying to keep Fraunhofer in her line of sight without making it obvious that she's watching him.

'For here or to go?'

'Sorry?'

'Would you like to drink it here, or take it out?' the *barista* says. He gives her a smile that suggests he's professionally immune to complicated – or slightly backward – customers.

Nina casts a look to the left. Fraunhofer is taking a mug of coffee from the counter.

'For here, please,' she says. She pays and grabs the coffee. Fraunhofer has taken a seat close to the counter, but sits with his back to her. She hovers for a second – the café is fairly full – but decides on a table near the window, one table away from Fraunhofer. A cardboard shelf displaying bags of coffee beans, which stands between her table and his, enables her to watch him without fear of being noticed.

But Nina needn't worry. He appears oblivious to her presence. He opens his laptop and switches it on. His fingers are thin and white, pink at the cuticles, and he taps away expertly at the keys. He appears withdrawn into himself, shoulders hunched, eyebrows pulled together into a frown. Nina takes in his profile. A slightly hook-shaped, but attractive nose; dark eyelashes framing blue? grey? eyes; a busy mouth, his lips working away in some silent incantation as he types insistently on his keyboard. He looks so harmless. And yet. Marie kissed that mouth, ran her hands through his short dark hair, grazed her soft cheek against his stubbly chin, allowed his thin fingers to touch her ... She probably overwhelmed him, blew his mind. And then abandoned him, left him to his own devices. Until the day he became so incensed by her rejection he battered her to death.

Then, he turns his head. Before Nina can look away, she sees the brief flicker of a question in his eyes, and she's afraid he might come right out and ask why she's staring at him, or worse, why she's been following him. But his eyes soften almost instantly, as though the question never quite surfaces into consciousness.

'Excuse me,' he says, and his voice is a little reedy, but pleasant. Melodious. 'May I have the sugar? Or do you still need it?'

He smiles and points at the sugar shaker in front of her. It takes her a moment to process what he's saying.

Then she says, 'Oh, no, please.' She hands him the sugar. He smiles and turns away.

Nina looks back down at her coffee and realises she can't bear the taste of it. She gets to her feet and, ignoring the sign politely requesting that customers clear their tables, slings her handbag over her shoulder and leaves the café, and heads back to the car and her newly acquired parking ticket.

22

When she arrives at Gärtnerstraße, Sara is already there, standing in the soft misty rain. Nina gets out of the car and pulls her hood up over her head. She goes around to the back of the car and takes out some folded-up cardboard boxes. Sara hasn't spotted her yet; she's smoking a cigarette, stamping her feet to keep the cold out. She's wearing a leather jacket and jeans, hair pulled into a ponytail, and has perfectly applied crimson lipstick. She looks like she's just stepped out of a fashion magazine. When she looks up and sees Nina, she flicks the cigarette into the kerb.

'Hi, honey,' she says and gives Nina a peck on either cheek. The smell of tobacco smoke that lingers on her is repellent and oddly pleasing at the same time. She takes a couple of boxes from Nina. 'I'm early, for a change. They've blocked off half the bloody streets for these celebrations, so I allowed myself plenty of time to get here.'

'I'm so glad you came.'

'No worries.' Sara looks up at the sky. 'I hate Berlin at this time of year,' she says.

Nina unlocks the door to number 31 and holds the door open for Sara. They step in and Sara looks around the stairwell. Two worse-for-wear prams are secured to a hook in the wall with bicycle locks. The walls are graffitied and there is a faint odour of damp. A dull syncopated thudding can be heard from somewhere above. Sara pulls a face. 'Pretty grim.'

'Cheap, though.'

'Well, it would have to be.' Sara goes up the stairs without touching the banister.

'We've got until the end of the month to clear the flat,' Nina says. 'The landlord agreed to terminate the rent contract early.'

'I suppose it's always good to have a deadline.'

They reach the second floor. Nina puts the key in the lock, closes her eyes and takes a few deep breaths.

'Take your time,' Sara says softly.

Nina turns the key and pushes open the door. Then she switches on the hall light. The smell of disinfectant has all but vanished, and there is a cold draught coming from the living room.

'Bloody hell, it's freezing in here,' Sara says, following her in.

It occurs to Nina that she forgot to close the window after her previous visit. She rushes into the living room, dropping the boxes on the way. 'Shit,' she says and shuts the window. She looks down at the floor. The rain has soaked the wooden floor, marking out a dark wet semicircle. It will have to be fixed before she hands in the keys to the landlord.

Sara comes over. 'We should switch all the radiators on,' she says, 'let it dry out a bit.'

Nina nods and turns the knob on the heater under the window. The radiator lets out a gurgling, knocking sound.

She worries that it might be broken, but she places her hand on top and after a few moments, feels the heat.

Thankfully, the boxes of papers and files are standing far enough from the open window to be undamaged. Nina looks at them and says, 'I think I'll start in the bedroom. Sort out her clothes.'

'Whatever you like,' Sara says. 'I'll see what needs to be done in the bathroom. Shouldn't take long, hopefully.' She places her hand on Nina's arm. 'This is good. Believe me, you'll feel a lot better afterwards.'

Nina gives her a hasty smile and heads into the bedroom. The light in here, like in the rest of the flat, is dusky. She switches on a lamp to give the room some structure, take away the shadows and fuzzy edges, and walks over to the wardrobe. She pulls open the double doors and the smell of Marie – a sweet, herbal, jasmine smell – slaps her in the face. The blood drains from her head, she's dizzy, out of breath, her heart drums a slow, drawn-out rhythm on the inside of her chest. She backs slowly towards the bed and sits down. Her muscles have turned to water. She doesn't understand – doesn't understand why now, why she didn't notice the smell this acutely before. She starts to shake, feels the need to lie down. She lets her eyelids slide shut as her mind clouds over. Everything is distant – her body weighs nothing, she is floating, drifting along the rush of blood in her head. Then Marie's voice:

'Nina, Nina.' Softly. In sing-song.

She smiles.

The voice again: 'Nina. Are you all right?' But now the voice is closer, harder. 'Nina.'

It takes a concentrated effort of will to open her eyes. Sara is standing over her, her red lips stark against her pale face.

'Nina. What's the matter?' She sits down on the bed and puts her hand on Nina's forehead. 'Are you sick?'

Nina sits up and tries to ignore the dizziness.

'No, I'm fine,' she says. Her irregular heartbeat is making her nauseous. Perhaps she should take some Atropine, just to get over the worst of it. 'I felt so overwhelmed, all of a sudden.'

Sara looks over to the open wardrobe. 'Maybe all this is just too personal,' she sighs. 'The clothes, I mean.' She turns back to look at Nina. 'Why don't you let me sort them out? I can easily bag the ones to throw out, and see which ones you might like to re-sell. Or is there anything you'd like to keep?'

Nina swallows, but the tightness in her throat remains. 'No. Just – just the green dress. I wanted to give that one to Bekka.'

Sara gives her a matter-of-fact hug and gets up. 'Right, then. Leave this to me. I'll finish up in the bathroom first. You can go and make a start in the living room. You'll have to decide what to do with the papers and whatnot.'

Nina stands up slowly. It was a mistake not to eat anything today. Six hundred calories is what her body needs to keep ticking over; anything less is pushing it.

'Are you really all right?' Sara asks. 'I mean, as much as I think you should get this over with, I don't want to bully you into doing anything if you're not feeling well.'

'No, I'm just tired. It's – like you said, I have to get this done.' Nina leaves the bedroom.

In the living room, the air is stuffy. Mildewy. Nina spots a patch of black mould in the corner of the ceiling. That feeling of guilt, never far from the surface, twists and rises inside her. She should never have encouraged Marie to take this flat. She should have got her somewhere nicer – cleaner – and offered to pay the difference, until Marie was on her feet. She had the money back then, the regular income, never having to think twice before buying a new pair of shoes. It makes her stomach turn to think she might have condemned her sister, then made such a monumental mistake, setting up her own practice. And now. Now it's all falling to pieces.

She kneels on the floor – it's draughty down here – and opens one of the boxes. Just a load of official-looking papers, bills, the rental contract, bank statements, a number of membership agreements: a local gym, a writers' affiliation, Greenpeace, the Youth Hostel Association. She closes the box. She might as well take it as it is; she'll have to sort through it properly at home and cancel any outstanding memberships. She can hear Sara rummaging in the bathroom, opening cabinet doors and the clink of glass. The glass that holds Marie's toothbrush. She suppresses the urge to cry and instead opens the next box. It's full of books, non-fiction, novels, poetry collections. She's not sure why the police took these; perhaps they thought they might find notes or slips of paper between the pages. But that's irrelevant now. She doesn't need to sort this box; the books can be donated. She shoves the two boxes she's looked through aside. There are three more.

Sara pops her head round the door. 'D'you have any bin

bags?' she asks. 'There's lots of stuff in the bathroom that can just be dumped.'

'Oh.'

Sara inclines her head. 'I'm not throwing away anything important,' she says. 'Please, you can trust me.'

Nina takes a breath. 'Of course. There should be some bin bags in the kitchen. In the cupboard under the sink. But I have some in my car, if –'

Sara smiles and is gone.

Nina covers her face with her hands, runs her tongue over her lips. She's very thirsty; perhaps it's all the dust. She takes a deep breath and opens another box. It's full of lever arch files, which, on closer inspection, turn out to be handout material and notes from Marie's time at university. Why did she keep these? Was she planning on going back and finishing her degree? There's so much they never discussed. Nina closes the flap and shoves the box across the floor. It hits the wall.

Sara comes in with two glasses of water. 'Here,' she says. 'Thirsty work.'

Nina takes a glass and finishes it in one go.

'More?' Sara asks.

Nina shakes her head. 'D'you think you might let me have a cigarette?'

Sara frowns but doesn't say anything. She goes out to the hall, gets her handbag and takes out a pack of Gauloises. She pulls a cigarette halfway out of the pack and offers it to Nina. 'If you must.'

Nina takes the cigarette and leans over to light it off Sara's lighter. She inhales and is surprised that she doesn't need to cough. Sara pulls the corners of her mouth down and then lights her own.

'Well?' she asks. 'How does it taste?'

'Awful. And incredible.' Nina's mind is afire and the tips of her fingers are fizzing. The second drag is better than the first, getting through to those hidden crevices of cravings that have been lying dormant for so many years.

'Enjoy,' Sara says. 'But make it your last.'

They sit and smoke in silence. After several minutes, Sara holds out her hand for Nina's glowing stub, takes it carefully between her fingers and crosses the room to open the window. She tosses both stubs out.

'I'm more or less done in there,' she says. 'There's a bag of clothes that are still wearable. They can go to charity. I can deal with that, if you like.'

'Thanks.'

'And then there's the stuff that can be thrown away, underwear, T-shirts, stuff that's just too – worn.'

Nina clears her throat.

Sara sits back down beside her on the floor. 'Do I sound horribly efficient?' she asks with a look of genuine concern. 'It's not – it's not as though I don't care.'

'I know,' Nina says. She feels a rush of love for her friend. Her emotions are so close to the surface these days, it's painful. 'And I don't think you're horribly anything. I couldn't do this on my own.'

Sara gives her a concerned smile. 'How are you getting on in here?'

Nina shrugs. 'One box can go straight in the bin, one

can go to a bookshop and the other one I have to take home. Tie up some loose ends.'

'Good, you're getting there, then. So what's left?'

Nina nods in the direction of a shelf lining the wall. 'The things on there. The picture frames I'll keep, the rest of the books can go in a box for the bookshop, um –' Her voice falters. She clears her throat again. The zippiness from the nicotine is ebbing away. 'My father's contracted a house clearance company. They'll be in next week to empty the place. We have to get out any personal items before they turn up.'

'You know, I think your parents are asking a lot of you, to do all this on your own,' Sara says.

Nina frowns. She hasn't thought of it like this. 'I suppose so. But they're getting old, and –'

'Hey,' Sara interrupts gently. 'You don't have to make excuses. Besides,' she gets up and wipes the back of her jeans with both hands. 'You have me to help you.' She looks around. 'Right. I'll start packing. You get back to the boxes.'

It feels nice to have someone in charge. Someone who will tell her what to do while expecting nothing in return. Nina pulls a box closer and opens it. It's the same one she took the journals and photo album from the last time she was here. It is only half full now and she takes out everything and places it on the floor. Among the items is a clear plastic bag containing photocopies of letters. Letters from Jakob Fraunhofer. A sticker on the bag states that the originals have been retained by the police for purposes of an ongoing enquiry. Her hands are shaking and she pictures him, lips working away as he writes, in dense, spiky handwriting, his love and desire for Marie. She looks over to Sara, who is emptying books off the shelf and dropping them into a box by her feet.

Sara turns around. 'Everything okay?'

'Of course.'

She smiles and turns back. Nina slips the bag into her handbag. She can't read them here, not with someone else present. The writing journals are next. A dozen or so; leather bound, surprisingly expensive-looking, the pages filled chaotically and margin-to-margin with Marie's inky writing. Between the journals, Nina finds a manila envelope stuffed with clippings, flyers and other papers she imagines were Marie's research material. It is marked "*Sakoku*" – whatever that means, someone's name perhaps – and contains material on a single theme: the GDR Ministry for State Security, the Stasi. Printouts of old newspaper articles, photographs of stern-faced grey-haired men sitting at desks or waving to crowds, and a batch of photocopies of typed documents with individual words, clauses or even whole sections blacked out. She presumes they might be Stasi files, but Nina can't be sure. Her eyes are blurry and skittery from her blackout – if that's what it was – in the bedroom.

'Urgh,' Sara says suddenly. 'Vile bunch.'

Nina startles. Sara, standing behind her, dips her head towards the black-and-white photo lying on top of the envelope.

'Party *officials*. Should've shot the lot,' she says dryly. Her parents fled East Berlin in the mid-1970s, in the modified chassis of a West Berliner's car. The lives of their aunts and uncles, cousins, grandparents – those who stayed behind

– were never the same afterwards, the Stasi made sure of that. Sara has an elderly uncle who spent ten months in the political prison in Hohenschönhausen. He still suffers from debilitating panic attacks, but because he's in the advanced stages of dementia, he doesn't have a clue as to why. Little wonder that Sara's views are so unforgiving.

'But why did Marie have stuff like that?' she asks, both hands reaching up to readjust her ponytail.

Nina lifts her shoulders in a shrug. 'I'm not sure. Research for her writing, I guess.'

'Nasty,' Sara says. 'Either way, that morally bankrupt lot won't do much to lift our mood.' She gets up, her eyes narrowed with contempt. 'Best get on with it – idle hands and all that.'

Nina replaces the papers in the envelope and gathers up the journals to put in the box. If she's honest, all she's doing is procrastinating. She should just throw everything out – what use is it to her? It's hopeless, all of it. She can feel the craving for another cigarette emerging in her brain, like a long-lost friend asking to be let in the back door.

Sara has gone back to wrapping the picture frames in newspaper. One photograph, still standing on a shelf to her left, shows Marie perched on a log, in a striped top and shorts, with Lake Schlachtensee in the background, close to where they grew up. The lighting is all wrong and the frame is slightly off-kilter, but Marie always liked this photo because of the goofy face she's pulling.

*

May, 2002

'Sebastian's asked me to move in with him.'

Marie didn't answer straight away and concentrated on rolling a cigarette. She'd started smoking a year earlier, at fifteen. Nina blamed herself. Anything she did, her sister invariably copied.

Marie lit up and took a deep drag.

'You don't like him, do you?' Nina said.

Marie shrugged and exhaled. She pushed her feet against the ground, making the log wobble slightly. 'Nah, he's all right. A bit old for you, I reckon.'

'He's only thirty. That's hardly old.'

Marie gave her a look that suggested the opposite. 'And he's a bit up his own arse.'

'Marie!'

'But he is though, isn't he?'

Nina shook her head. 'I don't think so.'

'Mind you.' Marie grinned. 'It's a nice, squeezable arse.'

Sara places a newspaper-wrapped frame in the box next to Nina.

'Was she any good?' she asks.

'What? Marie?'

'Yes. Her writing. I don't read much, to be honest. Not as much as I'd like to. You know how it is.'

'Her writing was wonderful.' She runs her hand over the journal. 'It glittered,' she says distantly. 'Quite sparse, you know, and dark. But unexpectedly funny in places. It always took me by surprise.'

Sara licks her thumb and rubs some dirt off her jeans. 'Maybe you could let me read something, one of her stories. You choose.'

Nina is touched by her friend's request, but struggles to find the words to explain that no one will ever read Marie's stories. That Nina made a promise she intends to keep, and that very soon Marie's work will be nothing but ashes. So, instead, she says, 'I'll see what I can find.'

'Oh, and that box over there has loads of drawings in it,' Sara says, pointing to the box closest to the wall. 'They're pretty impressive, too.'

Nina is puzzled. 'They're not Marie's. She didn't draw. They must belong to someone else.'

'Are you sure?' Sara says. 'I'm talking about the charcoal drawings, the ones signed M. Bergmann.'

Nina gets to her feet and pulls the box towards her. It's the only one she hasn't looked through, and she'd assumed it contained more files and the like. She opens it. Sketchpads lie on top of more lever arch files. She lifts one out and flips the cover back. Like Sara said, it's in charcoal, a portrait of a child. The lines are a little smudged, and Marie has played with ideas of abstraction, cubist-inspired. But it is instantly recognisable. It's a tender, careful drawing of Kai. Nina flips to the next page, and the next. All portraits, all of Kai and Rebekka, apart from one. She recognises the picture, from a photograph of Nina holding two-day old

Kai in the hospital. Except that Marie has drawn herself holding him, not her sister.

This time, she can't hold back the tears. She cries quietly, urgently, and it is a good few minutes before Sara notices and comes to sit beside her, unspeaking, her arm wrapped warmly around her shoulders.

*

It is almost six o'clock when they decide there's no more they can do. Boxes and bags for the dump have been clearly marked; the boxes Nina will take with her are piled at the front door. The rest will be left for the clearance company. When she goes to lift a box to carry it out of the flat, Nina feels a stinging pain in her shoulder.

'Shit.' She drops the box.

'What's up?' Sara asks.

'My back's giving out,' Nina tells her. She can't face explaining the whole Thiel episode.

Sara opens the front door. 'Here, let me take the heavy ones, Grandma.' She grins. 'You're getting old.'

One box at a time, they shift the lot into the shadowy hallway. Nina doesn't linger in the flat, doesn't take one last look, but instead, closes the door behind her and locks it with a sharp turn of the key. She looks at Sara.

'Sebastian wants another baby,' she says, and her voice resonates throughout the stairwell.

'Oh.' Babies aren't Sara's thing: she doesn't have children and doesn't want any, either.

'I think he's serious.'

'How about you?'

Nina lets out a small, sad laugh. 'I don't know, Sara, I really don't. He's such a wonderful dad, everyone says so. And maybe . . . maybe it has something to do with Marie's death. New beginnings. I don't know.' She takes a shaky breath. 'But I – I don't think I *can*. I can't have another baby. I don't have the energy.'

Sara puts her hands on Nina's shoulders. They are heavy and warm, grounding her. 'Then don't,' she says firmly. 'And don't let him pressure you, either. God –' she looks up to the ceiling and shakes her head, 'men are just so – so *pathetic* sometimes.'

They're interrupted by the sound of a door unlocking and a keychain being unbolted. Nina glances across the hall just as the door opens a fraction.

'Marie?' a voice asks.

Nina takes a step forward. 'No, Frau Lehmholz. It's Nina. Marie's sister. We met the other day, remember?'

Frau Lehmholz pokes her head out of the door, giving her the appearance of a turtle with its head outside the shell. 'Marie? Is that you?' She squints in Nina's direction.

'No, it's Nina,' she repeats. And adds gently, 'Marie doesn't live here anymore.'

'Did you bring my medicine?' Frau Lehmholz asks, annoyed. 'I've been waiting all day.'

Nina looks back at Sara. She shrugs.

'I don't have your prescription,' Nina tells the old woman. 'But if you get it for me, then I'll happily pop out and fetch your medicine.'

Frau Lehmholz looks as though she's about to cry. But

then her face darkens. 'Don't bother then,' she snaps, and retreats inside with a slam of the door.

'That was weird,' Sara says. 'Who's she?'

Nina stares at Frau Lehmholz's door. 'I didn't realise,' she murmurs. 'I – I spoke to her just recently. We had a cup of tea together and talked about Marie. She seemed so lucid, then –'

'Seemed pretty confused to me,' Sara says. 'Poor old thing.'

'Perhaps –'

'What?'

'No, nothing.' Nina picks up a box and heads down the stairs, making a mental note to contact someone about making a welfare check on Frau Lehmholz.

23

Nina scrapes the rest of her muesli from the side of the bowl and licks it off the spoon. She weighed 48.3 kilos this morning, better than expected, and has decided to reward herself with her full daily allowance. The persistent dizziness is beginning to get on her nerves, and the heart arrhythmia worries her slightly. But by next week, she should have hit the 47 mark. This gives her a comfortable three-kilo buffer, just in case.

Then she'll stop.

Kai comes into the kitchen, early morning chirpy as always.

'I think I'll have –' He places a forefinger on his chin and puts on his thinking face. Nina can't help but laugh.

'I think I'll have banana porridge and Nutella toast,' he says.

'Good morning to you too.'

'Sorry, Mama. Good morning. May I have banana porridge and Nutella toast, please?'

'Coming right up, young sir.' She places a saucepan on the stove and pours in some milk. 'Oh, would you go and ask Papa if he'd like some? Save me cooking twice.'

Kai turns to run out of the kitchen but Sebastian is already coming in the door.

'Morning,' he says. He has showered and shaved and looks rather handsome. All clean and scrubbed like that. Last night, he helped her burn Marie's papers, letters and journals out in the garden, including the letters from Fraunhofer. In the end, she couldn't bring herself to read them.

Sebastian built the fire quite close to the house to stop the rain from putting it out, never once complaining when the smoke drifted right up towards their bedroom window, never once suggesting, in word or deed, that this was somehow a childish, superstitious thing to do. He got on with it, tolerating the acrid stink of the wet fire as Nina stood watching Marie's personal life go up in flames. She kept nothing but the drawings. It was harder, much harder than she could have ever imagined, all her grief honed to a fine, white-hot point. When they were done, they went upstairs together, an almost forgotten intimacy between them, but Sebastian didn't make any advances towards sex; instead, he just held her close until she fell asleep.

But when she woke, things had shifted. The quality of pain had changed. It wasn't gone, not by a long stretch, but it has spread out more evenly, now more of a dull persistent ache than that scorching pain. As though some-thing had fallen into place overnight with a soft, satisfying *click*.

She smiles at Sebastian. 'No Bekka?'

'I tapped on her door on my way down. She's probably still getting dressed.'

She adds the porridge oats to the hot milk and stirs.

'What are you making?' he asks.

'Banana porridge. Kai's request.'

'And Nutella toast,' adds Kai.

Sebastian goes to him and strokes his hair. 'Good choice, Tarzan.'

Nina looks up at the kitchen clock. It's seven fifteen.

'I'd better go up and check on Bekka,' she says. 'She's got an exam this morning.'

'You want me to go?' Sebastian asks.

'No. You sit down and eat.' She spoons the porridge into two bowls. 'You'll just need to add the banana.'

'Aren't you having any, Mama?' Kai asks as she sets the bowls on the table.

'No, I was up early. I've already eaten.' She points at the muesli bowl, as evidence. 'Right, *bon appétit*, you two. I'll go and get Bekka out of bed.'

*

It is a long morning at the surgery. Before the first patient arrives (one of two women, both in for a check-up, which brings in no more than sixty euros apiece), Nina calls social services to arrange for a welfare check on Frau Lehmholz. They assure her they can add her to their list, but are equally clear that the list is a very long one.

The fewer patients Nina has, the more time she has on her hands to worry about not having more patients. Needing to distract herself, she begins her exercises. She could, of course, tidy up the cabinets, make an inventory of gloves, and spatulas, and swabs, and needles; she could answer her accountant's emails; she could return the calls from the various pharma company reps, to refill her stock of samples. She could do all of the above, but instead, she takes off her white coat and lies down on the floor. Her abdominal muscles are hard and strong; it takes some fifty or so sit-ups for them to start burning. She has counted eighty-six when she hears a sharp knock and the door opens.

'Oh, sorry, I didn't mean to –'

Nina scrambles to her feet and smiles awkwardly. 'I – I thought I'd –'

'No, that's great. I mean,' Anita pats her own stomach, 'I could use some exercise myself.'

Flushed, Nina goes around behind her desk and sits down. Anita steps forward, clasping her hands together in front of her.

'Dr Bergmann, I was wondering . . .'

'Yes?'

'You see, I was printing out the prescription for Frau Markert – for the Dulcolax?'

Nina nods. 'For her constipation. She phoned earlier and I said I'd write her a prescription.'

'Yes, but, I was wondering, because Frau Markert's pregnant, and –'

'It's perfectly safe for pregnant women to take.'

'Well, yes, but she's in the thirty-first week, and I remember her telling me a couple of weeks ago, when I was taking her blood pressure, that this is her third attempt. At having a baby? She's had two miscarriages. And when

I saw you'd prescribed the Dulcolax, I just thought, you know, maybe she shouldn't be taking that.'

Nina's heart lurches. Anita is right. She's absolutely right. With a risk of miscarriage or premature birth, the patient shouldn't go anywhere near laxatives like that. How could she have missed it? She, who is usually so scrupulous, so conscientious about what she prescribes to whom. A Freudian would say that this was – in truth – no mistake at all. That she is on a path to self-destruction, and that what she really needs, *really*, is a malpractice suit to finish her off. She feels the heat rising up her already uncomfortably flushed face.

'You're absolutely right, Anita,' she says. 'Thank you. I wasn't thinking. I –'

Anita is blushing, her discomfort evident in the twisting of her hands in front of her. 'It's just, I didn't want to do anything wrong. I'm really sorry.'

'There's nothing for you to be sorry about.' She feels utterly, desperately sick. 'Could you get me Frau Markert's phone number please? I'll give her a call and tell her to drink plenty of water and make sure she's getting enough fibre.'

Anita nods, then opens her mouth as though to speak, but instead turns and almost runs from the room. Nina takes a patient file from her pile, but can't bring herself to open it. The energy she felt a few moments ago escapes her body in one unstoppable rush leaving her with nothing other than horror at her own professional misjudgement. Perhaps she should lock up for the day, go home, have a bath. But even the thought of getting up and crossing the room exhausts her. She drags her eyes away from the file to the window. The bottom half of the windowpane is frosted to prevent anyone looking into the examination room from the outside; through the clear glass at the top she can see a flat leaden sky. She feels the weight of it, it makes her weariness complete.

Just then, there's another knock at the door.

She turns her head. 'Yes, Anita? What can I –'

'Sorry, I don't mean to be a nuisance, Dr Bergmann.' It's Franzen. He wears a discreetly elegant tan raincoat, and his shoulders are spotted with rain. 'Do you have a minute?' As usual, his face gives away absolutely nothing.

'Oh.' The sight of him brings her close to tears and she realises how good it feels to see him. She nods and tucks a strand behind her ear. 'Yes. Please, come in. I'm –' She gestures in a lazy sweeping motion at the papers on her desk.

Franzen steps in. He has a leather briefcase with him, which he opens and – without a word – pulls out a laptop. 'Do you mind?' he asks, and places it on her desk without waiting for an answer.

'What is this?' she asks, unnerved.

'It's – well, it's best if I just show you.' He waits for the laptop to boot. 'Would you mind?' he says again and turns the screen to face her. 'I'd like you to look at something.'

'Look at what?' she asks, with a small lurch in her stomach warning her that she might not like whatever it is he has to show her. But he doesn't answer, just comes to stand behind her.

He double-clicks on an icon and a YouTube video appears.

'The recording isn't very good,' he says. 'A bit shaky. It was taken on a mobile phone.'

Nina bends closer to the screen, confused. The video shows around thirty people facing forward in what looks like some kind of hall; a school hall perhaps, or a community centre. The light is dim, and, as Franzen said, the image is shaky. The sound quality is poor and Nina can only hear the voice of a man off-screen. He speaks in a rant, angry and loveless, but when he pauses, the crowd laughs and cheers.

Nina doesn't understand what she's looking at. Why is he showing this to her? She opens her mouth to speak, but Franzen gets in first.

'It's a meeting of *Neue Ordnung*, New Order, a right-wing extremist organisation.'

'Neo-Nazis?'

He nods.

'And why are you showing it to me?'

Franzen fast-forwards a few minutes. 'Here.' He freezes the video on an image of the speaker.

On the screen, Nina sees a man, teeth bared and eyes torn open in a grimace of fervour. 'Who is that?' she asks, instinctively recoiling from him.

Franzen rubs his chin. It's the first time she's seen him unshaven and she can't help but think that it doesn't suit him. 'Günther Lehmholz,' he says matter-of-factly.

'Lehmholz?' Nina's thoughts can't connect. 'The old woman's son?' Her ears are buzzing.

'Yes. My colleague, Herr Maslowski, thought he recognised the name from a couple of years back, and it turns out his instincts were right. This man Lehmholz is a long-standing member of *Neue Ordnung*.'

'But why are you showing me this?' she asks. She is suddenly and intensely thirsty, her head is spinning. 'I think I need –'

'Please, just another minute. There's something else.'

Franzen presses play, and the camera scans the crowd once again. Almost immediately, he pauses the video and points at the screen. 'Here. Behind this man, can you see?' He removes his finger and straightens up, standing so close behind her she can feel his body heat.

Her stomach flips. 'Oh my god,' she whispers.

'Is it her?'

Nina shakes her head, not in response to his question, but to the image in front of her. On a chair in one of the back rows sits a woman, dressed in black, staring ahead with her mouth slightly open and her eyebrows pulled together.

'Dr Bergmann?'

She stares at the screen until her eyes sting. She is trembling.

'Dr Bergmann.' Franzen's voice is calm. 'Can you confirm that this is your sister, Marie?'

Nina closes her eyes and breathes in and out, as deeply as she can. The buzzing in her ears gets louder. Then she nods. 'Yes.' The word comes out as a croak. 'Yes, but –'

'That's what I thought,' he continues in that calm tone, as though what he has made her watch isn't causing her heart to jolt and tilt inside her ribcage. He crosses the room and fills a glass with water from the sink in the corner. When he places the glass in front of her, all she can do is stare at it.

Franzen closes the laptop. He takes a seat opposite and places his hands, palms together, on the desk between them. 'This is what we know. We spoke to the informant on the assumption that this is, indeed, your sister. We didn't give him any details. He said he saw Marie twice, maybe three times at the meetings, he isn't sure. She came and went without speaking much. Unfortunately, we can't lean on him too heavily. The anti-extremist division is very – how should I put it? – *protective* of their informants.'

'But she's my sister!' she bursts out, unable to control the volume of her voice. 'And this is a murder case!'

'I know.' Franzen presses his lips together for a moment. 'I know, and this is one of the many things that stand in the way of our work. Politics before truth.' He sighs. 'But let's not get into that here. The fact is, these organisations are extremely difficult to penetrate. They don't just let people walk in off the streets. So –'

Nina interrupts him. 'Marie was not a Nazi.' Her voice is almost a growl. 'I don't care what you showed me. That was –' she shakes her head rapidly, 'that was not really Marie.'

Franzen nods. 'I understand.'

A pause.

'Do you?' she says, 'because I don't.'

She must have spoken more aggressively, or more frenzied, than she thought, because Franzen opens his hands, palms facing upwards. It is a gesture intended to calm her.

'Please,' he says gently. 'Let me tell you what we are thinking. It's possible that Marie encountered Lehmholz via his mother. She and the old lady were quite close, you told me.'

Nina nods her head.

'We've ruled out Lehmholz as a suspect – he's been in South Africa for the past three months.' He pauses.

He doesn't live in Berlin any more, so I don't get to see him as often as I'd like. That's what Frau Lehmholz told her. Had she known about her son's involvement with the neo-Nazis? Is he connected with the outcast supremacists of South Africa now? Nina's mind is contracting and expanding at the same time. She has the feeling she's in some dream, where nothing and everything makes sense.

'Are you all right?' Franzen asks. 'Maybe you should have some water.' He gestures towards the glass in front of her.

Nina reaches for the glass and empties it in a few gulps. Her insides are sick and light. When Franzen continues, she hears his voice as if through a layer of cotton wool, dull and edgeless.

'We're thinking Marie met Lehmholz in connection with his mother and got access to *Neue Ordnung* through him. To be honest, I'd hoped you might be able to tell us what she was doing there – right-wing extremism doesn't quite square with what we know about her. So,' he tilts his head at her, 'we're at a bit of a loss. Is there anything you can think of that might shed some light on this?'

The buzzing in her ears stops suddenly – so suddenly,

the quiet is uncanny. She hears the clicking of Anita's typing from beyond the closed door, Franzen's calm and steady breathing, a mobile ring-tone from the pavement below.

'No,' she says finally, to break the silence. 'I can't think of anything.'

24

Ten minutes after Franzen departs, Nina steps out onto the pavement. The sky is still low and grey, the wind blows in occasional icy gusts, sending swirls of yellowed leaves across her path. She walks with no particular destination in mind, head down against the wind, a hand clutching the collar of her coat shut. Past a primary school, grand four-storey apartment buildings, one or two old villas tucked in and set back from the street. She walks hard. Needs to clear her head. Needs to get her life back under control.

The wind picks up, stinging her cheeks, and a couple of raindrops fall from the sky. Apart from an occasional car sweeping past, she's alone. Most people wouldn't go out in this weather if they had a choice. The rain picks up, too; soon Nina's hair and face are drenched. But she doesn't turn back. Instead, she crosses the road, and finds herself passing through a hedgerow. She stops abruptly when she realises where she is. The local cemetery. She shivers; her subconscious is so predictable, it's almost comical. She turns to leave, but is hit by dizziness and for a moment loses her bearings. Placing her red-cold hands on her thighs, she bends forward and breathes in deeply. Slowly, the giddiness subsides.

A black car drives past, slowing to the speed limit in the proximity of the primary school. Nina starts walking again, leaning into the rain, careful not to slip on the slick cobblestones. Her mind is fogging over, so she picks up her pace to clear it. She forces her thoughts into focus, tries to push past the grainy image of that video, the bared teeth of Lehmholz, his coarse, grinding voice – and her sister, so *female*, in the midst of all that ugliness, her lips parted, forehead creased. The video was taken four months ago, Franzen said. It's an effort to calculate the timeline, the cold wind is making her skull ache. July. Marie was at that meeting in July. But why didn't she mention it to Nina? This was a big deal, something so out of the ordinary – surely she would have mentioned to her sister that she'd attended a neo-Nazi meeting. It is incredible to even consider such a thing. They spoke about everything. Everything, except –

Nina comes to an abrupt stop, almost laughs out loud. It must have been research for Marie's writing. Of course! It's been staring her in the face the whole time. She found research on the Stasi amid Marie's papers, and now, here's research on neo-Nazis – it makes perfect sense. Six months ago, Marie had joked about what her online search history would look like to someone who didn't know her: what it feels like to drown, nineteenth-century prostitution laws, how to infiltrate global corporations, the psychological profile of cult leaders . . .

Nina's nose is running. She fumbles in her pocket for a tissue, her hands numb with cold. She needs to call Franzen, to explain everything. She'll call him tonight, when she's had a chance to rest her mind, so she can be sure to articulate it all properly. She turns a corner and sees a black car on the street ahead of her, idling in a no-parking zone, its red brake lights luminous through the rain. It's the same car that just drove past, she's almost certain. She stops and waits to see if it will drive off again, but it doesn't. *Thiel has a car.* Panicked, she turns and heads back; it's a ten-minute walk to her office from here. Behind her, she hears the engine growing louder and the sound of tyres on the wet road as the car makes a U-turn. Her breath catches in her throat as she hurries on, letting out a small gasp of relief as she spots a newsagent on the far corner.

But the car is crawling closer, a quick glance back puts it at less than twenty metres behind her. If she starts running, she might make it to the newsagent before the car catches up with her. She plunges forward, blood pounding in her ears, the horizontal rain blinding her. The car draws level – she hears the splash of the tyres beside her – and she loses her footing, falling hard onto her right knee. Pain flashes through her body.

'Nina?'

The voice is vaguely familiar, but she can't place it.

'Nina Bergmann? It's Bernhard. Are you all right?'

A moment later, she's being lifted from the ground.

'That looked painful,' Bernhard says, placing his arm around her waist to help her up. 'And you are soaked through.'

Her breath is unsteady as she lets him guide her to his car. But when he opens the passenger door, she hesitates. 'I'll get the seat wet,' she says.

He frowns. 'Never mind that, but we have to get you warmed up.' He looks around. 'There's a café over there.' He points across the street.

'It's okay, really,' Nina says, aware that her teeth are chattering. She bends and flexes her right leg and winces.

'I insist,' he says. 'Then when you've dried out a bit, I'll give you a lift.'

She leans on him as they cross the road. The café – which turns out to be a tea house – is set back from the street by a quaint courtyard with an ancient chestnut tree set in the centre. Inside, Bernhard helps her to a chair. Small table lamps are lit, giving the place a cosy autumnal feel. The air is filled with a warm, aromatic tea smell.

'Do you need ice for that?' Bernhard asks, nodding towards Nina's knee.

'No, it'll be fine. I just grazed it.' She puts a hand to her knee; it's hot and throbbing beneath the damp fabric. She'll have a nasty bruise tomorrow.

The waitress comes over and they order. Earl Grey and a scone for Bernhard, Oolong for Nina.

'I was heading back from a meeting in Dahlem and thought I spotted you on Laubacher Straße,' he says when the waitress has left. 'And you looked a little forlorn in the rain, so I pulled over to wait and offer you a lift.'

'My practice is two streets across. I was out for a walk and got caught without an umbrella.' Nina attempts a smile but still feels utterly shaken.

'This is a nice area,' Bernhard says, casting a glance towards the street outside.

'Yes. It was my husband's idea that I set up here.'

He raises his eyebrows. They're silver-grey and well-trimmed. 'You don't like the neighbourhood?'

'I do, but –' She stops. She doesn't want to start discussing the horrendous rents. 'I do like it.'

They lapse into silence as they wait for the tea. Apart from an elderly woman at a table by the window, the place is empty. Nina looks out of the window. The rain has paused, yielding to a grey November mist that has curled up and around the chestnut tree outside. She shivers, glad to be indoors. She turns back as the waitress places the tea on the table, and notices Bernhard watching her intently.

'You look nothing like her,' he says. 'Marie.'

It catches her off-guard. Then she remembers. 'Of course, you met her, didn't you?'

'Briefly,' he replies. 'But I remember thinking, when I first saw you, how striking the difference was. Dark and fair. Like that fairy tale, Snow White and Rose Red? Snow White, the blonde girl, is quiet and shy and loves reading, and her sister Rose Red, the brunette, is outspoken and cheerful. Then ... *blah blah blah* ... evil dwarf ... bear, and they live happily ever after.' He chuckles. 'I used to read it to Sophie all the time. All the Grimm stories. She loved them, especially the gruesome ones.'

He smiles as he raises his teacup to his lips, but it is a private smile. A sad smile. Nina knows the fairy tale. She used to read it to Marie, who also loved it, and then to Rebekka and Kai. She wonders vaguely how old Bernhard's daughter would be now if she'd lived. Probably only a few years younger than herself.

'I was thinking of calling you a little while back,' she

admits. 'I got frustrated.' Her voice is low. 'With the police investigation.'

He doesn't speak.

'But then they called to say they have a suspect,' she continues. Yes, she should focus on Fraunhofer. Forget about the video. 'So I'm glad I didn't have to bother you, after all.'

'It wouldn't have been a bother.'

Nina sips her tea. It has a pleasant fragrance, though it tastes somewhat bitter. She picks up a stick with sugar crystals from the holder on the table. The crystals are the colour of amber. 'I know,' she says, putting the stick back. Her mother's reproach about Bernhard being a busy man comes to mind.

'But – that's good news, isn't it?' he says. 'About the suspect.'

'Yes, I suppose so.'

Marie's face on the video – alert, curious, sceptical. Always becoming, never just being. Nina needs to call Franzen, stop him from letting the investigation going off on some meaningless tangent. Marie wasn't one of them, Nina is sure of it. Her sister was too honest, too joyful to believe in the paranoid doctrines of those men. She brushes back a wet strand of hair that has fallen across her face. Her forehead feels hot. She might be running a fever.

'So, have they made an arrest?' Bernhard asks.

'Um, no. I – I don't think so. He's "helping with enquiries", they said. But he doesn't have an alibi, and it seems he was stalking Marie, although he denies attacking her.'

'Well, I hope they have their man. For your sake. And your family's. I wouldn't want anyone to go through what Gloria and I went through after Sophie was killed.'

He sounds angry, resentful, but something in his voice snags and Nina realises he's close to tears.

'Oh my goodness, I've upset you. I'm so sorry, Bernhard, that was thoughtless of me.'

He shakes his head. 'No,' he says and clears his throat. 'You have absolutely nothing to be sorry about.'

A long silence follows. Nina warms her hands on her cup, knowing she should probably finish her tea and take her leave. But it feels so good to just sit here, with someone who understands what she's feeling, someone who doesn't need to be told about the howling, gut-wrenching pain that feeds off itself, swelling and twisting into shapes grotesque and untameable, something that breaks you so profoundly you will never be the same again.

She picks up her cup, then places it quickly back onto the saucer. 'I thought we were so close,' she bursts out. 'I thought we knew everything about each other. But now – it seems as though I knew nothing about her.'

The woman sitting by the window coughs a little too loudly. Nina shudders and wraps her arms around herself. 'It sounds stupid, but I feel . . . betrayed somehow.'

Bernhard leans in closer. 'I'm sorry, Nina. I'm not sure what you mean.'

'I went to Marie's flat on Wednesday to clear it out,' she tells him. 'She had things, old stuff from uni, drawings . . . things I never knew about.' She feels something surging up inside, fluttering in her throat, eager to get out. 'And the police think she might have been involved with neo-Nazis, and that's just *ridiculous*! Because there's no way she would've ... it just isn't ...'

Bernhard's eyes open a fraction wider, but he doesn't speak.

Nina continues, the words spilling out of her now: 'And then there's this woman, her neighbour, she told me things. About Marie. But the other day –' She looks up at Bernhard, knowing she's making little sense. She expects him to make some excuse to leave.

But instead he says, 'Carry on. Please.' And when she doesn't speak, he continues, 'Nina. I don't know anything, so I can't judge anything. Talk. Let it out.'

'I thought she might know who did this to Marie. But it turns out ...' She waves a hand across her face. 'She's very old. Confused. But that's not what it was. She ... she made me realise that there were things about my sister I hardly knew. As if Marie chose to show me only a very specific part of herself. Like she was acting out a role for me. And now it's too late for me to find out who she really was.' These last words leave her mouth in a whisper.

'But we all have different roles, don't we?' Bernhard says. His voice is soft but resonant, originating somewhere deep inside him. 'You, Nina, play the role of mother, daughter, wife. And the Nina your parents know is different, surely, than the Nina your husband knows. The Nina your patients know. The Nina your sister knew. Yet there's nothing dishonest about that, is there?' He reaches out his hand as though to place it on hers, but seems to change his mind. He picks up his teacup instead. 'And if I may offer you some advice – think of it as fatherly advice – remember the Marie *you* knew. Trying to fill in gaps after the fact, gaps you never realised existed, might only distort your otherwise positive memories of her.' He stops abruptly. 'I'm sorry, I hope you don't think I've overstepped a line.'

'No,' Nina says. A bubble of hysteria rises up, but she suppresses it in time. These erratic mood swings, they're exhausting. She lets out a shaky breath. 'No, in fact, I think that's exactly what I needed to hear.'

Bernhard stares into his cup. 'Sophie's death took a real toll on our marriage. I would get hopelessly morose every year on the anniversary of her death – even worse on her birthdays, wondering what she would be like at twelve, sixteen, twenty-one years of age. What would her job be, would she have married young, or perhaps waited? When would she have given us grandchildren? Or perhaps none at all?' He blinks rapidly. 'It got too much for Gloria. She said I wasn't letting it heal, like picking at a scab until it becomes inflamed and septic. She told me that we should take comfort in the joy Sophie gave us when she was alive.' He looks straight at Nina. 'And she was right. Anything else is self-destructive.'

Nina feels herself blushing. She's oddly ashamed at her own drama. She can't even imagine how people continue to live after losing a child.

Bernhard looks at his watch and then back at Nina. 'I'm glad we bumped into each other,' he says with an affectionate smile. 'But I'm afraid I'll have to be off. I have a tight schedule today.'

She nods. 'Yes. I'd better get back myself.' They get up, and after a polite back-and-forth, she agrees to let him pay for her tea.

'I presume I'll be seeing you on Saturday?' he says when he comes back from the counter.

'Saturday?'

'The dinner party. At your parents'. For the celebrations.'

Why does this keep slipping her mind? 'Yes, of course, the dinner party. You'll be there?'

'We will indeed. Gloria and I.'

He helps her into her coat. She catches a hint of his cologne, and has to resist the temptation to turn and bury her face in his chest.

*

In the afternoon, Anita informs Nina of one more cancellation. However, there is a walk-in patient, making a total number of four women she sees that afternoon. At ten past three, almost two hours before she would normally close the surgery, she decides it isn't worth sitting around waiting for more walk-ins, and tells Anita that she's welcome to go home.

'And have a nice weekend,' she adds. 'Any plans?'

Anita shrugs. 'Nothing special. We'll probably come into town for the festival at the Brandenburg Gate. My wife wants to go, anyway. To be honest, I'll be glad when it's all over.'

'I know how you feel,' Nina says, although she means something different. 'Have fun, whatever you decide to do.'

'Thanks. You too.' Anita looks at her, hesitates, but then says, 'I'm sure things will get better. More patients, I mean.'

Nina attempts a smile. 'I'm sure they will.' She doesn't mention that she'll be paying Anita's wages out of her savings next month.

They lock up together. Outside, the air is sharp. Anita heads left towards the U-Bahn, and Nina tries to remember where she parked the car this morning. Standing alone on the pavement, she glances around to make sure no one is lying in wait for her. Satisfied that she's alone, she starts to head off down the street before her mobile rings loudly, making her jump. She answers quickly.

'Dr Bergmann? It's Kommissar Franzen. I'm just checking in to make sure everything's all right.'

'Herr Franzen. Yes, everything's fine. I'm –' A flock of pigeons on the square in front of her takes noisy flight and her heart plunges. Then a dog, followed by its owner, turns the corner. The dog chases the pigeons in a delighted frenzy. 'I've just locked up. I'm on my way home.'

'About earlier,' he says, 'I realise it might have been upsetting for you. But in my experience, it's best to put everything out there, see where it takes us.'

'I understand.' Should she tell him her thoughts about the video now? About how Marie can only have been present at those meetings for her research? She holds her breath, releases it in cloud of white mist. Her right eyelid flickers. She's so tired. She'll call him tonight, or tomorrow. So instead, she asks, 'Is there any news on Fraunhofer?'

'Afraid not. The public prosecutor wants a psychiatric

report on him before she presses charges. I'm afraid nothing's going to happen until after the weekend. But I also wanted to assure you that finding Thiel is still very much a priority. If my colleagues manage to track down his wife Jessica, we're sure to find him. Until then ... please just stay safe.'

At the sound of Jessica's name, Nina's heart flip-flops. She takes a step back and leans heavily against the building.

'Dr Bergmann? Are you still there?'

'Yes,' she manages to whisper. The thoughts tumble in her brain. 'Herr Franzen,' she's finally able to say, 'can I call you back in a couple of minutes?'

'Of course, I –'

But she cancels the call before he can finish.

She fumbles the keys with freezing fingers and it takes an age to unlock the office door. Then another age checking through the filing cabinet. But then – then she finds it. Jessica Thiel's file. Her hands tremble as she flicks through the pages, looking for the patient information form. Her mind is a mess, she can feel her brain trying to absorb and shape something. Something significant. She scans the form to anchor her thoughts. She finds the anchor at the bottom of the second page.

"Please indicate whether the practice has been recommended to you, and if so, by whom."

And in Jessica Thiel's rounded, girlish handwriting, the words: *Dora Diamant.*

Nina has to sit down before she returns Franzen's call.

25

On Saturday afternoon, Nina helps Rebekka get ready for the evening. There isn't really much getting ready to do: Rebekka will be wearing the black dress inspected and approved by Antonia, along with a neat white apron to match Hannah's. But Rebekka is nervous and excited, and this has manifested itself in her indecision how to wear her hair.

'Maybe a ponytail,' she says, looking up at Nina in the mirror. On Rebekka's insistence, Nina has taken the large mirror from the hall and set it up in front of the living room window, 'for the light'. Rebekka sits on a stool looking into the mirror. Nina stands behind her with hairbrush and clips at the ready.

'Or a bun. That would look good, wouldn't it? Suit the whole "maid" look.'

Nina scrapes Rebekka's lovely thick hair into a ponytail, then twists it around itself and secures it with bobby pins. 'How's that?'

Rebekka turns her head to the left, to the right, not taking her eyes off her reflection. 'I don't know,' she says, then poses a smile, and a pout.

Nina feels ragged. She slept three, maybe four hours

last night, and those few hours were distorted by half-grasped dreams, thoughts, memories, in which all seemed perfectly clear one moment, only to fog over and crumble into nothingness the next. Jessica Thiel knew Marie. Had they been friends? Had Jessica used Marie's pen-name as some kind of joke? No, she decides, Jessica didn't seem the type. Too uncertain of herself, too timid for that sort of humour. But her husband – a violent, choleric thug, more than capable of using his fists against a woman. No wonder his wife had such a defeated air. In one of count-less dreams, Nina saw him pinning Marie against a wall, holding her arm twisted behind her back as her mouth gaped open in terror and pain. She'd woken at dawn with her heart thumping.

'Ow, Mama, that hurts!'

Nina looks down and realises she's pushing a bobby pin into Rebekka's skull.

'Sorry.' She loosens the pin and then slides it gently into the bun.

'No,' Rebekka says decisively. 'It makes my face look fat. Maybe I should curl it and then pin it up.'

Nina checks her watch and yawns. 'Well, you've got just over half an hour before you have to leave the house. If you want me to curl it, fine, but then that's it. No more changing your mind.'

She starts removing the pins. When she told Franzen about Marie's connection with Jessica Thiel, he sounded interested, but guarded. As usual, he was impossible to read. That's probably a prerequisite for his job, but it's frustrating beyond belief. The hunt for Thiel has been moved up the priority list, he told her, but there were other things he wasn't at liberty to discuss. 'We're doing our best, Dr Bergmann,' he said. 'Trust me.'

A sharp jolt of pain in her palm jolts her out of her thoughts. She has pressed a hairpin so tightly in her fist she has drawn blood.

Thankfully, Rebekka hasn't noticed. 'Okay, Mama. Final decision. Curl and up.' She demonstrates with her hands. 'But plenty of hairspray, okay?'

Twenty-five minutes later, Rebekka's hair has been styled to her (near) satisfaction, they have had the obligatory argument, negotiations and compromise regarding make-up – a little mascara, no rouge, a touch of lip gloss, absolutely *no* perfume – and Rebekka heads for the study to present herself to her father.

'Never a prettier maid,' he says, laughing and winking at her.

'Maid to be a lady,' Rebekka responds.

'Maid to measure.'

'All maid up and nowhere to go.'

'Listen,' Nina says, slightly sorry to be spoiling their fun. 'Don't let Omi hear you say that. She prefers the term "housekeeper".'

'Why?' asks Rebekka.

'I don't know. Middle-class guilt, I suppose.'

'Whatever,' Rebekka says, going back into the living room to take a last look in the mirror. 'As long as I get the fifty euros, she can call me what she likes.'

Sebastian laughs. Nina helps Rebekka into her coat, insisting she take an umbrella, just in case.

'We'll see you at around nine,' she says, kissing her daughter on the cheek. 'Everyone else will be coming straight from the festival at Brandenburg Gate, so Papa and I will probably be there first.'

'Okay. Later, then.' Rebekka steps out into the cold. 'God, I hope I don't spill anyone's soup in their lap,' she says, pulling a face.

'You won't. You'll have fun. Now, off you go, or you'll be late.'

Nina gives her a small wave and watches Bekka walk towards the bus stop. She looks so grown up, with her straight-backed, confident gait. What happened to her little girl? You stand so close to your children, she thinks, that you fail to see them growing. It's almost the cruellest price to pay. One minute, they're still in nappies, the next they're wearing bras and braces, and menstruating, and picking up on hidden emotions with some adult radar. At this moment, she regrets not having taken more photographs, not having bothered getting out the camcorder (but the battery was never fully charged, the memory card was full, the cables never where they should be), and decides she has no excuses not to get out her phone more often. Better late than never; at least she won't lose out on Kai's vanishing childhood in that way.

She wonders where these emotions are coming from. Was she feeling like this before Sebastian mentioned having another baby? Or did this trigger some uncon-scious need, some underlying longing to start again, from the beginning? Perhaps – and Nina entertains this thought only for a single, painful second – she wants to replace the baby Marie couldn't have.

*

Nina stands at the sink brushing her teeth while Sebastian takes a shower. The mirror has steamed up, so she wipes it with her hand, creating a circle that reflects only her face, neck and the tops of her shoulders. Her eyes are still puffy from lack of sleep. As she counts brushstrokes in her head – a habit she acquired in childhood and has never abandoned – she notices how nicely pronounced her collarbone has become. She traces the bone with the fingers of her free hand, tapping softly and listening out for the slight, hollow sound. She spits and rinses. Sebastian steps out of the shower and wraps a towel around his waist.

'I'm looking forward to tonight,' he says, coming to stand behind her. He leans against her to wipe the mirror at his eye level.

'Are you?' Nina says. She doesn't what to wear to the dinner. The dress code is, naturally, black tie, and she has a few evening dresses to choose from. But two of them are off-the-shoulder, and the others have spaghetti straps. She worries that her mother will notice the weight loss and she could kick herself for not planning ahead. This morning, on the scales, she was 800 grams away from her target. She should have bought a stole, or an evening jacket. She'll have to wear the black silk cardigan, although she hasn't even taken it out the wardrobe for years and it probably smells of mothballs.

'Sure. There'll be some interesting people there,' Sebastian says and gently nudges her out of the way so he can start shaving. 'And the food's bound to be great.'

Nina steps through to the bedroom and pats her legs dry, carefully avoiding the bruise on her right knee. Then she slips into her underwear and a tracksuit. Out of the corner of her eye, she notices Sebastian watching her.

'I'm going to do my hair before I get dressed,' she explains.

'You don't want to overdo it,' he says, spreading shaving foam over his lower face.

'No,' she replies. 'I was thinking of the dark blue dress, you know, the one with the sequins at the front.'

'I don't mean that,' he says. 'I mean the diet.' He strokes his own stomach. 'It's not as though I don't admire your discipline. I get to the gym twice a month these days if I'm lucky. But you don't want to get *too* thin.' He grins at her. 'Your boobs will shrink.'

Heat rises to the top of her head.

'I, I'm not –'

She's saved by the doorbell.

Sebastian looks at her. 'You expecting anyone?'

'No,' she replies. 'You don't think it's Vanessa, do you?'

Vanessa – the mother of Kai's friend Jakob – came to pick up Kai earlier for a sleepover. 'Did you make sure to give her your mobile number?' Nina adds.

'Of course,' he replies, giving his jaw a last scrape with the shaver. He turns to her. 'I can hardly get the door like this, can I?'

She gets up and goes downstairs to open the front door. It is Franzen.

'May I come in?' he asks.

Her heart skips and she steps aside to let him in. A gust of damp, icy air blows in behind him.

'I'm very sorry to intrude,' he says, as Nina closes the front door and gestures towards the living room. 'I thought I should come in person, rather than phone.'

He's come to tell her that they've found Thiel, or that they've charged Fraunhofer with Marie's murder and, suddenly, Nina falls back into last night's dream, except now she is picturing Fraunhofer's slim, solemn face, twisted into rage and violence, his thin white hands curled into bony fists as he beats the life out of Marie.

'Would you like to sit down?' he asks, placing his hand gently on her arm.

'Oh. Yes.' She takes a seat on the sofa, Franzen opposite, like the last time he was here.

There are footsteps on the stairs. Franzen looks at the door.

'My husband,' Nina says.

'Good,' Franzen says. 'It's better if you both hear this.'

'Have you spoken to my parents yet?' she asks.

He shakes his head. 'No. I recall your father mentioning that he's involved in some . . . event, today.'

Sebastian comes in, wearing his black dinner suit but with the bow tie still loose at his throat. He looks at Franzen, and frowns. Franzen stands up and holds out his hand to shake.

'Hello, Herr Lanz,' he says. 'I was just telling your wife that I thought it better to come by in person. I do apologise if I'm intruding.'

Sebastian takes his hand. 'Are you on duty today?'

'Afraid so.' Franzen lets out a quiet laugh. 'It's the kind of job that doesn't take account of weekends and national holidays.'

'Please, sit down,' Sebastian says, and Franzen takes his seat. Sebastian sits beside Nina, taking her hand and interlacing his fingers in hers. 'So,' he continues, and she wonders how he can stay so calm, 'what can we do for you?'

'Well, the first thing I can tell you is that we've located Frau Thiel.'

Nina lets out a small gasp. 'Where? Is she all right?'

Franzen nods. 'She's staying at a women's refuge. The women who run the place are very protective, understandably – their address is only available on a need-to-know basis –'

'Even to the police?' Sebastian sounds incredulous.

'Yes,' Franzen continues. 'But they allowed a female officer to go and interview her. Frau Thiel recalls meeting a young woman at a café several months ago, by the name of Dora. They got chatting, and the woman gave her your card, Dr Bergmann. Apparently, Frau Thiel was worried she might be pregnant and, well, it wasn't something she was happy about.'

Out of the corner of her eye, Nina sees Sebastian turning to her and raising a single eyebrow. She remains facing forward. 'I see.'

'Frau Thiel gave a description of Dora that matches that of Marie. She had no idea what had happened to Marie – the murder, I mean. She was quite distressed about it, by all accounts. But she did give her husband an alibi for the day of the attack. He was sleeping off a hangover on the day in question. He didn't leave their flat until late afternoon.'

Nina squeezes Sebastian's hand so hard her fingers begin to feel numb. As hard, she thinks, as she squeezed his hand when she was in labour with Kai.

'Perhaps she's frightened,' she says, releasing her grip to place her hands on her lap. 'Perhaps she's giving him an alibi because she's afraid of her husband finding out.'

Franzen tugs at his earlobe and looks quite uncomfortable.

Sebastian stands up, crosses his arms across his chest. 'I think my wife has a valid point,' he says. 'It's quite possible that the woman is lying, surely. Which would be understandable.'

Franzen fixes him with a stare, and then also gets to his feet. 'Herr Lanz, please sit down.'

Sebastian hesitates, but then sits back down and drapes his arm around Nina's shoulders.

Franzen returns to his chair. He looks at her. 'Herr Thiel was killed in the early hours of this morning in road traffic accident. The driver of the car he was in careered headfirst into a tree. The pathologist's report isn't final yet, but they both evidently had high levels of alcohol in their blood.'

Nina's hand flies up to cover her mouth.

'God in heaven,' Sebastian murmurs.

'I'm sorry if this comes as a shock,' Franzen continues. 'You will receive official confirmation by the prosecution service that the case against him has been discontinued.

But I thought you might like to know as soon as possible. I'm sure this has been a concern for you. I'm sorry, perhaps I should've told you this news first.'

Sebastian lets out a grunt of disapproval and turns to Nina. 'Are you all right?'

She nods, barely. She can't find her voice. This wasn't what she'd expected. But then, surely, Marie's murderer must be Jakob Fraunhofer, and the relief at this thought, at the clarity of the circumstances, gives rise to a kind of elation.

'There's more, I'm afraid.' Franzen takes a deep breath as if to drag down the bubble of hope inside her. 'Jakob Fraunhofer is no longer a focus of our enquiry.'

No one speaks. Nina can hear the dishwasher go through a rinse cycle, a whoosh followed by a dull thumping sound. Sebastian probably put a wooden spoon or something in the cutlery tray, and now it's hitting off the spinning arm. Or perhaps it's the sound the dishwasher always makes, she can't be sure. She can feel her pulse in her throat, or rather, in that fleshy part on the underside of her tongue. What's the term for that? She can't remember.

'He's been dropped from the investigation?' Sebastian says. 'What? Completely?'

Franzen nods. He looks sad at having to convey this information to them.

'He had an alibi without knowing it. A Russian import-export shop on Schönhauser Allee had an illegal CCTV camera installed, facing the street. Anyway, Fraunhofer had claimed that he went for a long walk up Schönhauser Allee on the morning of the attack, without meeting anyone who could corroborate this. My colleague, Kommissar Maslowski, saw a copy of a complaint someone had made about the camera, so we decided to check it out. And there he was, Fraunhofer, on the morning of the attack, heading north shortly before nine a.m., and back south again at ten.'

'That was lucky,' Sebastian says dryly. 'Your colleague coming across the complaint like that.'

Franzen holds his hands out, palms facing upwards. 'That's the way these things work sometimes.' He sounds tired, unwilling to engage with Sebastian's hostility.

Nina's mind has fogged over. She clears her throat. 'But wouldn't that still give him enough time to get to Marie's?' she asks. 'Frau Lehmholz only found her at eleven.'

Franzen shakes his head. 'No. Even if he borrowed someone's car, or took a taxi, he wouldn't have made it to Marie's flat much before ten-thirty, ten-twenty at the earliest. And we know that he was at work at half past ten.' He pauses, then looks straight at her. 'Truly, I'm sorry.'

Nina looks away.

Sebastian leans back and crosses his arms over his chest once more. 'What happens now? Are there any, what would you call them, second-order suspects?'

'No. There's the man Frau Lehmholz saw, or claims to have seen. But –' Franzen sighs. 'To be honest, it doesn't look promising. I'm sorry I'm not able to give you better news.'

Nina realises that she's freezing. She's afraid that if she opens her mouth to speak again, her teeth will start chattering.

Franzen stands up and says in a brusque tone, 'I don't want to take up any more of your time. I'll contact you if there are any developments.'

Sebastian also gets to his feet. 'Thanks for coming by.' He holds out his hand. Franzen shakes it and nods at Nina.

'But what about that letter from Robert?' The sentence bursts from her mouth.

Franzen and Sebastian turn to look at her.

'The letter, it was among her things. You must have read it. Robert was still in love with her. That's a motive, isn't it? Even if he wasn't the father of her baby. *Especially* if he wasn't the father of her baby.'

'Nina,' Sebastian says with an odd tilt to his voice. 'Robert has an alibi.'

'What?'

Franzen frowns. 'I told you this, when I came to see you. The Max Planck Institute in Leipzig was hosting a conference on the day Marie was attacked. There are some twenty people who can corroborate Robert's presence there.'

'But . . .' She blinks several times. Did he tell her that? She would have remembered, surely. She gets to her feet. And suddenly she's on a roll, making connections she hasn't made before. 'But what about his new girlfriend? You said yourself you don't know the gender of the attacker. The murderer. It could've been Robert's girlfriend! Hmm? She might have been jealous about Marie and Robert's past, about the two of them wanting to stay friends. That's enough to drive someone to –'

'Frau Bergmann.' Franzen voice is all smooth edges

now. 'I do understand, believe me. And yet I'm going to be quite frank with you. You are clutching at straws. This is not unreasonable behaviour, under the circumstances. But we have exhausted all possible leads, asked all possible questions and explored all possible avenues. Not to solve a case is an extremely frustrating outcome for any police officer, and I realise that what is frustrating for me is unimaginably painful for you. The case will remain open, but for now, there is nothing more we can do. I'm sorry.'

She sits back down, heavily. Her outburst has left her stunned.

Sebastian speaks. 'Thank you, Kommissar Franzen. I think it would be best if –'

Franzen gives Nina a last look, catching her eye. 'I'm sorry,' he repeats. 'Truly.'

He follows Sebastian out and a moment later, Nina hears the door clicking shut.

When Sebastian comes back in, she says, 'I don't want to go there tonight.' She sounds like a sulky child, but she doesn't care.

Sebastian puts a hand out to stroke her hair. Then he crouches down in front of her and puts his hands over hers. 'You know that's not an option,' he says.

'But what if I was ill?'

'But you're not. Listen –' He pauses. 'Listen. Life doesn't stop here. I'm just as upset as you are about the investigation. But there's nothing we can do about that now. Believe me, if I'd known what Franzen was going to tell us . . .' He squeezes her hands. 'This evening is very important for your parents, you know that. And it's not going to be as bad as you think. If anything, it'll be a distraction.' He stands up. 'Besides, would you want to miss seeing Bekka in action?' he asks, smiling. 'With the little apron and everything?'

She shakes her head slowly and feels her teeth rattle in her skull.

'I'm going to make us a drink,' he continues. 'Consider it medicinal. Come on –' He takes her hands and pulls her to her feet. She doesn't resist. 'You go and get ready. Gin and tonic okay?'

She nods, although she hasn't really processed what he said.

Sebastian goes out to the kitchen and Nina heads upstairs. In the bathroom, she brushes out her hair and starts backcombing individual strands. Yes, she is clutching at straws. Of course she is. She would drown otherwise. She tries not to think of Thiel, lying cold and rigid in a sliding drawer somewhere. She rubs her shoulder where he twisted it – she can still feel a twinge now and again when she lifts something heavy, but soon, the twinge will be gone. Did Franzen honestly think she'd be pleased to hear the man was dead? Maybe she *should* be pleased, or at least relieved. But she doesn't feel relief. She feels nothing. It is not an unpleasant feeling. She's not happy that he's dead, but she's not sorry, either. She pins up a strand of hair with a hairpin. Takes a few deep breaths. She feels something tugging inside her. This is it. *There's nothing more we can do*.

Sebastian shouts up the stairs that the drinks are ready and that she needs to get a move on. Nina calls down that she'll be another ten minutes, then pins up the rest of her hair and appraises her reflection. It'll do. Eyeliner, mascara, lipstick – she applies it automatically. What does Jakob Fraunhofer feel over Marie's death? Is he grieving? She hadn't considered this before, all those other people who knew Marie and might be in mourning for her. She switches off the bathroom light on her way out and steps out of her tracksuit. *Life doesn't stop here.* She lets her hand glide down her belly, then to the side, her fingers skating one, two, three, four over the hip bone that protrudes over the elastic of her knickers. Life doesn't stop here. Sebastian is right. Not just her life, but his, Rebekka's, Kai's, Jakob Fraunhofer's.

It would be a way out. To have another baby. As a father, Sebastian is delightful and delighted. Her practice will either survive or not. Perhaps she shouldn't rule out the idea. Perhaps – and the thought is as shocking as a firework, an alarming crack and bang, but then fizzling out into nothing – Sebastian understands her better than she does herself. Something tugs inside her and snaps, but faintly, soundlessly. This is it. She slips the blue dress from its hanger and rubs the fabric – soft, silky – between forefinger and thumb. She needs to let go. Her heart is so small and dry, it's barely more than a flutter inside her. A baby. It would be nice, at least, to have the option. She puts on the dress and looks in the mirror. As she feared, the thin straps show the boniness of her shoulders. She opens the wardrobe and roots around for the cardigan, which she finds right at the back, hanging in a plastic cover. She takes it out and smells it. No mothballs, just a faint whiff of dry-cleaning chemicals. She shrugs it on and goes downstairs to join Sebastian.

26

Hannah opens the door to them.

'Good evening,' she says, smiling, and helps Nina out of her coat.

'Hello, Hannah.' Nina hands her the scarf. 'Thank you.'

The dark rich smell of roasted duck fills the spacious hallway. It is intensely appetising and sickening at the same time.

'How's Rebekka doing?' Sebastian asks. 'Help or hindrance?'

Hannah puts her head to one side. 'She's a lovely girl. Far more use to me than those students Frau Bergmann usually gets in to help on these occasions.'

She gives Nina a big smile, just as Antonia comes into the hall from the adjacent dining room.

'The fridge is out,' she snaps.

'No, Frau Bergmann,' Hannah says, hurrying past them to hang up the coats. 'I adjusted the temperature a little so the canapés wouldn't get too hard. From the cold.'

'Well, you must have switched it off completely. I checked the wine and it's barely cool. Why don't you ask me before you interfere like that?'

'I'll go and see.' Hannah scoots down the hall towards the kitchen.

'And please don't roll your eyes at me,' Antonia says, loud enough for Hannah to hear.

Sebastian steps forward and kisses her on the cheek. 'Don't worry about the wine,' he says. 'Pop it on the terrace for half an hour. It's certainly cold enough out there.'

She gives him a smile. 'I do apologise, Sebastian. I shouldn't be griping like this. But it's hard not to be a little nervous, you know?'

She turns to lead them into the drawing room. Sebastian catches Nina's eye and winks. Nina is aware that she's ever so slightly unsteady on her feet, but feels glad she had a drink before coming.

In the drawing room, the fire has been lit and the lights dimmed. The room seems drowsily elegant, as though the immaculate yet cosy style of the place is somehow accidental and it hasn't taken Antonia hours and hours to get the ambience exactly right. Nina takes a seat closest to the fireplace. She's cold in her thin dress, in spite of the cardigan. Sebastian remains standing, and Antonia takes a seat opposite Nina. Despite her claims of nervousness, she looks perfectly calm, ankles crossed, hands folded in her lap.

'You look nice,' she says to Nina.

'Thanks, Mama. So do you.' It's true. She's wearing a simple black dress, Armani perhaps, the neckline showing just enough cleavage to suggest a certain confidence in her appearance, but not so much as to indicate that she thinks she's younger than she is. She has perfect style, from her pearl-drop earrings to the unobtrusively matching buckles on her shoes.

'How was Papa's speech, by the way?' Nina asks, remembering suddenly.

'Oh.' Antonia looks away into the fire.

'Not good?' Sebastian asks.

Antonia sighs. 'They decided to drop it,' she says. 'Papa was brief about it on the phone. They claimed a scheduling conflict or something, but I assume it had more to do with that arrest. The spy, you know? Papa was responsible for his most recent promotion.' She looks at Nina and then up at Sebastian. 'Naturally, he had no idea. Best not mention it when he comes.'

'Too bad,' Sebastian says.

'Yes. After all that effort.' She gets up. 'I suggested he give a condensed version after dinner, but – oh, never mind.' She waves her hand across her face. 'From tomorrow, he'll be out of my hair for a couple of days, at least.'

'What do you mean?' Nina asks.

'I booked him a golfing holiday. Four days in Mallorca. I thought he might need it after all this. He's off first thing tomorrow morning.'

'Wouldn't mind that myself,' Sebastian says. 'You didn't fancy joining him, Antonia?'

She puts her head to one side and gives him a coy smile. 'I'll be glad of the peace and quiet, if I'm honest.' Then she straightens her posture abruptly. 'Now we just have to get this dinner over with. Like I said to Nina, a simple reception would've been fine, as far as I'm concerned. But Hans insisted that everyone was bound to be starving after standing about in the cold for hours.'

'Well, he has a point,' Sebastian says with a chuckle.

'Speaking of which, when are you expecting them?'

She checks the slim gold watch on her wrist. 'In about fifteen minutes. Goodness, I'd better see how Hannah and Bekka are getting on.' She crosses the room. 'Oh, would you mind fixing yourselves a drink?' She indicates the drinks cabinet. 'I don't mean to abandon you, but –'

'Not to worry,' Sebastian says. 'We'll be fine.'

She leaves the room and Sebastian pours himself a whisky. 'G and T?' he asks.

Nina nods and he fixes her drink. The kitchen is two rooms away, separated from them by the commanding dining room, but they can still hear Antonia conversing urgently with Hannah. Nina takes a sip. The bubbles of tonic fizz on her tongue.

'She doesn't know, does she?' she says after a few moments' silence. 'About Fraunhofer.'

'It doesn't seem so,' Sebastian replies. He sits down in a large leather armchair, Hans's favourite. 'And I don't think we should mention Franzen's visit. Not tonight. It can wait until tomorrow.'

'That was very considerate of him,' Nina says, 'to remember that my father's involved in the celebrations.'

Sebastian raises his glass to her. 'I think he just wanted an excuse to come and see you.'

She doesn't look at him. She's blushing – it's a weird sensation, her face hot and the rest of her body cold. She takes another sip. 'That's ridiculous,' she says quietly.

Sebastian lets out a soft laugh. 'I don't mind. Not at all. It's a compliment when other guys have the hots for my wife.'

'He hasn't got the "hots" for me,' she retorts, annoyed.

'You don't –' he begins, but is interrupted by Rebekka, as she comes into the room.

'Good evening, Madam. Good evening, Sir,' she says, doing a goofy bob of a curtsey.

Nina gets up, teeters slightly, but manages to stabilise herself on the arm of the chair. Two gin and tonics on an empty stomach. 'Stupid heels,' she says, nodding at her shoes, but neither Sebastian nor Rebekka seem to have noticed.

'It's amazing,' Rebekka is saying, 'how much work there is. Hannah's been up since six this morning, cooking, and there's still loads to do.' Her cheeks are flushed with excitement. 'You wouldn't think, just for a dinner party.'

Sebastian laughs. 'Well, if you pick up any useful tips, make sure to try them out at home.'

'Of course, Papa,' she says, and grins. 'If you pay me fifty euros.'

Nina goes over to her and fixes a strand of hair back into a pin. 'You're not getting tired, are you?'

Rebekka rolls her eyes. 'No, Mama. I'm having a ball. By the way, you have to try the stuffed cherry tomatoes. I made them all by myself.'

Nina wants to know what else is on the menu, but Rebekka skips back out of the room before she has a chance to ask.

'Looks like she's enjoying herself,' Sebastian says.

They hear the sound of car doors slamming outside. Antonia dashes in from the dining room, wiping her hands.

'They're here,' she says. She takes a deep breath and goes out into the hall.

Nina looks at Sebastian, but he shrugs, and so they stay where they are. A rush of cold air from outside hits the fire, making the flames dance about. More car doors slamming. They must have arrived in convoy. In the hall, Antonia is greeting the guests, her voice bright and chirpy, no trace of the nerves she claimed to be feeling earlier. But then, she has been doing this for years. Nina remembers the parties – formal and casual – that her parents gave while she was growing up here. And as far back as she can remember, she would be among them, in her best clothes, awkward and diffident when she was small, overwhelmed by the adult talk and the smoke-filled rooms (in the days before her mother felt socially validated enough to ban smoking in the house), and then less timid over time as she learned the art of small-talk, of being graceful and accommodating.

In contrast to Marie, who, even as a small girl, enchanted guests by singing to them, scandalising their parents by running naked through the house at the age of five, and – from the onset of puberty – generally upsetting everyone by making vehement noises of disgust when meat was served for dinner, or initiating aggressive debates on abortion, child labour, female genital mutilation, the destruction of the environment, or any other topic in the newspapers that had irked her. Nina remembers how her sister was always too rebellious, too spirited to keep the peace in these formal, mannered settings, not caring when she was punished for striking out, breaking family conventions – and she feels a wild tug of longing for her. She wonders, vaguely, whether her parents' social life is still as busy as it used to be; she senses not, but realises this is one of the many things she no longer discusses with them.

Hans leads the guests in from the hall, and suddenly, the room is full. There are twelve guests in total, including Sebastian and Nina. Introductions are made, but she can't hold on to most of the names. She recognises the state secretary, Helmut Zweck, who is accompanied by his wife Claudia. There is only one couple younger than her and Sebastian: a press officer, Sabine Till, who remains standing in the background next to her partner, Justus Rielke. Gloria and Bernhard Klopp enter last. Bernhard spots Nina on the other side of the room and throws her a smile.

They have brought with them the smell of a November evening; damp-cold, a few of them carrying the musty odour of cigarette smoke. They're all talking about the celebrations at Brandenburg Gate, the speeches and fireworks. Nina glances at her father. He must be painfully disappointed that his speech was dropped, but he doesn't show it. He stands with his back to the fireplace, listening to Zweck tell him, in a loud bass of a voice, how Angela Merkel had complained that her legs were freezing and how she wished she'd worn her ski suit. Nina is gripped with the bizarreness of the situation, the sensation that she's standing to one side of herself, looking on at these happy hungry dinner guests, with Thiel's body lying in a morgue somewhere, Jakob Fraunhofer stunned and relieved at this auspicious twist of fate, and Marie's murderer still at large, somewhere in this city perhaps, free as a bird.

Her father's voice cuts through her thoughts, sending

a collection of little black dots into her line of vision. Her heart thumps sharply, three times, four times, before retreating back into a steady rhythm.

'Here's my girl!' he declares over the chatter as Rebekka enters the room, carrying a tray of filled champagne glasses.

All eyes turn to look at her, and Rebekka pinkens and gives a shy smile.

'Our granddaughter, Bekka,' Antonia says proudly, giving Rebekka an encouraging nod.

Hannah comes in behind her with the canapés, two huge silver trays with bite-sized delicacies. Nina smiles and shakes her head as Hannah passes, while Sebastian shoves one in his mouth and balances another two on the palm of his hand.

Rebekka walks around the room, smiling back at the guests. Gripping the sides of the tray tightly, she offers each one a glass of champagne. Someone asks her age, and Rebekka replies quietly and politely. But when she gets to Bernhard and Gloria, she hesitates, her nerves getting the better of her. The glasses begin to wobble on the tray, and before she can steady herself, it happens: first one, then another glass falls off the tray, and they hit the polished wooden floor in an explosion of expensive, mouth-blown slivers of Venetian glass.

Antonia rushes forward, holding her arms out as though to prevent anyone from stepping on the glass splinters and cutting themselves. 'Never mind, never mind,' she says to a distraught Rebekka. 'Hannah, go and get a cloth and dustpan.'

Rebekka, close to tears, ignores Nina's outstretched arm

and, head down, dashes out of the room. Hannah follows her out.

'Shards bring good luck, isn't that what they say?' Hans asks. People laugh politely but sincerely; the mood in the room is lively and hardly likely to be spoiled by a couple of broken glasses and spilled champagne.

'Gloria, Bernhard, let's get you another drink, shall we?' he continues.

Hannah comes back with another tray. She offers Herr and Frau Klopp their drinks and steps over to Antonia. 'I'll clean up as soon as the guests have been seated for dinner,' she says quietly. 'We can start any time.'

Antonia smiles and nods. She claps her hands together to get everyone's attention. 'Please,' she says, 'dinner awaits.'

Her announcement is followed by a collective murmur of approval. Hans offers Frau Zweck his arm and leads her into the dining room; the other guests follow. The mahogany dining table has been extended to its fullest, making the large room appear almost cosy, and the table setting is spectacular in white and silver. A floral centrepiece in the colours of the national flag – black, red and yellow – is eye-catching. The guests find their seats, and Hannah and Bekka bring in the first course. It is a simple consommé, Nina notes gratefully. Bekka is serving the guests on the opposite side of the table, fully focused, her flushed cheeks perhaps a remnant of her embarrassment. Hannah fetches a bottle of white wine from a sideboard and begins to fill the glasses.

'*Bon appétit*,' Hans says, and there is a brief silence as everyone begins eating.

Nina lifts the spoon to her mouth and she is forced to revise her opinion as soon as she tastes the broth. There is nothing simple about this consommé. It's delicious – earthy, rich and salty – intended to whet the appetite. It succeeds. Her stomach rumbles and whines, and she glances from side to side, hoping no one heard. And, it seems, no one has. At the head of the table, Antonia has struck up a conversation with the state secretary, but they keep their voices low and Nina is too far away to catch their words. As if on cue, her father begins to talk to Gloria Klopp, sat to his left, about some mutual acquaintance at the Ministry of Justice. Nina doesn't know how many of the guests her parents have met before, and she can't tell just by observing them. Her parents are professionals in the art of hosting.

Hannah and Rebekka come in to clear the soup bowls. Nina tries to catch Rebekka's eye, but she keeps her head down, looking up only occasionally to take note of how Hannah is stacking the bowls, sliding out the spoons and placing them on the uppermost bowl. She looks terrified, all buoyancy and pleasure gone. This wasn't such a good idea, after all, Nina thinks with vague unease. Perhaps Bekka is too young, weighed down too heavily by some imagined expectation of perfect performance in what is, after all, only a dinner party. Hannah leads the way out of the dining room, Rebekka following nervously behind, and they return minutes later with plates of salmon pâté.

Nina looks down at her plate. It's a small portion, half the size of a pack of cards, but as she slides the tip of her fork into the pâté and lifts it to her mouth, she tastes the double cream immediately. She puts the fork back down and smears most of the pâté around the plate. The other guests are eating with too much gusto to pay any attention to her.

'That was utterly delicious, Antonia,' Bernhard says, when his plate is empty. He places his napkin down. 'And now, with your permission, I shall go and personally compliment the chef and her charming young sous-chef.' He stands up. 'And make sure they serve me an extra-large portion of whatever's coming up next.'

A few of the dinner guests laugh obligingly as he heads towards the kitchen. Nina recalls the state she was in when he came across her in the rain; how comforting his presence was at the tea house, the feeling of being able to let go and yet feel perfectly safe. She's glad he's gone to the kitchen to see Bekka. He's sure to put her at ease.

A few minutes later, he returns, gives everyone a thumbs-up and earns another laugh. He seems different this evening, boyish almost. Like the class clown. Perhaps, as he himself suggested, everyone has different roles for different situations, and this is one of the roles he plays in company.

Hans gets to his feet just as Hannah and Rebekka return. Bekka looks flushed and exhausted, but manages a strained smile as she clears Sebastian's plate.

'A toast,' Hans says and raises his glass. 'Here's to a free, united Germany.' The other guests follow suit. As Nina drains her glass, she rides the sensation of her limbs turning to wax.

*

During the break between courses, Nina takes the opportunity to go to the bathroom. Rather than going to the downstairs toilet, she climbs the stairs and heads towards the bathroom next to her old bedroom. She uses the toilet and washes her hands, noticing that the hand towel is fresh and clean. How much effort they put into the upkeep of this house! Cleaning a bathroom nobody uses, probably replacing the towel weekly, even though it's no dirtier than the one replacing it. Nina closes the door behind her and, standing in the hall, can't resist opening the door to her old bedroom.

Most of the furniture has long since been replaced; the room now functions as a guest room. But the bed is the same. Different linen, but the same bed. The bed where she once had a rare tickle fight with her father, one of the few times he tucked her in at night – a faded, dusty memory. The bed Marie would join her in for comfort during a thunderstorm. The bed where Markus, the boyfriend she'd sneaked in one night when her parents were at the opera, told her the distressing truth about her fourteen-year-old body. ('Not *fat*, exactly, just a bit chubby.')

What will she do with Bekka's room when she leaves home? With Kai's room? Will she change the linen on beds no one has slept in? Nina feels a throb of panic at the back of her throat. A burst of laughter drifts up from the dining room, and she shuts the door of her old bedroom and hurries downstairs.

Rebekka is coming through the door leading from the kitchen, a plate in either hand. Nina smiles at her, but Rebekka looks away and frowns, preoccupied, probably trying to avoid putting her thumbs in the gravy on the plates. Gravy. Breast of goose. Red cabbage. Two perfectly formed dumplings. The smell is rich and delicious, a hint of cloves and juniper, the gravy not thickened with flour – Nina is fairly sure of this – but reduced for hours and textured with butter.

'That's interesting, but not quite the point I'm making.' It's Justus Rielke addressing the man opposite him, presumably picking up on a conversation that began while Nina was upstairs. His tone is a little strained, as though he's trying to control his temper.

'In fact,' Rielke continues, his voice solidifying, 'the *sakoku* policy in Japan lasted for over two hundred years. It guaranteed social peace during most of that period, and certainly prevented the colonialists from depleting the country of its natural resources.'

'The what policy?' Claudia Zweck asks.

Rielke clears his throat and nods his head, as though accepting an invitation to lecture. '*Sakoku*. It means "locked country". It was Japanese foreign policy between the seventeenth and nineteenth centuries, under which foreigners were not entitled to enter the country and Japanese were not entitled to leave. On penalty of death.'

As Hannah leans in to top up her glass of *Spätburgunder*, Nina realises she has come across the term *sakoku* before. But she's really rather tipsy, and so despite a good few moments of concentrated thinking, she can't place it. Probably one of Rebekka's school projects. The one she did with Emily, or was it Emilia?

State Secretary Zweck finishes chewing a mouthful of dumpling. 'I rather think Herr Rielke is treating us to a quote from his PhD thesis, am I right, young man?'

Nina raises her eyes and catches a glimpse of Sabine Till, Rielke's girlfriend, whose face is a picture of awkwardness.

'Well, yes.' Rielke clears his throat again. 'But the point I'm trying to clarify, is –'

Zweck interrupts him. 'And I'm sure your *point* will make an interesting essay.' His voice is deep, commanding. 'But any link between *sakoku* and the policies of the former GDR would be tenuous, to put it mildly. I'm sure everyone here would agree.'

'Actually,' Rielke says, his tone sharp again, 'I can't take credit for making the link myself.' He glances across the table. 'Herr Klopp here has very kindly been advising me on my thesis. It was in fact his suggestion.'

All eyes rest on Bernhard. He looks a little taken aback, but then he smiles, the starburst of wrinkles around the corners of his eyes making him look young and mischievous. 'And if I'd thought for one moment you would use it for entertainment at dinner parties, my young friend, I wouldn't have said a thing.'

There is a murmur of laughter around the table. Rielke opens his mouth to speak, but Antonia is quicker.

'More wine, anyone?' Her voice is clear as a bell, practised in the art of suppressing any dinner party unpleasantness before it even starts, and Rielke closes his mouth and goes back to his meal, attacking – rather intensely – the breast of goose on his plate.

27

Claudia Zweck declines dessert, a raspberry and lemon mousse, insisting to Antonia that the meal was absolutely spectacular but that if she ate another bite, she would burst the seams of her dress.

'I do hope you don't think it rude of me,' she says, waving a small pale hand glinting with rings in front of her face.

'Of course not,' Antonia replies. 'I do believe Herr Klopp has reserved double portions.'

For a moment, Nina considers following Frau Zweck's cue, but resists. Her mother would not forgive her so graciously. So instead, when Hannah places the dessert in front of her, she mumbles something about how delicious it looks – which indeed it does, a perfectly round fluffy slice of pink mousse on an equally round slice of white, expertly eased from its mould and topped with a sprig of mint – and toys with the mousse on her plate until it is no more than a mush of crushed pink. She looks over to her mother, who sits at the top of the table like a queen, the satisfaction over the success of the dinner party evident in the smile that now doesn't leave her face – the corners of her mouth pulled up a fraction while she talks to Zweck on her right. At one point, Bernhard places his hand over hers and squeezes it, saying something Nina can't hear from where she's sitting. Her mother beams.

When dessert is finished, Hans suggests coffee and cognac in the living room. Warmed and satiated by excellent food and wine, everyone gets to their feet and follows him through. Nina tells Sebastian she's going to check on Bekka, and he strokes her face and smiles.

'You okay?'

She nods. 'Yes. Yes, I think I am.'

'Give Bekka a kiss from me,' he says, and turns to follow the others into the living room.

Rebekka is standing at the sink, rinsing dishes. The heat in the kitchen and the steam rising from the hot water in the sink has taken the bounce out of the curls in her hair. A few strands stick to the sides of her face. Nina walks over to her, slowly – it is only now, on her feet, that she's aware of how much she has drunk, and she's not used to negotiating high heels in this condition – and puts her arms around her daughter's waist from behind. She leans in to her.

'Great job tonight, Bekka.'

Rebekka rinses a plate clean under the running tap. Her hands are bright red.

'Isn't that water too hot?' Nina asks, concerned.

Bekka shakes her head and slots the plate into a rack on the draining board. 'Mama?' Her voice is small.

'Yes, sweetie?'

'I – there's . . .' she trails off.

Nina spins her around gently and places her hands on

either side of Rebekka's face. Her cheeks are burning.

'What is it?' She lowers her head until her forehead is touching Rebekka's. Rebekka recoils slightly and Nina realises her breath must smell of alcohol, and that this is also the first time Rebekka has ever seen her mother drunk. The thought makes Nina giggle. Drunken parents, a teenager's nightmare. She feels good. In fact, standing here, resting her head against Rebekka's, she's grateful for Franzen's visit earlier. It's over. It's finally over. Perhaps now they can get back to normal. And she's grateful for what she has: a sexy, loving partner; two beautiful, adorable children; a gorgeous home. And there could be so much more, if she just reaches out and takes it. Her mind flows back and forth, gently, lazily.

'Mama?'

Nina finds that she has closed her eyes. She wills them open. Rebekka pulls her head back.

'I . . . I did something stupid,' she says miserably.

Nina puts her head to one side in a show of sympathy. 'The champagne glasses you mean? Oh, sweetie, never mind about that. Omi and Opa aren't cross. In fact, they've been singing your praises all evening. You did a great job.'

She plants her lips on Rebekka's cheek and holds the kiss, still swaying slightly.

'No, Mama, it's not that. It's –'

'Frau Bergmann?'

Nina turns her head. 'Oh, Hannah, great job, both of you. The food was –' She makes an exaggerated gesture with finger and thumb, bringing them to her mouth and kissing them off. 'Mmwah.'

Hannah places her hand on Nina's arm. 'Rebekka's tired, Frau Bergmann. She's worked so hard this evening. The best helper I've ever had, but I think it's best if she goes to bed now. Perhaps you'd like to join the others? For coffee? I made it strong.'

'Yes, yes, of course.'

'Rebekka,' Hannah says, 'Your bed's all made up. Upstairs, in the spare room. Why don't you –'

Nina claps her hands together. 'My bedroom! Oh, you're going to be sleeping in my old room!' She feels oddly emotional. She puts her hand out and strokes loose curls of hair behind Rebekka's ear. 'Well done, Bekka. Now, sleep tight, sweetie, and Papa and I will see you tomorrow.'

She turns and walks, with slow concentration, out of the kitchen and through to the living room.

*

Sebastian holds the door open for Nina, and she climbs into the taxi. She falls back onto the seat, but then, with great effort, leans forward to take off her shoes. The relief is delicious. She clenches and unclenches her toes a few times and rubs them between her fingers. A small ladder has begun to crawl up her stocking from the big toe on her right foot.

Sebastian gets in beside her and the taxi pulls away. Nina looks up at the digital clock above the rear-view mirror; the red digits dance around for a moment, but she manages to bring them into focus for long enough to see that it is four minutes past two. She slumps back onto the seat and then nestles into Sebastian.

'Great evening,' he says, adjusting his position so that she fits snugly into his shoulder. He loosens his bowtie with his left hand and opens the top button on his shirt.

'Mmm.'

'I bet you're glad I made you come.'

Nina puts her hand on his thigh, feels with pleasure how firm and toned it is.

'Bekka was great, wasn't she? I should have taken a photo of her in that apron. Would've been good blackmail material.'

'Yes, it would.' She laughs at the thought. 'But I was so proud of her, too.'

'That Rielke, though,' he continues, 'what a prize dick. Pompous little know-it-all with his student haircut.' He turns his head and kisses her on the forehead. 'You certainly enjoyed the wine tonight, didn't you?'

Nina lets out a soft giggle. 'I certainly did.'

'It's nice to see you so ... mellow, for a change,' he says. 'Not too mellow, I hope, for –'

She slides her hand up his thigh. 'No, not too mellow at all.'

They sit in silence for a while, as the taxi coasts down the empty residential streets of Zehlendorf, the tyres bumping along the cobbled surface, until the driver takes a right turn and accelerates hard as he prepares to join the inner-city motorway. He stays in the outside lane. Is he keen to get the fare over with so he can go home, or does he just enjoy the freedom to drive fast on night-time roads? Large orange lampposts illuminate the motorway with a light made all the more artificial by the shadows of the forest looming on either side.

Nina closes her eyes. Tomorrow, she decides, she'll increase her allowance to one thousand calories. That way, she can ease herself into eating more without feeling guilty, or worrying that her weight will soar out of control. Four hundred extra, that's half a chocolate bar (chocolate!), or a big cheese sandwich, or a small portion of spaghetti with pesto. She melts further into Sebastian's arm, overcome with relief at her decision. She had imagined it taking a concentrated effort of will to get to this point, and now it seems so easy, so ridiculously easy.

'What are you counting?' Sebastian asks.

'Hmm?' She opens her eyes lazily. 'What?'

'You're counting on your fingers. You always do that when you're adding up something in your head.'

'I don't, do I?'

'Yes. Always,' he says, smiling.

'You never told me that before.'

'I thought you knew. Now,' he says, 'why don't you stop counting whatever it is and put your hand back where it was.'

He guides her hand back to the top of his thigh. They fall back into silence as the taxi exits the motorway and heads up a city street towards the elegance of Charlottenburg.

'Speaking of counting,' Sebastian says after a moment, 'while I've got you in a good mood.'

Nina smiles up at him.

'I ran into Jan on Friday.'

Jan Steinmacher, Sebastian's former tennis partner and her accountant. 'Oh.'

Sebastian slips his arm around her shoulder. 'He seems to think perhaps you're hiding from him.'

Nina withdraws her hand from his thigh and begins cleaning imaginary dirt from under her fingernails.

'Listen,' he says. 'He's not your enemy. He can only do his job if you let him know how things stand.'

The weight of his arm is oppressively heavy on her shoulder. She shifts her position.

'Not now, Basti, okay?'

'Yeah, you're right. It's late. But –' He removes his arm in a grand sweeping movement. The taxi pulls up outside their house. 'We talked about options, remember? We can always put some of my money towards it, if that's what it takes.'

The taxi driver turns in his seat.

Sebastian hands him a twenty-euro note and then gets out of the car. Nina picks up her shoes and steps out. The ground is icy and hard beneath her stockinged feet, sending a spike of cold up through her body. She tiptoes unsteadily to the front door and waits for Sebastian to unlock it. She feels a little sick now, and really just wants to go to bed. Sebastian opens the door and they step into the house. She drops her shoes at the foot of the stairs, annoyed to be feeling sick, when moments earlier, she was happily anticipating sex with Sebastian.

'Water?' he asks, hanging his coat up on the rack.

Nina nods. He comes and puts his arms around her. She inhales his smell, and abruptly, thankfully, the sickness abates. She slides her hands over his buttocks. Maybe they should have sex right here, on the stairs, like the day they first got the keys to the house and Rebekka was at kindergarten, and they closed the front door behind them and, without speaking, went for it, right here on the stairs, and then, once more, in the empty living room, Sebastian with his trousers around his ankles and her, naked from the waist down.

She lifts her head and kisses him; a full, all-consuming kiss, their heads twisting left, then right; she tastes cognac in his mouth, and coffee, and feels, as she presses against him, the erection straining against his trousers. They release, briefly, as she strips off her cardigan and reaches behind awkwardly to get to the zip of her dress. Sebastian fumbles with his belt, unbuttons his trousers, leans into her, pushes her gently onto the stairs with the weight of his body. He teases her earlobe with his teeth.

'Oh god, Nina,' he says, his voice hoarse with sex. 'Where have you been?'

It is short, hard and sweet. She doesn't have time to come, the drink has slowed her down too much, and she's left with a tingling ache between her legs. But she's happy all the same. Happy, and exhausted. Sebastian pulls up his trousers and goes to the kitchen, returning moments later with two glasses of water. She takes one and drinks it, noticing how thirsty she is. Sebastian takes a seat next to her on the stairs. The hall is dark; neither of them switched on the light when they came in.

'Why don't you give him a call first thing tomorrow,' he says.

'Who?'

'Jan. Let him know you're still in the land of the living.'

Nina shivers. She picks up her dress and drapes it over

her knees. 'Yes, okay. I'll call him.' She breathes out heavily. 'All right?'

Sebastian drains his glass and puts it down beside him. 'All I'm saying is that any problems you're having won't go away if you ignore them,' he says. 'Just give Jan a call, eh?'

He reaches out to stroke her shoulder, but she pulls away.

'Exactly what problems am I having?' She looks at him. 'What, so you're an expert in small business financing now, are you?'

Sebastian turns towards her, and their eyes lock briefly. He looks away first.

'I didn't mean . . .' he says. 'I just thought, you seemed so reasonable tonight.'

'Ha!' She lets out a short, sharp laugh. 'As opposed to unreasonable normally. Is that the point you're making?' Precisely as she says these words, she's willing herself to shut up.

He lifts his hands to his face. 'No, I'm sorry. Look, forget it. Pretend I never mentioned anything.'

'Well, it's too late for that. We don't want to *ignore* anything, do we?' *Shut up, shut up.*

Sebastian gets up, bends down to pick up his glass and says quietly, 'I thought perhaps you were back to normal, but I guess I was wrong.'

He begins to walk down the hall towards the kitchen. Nina jumps up, dress in hand, and follows him.

'Basti,' she calls. 'Basti! Don't –' She catches up with him and grabs his arm.

'Don't what?' he asks, looking down at her hand on his arm.

'I'm sorry,' she says. 'I'm sorry.' She tugs at his sleeve. 'Come on, let's go into the living room. Do it on the floor, like that time – d'you remember?'

Sebastian jerks away. She loses her grip on his shirt.

'You're kidding,' he says firmly. 'I'm not in the mood.'

She reaches out again. 'Come on, Basti, I didn't . . . you were too quick just now. It's only fair.' She puts both hands on his arm. She's still naked and can feel herself shivering, exposed now, but the cold hardly matters.

Sebastian half turns to face her. 'No. I can't do this, Nina. Up one moment, down the next. I can't handle that. Now,' he removes her hands, 'I would suggest you go to bed.'

But she doesn't give up. She steps forward and cups his face with her hands, trying to draw him down. 'Basti, my Basti,' she whispers, pressing against him, 'please come in there with me.'

'No, Nina. I've had enough of your drama.'

He takes hold of her wrists and pulls her arms down. She resists. He grabs them again and flings them away.

'Why are you being so mean?' she whines.

'You're drunk. Go to bed.'

'But why won't you come in there with me?' Her tongue is thick and stupid in her mouth, her words are slurred.

'I'll tell you why.' His mouth twists. 'Look at you. You're disgusting.'

She actually feels herself shrinking at his words.

He tries to turn, but she steps in to block him. Then he

pulls back and – she catches a glint of confusion, almost surprise in his face at how easy this is to do – he shoves her, hard, with both hands, so that she loses her balance and falls backwards onto the floor with a thud. It is so strange, so shocking an action, that for a moment, neither of them speaks. Then, Sebastian rubs his face and says, in a voice that threatens to break at any moment, 'I can't handle this.'

He steps over her and heads upstairs.

28

With each short exhalation, Nina's breath is transformed into a white cloud; with each sharp gasp for air, it is as though she's inhaling ice. It stings her lungs. Her feet pound flat on the gravelly path, the crunch sounding unnaturally loud. There are only a few other runners in the park at this hour, in this weather, for the most part plugged into music clipped onto waistbands or upper arms. Occasionally, when one of them overtakes her, she can hear the earplugs exuding a bass line that thumps in perfect synchronicity with their stride. She wishes she were a runner – purposeful, aligned, focused – but she's not. For Nina, running is misery. She breathes through her mouth, but soon, it feels unbearably dry, so she closes her mouth again, but can't seem to get enough air in her lungs, so she opens her mouth again. She should have brought some water, though none of the other runners seem to be as desperately thirsty as she is.

But running burns calories, hundreds of them; her metabolic rate will remain high hours after she has come to a standstill. And she has plenty to burn off. After Sebastian went to bed, leaving her drunk and naked on the floor, she consumed one litre of Strawberries & Cream

Häagen-Dazs; half a jar of peanut butter; six slices of toast with butter; a family-sized packet of crisps; the remains of the cooking sherry; one large wedge of camembert; what was left of a pack of frosted cornflakes, eaten – no, shovelled in – by the handful until her mouth was sore from spiky crumbs of sugar.

Afterwards, the bathroom.

She feels a stitch in her side, and she digs her fingers into her abdomen just beneath the ribcage. The stitch fades for a moment, but returns even more acutely when she releases her fingers. She keeps on running, wincing at the pain, then applies renewed pressure to her abdomen until her fingers are almost hooked beneath her lower ribs.

She woke up several hours later, shivering on the tiled floor, lumps of half-digested food swimming in the toilet bowl, the smell of gastric acid in her nose. She cleaned the toilet as best she could and went upstairs to bed. Sebastian was in the spare room. And that was where he stayed for the whole of Sunday, while she tried to have as normal a day as possible.

'Walk it off or take a break,' a voice beside her says in passing now, a voice that is not at all breathless, although it should be, surely, because wasn't this guy already lapping the small lake when she arrived twenty minutes ago? She nods her head in appreciation for the advice, although the runner – a man whose knock-knees are accentuated by the tight Lycra leggings he's wearing – is already twenty, thirty metres ahead of her by now, running confidently, elegantly, a metre or so per stride, covering ground at an effortless pace. She comes to a standstill and leans forward, resting her hands on her thighs, feeding her body with oxygen in large, shuddering breaths.

How could he have done that?

Back in the days when relationships were straight-forward, before the sticky complexities of children and mortgages and jobs and loyalty and love had spun themselves around her; back in the days when you stuck with a good relationship and left a bad, Nina swore to herself that there were two things she would never, under any circumstances, tolerate: sexual disloyalty and physical violence. And yet, she herself is guilty of the first. And as for the second: had Sebastian actually raised his hand to her? Really? They had an argument, they were both drunk, and she wouldn't shut up, just *shut up*, and she flew about in his face like one of those fruit flies drawn to the smell of your breath, and then, when he could stand no more, he used his physical strength against her, pushed her to the floor. *What should I make of that, Marie?* Was this an act of domestic violence? Or was he putting an end to an argument she started, an argument neither of them, really, wanted to be having? It's not like he bit her or punched her, or physically beat her.

She remains bent over, although her breathing is steady again and the stitch has become a mere twinge in her belly. She starts moving only when a small dog, off its lead despite park regulations, comes sniffing about her ankles. Left foot, right foot, left foot, right foot. After a few minutes, her mouth is dry again. She must be dehydrated still, from the alcohol, the vomiting. But how can she go home? Can she go home ever again? She stops her efforts

270

at running and checks the time. It's eight thirty. Sebastian will be leaving the house to go to work.

She opens her mouth and releases a noise – half wail, half roar – that causes a family of ducks to take flight across the lake.

*

'Dr Bergmann?'

Anita stands at the door to the examination room. Nina still has her hand on top of the phone, although she replaced the receiver several minutes ago. The conversation with Jan Steinmacher went better than anticipated – at least, there wasn't too much talk of numbers, rather he was full of encouragement and ideas for kickstarting the sluggish business. Updating her website, perhaps subletting a spare room in the practice to a wellness therapist to pluck, wax, massage all those women coming in and out (there was talk of search engine optimisation, creating needs, identifying target groups, synergies etc.). Nina said she would think about it. The day has been long and headachy; perhaps she'll take a hot bath when she gets home.

Home – to Sebastian and the children. The last time she saw him was at three o'clock in the morning, when he stepped over her after having shoved her onto the floor. *He didn't mean to hurt me. He was drunk, I was drunk, he didn't know his own strength, if I had been sober I would have kept my balance. If I had been sober I would never have niggled at him, provoked him and he wouldn't have pushed me. But he did push me. Hard.*

She has wept several times during the day, between patients, and now she feels dried up on the inside. She couldn't cry any more even if she wanted to.

She takes her hand from the phone and looks up at Anita.

'Yes?'

Anita places her right arm across her chest, resting her hand on her left shoulder, like a teenage girl in a swimming costume trying to hide her budding breasts. This month, her hair is cornflower blue. She looks down at the floor and Nina knows that whatever she has to say, it isn't good news.

'Um.' She looks at Nina unhappily, and then back down at the floor. She takes a quick breath. 'The thing is, Dr Bergmann, you see, there's this new doctor's office opening in Löwenberg. It's a joint surgery, six different specialists, and, well, the new administrator there is my aunt, and she said they were looking for staff, medical receptionists, and it's only ten minutes from where I live, so anyway, they asked if I was interested, because there aren't many people, receptionists, who would commute from Berlin to Brandenburg. Mostly, it's the other way around, and, so I said I'd talk to you first.'

She drops her right arm and both arms now dangle loosely by her side. 'I'd be willing to stay on till you got a replacement, of course,' she adds.

'Oh.' Nina coughs and swallows. 'Well, yes, of course you should take the job. You commute, what, an hour to work at the moment?'

Anita squeezes her lips together and nods.

'Then, it's settled, isn't it?' Nina attempts a smile. 'Would you be able to stay until the end of the year?'

Anita nods hurriedly. 'Yes, yes. And longer, if I need to work in a replacement.'

Nina clasps her hands together and places them on the desk in front of her. 'I'll be sorry to lose you, Anita,' she says.

Anita takes a step forward. 'I'm very sorry, Dr Bergmann. I don't want you thinking that I'm deserting you. It's just ... it's such a good opportunity for me. I'm really so sorry.'

Nina gets to her feet. Too quickly, because she feels the blood rush from her head. She holds onto the desk until the giddiness passes. 'Don't be sorry, Anita,' she says. 'It's been great to have you here. You'll be an asset to anyone. I hope this works out for you.'

Anita blushes a little, does an awkward half turn towards the open door. 'I've left some papers for you to sign on the counter.'

'Okay, thanks,' Nina says. 'Have a good evening.'

'And you, Dr Bergmann, and thank you.'

She gives a small shrug, then turns and leaves.

*

It's dark by the time she gets home. Sebastian isn't in; instead, she finds a note stuck to the fridge telling her that Kai is having dinner with his friend next door and that Rebekka will make her own way home after piano lessons. He doesn't mention where he is, or when – *if* – he'll be back. Nina rests her head against the fridge door. Perhaps he isn't angry, she thinks. Perhaps he's avoiding her because he feels ashamed. A low moan escapes her mouth, and she holds her breath, willing him to walk in through the front door right now, so that she can hold him and stroke his hair and tell him he has nothing to be ashamed of. But eventually, she is forced to breathe out.

She opens the fridge. It's gapingly empty. She hasn't even left a drop of milk or a slice of bread for her own children. No wonder Kai is having to eat next door. The blood drains from her body as an intense shame takes hold of her, boils and bubbles on the inside. As it burns, the shame rushes and rings in her ears, rooting her to the spot, before she grasps that the ringing sound is, in fact, her mobile; the tone muffled by the heavy fabric of her coat which hangs at the door. She still doesn't move. Instead, she crouches down, leaning against the fridge door, and draws long, strained breaths until the ringing stops. Then, more clearly, more urgently, the sound of the landline phone ringing. She waits – five, six, seven rings – until the answerphone clicks on. Sebastian's voice.

'You've reached the Lanz-Bergmann family. Please leave a message and we'll call back.'

Then: 'Hi, this is Sara for Nina. Well, I can't reach you on your mobile, and I'm off to NYC tomorrow morning. Hope everything's okay. Um, yeah, please call me tonight. But I'll email you from New York as soon as I can. Speak soon. Love you.'

Slowly, Nina gets to her feet, letting her circulation adjust to the shift in position before walking down the hall and up the stairs. She heads straight for the bathroom, locks the door behind her and turns on the hot water tap. When the bathroom mirror and windows have misted up, she gets out of her clothes and steps into the tub. The water is very hot; it turns her skin pink and makes it itch, but she slowly, slowly lowers herself in. She closes her eyes.

*

March, 2000

It was a little after midnight. Nina got home to her flat to find Marie curled up on her doormat. Nina guessed immediately that she had run away from home. Marie refused to talk at first, just cried and cried until she started shivering, and Nina made her take a bath to warm up.

She didn't want Nina to add any scented oil or bubble bath, and her soft young skin appeared almost translucent when it was submerged in the water. Nina used a flannel to wipe the tear streaks off her face, and then sponged down her arms, legs and back.

'They hate me,' were the first words Marie said. 'And I hate them.'

'Shh, nobody hates anyone,' Nina murmured. Then, 'Did you have a fight?', picturing her parents, pale and frigid, attempting to suppress any visible anger until they threatened to implode with the sheer effort of absorbing Marie's whirling, shrieking fury.

Marie took a deep breath and ducked her head under the water, closing her eyes below the surface, her short dark hair haloing her face. She held her breath for so long that Nina was tempted to grab her shoulders and hoist her back up. When she resurfaced, she let the air out of her lungs in a rush. She looked up at Nina.

'What do you reckon?' she said.

Nina stroked her wet hair, gently rubbing in some shampoo. 'I'll have to call them and let them know you're okay,' she said.

Marie stared down into the water. 'You're going to make me go back, aren't you?'

'Oh, honey,' Nina replied. 'I'm sorry.'

The door handle rattles. Then, a knock, and, 'Mama, are you in there?'

Nina's eyes fly open. The bathwater is tepid. 'Yes.' It's an effort to raise her voice enough to be heard through the door. 'Yes, Bekka. I'm in the bath. I'll be out in a minute.'

A pause.

'Okay. But Frau Willmers is at the door asking if Kai can stay for another half an hour,' Rebekka says, adding more quietly, 'to watch TV.'

'Tell her it's fine.'

Rebekka doesn't say anything more and Nina assumes she's gone back downstairs. She moves her legs to get the water to yield the rest of its warmth, then slides her head back down until only eyes, nose and mouth are above the surface. The water is tight around her ears; an irregular drip from the tap and her breathing are the only sounds. She closes her eyes and for a moment, she is gone. Elsewhere. Beyond her body, her family, her marriage, her mother-hood . . . It is perfectly still. But no. She hears something. A dull thump, an indistinct voice. She sits up quickly and takes some deep panicky breaths, as though she has just almost drowned and only managed to break through to the surface at the last moment.

'. . . talk to you, Mama.'

It's Rebekka's voice on the other side of the door. Has she been talking this whole time?

'Bekka, Bekka, what is it?'

'Forget it,' she says through the door. 'It doesn't matter.'

'Bekka,' Nina says, more loudly, but there is no response from her daughter.

29

Nina stops at a red light. In front of her, several metres ahead of the slip road leading onto the inner-city autobahn that takes her home in under ten minutes on a good day, she sees a large yellow traffic sign. *Umleitung.* The autobahn is closed off and traffic is being rerouted north-eastwards up Mecklenburgische Straße, a wide, ugly street lined with squat, one-storey buildings – carpet warehouses and DIY superstores and the occasional McDonald's. She sighs, shivers, and tries to concentrate on generating a mental map of side streets and short cuts that will enable her to avoid the busy main roads on her way home. But although this is a part of the city she has been living in – and driving, walking and cycling in – for the best part of her adult life, her mental map freezes up several times, suddenly unsure of whether or not Kahlstraße is a one-way street – and if so, in which direction? – or if Wilhelmsaue is a cul-de-sac, only passable on foot, or on a bike – or was that Maxdorfer Steig?

The driver in the car behind beeps his horn; the car behind that one follows suit. Nina changes into first gear and accelerates just as the light changes back to red, leaving a column of angry drivers stuck at the traffic light in her wake. She continues on up Mecklenburgische Straße, which would lead her in the opposite direction to home. The street seems to go on for ever, its blandness underlined by the rows of now-naked trees that claw the low sky. It begins to rain; she switches on the headlights and wipers. The wipers whisper and groan across the windscreen. She has to turn left at some point, but decides to stay on the main road, after all, stick with the route she's sure of, even if it takes her three times longer than usual to get home.

Warm air blows out of the ventilator on either side of the steering wheel in a monotonous whoosh, but she's freezing, nonetheless. A chill penetrated her body a while back, all the way deep into her bones, and there is nothing she can do – no amount of clothing, or heating – to prevent herself from feeling constantly cold.

She managed to drag herself out of the bath last night, her skin wrinkled and bloated, when the temperature had dropped to a numbing cool. She stepped out of the bath and immediately began shivering so fiercely that it was an effort to detach the bathrobe from its hook on the back of the door, and an even greater effort to force her damp arms through the sleeves. She didn't bother wrapping a towel around her head; the hair on her scalp was almost dry, while the hair from her ears downward hung like heavy rats' tails, plastered to the sides of her face, dripping water onto her towelled shoulders.

She opened the bathroom door and found herself face to face with Sebastian.

He didn't look her in the eye. 'I've just put Kai to bed,' he said. 'Bekka's in her room.'

She swallowed, didn't know what to say.

'I'm going out,' he added and went to walk past her towards the stairs.

She reached out to place a hand on his arm, but he sidestepped her without stopping.

'I rang Jan today,' she said, noticing how helpless her voice sounded.

'Good for you,' he said, not breaking his stride; increasing it, in fact, as he lunged down the stairs, taking two at a time, eager, it seemed, to get away from her as quickly as possible.

She reaches the busy junction at Berliner Straße, where she needs to take a left. But there is a broken-down car in the left lane, and she's somehow, involuntarily, swept up by the other drivers and misses her turning. So here she is, in the middle of the junction, able only – if she follows traffic regulations – to drive straight ahead, or else turn right. She turns right. Immediately, she knows where she's heading. She looks at the clock on the dashboard, but it just flashes 0:00. Great. The car really is giving up the ghost as well. She tries to estimate the time. She left the surgery at one, closing early. Anita offered to stay behind and straighten out the patient database, put it in order and make it more easily understandable for whomever replaces her when she leaves. So far, Nina has consciously avoided thinking about the fact that Anita will be gone in just over six weeks.

She fumbles in her handbag on the passenger seat and pulls out her mobile, looks up and has to swerve violently to the left to avoid hitting a man who is getting into his double-parked car. The front wheel of her car hits the kerb on the central reservation, just missing a tree, and she's jerked a couple of inches up out of her seat. The engine stalls; a cacophony of hooting begins behind her.

She takes a deep breath, puts the gear in neutral and restarts the engine. *Calm down. Nothing's happened, everything's fine.* She gathers speed again and when she stops at the next red light, she checks the time on her mobile. 1:32. Meaning she has over two hours before she has to pick up Kai from school.

When she turns onto Gärtnerstraße, the rain has stopped. There is a space between two parked cars in front of number 31, not quite big enough for her car to park properly, so she bumps up the two front wheels onto the pavement at a slant and switches off the engine. She doesn't hesitate, gets out of the car and strides towards the front door of the building, although her legs still feel stiff after yesterday's run in the park. The strap of her handbag digs into her right shoulder. It is heavy. She stopped off at an electrical appliance shop on Grünberger Straße – not one of those huge, brightly lit and low-ceilinged warehouse-style megastores with gaudy advertising banners and stunningly incompetent staff, but a small, dilapidated corner shop displaying faded signs for *VEB Robotron* radios, in which an impossibly old man took an age selecting an assortment of different battery types. She grabbed the batteries before he could even offer to put them in a bag and tossed a couple of twenty-euro notes on the counter, calling a thank you, but leaving the shop without waiting for her change.

She scans the scuffed brass plate with doorbells and residents' names, and with a stiff, cool finger rings the bell marked "Lehmholz". The nameplate on the adjacent bell is empty. The intercom crackles into life more quickly than she expected.

'Hello? Who is it?'

She moves in towards the loudspeaker, her mouth almost touching the brass plate. 'Hello, Frau Lehmholz? It's Nina Bergmann. Marie's sister. I thought I'd ... I'd pay you a visit.'

There is a pause. The intercom is silent. Then a *click-click*, and Nina places her hand on the doorknob, waiting for the noisy buzzer. When it sounds, she gives the door a hard push and enters.

Frau Lehmholz is waiting on the landing. She smiles when she sees Nina coming up the stairs. Nina smiles back, picks up her pace despite the protest of her sore thigh muscles. When she reaches the second floor, she's unsure whether to offer her hand or to embrace the old woman. She settles for an awkward in-between: a hand on her left shoulder, which feels shockingly bony beneath the woollen cardigan, and a grasp of the wrinkled right hand. But Frau Lehmholz is not a woman of half-measures. She pulls Nina towards her and hugs her closely. Nina's chin touches the top of her head.

'So nice of you to come,' she says into Nina's chest.

Surprised by her warmth, both physical and emotional, Nina hugs her back as tightly as she dares without running the risk of snapping her in two. She's fiercely grateful that Frau Lehmholz appears to be 'with it', as Rebekka would say.

'You're lucky,' Frau Lehmholz says, releasing herself from the embrace. 'I can't hear a thing,' she pats the hearing aid she's wearing on her belt, 'but I was just coming out of the toilet and I saw the light flashing.'

Nina frowns. Frau Lehmholz gives her a girlish smile and leads her into the flat, pointing to a round light bulb above the intercom system at the front door that Nina hadn't noticed on her first visit.

'I had this installed a few years ago, when my hearing first started going,' she says. 'It's linked to another light in the kitchen, but that one's been broken for ages. It lets me know when someone's ringing the doorbell.' She shrugs. 'But, of course, it's only of use if I happen to be looking at the stupid thing while the bell is ringing.'

She shakes her head, crestfallen, as if suddenly disappointed by the unkept promises made by modern technology. 'Never mind,' she adds, more to herself than to Nina, and starts walking towards the living room door.

Nina follows her, looking around, oddly pleased that the place is familiar, that her mind doesn't have to bother with the effort of processing wholly novel information. The light is lazy, as it was during her first visit, lending the apartment a pleasantly cavernous feel. However, when she reaches the living room and follows Frau Lehmholz in, she's struck by the disorderliness of the place.

Used tissues lie crumpled on the floor surrounding the armchair, crusted with a brownish substance Nina assumes must be dried blood – from a nosebleed maybe, or perhaps Frau Lehmholz has a more serious chest condition? She should enquire delicately, if the opportunity arises. People don't like to be reminded of their physical deterioration. The horizontal surfaces on various items of furniture – the armoire, bookshelves, coffee table – are covered in a carpet of dust. Everything looks shabbier than on her previous visit. The only clean item, one that seems to be freshly polished, is the photograph of Frau Lehmholz and her husband. As Nina steps forwards, the light from the overhead lamp catches on the glass and reflects a brilliant flash into her eyes.

'Sit down, please,' Frau Lehmholz says, who has eased herself into her armchair.

Nina sits down in the same spot she sat in last time, on the sofa opposite. The room smells of mildew and cat food, although Nina can't remember Frau Lehmholz mentioning a pet.

'I –' she begins, not knowing quite how to start the conversation. 'I was wondering if social services have been in touch?'

Frau Lehmholz looks at her with pale, cloudy eyes. 'I'm afraid we won't be able to have much of a chat,' she says. 'I can't hear a thing.' She nods towards her hearing aid. 'The batteries died a few days ago.'

Nina, happy to have something to do, heaves her handbag onto her lap.

'Here.' She scoops out two handfuls of batteries and dumps them on the sofa beside her. The old man in the shop recommended zinc air cells for hearing aids, so she bought an assortment of these (they varied in colour), but also some standard AAA and AA batteries, just in case. She looks up at Frau Lehmholz. The old woman raises an

284

emaciated, leather-skinned hand to her mouth and holds it there, quivering slightly, her mouth in the shape of an *O*. She looks straight at Nina.

'So like your sister,' she says. 'She was so thoughtful, so . . . *sweet*.' This last word is said in a reverent hush.

The old woman's affection brings Nina close to tears. But she doesn't want to cry, not now, not knowing if Frau Lehmholz will be this clear of mind another time. She needs to make use of her lucidity, while it's here. She gestures to Frau Lehmholz to remove her hearing aid, and begins trying out the different batteries to see which one fits. The old man in the shop was right – the device requires a zinc air cell, of which she has bought five different sizes, all designated by different coloured sealing tabs: blue, red, green, brown and yellow.

'It's the green one, dear,' Frau Lehmholz says, pointing.

Nina slots the battery into place and hands the device back. Frau Lehmholz takes it, clips in onto her belt, and switches it on. She winces – perhaps the volume is turned up too high – and after fiddling with a small knob, relaxes into a smile.

'There, that should do it,' she says. 'Now, dear, do say something, so I know this thing is working properly.'

'Um –' Nina is not sure what to say. She nods at the batteries beside her. 'Do you think you might have a use for these?'

Frau Lehmholz peers towards the pile of batteries. 'These'll fit my remote control,' she says. 'If you wouldn't mind leaving those ones, I'd be grateful. I don't get out much.'

'Of course.' Perhaps Nina should offer to go shopping,

get some groceries, or fill those prescriptions she mentioned last time. But she wants to ask her some questions first. That's why she's here.

She clears her throat and leans forward slightly, suppressing a growing feeling of – what? Unease? Guilt, that she wants to suck some information out of a woman who might drop dead at any moment, or else – more probably – sink back into the pitiless clutches of dementia? She clears her throat again, wondering if she should supply some other reason for why she's here. In the end, she decides to be honest.

'I've come to ask you about that man you saw in Marie's flat. The one you mentioned the last time I was here.' She pauses for the woman's reaction, concerned that she might take offence.

But Frau Lehmholz sits there, hands folded over her stomach, smiling. Perhaps the hearing aid isn't working properly.

'You said that you saw a man in Marie's flat once. A tall man. Remember?'

Frau Lehmholz nods slowly. 'Yes, I remember. Why do you ask?'

'I'd like to know if you can recall anything else about him,' Nina says. 'His name, perhaps.'

Frau Lehmholz drops her gaze to the floor. Nina watches her face intently, as she rummages around in her mind, opening one drawer of memories after the other. Nina becomes aware that she has placed her fingers on her temples, as though by some magic this posture will help Frau Lehmholz retrieve the one, all-important detail. After what seems like an age, the old woman lifts her head and leans back in her chair.

'No,' she says. 'Nothing.'

'Are you sure?' Nina's disappointment is like a physical pain. 'It really is so important. You said it was a short name. Can you think of the first initial? Was it a common name? Perhaps it rhymes with something? Was it Thiel, perhaps?'

Clutching at straws.

A shadow of irritation passes over the old woman's face. 'No. I can't remember. It was a short name, yes. A snatch of a name. But that's all I can tell you. And you badgering me won't help. You can't force these things. That I do know.'

'I'm sorry.' Nina can barely hold back her tears. She swallows and begins putting the batteries back into her handbag, except for the AA ones; these she places on the coffee table. Then Frau Lehmholz speaks, quietly:

'No, dear. What was your name again, Nina? No, Nina, I'm the one who should be sorry. Don't hold it against me. Please. It's just – I get so *angry* with myself, with my stupid, *stupid* brain.' She lifts a hand to her head and raps her knuckles against it, hard, as though to shift some lost memories. Then she leans forward and grabs onto Nina's hand. Her fingernails are sharp, and dig into Nina's flesh. 'Don't go just yet,' she says. 'Keep me company for a while? Have a cup of tea with me?'

And without waiting for an answer, she lets go of Nina's hand, shuffles forward on her chair and, with a heavy breath, positions her walking cane in her hand.

'Let me make the tea,' Nina says, jumping up before

Frau Lehmholz has quite managed to heave herself out of her chair. 'I'll be right back.'

She crosses the hall into the kitchen and fills the kettle. It was a dead end; she knew it even before she came here, spurred on by some desperate hope that if she found out the man's name, it would somehow turn back the clock – not to before Marie's death, this she understands, but to before all the pain and despair she has caused since then. She was foolish to believe that a confused old woman could recall a name she'd heard only once; foolish to believe that the man's name would solve anything anyway. He might not even be the one, who . . . who . . . she can't bring herself to think it.

But the name – the hope of it was all she's had to keep her from falling. She's light-headed; she drops her chin onto her chest just as the kettle clicks off, but then her head starts spinning, or rather, *she* starts spinning, her entire body is whirling around the cramped kitchen, and she's actually enjoying the sensation, hearing only the wind whooshing past her ears, feeling only her heartbeat ricocheting off the sides of her ribcage. But then the nausea hits, and she reaches out to steady herself on the kitchen counter, loses her balance, and falls, the side of her head narrowly missing the corner of the square kitchen table on her way down. She lies there for a minute, or maybe ten, she can't be sure, until she hears Frau Lehmholz calling her name.

'Nina? Nina? Did you find the tea? It's on the shelf above the sink.'

Nina gets to her feet slowly, mentally sweeping the inside of her body for any vestigial signs of vertigo.

'Oh yes, I see it,' she calls back across the hall, and her voice sounds strangely high-pitched. 'I'll be in in a minute.'

She switches the kettle back on. It only takes a couple of seconds for the water to reboil. She picks up the teacups, but her hands are trembling hard, and a splash escapes from one of the cups and scalds her hand. She looks around and finds a small tray propped up against the splashback. When she re-enters the living room, Frau Lehmholz looks at her with concern.

'Are you feeling all right, dear?' she asks. 'You look dreadfully pale.'

'I'm a little tired, that's all.' Nina places the tray on the table. 'I'm sorry it took so long.'

'Oh, never mind,' Frau Lehmholz says. 'I closed my eyes for a moment, and I wasn't sure if I'd fallen asleep. But you're here now.'

They sit in silence and sip tea. An ancient-looking wooden clock that hangs on the wall beside Frau Lehmholz's collection of postcards chimes out a melodious dong. Nina looks up. It is half-past two. She has to be at Kai's school in an hour.

'You seem terribly troubled, dear,' Frau Lehmholz remarks, before Nina can think of a polite way to make her excuses and leave.

Nina doesn't reply. She hears the ticking of the clock, only now aware of how loud it sounds. She glances at Frau Lehmholz and finds her staring. She feels awkward and ashamed, as though these pale eyes can see right through her, right through to her shameful hopelessness and unbearable loneliness. She averts her eyes, can't bear the exposure.

'You can't just ignore it,' the old woman continues. 'If you pretend it isn't there, it eats away at you, little by little.'

Nina fixes her gaze on a corner of the coffee table. It looks bruised and scarred; tiny dents and scratches reveal the yellowish untreated wood beneath the dark varnished surface.

'I stopped living for a while after Manfred died,' Frau Lehmholz says, her voice lucid. 'I didn't die, I stopped living. It isn't the same thing. I stopped eating, I stopped sleeping, I stopped laughing – I would have stopped breathing if I'd had the choice. And then, one day, as though I'd actually heard the sound of gnawing, I realised it was eating me alive. The grief. So I had to take the decision not to provide it with any more nourishment, before it devoured me completely. I can't tell you exactly how I did it – it was slow, and painful – but I know that as soon as I realised what was happening to me, I was able to fight it.'

She stops talking. The clock keeps ticking, replacing her words. Nina looks up from the table and feels her facial muscles contracting into what must be a hideous grimace of sorrow. She opens her mouth. A wail is released.

Frau Lehmholz leans forward in her chair and opens her arms. Nina releases her tears with a desperate moan, and flops forward onto her knees. She grabs Frau Lehmholz around the waist.

'I ... I ...' She holds onto her as if she were clinging to a rock in a torrent. 'I can't ... I don't ...'

'Hush, my dear, hush.' The old woman's spidery hand strokes the back of Nina's head.

'I can't stop it! I can't stop it!' Nina says into the folds of the woman's skirt. She gives herself over to another bout of crying. Frau Lehmholz doesn't speak, just sits and strokes. When she feels the tears receding, Nina lifts her head slightly, but doesn't quite look up. She speaks into the woman's chest.

'I can't control it, I don't know what to do. I have to hide it from everyone. The children. It's so hard. They don't know how *hard* it is! And Sebastian, Sebastian – he pushed me. How could he *do* that? *How?* I needed him, I was depending on him and he turned on me. How could he *do* that?'

The words come out twisted, in a spray of snot and tears. She sounds crazed, pitiful, but there's nothing she can do to stop it.

Frau Lehmholz shifts her position beneath Nina's head. Then she hands her a tissue.

'I think you must be very lonely, dear,' she says. 'You should speak with your husband, tell him what you're telling me. Men can be rather ... *clumsy*, in such matters. Not because they don't care, but because, well, you know, if they can't master a situation, they'd rather pretend it isn't there. And then it can be too late.'

But Nina is not listening, not really. She wipes her nose with the tissue.

'I'm not even sure if he's Kai's father.' Her voice is calmer, her thoughts more structured now. 'I had – I made a mistake, and I don't know for sure. I've never told anyone, not even Marie. Telling would make it real. But it scares me. It really terrifies me.'

Frau Lehmholz keeps stroking her hair. 'That's right, you talk, let it all out. You'll feel better for it, believe me.'

They remain in this position for a while, Nina's head resting on the hard, bony lap of Frau Lehmholz, inhaling her smell, which, although tainted by the whiff of underlying cell decay, is warm and comforting. She's lulled by the relief of her confession, despite the rawness it has left behind. Then, as Nina feels herself sliding away from utter distress and towards sleep, Frau Lehmholz speaks.

'But, to be honest, dear, it doesn't surprise me.'

Nina sniffs and murmurs, 'Mmm?'

'You see, if you behave like a whore, you only have yourself to blame for the consequences.'

Nina jerks her head up. *Whore?* She must have misheard.

'Yes, quite. All those men, in and out of your flat, in and out of your bed. God knows where you picked them up from.' She spits these words out in a hiss. 'Those street walker clothes you insist on wearing. What did you expect?'

Nina sits back on heels. 'I'm sorry, I – I'm not sure –'

'Indeed,' Frau Lehmholz continues, more loudly. 'I'm a respectable woman and I must say I am shocked, if not to say disgusted. In truth, it's best that you leave, right now.'

'Frau Lehmholz –'

'I said, *leave*!' Her voice has risen to a shriek. 'And take your filthy ways with you!'

Stunned, Nina gets to her feet, ignoring the giddiness that now always accompanies sudden movement. Frau

Lehmholz is trying to get out of her chair, but her cane slips away as she puts her weight on it and she topples over. Nina lunges forward to assist her, but this leads to more yelling.

'Don't touch me, you dirty slut! Get out, before I call the police!'

Nina grabs her handbag and coat, and runs out into the hall, yanks open the front door and slams it shut. From behind the door to Marie's old flat, she can hear the motorised hum of a floor-sanding machine.

30

Nina waits outside the school gates, concerned that Kai might comment on her appearance and start worrying. She did her best in the car, pulling her hair into a fresh ponytail and taking deep breaths to try and calm her nerves, which are dancing and jangling throughout her body, right into her fingertips. But her eyes remain bloodshot, her nose red and swollen.

She spots Kai as soon as he appears from behind the heavy oak doors, amid a cloud of laughing, shouting children. He sees her and comes bouncing down the concrete steps, so quickly she has to make an effort to suppress an image of him stumbling and crashing down.

'Mama!' he calls, and she opens her arms to receive him.

'Hello sweetie.' She gives him a tight hug and then straightens up and walks briskly, his hand in hers, towards the car. He doesn't get a chance to look up at her face.

'Hop in,' she says.

Kai clambers into the back and onto his booster seat. Nina gets in the driver's seat and resists the temptation to turn around and help him fasten his seatbelt. Finally, he snaps it into place and they set off towards home.

She doesn't feel better for the confession, if that's what it was. She feels hollowed out, raw, as though something has been scraped from her insides. She feels betrayed by an old woman's madness. As if she doesn't have her own madness to contend with! She's completely exhausted, and finds it hard to believe that it is only early afternoon. If it weren't for her son, she would go straight to bed once she got home. She looks up at Kai's reflection in the rear-view mirror. He catches her eyes with his own.

'Can we have schnitzel for supper?' he asks.

Nina wipes her nose with the back of her hand. 'Of course. Anything you like.'

'Cos Papa likes it too.' Then, when she doesn't reply, 'Can I help you hammer the meat?'

'Yes,' she says. 'If you promise to be careful.'

'Because we don't want finger-schnitzel for supper,' he says earnestly.

Nina almost start crying at hearing this long-running family joke, which began when Sebastian once flattened the tip of his index finger while tenderising the meat. But she manages to turn the feeling into a tight laugh. 'No, we certainly don't.'

When they get home, Kai scurries past Nina and drops his school bag on the floor.

She calls out, 'Bekka?' but there is no answer. Rebekka has a short school day on Mondays, but she's probably hanging out with her friends.

'Can we make the schnitzel now, Mama?' Kai asks, sitting on the stairs and struggling with the buckle on his shoe. Much like Sebastian, Kai isn't particularly dextrous with his hands. This thought grates against her raw insides, makes her catch her breath.

'Um, maybe we should wait for Bekka to come home,' she says. 'Then she can help us.'

Kai shrugs and flicks off his shoe in the direction of the open shoe cabinet, cheering '*Yesss*' to himself as it hits the target.

'We can watch some TV together, if you like,' Nina suggests.

Kai looks up at her, his face briefly betraying incredulity at her suggestion, as though she'd just offered to give him his Christmas presents early, followed by a widening of his eyes and an eager nod.

He hurries into the living room, evidently fearful she might change her mind at the last moment, and switches on the TV. Nina joins him on the sofa and puts her arm around his shoulder.

They settle in to watch a stream of flickering, boisterous cartoons that Nina finds exhausting. Outside, the sky is darkening; soon, there will be no light left in the room, save for the sharp brightness smashing out of the TV set and bouncing onto their faces. But the warmth of him leaning in against her, the smell of his hair and skin, keeps her there, immobile, not healing her, exactly – she's too abraded for that – but grounding her, holding her down gently like the weight on a helium-filled balloon. If she has to be somewhere, this is where she wants to be, beside her little boy who isn't really that little anymore, until finally, he stretches out his legs in front of him and announces, 'Mama, I'm hungry.'

Nina checks the time. It is half-past six.

'Can we make schnitzel now? I don't want to wait for Bekka,' he says.

Nina nods. She can't summon the strength to feel angry that Rebekka hasn't called, at least, to say when she'll be home.

'Let's go,' she says, and leads the way into the kitchen. They flatten four slices of veal between sheets of clingfilm, taking turns with the meat mallet, until the slices are almost as thin as human skin – Nina holds each slice up to the light to demonstrate its transparency to Kai. Then they dip two of them in cornflour, beaten egg and breadcrumbs, their hands getting slimy and sticky in the process.

'Schnitzel goes soggy once it's cooked,' she tells Kai, as she heats butter in a cast iron pan. 'So we'll just cook for you and me. Papa and Bekka can have theirs when they get home.'

She doesn't know when Sebastian will be home. She hasn't seen him since their brief encounter on the landing, and it's entirely possible that he might not come home at all tonight.

'You and me, Mama,' Kai repeats. 'Let's cook!'

Nina switches on the extractor fan above the stove and slides the first slice of breaded meat into the hot pan. The smell hits her like a physical force; she had forgotten – forgotten! – that she's preparing a meal she won't be able to eat. This lapse of control, the smell of fried breadcrumbs and browning butter – delicious and disgusting at once – panics her. A small moan escapes the back of her throat.

*

May, 1997

It was a week after her twentieth birthday. A month before her first-year exams. Marie was sitting on Nina's bed, jeans and T-shirt filthy from playing outdoors.

'I've decided,' Marie said, giving Nina her most serious look, eyebrows pulled down in a curly V, lips pouting slightly.

Nina lowered the textbook she'd been trying to read. She'd been staring at the same paragraph for twenty minutes but it was refusing to make sense. 'You've decided what?'

'From now on, I'm going to eat whatever you eat.'

Nina flushed and turned back to her book. 'That's silly, Marie.'

Marie puffed a short snort of air through her nose. 'I don't think it's silly. And I've decided.'

Then she bounced off the bed, leaving a mud-brown smudge on the bedspread.

'Mama?' Kai's voice is barely audible above the sizzling of the meat and the growl of the extractor fan. 'Are you okay, Mama?'

She breathes in through her mouth to try to block out the smell.

'Yes, I'm fine,' she says, struggling to stay here, in the kitchen, with Kai. 'I had a sudden headache, that's all.'

'Like when you eat ice cream too fast?'

'Exactly.' She forces herself to slide the spatula underneath the schnitzel and turn it in the pan. 'Would you get me a plate, please?' she asks, desperate now to get away from the stove, the smell, the meat.

Kai pulls a chair over to a cabinet and retrieves a plate, setting it down next to her. She lifts the schnitzel onto the plate and hands it to him.

'You'll need a knife and fork,' she says. 'And you can eat in the living room. We won't tell Papa.'

'What about you?' he asks, glancing up at her, and then down at the plate in his hand.

'I think I'll wait for this headache to pass,' she says. 'Then I can eat with Bekka and Papa when they come home.'

Kai gives her a look in which she can detect uneasiness, as though he has now started wondering whether all these special privileges might be leading up to something very bad. She leans down and kisses his forehead. 'And we can watch TV while you're eating,' she whispers.

Delight triumphs over uneasiness, and he grabs some cutlery from the drawer and rushes into the living room.

*

At seven forty-five, when Kai starts emitting a series of large, unselfconscious yawns, Nina becomes worried. It is a clawing feeling, unpleasantly familiar, a feeling she has recognised since the day Rebekka, aged three, slipped her hand in a supermarket and disappeared into the labyrinth of aisles. She finally found her, after a frenzied, hysterical search, behind the cheese counter, where she had befriended a plump, rosy-faced sales assistant and was chomping on a wedge of Gouda.

Since that day, Nina has experienced this feeling innumerable times – glancing up from a newspaper on a playground bench and not being able to spot Kai instantly; scanning crowds of over-buoyant, vociferous children for the familiar face of third-year Rebekka, as they were released in potent, unstoppable waves from a long school day of forced immobility and overheated classrooms. A heart-stopping throb of panic, more often short-lived than not, but forceful enough to have made her wonder at times whether, over the years, the mere accumulation of such moments might add up to a shrivelling of her own life-resources.

She reaches over to the phone and dials Rebekka's mobile. It rings and rings. She hangs up when the voicemail comes on. The phone is probably wedged at the bottom of a school rucksack, or on vibrate or something. Nina tries to subdue the mixture of dread and anger that scrapes at her, and notices only then that Kai has fallen asleep on the sofa beside her. She picks him up, as gently as possible, holding him as she did when he was a baby.

He opens his eyes, says, 'I fell asleep,' and Nina shushes him. He's heavy; she negotiates the stairs with difficulty, but finally reaches his bedroom and sets him down on his bed. She slides his socks off but leaves him in the rest of his clothes and pulls his blanket up, kissing him on his smooth cheek, inhaling his soft, warm breath, before leaving the room.

Downstairs, pacing the floor, she dials Rebekka's number again. This time, there is no ringing tone; the phone is switched off. Or the battery is dead. Her finger hovers over Sebastian's number, but she decides against calling him. She tells herself to calm down. She's thirsty. She goes to the kitchen; the lingering smell of cold frying makes her queasy. She opens the kitchen window wide and breathes in the icy air. Then she pours a large glass of Diet Coke and drinks it as quickly as the fizz will allow. She burps and pours another glass.

Twelve minutes past eight. It isn't late, by any standards, not for a fourteen-year-old to be out and about, but it is after dark and Nina just wishes she knew where Rebekka was. Before she can stop it, she imagines Bekka stepping out onto a road, in the dark, a car hitting her before it has a chance to stop, metal against bone, a body flung through the air like a ragdoll ... And then Nina forces herself to imagine Rebekka walking through the front door, apologising for being late and not calling, or perhaps in one of her moods and stomping upstairs – either way, Nina makes herself imagine the relief she will feel on seeing her daughter safe and sound.

Fourteen minutes past. She retreats to the living room and picks up the phone again. She tries Bekka. Voicemail. That's something, at least. She leaves a short message, trying to keep the panic out of her voice. She sends a text to the same effect. Then she calls Sebastian. Straight to voicemail. She hangs up before the beep. She's suddenly angry, enraged that she's here on her own, that Sebastian isn't experiencing the sharp, clawing worry that something might have happened to their daughter. She makes herself sit down and watch TV. The children's channel switches to light comedy after eight p.m. She flicks to a news channel and turns the volume to mute, looks instead at the headlines skimming from right to left across the bottom of the screen. A house fire in North Rhine-Westphalia; three dead, including two children. Severe flooding in Malawi; hundreds dead, tens of thousands displaced. An estimated 1.5 million famine victims in North Korea. Slow to negative economic growth forecast in Brazil following a downgrade by Moody's. Sports: Bayern Munich heads up the league.

Her vision blurs, and she closes her eyes to rest them. A car slows in front of the house, but accelerates again and drives away. She dozes and wakes, dozes and wakes, and at just after ten, she begins to cry.

Then the phone rings. She snatches up the receiver.

'Bekka?' Her voice is hoarse and thick.

'No. It's me.'

'Mama? Have you spoken to Bekka? Have you any idea –'

'She's here, with me.' Her mother's voice is frosty, but to Nina's ears, it is the sweetest thing she has ever said. 'She turned up on our doorstep about twenty minutes ago, frozen through, poor thing.'

'What? Where? I've been ... can I speak to her?' Nina is finding it difficult to put her words in order.

'You should come right away. I should also tell you that I've called the police. They're on their way here.'

'The police? What –'

'Bekka's fine. I'll explain everything when you get here. Don't be long.'

And with that instruction, her mother puts down the phone.

31

When her mother opens the front door, Nina can see immediately that she has been crying. Her nose is swollen and pinkish; her cheeks reveal faded streaks of mascara, remnants of little brooks of tears she hasn't bothered rinsing away. But her expression is hard.

'You took your time,' she says, but Nina shaves past her and rushes into the living room. Kommissar Franzen is sitting in a chair close to the fireplace, perhaps to warm himself, although the fire appears to be almost burned out: two ashy, amber-glowing logs emit a sporadic flame or two. He looks up as Nina come in.

'Where's Bekka?' she asks – no, *demands*. 'Where's Bekka?' she repeats when no one speaks.

'I put her to bed,' Antonia says from the doorway. 'She was absolutely exhausted. I shouldn't wonder if she's caught pneumonia.'

'I need to see her,' Nina says and begins to head past her mother towards the hall, but then Franzen speaks.

'Please,' he says, and his voice tugs at her, making forward motion impossible. 'Please, Dr Bergmann. Sit down. I need to speak with you.'

Nina turns and takes a seat on the sofa. Her mother

hovers near the door, but then decides to sit down as well.

'Where's Sebastian?' she asks.

'He's on his way,' Nina tells her. 'He should be here any moment.'

She finally reached him on his mobile as she sat in the car, tearing through Berlin, her senses sharpened to a single, furious point, her whole body twitching and fizzing as if to some white-heated rhythm, the speed dial at a hundred and twenty and climbing as soon as she hit the autobahn. She'd left Kai asleep upstairs, after persuading a reluctant next-door neighbour to plug in the old baby monitor in her kitchen, claiming an emergency and that she would be back within the hour. She felt terrible, doing this, leaving her little boy to perhaps wake up alone in a dark, empty house, but she couldn't take him along, either, not until she knew what was going on.

She pressed Sebastian's number, then the speaker, propped the phone on the passenger seat and waited for him to pick up – *pick up, for Christ's sake!* – chanting *Bekka's fine, Bekka's fine* under her breath, while the phone rang and rang and –

'Yeah, you called earlier. What is it?'

'Sebastian,' she shouted in the direction of the phone, her voice harsh. 'Bekka's at my parents' house. She – she didn't come home. She went there instead. They've called the police. I'm in the car. I'll be there in five minutes. You'd better come.'

'What? Slow down. What's with Bekka?' Despite the slur in his voice that told her he'd been drinking, his obvious alarm seeped through, making her want to cry. 'And where's Kai?'

'I'll be there in five minutes,' she repeated. 'Just come.' And she reached across and switched off her phone.

Kommissar Franzen looks across at her now. A fine, dark stubble shadows the lower half of his face, and his eyes, usually so attentive and clear, appear a little startled. Every blink seems slowed down by a millisecond.

'It's all right,' he says. 'Your daughter is all right.'

She looks straight at him, ignoring the zillions of little black dots that now flood her vision, letting him know in no uncertain terms that no, everything is not all right.

'Bekka –' she begins, but her voice cracks and she has to clear her throat.

'Bekka's fine,' he says, and Nina is vaguely aware of a sigh, or sniffle, coming from her mother's direction. 'She turned up here about an hour ago, and when I arrived –'

'She was absolutely frozen through,' Antonia interrupts. 'In a real state. You should have seen her! Oh, I wish Hans were here!'

Franzen puts out a hand, palm facing the floor; whether to reassure Nina or to stop her mother, she can't tell.

'She was fine when I arrived,' he continues softly. 'We talked – she told me what she had to say – and I agreed with Frau Bergmann,' he nods in Antonia's direction, 'that she should go to bed and get some sleep.'

'I had to give her Papa's electric blanket,' Antonia says. 'Her feet were like ice. Why wasn't she wearing proper boots in this weather, instead of those, those ridiculous trainers?' She spits this out at Nina.

But Nina doesn't turn her head; she keeps her eyes fixed on Franzen's face. She's afraid she might faint and she needs his eyes to anchor her. She wants to ask him why Rebekka came here instead of her own home, but she's afraid he might know the answer.

Then her mother starts crying. It's a soft, wretched noise that makes her sound like what she is: an old woman so filled with sadness that she no longer cares who witnesses her in this state. This surrender of pretence touches and unsettles Nina, and she's reminded of the first time she saw her mother crying, when she was eight years old and her father hadn't come home for two nights running. She and her mother were having supper in the dining room, when her mother just put her face in her hands and started crying, without warning, without explanation, leaving Nina feeling both horrified and impotent. This is how she feels now, and, like then, is frightened by her own inability to provide comfort.

'Frau Bergmann,' Franzen begins, but is interrupted by the crunch of tyres on gravel in front of the house. A car door slams and then suddenly Sebastian crashes in, bringing with him the cold night. The change in atmosphere in the room is abrupt and palpable; a prickling tension appears from nowhere; there is movement, shuffling, a shifting of positions.

'Where's Bekka?' Sebastian demands, echoing Nina's question of some five minutes ago.

Antonia gets to her feet, still weeping, and almost falls into him, expecting and receiving an embrace.

'Nina, what's going on?' he says over her shoulder. He sounds angry and tired.

Franzen stands up. 'Your daughter is fine, Herr Lanz. I was just explaining to your wife. Please,' he gestures to the sofa, 'please sit down.'

Sebastian releases Antonia from his arms and walks over to Franzen. 'I want to know *right now* what is going on!'

Nina recognises his body language. He's looking for a fight. With her.

'Please, Herr Lanz,' Franzen's eyes flash briefly, 'sit down.'

Sebastian hesitates, but then backs down and takes a seat next to Nina on the sofa. She can smell the whisky on him and knows he really shouldn't have driven. But the state she's in herself, who is she to judge?

Franzen also sits down. 'Frau Bergmann,' he says to Antonia, who lurches, rather helplessly, where Sebastian left her, 'Perhaps you could make us some coffee. You already know everything I'm about to tell your daughter and son-in-law.'

Antonia sucks in her lips, giving her head a little shake to regain her composure, then leaves the room.

'Where's Kai?' Sebastian asks, looking around as though he might find him hiding somewhere in the room.

'He's at home,' Nina tells him. 'He was already asleep when my mother called, so I asked Johanna from next door to sit with him.' She doesn't mention the baby monitor. His fuse seems short enough as it is.

There is a brief silence; then Franzen speaks.

'Rebekka told me something,' he says, 'which might be turn out to be significant for our investigation.'

'Bekka?' Nina asks.

Franzen nods. 'She told me that she recognised someone at the dinner party your parents held here on Saturday. It was one of the guests – she wasn't sure of his name, but when she described him, Frau Bergmann knew right away who she was talking about. It was Bernhard Klopp.'

Nina is struggling to process what he is saying. Her heart is racing and her mind is being tugged backwards and forwards at great speed. Bernhard Klopp. She starts shivering.

'Perhaps you'd like a blanket?' Franzen asks and points to a beige and brown plaid cashmere throw that's draped over Sebastian's side of the sofa. Nina shakes her head, but Franzen gets up and takes the throw, shaking it out before he hands it to her. She wraps it around her shoulders.

'Where would Rebekka know Bernhard Klopp from?' Sebastian asks.

'She saw him several months ago. Having an argument with Marie.'

Nina is falling, falling. She digs her nails into the sofa.

Sebastian puts his hands over his face and rubs it several times. Then he looks up. 'Let me get this straight. Rebekka saw this man having an argument with my sister-in-law, who is then attacked, who then dies, and Rebekka didn't think this important to mention?'

Franzen sighs. 'Here's the thing,' he says. 'Rebekka was in a bar with Marie.' He holds up his hand as if to ward off the inevitable reaction from Nina and Sebastian. 'She had told you that she was spending the night with a friend, but in truth, she went out with Marie. I need you to know how bad she feels about this, about lying to you, but I think we all know it's one of those things teenagers do.'

Nina looks over to Sebastian. He's clenching and unclenching his jaw. He looks ready to fly into a rage, and she hopes Franzen will be able to disarm him before he does. Nina knows that if she speaks, she will just shorten that fuse.

'Bekka's a teenager, sure, but Marie –' Sebastian shakes his head from side to side. 'Marie was no fucking teenager. What the hell was she thinking?' He jumps to his feet and starts pacing the floor.

'I understand how you feel, Herr Lanz,' Franzen says. 'But it's important we focus now on the information Rebekka has provided.'

Nina clears her throat. 'But Bernhard Klopp told me he hardly knew Marie,' she says, noticing how small her voice sounds, and at the same time, realising how short and snatchy the name 'Klopp' feels on her tongue.

Franzen is still looking at Sebastian, a shadow of concern on his face. He turns to Nina. 'She was in a bar with Marie – she says she wasn't drinking, and I believe her – and she left the table to go to the toilet. When she came back out, Marie was standing near the bar, talking to a man. She says that it didn't look like a friendly conversation, so she wasn't sure whether to go over to them. She says she was afraid that if there was some sort of trouble, she would get found out, and she was terrified of either of you finding out. So she hung back and waited, and then the man grabbed Marie's wrist and twisted it. Rebekka could tell from her aunt's expression that it must have hurt, so she decided to see if she could help, call the police if necessary, but before she got back to Marie, the man had left.'

'And what did the man want?' Sebastian asks. 'What did Marie tell Bekka?'

'Oh, she said it was just some loser coming on to her. Then they finished their drinks and went to Marie's flat for the rest of the night. And on Saturday evening, Rebekka recognised this man among the dinner guests.'

'Is she absolutely sure?' Nina says, straining to raise her voice beyond a whisper.

'She is absolutely sure. She said she knew she recognised him from somewhere when she first saw him among the guests –'

When she spilled the drinks.

'But then she told me he'd come into the kitchen during the dinner party and was asking her all sorts of questions. She was absolutely sure then that this was the man she'd seen with Marie.'

Nina is assaulted by a series of flashes in front of her eyes. 'What kind of questions?'

'About Marie. About how Rebekka was coping. But she's very upset and her story's a little muddled. We'll have to confirm it, obviously,' Franzen says. 'I'm afraid she'll have to make an official identification. But she was very, very sure about him, yes.'

'But –' Nina looks to Sebastian for some kind of assistance, some reassurance, but he's still fighting his own anger. The whole time, Klopp was squeezing her for information about the investigation. The sense of betrayal is overwhelming. She can hardly push the words out. 'But he lost a child himself.'

Sebastian lets out a snort. 'I'm going up to see Bekka now,' he says and turns, heading towards the door. At that moment, Antonia appears in the doorway, holding a tray with four mugs of coffee. Nina had forgotten all about her.

'No,' her mother says, and she's no longer a desperate old woman. 'No. You will leave her to sleep.'

'I want –' Sebastian begins, but Antonia blocks his path.

'You will sit down and think about what's best for Bekka now. And you might like to think about why she found it so impossible to tell her parents what she told me, and why she came here tonight after wandering about in the freezing cold for hours on end, rather than going to her own home.'

She tried to tell me. She tried to tell me but I wasn't listening.

Nina glances over at Sebastian. He looks deflated; he seems to have shrunk as Antonia passes by him and places the tray on the coffee table.

'Fine,' he says, 'but I don't want any coffee now. I'm having a drink.' He crosses the room and pours himself a glass of whisky from a crystal decanter on the sideboard. Antonia offers coffee to Franzen and Nina, and then sits down.

'This could this be the same man Marie's neighbour saw,' Nina says. It isn't a question.

'Possibly,' Franzen takes a sip of coffee, 'but I don't want to start speculating at this point.'

'What happens now?' Antonia asks. 'Will you arrest

him?' A look of acute pain crosses her face, as though it has only now struck her that, just a few days ago, she might have sat down to dinner with her daughter's killer.

'No, we won't do anything tonight,' Franzen assures her. He takes a sip of coffee and then puts his cup down. 'We'll need a proper statement from Rebekka, in writing, and then we'll arrange for the identification process. I'll speak with Frau Lehmholz again, of course. But right now, I can only treat this as a significant lead. We have no hard evidence that Herr Klopp had anything to do with Marie's death.'

'Yet.' Antonia's voice has regained its stiffness.

'Yet, Frau Bergmann,' Franzen says in agreement. He stands up. 'I should be going,' he says. 'It's late.'

Nina goes to get up, but Franzen shakes his head. 'Please stay where you are. I'll see myself out. Perhaps you can bring Rebekka to the station tomorrow morning, say ten o'clock?'

She nods. Her mother remains seated, staring into her cup.

'Thank you,' Franzen says, and adds, 'I hope you all manage to get some sleep. I'll see you tomorrow.'

And he leaves. Nina hears the front door closing thoughtfully behind him.

Her mother stands up and crosses the room towards the living room door. 'I'll drive Bekka home after breakfast in the morning,' she says. 'Goodnight.'

32

Sebastian and Nina are left in the room together. He's standing at the sideboard with his back to her, drink in hand, staring at or through the black of the windowpane; she's on the sofa, hunched beneath the blanket and the weight of tension that failed to leave the room with Franzen and her mother.

'We need to talk,' she hears herself say, before she has a chance to reflect on exactly what it is she needs to say. Something painful, she knows that much.

Sebastian draws a deep breath. 'Okay,' he says, still with his back to her. 'Shoot.'

A wash of misery engulfs her. She closes her eyes for a moment and finds it near impossible to open them again. 'Not now,' she murmurs. 'Tomorrow.'

She opens her eyes in time to see Sebastian spinning around. 'Why wait?' he says in a mock jovial tone. 'Let's talk now. Let's talk *all* about it.'

As he speaks, he waves his glass around in his hand; a few amber drops escape and begin to soak into the rug.

'No, Basti, please, I'm tired. We need to go home. Kai might wake up.'

Sebastian takes a few unsteady steps forward. 'You know

what, Nina. This is killing me. This –' He stops a couple of feet in front of her and waves his glass around again, in an exaggerated circular movement, 'All this is killing me.'

She looks down at her coffee, wondering lazily if this is full-fat, semi-skimmed or skimmed milk, and realises that she is beyond caring.

'You're drunk,' she says.

Sebastian drains his glass and returns to the sideboard for a refill. 'Yeah,' he says, 'Big fucking deal.'

Nina gets to her feet. When she removes the blanket from her shoulders, it's as though she has stepped naked into a meat locker; her body heat, which was so cosily trapped beneath the layer of the cashmere throw, escapes into the air in a single inexorable wave; the hairs on her arms shoot upwards as if electrified; she feels her nipples contracting.

'I'm going home,' she says, squeezing out the words before her teeth start chattering.

Sebastian turns to look at her. 'You do that,' he says. 'To be honest, I'm out of ideas. I'm sick of trying. I don't know what to do anymore. My guess is you're enjoying your self-pity. Looks to me like you don't want my help at all.'

She swallows, although her mouth and throat are so dry it is almost painful. 'What did you expect?' she says. 'That I'd have a good cry and forget all about her? Visit her grave once a year with some fresh flowers? Go on like nothing's happened, or, perhaps not quite nothing, but just some minor annoyance? Shit happens and all that?'

'Stop it!' he yells. He thumps the sideboard with his fist, making her jump. 'You're so fucking *obsessed* with her that

314

you can't see what you're doing to us. But I point blank *refuse* to sit around and watch while you drag us all down with you. Me. The kids. Our whole fucking lives.'

'What are you saying?' She's walking along the edge of a steep cliff; she imagines falling off, plunging weightlessly through the air. The image is exquisite.

'Let me tell you about dear blessed Marie,' Sebastian says, and the set of his voice makes her want to cover her ears and scream, to drown him out, but she can't seem to move.

'That time you went to hospital to have your appendix out,' he continues. 'Marie came around to "help" with the children, remember?'

She nods slowly. A high-pitched whistling noise increases in volume in her ears.

'Picked them up?' Sebastian is saying. 'Made them fish fingers and pasta with ketchup, like I was some incompetent oaf who couldn't cook a decent meal for his own children?' He pauses; his voice is trembling slightly. '*Auntie* Marie and I shared a couple of bottles of Merlot one night, and then *Auntie* Marie unzipped my trousers and put her hand on my cock and her tongue in my ear, and I'll be honest, it wasn't unpleasant, in fact, it was very pleasant indeed, arousing you might call it, and do you know what I did, Nina? Do you?'

'You're lying,' she says slowly. Her heart is beating erratically now; she feels sick, a thick glob of nausea spreading in her gut. 'You're drunk and you're angry and you're jealous.'

'Yeah, yeah,' he almost snarls. 'I'll tell you what I did. I pushed her off me, threw her off the sofa.' He laughs – a short, angry bark. 'And she swore, and she started crying. And then she begged me, *begged* me, never to tell you. But to be honest, I knew she would be a lot more fun than you, you cold bony bitch.'

He stops talking, and an exhausted hush descends on the room. Only the whistling in Nina's ears is getting louder and louder. She wonders, vaguely, whether he hears it, too.

'I would've known,' she whispers.

'I never told you,' he says finally, 'because I knew how much it would hurt you. And whatever you might think of me, I never, ever wanted to do that.'

He takes a step forward and reaches out to touch her arm, and this contact ignites something inside her – or perhaps it simply coincides with a sudden quickening of her heart rate – but his touch stings, makes her draw her arm back and look down at it, to see if he has perhaps left a mark.

'I'm not glad she's dead,' he says. 'But I can't say I'll miss her, the selfish, spoilt little slut.'

Something inside her crumbles. She thinks it is in the region of her heart, but it can't be her heart, because she can still feel it hammering hard inside her chest.

Sebastian walks towards the sideboard. 'You have to sort yourself out, Nina. I'm serious. You need to get some help, or I'll have to take my children somewhere safe until you're better.'

'*Your* children?'

He places his glass down with a clunk. 'To be quite honest, I don't know if I can trust you around them anymore.'

Nina takes a step towards him and then stops abruptly. Her head is swimming. For a moment, she's trapped between a longing for reconciliation and the desire to hurt him as much as he is hurting her.

'I think a trial separation might be in order,' he says matter-of-factly. He's planned this speech, she realises. 'You could stay with your parents – the house is big enough. The kids and I could do with some peace.'

A desperate, frightened energy seeps through her body. She closes her eyes briefly to dispel the dizziness, then takes another step towards him.

'Let me tell you something,' she says, urgently, before she changes her mind, 'if you can stand any more of this little truth-or-dare game you seem so fond of: that conference in Zurich, seven years ago? That conference you insisted I go to, the one in fact you forced me to go to, because you said we needed time apart, to clear our heads, remember?' She can feel her upper lip curling into a snarl. 'Well, I fucked someone else. I had mind-blowing sex, lots of it, with a man who treated me with tenderness and respect.' Her voice catches on a sob, but she swallows and continues. 'And then I came back, and you pleaded with me to give us another chance. Said we owed it to Bekka to make our marriage work. Plucked at my guilt and shame and my love for my child. And then we did that obligatory making-up sex thing and three months later I still hadn't had my period and, guess what, I was pregnant –' She draws in a giant gulp of air. 'So, the moral of that story is . . . Basti dear, don't be so sure that Kai is *your* son.'

She feels the blow before Sebastian's hand makes contact

with her face; molecules of air being propelled every which way by the force of his hand; tiny reverberations that alter the stillness in the room for mere nanoseconds. As her body reels across the room, she sees her mother standing in the doorway, notices her blood-red slippers and the expensive shine of her satin dressing gown, and before she hits the floor and loses consciousness, she feels acutely and profoundly ashamed that her mother should be witness to her like this.

33

For hours now, she has been in a steady rhythm of dozing and waking, dozing and waking. She's not tired – not physically – because she has been sleeping for around twelve hours a night. Boredom-induced fatigue, she guesses. Antonia is looking after the children and brings them to visit her in hospital every day, but they're only allowed to stay for an hour.

Nina has been told it isn't good for her to lie in bed all day, that activity will accelerate her recovery, but the few times she has been up and about, wrapping her body in layers upon layers of clothes before taking short, chilly walks in the gardens, or meandering around the building until she feels sufficiently well-informed of the its geography to be able give visitors a guided tour of geriatrics, paediatrics, cardiology, oncology, radiology, intensive care and, of course, obstetrics and gynaecology, she has returned to bed feeling drained.

Yesterday, she discovered the physical therapy suite, and asked if she could use the weight machine or the treadmill, thinking this would at least give her activity some shape, some meaning, but she was told she would need another three weeks of intensive counselling and a weight gain of at least two kilos before they would allow her anywhere near physical exercise machinery.

She regained consciousness in the ambulance, waking to find an oxygen mask strapped to her face and a blood-pressure cuff on her arm, which was inflating to its fullest just as she opened her eyes. Cutting through the shrill whistling inside her head, and the discordant wail of the siren, she heard a voice; the medic:

'She's bradycardic. Blood pressure's way low. What do you know about her medical history? Medication? Allergies?'

And Hannah's voice (Hannah? Where did she come from?), close to hysterical: *'I don't know! I don't know! Frau Bergmann said she collapsed. Will she be all right?'*

And she closed her eyes again, dipped in and out of consciousness, a delicious, seductive feeling, sliding up and under, until she awoke fully in the emergency room and was forced to confess that she'd lost a lot of weight in a very short time, and was then hydrated and fed a glucose solution intravenously, and was made to have a short, tiring conversation with the on-call psychiatrist, who diagnosed the eating disorder she could have told them about if only they'd asked. The red mark on her cheek took days to fade, but perhaps it was from where the medic pushed the oxygen mask on her face.

The food is very good – buttery mashed potatoes and raspberry tiramisu are certainly not standard hospital fare. She's fully aware that each meal far exceeds the number of calories she has been granting herself on a daily basis for the past two months, but she's cooperating fully. Nina held Rebekka's hands on her last visit and saw the fear and anxiety on her daughter's face as she comprehended that her mother had been voluntarily starving herself. She promised Rebekka that she would get better – and she meant it. Kai seems less troubled; perhaps he's just too young to make sense of what's been happening, but Nina knows she'll have to keep a close eye on him. She would never be able to forgive herself if she has caused him any lasting emotional damage.

She is weighed twice daily: once in the mornings, just before breakfast and then again in the afternoon, when she travels two floors down in the lift to see Frau Dr Rossmann, the in-house psychiatrist. Dr Rossmann is surprisingly fun, with a wealth of jokes about elephants. She makes Nina laugh, and she makes Nina cry; mostly when they talk about Rebekka and Kai, but sometimes because Nina regrets not having had a therapist like Dr Rossmann twenty years ago. She doesn't cry about Marie any more.

Even so, she cries a lot, but Dr Rossmann tells her to 'go with it' when she feels upset or emotional, explaining that much like the transient depression many women face after childbirth, her weepiness is, among other things, likely due to a radical change in hormone levels that results from the re-nourishment process. Dr Rossmann encourages her to drink plenty of water, to restock her tears, if necessary. Therapy, thankfully, is a combination of chatting about life in general, and the cognitive-behavioural strategies Nina is gradually learning to implement.

She is always a little melancholic when she heads back to her room, to lie and read and watch TV and doze.

A couple of novels lie on the small white table next to her bed, and Nina is grateful to Anita who thoughtfully brought them in for her. She's also extremely grateful to Jan Steinmacher, who must have completed and returned the medical insurance form that grants her this single-occupancy room at the hospital.

She opens her eyes when she hears a gentle knock on the door. She calls, 'Come in' and there is Kommissar Franzen holding a bunch of flowers, which he gestures with, looking somewhat unsure of himself.

'I hope this isn't a bad time,' he says, standing at the door.

'No. Not at all.' Nina sits up, wondering if she should excuse herself briefly, so she can check her reflection in the bathroom mirror.

'You look ... well,' he says. 'Much better, I mean.'

She smiles. 'Thank you. Please,' she says, gesturing towards the two chairs that stand close to a small round table by the window. 'Grab a chair.'

He takes a chair and is about to pull it closer, but Nina swings her legs out of bed.

'Why don't we sit at the table?' she says, smoothing down her sweatshirt with one hand. 'It's not as though I'm bedridden or anything.'

'That's good to hear,' he says, as he takes a seat. 'Oh, these are for you,' he adds, handing her the flowers.

Nina takes them, blushing slightly. 'Thanks, I'll just –' And she goes into the bathroom cubicle, which is scrubbed and disinfected every day. She runs the tap and places the flowers in the water, then quickly brushes her hair and traces the shape of her eyebrows with a wet finger.

Franzen is staring out of the window when she comes back.

'Snow,' he says.

'Yes,' she agrees. 'I remember you mentioning that it would be a harsh winter.'

He turns to look at her. 'Did I?' Then, 'You have a good memory.'

They lapse into silence, but she doesn't mind, because she's glad of his company, however taciturn. For a while, they sit and watch the snowflakes. The light outside is acute and wintry, making the airborne snowflakes look almost dirty against the background of the pure white sky.

'There was some –' He clears his throat. 'Some disagreement over whether I should come and talk to you.'

'Oh?'

'Well, the inquiry. Some thought that these things might ... trouble you, impede your recovery. Whatever.' He looks straight at her. 'I thought you should know.'

She nods slowly. 'Okay,' she says, but she feels a surge of fear at what he might tell her.

'Last week, when Rebekka formally identified a photograph of Bernhard Klopp as the man she had seen arguing with Marie, we contacted him and requested that he appear at the police station. He didn't show up.'

Another pause. Nina wonders who these 'some' might be, who didn't think her capable of dealing with this news. But before she has time to consider it further, Franzen is speaking again.

'We went to his house, but he wasn't at home. His wife didn't know where he was, and from the state of distress she was in, we believed her. She was very cooperative, though; gave us the address of a weekend cottage they have in Brandenburg. When we got there, we discovered that Klopp had locked himself in his garage and left the engine running. We found a note.'

Nina gasps, horrified by the image that instantly recalls what happened to Thiel.

'He was unconscious, but alive. And he's made a full confession.'

She lowers her eyelids, takes some deep breaths.

'Are you all right, Dr Bergmann?' Franzen asks.

'Yes. I –' She nods, vigorously. 'Yes. I'm fine. Please go on.'

'Well, the story is that Klopp met Marie some months earlier, at a wine reception.'

'It was an awards ceremony – for poetry,' she says. 'Frau Klopp mentioned it a while back.'

'He and Marie "embarked on an affair", as he put it, during the course of which he told her that he had worked as a secret informal collaborator with the Stasi. Right up until '89.'

'*Sakoku.*'

'Sorry?'

'It's something to do with Japanese people not being allowed to leave their own country hundreds of years ago. I can't – I don't really know much more than that. But someone mentioned it at my parents' dinner party and said that Klopp had first mentioned it to him.'

Franzen tilts his head. 'I'm not sure . . .'

'I know, I'm not really making sense. It's a word, a Japanese word I first came across in Marie's writing. I thought it was someone's name.' It's hurting her to talk about, to think about it. Dr Rossmann has encouraged her to set herself a pain threshold, to let the thoughts and memories and feelings out, and the guilt – yes, the guilt, too – but not to push herself too far. That it's okay to keep things buried for as long as she needs to. But talking about it now, with Franzen, it's tolerable. The pain is there but it doesn't overwhelm her. 'Klopp must have mentioned it to Marie when she was doing research for one of her stories,' she says. 'But I should have remembered. I would have made the connection much earlier if I'd been –'

'Nothing about this is your fault,' Franzen says, his eyes on her face.

'I know. I *do* know that.' She swallows. 'Do you . . . has anyone read Klopp's file? From the Stasi, I mean?' She wants to know exactly what his role as "collaborator" involved.

Franzen shakes his head. 'He would've destroyed it as soon as the Wall fell. He had direct access to it, in his position. But he says his job was to squeeze secrets out of his targets, but using psychological, "hands-off" methods, rather than violence. Make of that what you will.'

'Hands off?' Nina says, her breathing rapid. 'He beat my sister to a pulp.'

'His words. I'm sorry, I don't mean to upset you.' He pauses, as if allowing them both time to absorb the hurt. 'Marie told him she wanted to write a book about it, that his story had "inspired" her. He'd thought it was true love – as he put it – up until that point, which is why he confided in her in the first place. He thought that by giving her money – in fact, it was more than we found in her account; she'd obviously spent quite a bit of it – he thought she'd drop the story, or maybe he imagined she'd stay with him. I don't know. But she broke it off. What Rebekka witnessed, in the bar, was the first of many arguments. The final one, well, he claims he lost control. And again,' he raises his palms towards her, 'those are not the words I would choose to describe what he did to your sister.'

She looks out of the window for a long moment, knowing he will be patient, will let her take her time. Outside, two floors down, she sees a young man struggling to fold a pram into the back of his car. In his effort, he exhales large clouds of white. Still looking out of the window, she forces herself to ask, 'And her baby?'

'He wasn't aware she was pregnant,' Franzen says, 'but we know now that the DNA matches.'

The room tilts around her, as though she were out at sea. If Marie had lived, this brutal, duplicitous man would have been the father of her baby. The baby she seemed to want so badly, the baby who never had a chance. Nina didn't think she could feel any more sadness, but she was wrong. Grief, like love, is boundless, she understands that now.

For a long time, she can't speak. At least, it seems like a long time, but she's lost her ability to distinguish between one moment and the next. She blinks, notices the light

326

has begun to drain from the sky outside. When she next speaks, she isn't sure Franzen is even still in the room.

'Will he be well enough to stand trial?'

Franzen is still there. 'Most certainly. He has minor lung damage, but he should make a full recovery, according to the doctors. So, yes, he will stand trial for murder.'

Nina lets out a long breath. She doesn't want to think about the trial. She starts to tremble, as though the air in the room has suddenly dropped to below zero. Franzen reaches out and puts a hand on her arm.

'It's likely to be tough,' he says, with genuine concern. 'You should make sure you have someone to support you through it.'

Nina looks down at his hand, his perfectly shaped nails, and realises he has stilled her whole body with his touch. She waits a moment, then says, 'Dr Rossmann, the psychiatrist here, she's been great.'

Franzen clears his throat. 'I can put you in touch with a liaison officer, if you like. We offered this to your parents at the start of the investigation, as next of kin, but they declined, and . . .' His eyes slide to the floor, apologetically.

'I would appreciate that. Thank you.'

He raises his head and smiles. 'And how long will you be –?'

'Another two weeks. Then they're sending me to a treatment centre for a month. On the Baltic coast.' She lets out a small laugh. 'The seaside. Imagine.'

'And your children?'

'They're with my mother. They're staying with her until

I get better. Then we'll –' She goes to look of the window again, but catches her reflection and turns away. She fights against tears and wins. 'My mother wants me to press charges, have his custody revoked, but it's . . . it's hard. For the children.'

'You don't owe me any explanation,' Franzen says.

'I know,' she says quietly. What she wants him to understand is that, first, she has to sift through years of her life with Sebastian. She has to figure out a different way of existing. If – and only if – she can trust him not to harm the children, she will let him back into their lives. Because they might need a father. She certainly did.

Franzen nods. He stretches out his hand and places it lightly on hers. 'I understand.' Then he gets up. 'Well, I felt it important to let you know what's happened,' he says. 'And to say goodbye.'

She looks up at him. 'Thank you,' she says. 'For coming to see me. Perhaps – perhaps you'd like to visit me again?'

'I'm afraid I'll also be away for the next month.' He gives her a genuine, wide smile. 'I'm off on my honeymoon.'

'You got married?' Nina has to work hard not to frown.

'Actually, it was several weeks ago, but I wasn't granted any leave. What with the ongoing enquiry and all. In fact,' he says, 'you saw me on my wedding day. At *Café Bilderbuch.*'

Nina blinks a few times. 'I had no idea.'

'Ayla and I – Ayla's my wife – had just come back from the registry office.'

'Oh my word.' Nina swallows. 'Congratulations.'

'Thank you.' He smiles again, and Nina sees how very

328

happy he is to talk about his new wife. 'Her family's from Istanbul. So that's where we're headed. I haven't met her parents yet, so I'm excited and a little bit terrified at the same time.' He lets out a gentle laugh. 'I just have to hope they like me.'

She laughs back, a little wearily. 'I'm sure they will.'

He holds out his hand for her to shake.

'I see you're not wearing a ring,' she can't help remarking, desperate to take her focus away from the thought that his might be their last ever meeting.

'I'm allergic to metal on the skin,' he responds. 'Except for platinum, and my police salary doesn't stretch to that.'

*

July, 2019

The flame of the candle was perfectly still. Nina took a sip of wine and glanced out across the street. From here, on the second floor of Marie's balcony, she could see into the park on Boxhagener Platz. Wisps of smoke from illegal barbeques drifted into the sky. The air was balmy, and the happy drunken laughs and shouts coming from the park fit the mellow summer mood perfectly. She felt more relaxed than she had in ages. In fact, she felt as though she could stay sitting here forever.

'I spoke to Bekka the other day,' Marie said. 'She wants to sleep over, while the school holidays are still on.'

'Have you two been making secret plans or something?' Nina said and boxed her sister playfully on the arm. Despite Sebastian's misgivings, Nina was pleased that Bekka and Marie got along so well. The relationship brought out the best in both of them, she thought.

Marie grinned. Her lips were stained bluish from the Beaujolais. 'Everyone's entitled to a secret or two.'

Nina boxed her again. 'Ha! Not on my watch.'

Marie opened her eyes wide in mock pain and rubbed her arm. Then she glanced at Nina with a half-smile on her face. 'No, I guess not,' she said, and refilled their glasses.

Nina tipped her head back and closed her eyes. The droning bass from a neighbour's stereo reverberated in the pit of her stomach. It felt good, soothing. When she opened her eyes again, Marie was looking at her intently.

'What?' Nina asked with a smile.

Marie's eyes flitted to the side and then back, like she was deciding something. Then she said, tentatively, 'You remember when you and Sebastian were separated?'

Nina blinked, taken aback by such an unexpected question. 'What are you talking about?'

'You know, years ago. Bekka was still in kindergarten.'

Nina frowned. 'We weren't separated. We were ... we were taking a break. Things were –' She gestured in the air with her hands, then stopped and looked at Marie. 'Why are you bringing this up? Has this got something to do with Robert? Did he –?'

Marie shook her head. 'No, nothing like that. I was just ...' She lifted a shoulder, then took a sip of wine. 'You never talked about it, that's all.'

'There was nothing to talk about. We weren't getting on, we took a break, we got back together. That's all.' She was struggling to hide her irritation. Moments earlier, she had felt so relaxed, and now this. Marie often said whatever was on her mind, without reflecting on how it might be received. Usually, Nina found Marie's candour refreshing and open-hearted, but at times it was too close to the bone. It's true she'd never talked to Marie about this – one of the few things she had never shared – but it was an episode best left in the past.

Marie was still looking at her.

'Like I said,' Nina said dryly, 'there was nothing to talk about.'

Marie lit another cigarette, ignoring her sister's tone. 'Was he screwing around?'

'What?' Nina gasped. 'No! Where's this coming from? Sebastian's not the type.'

'They're all the type.' Marie let out a little snort. 'If you ask me.'

'Nobody asked you,' Nina snapped.

Marie's face fell. She stubbed out her cigarette, causing crumbs of burning tobacco to jump out of the ashtray. 'Oh, Nina, I'm sorry!' She leaned forward and squeezed her sister's knee, giving her a lopsided smile. 'Me and my big mouth, eh?'

Nina sighed. She wasn't in the mood to hold on to her anger, and it hadn't been Marie's intention to upset her. 'No worries,' she said. 'Sorry I snapped at you.'

In the distance, church bells struck out eleven.

Nina straightened up. 'Shit. I'd better be off.'

Marie stuck her bottom lip out. 'It's not even midnight!' she needled. 'Who are you, Cinderella?'

'I wish,' Nina said. 'No. Bekka's got a piano recital tomorrow at nine and I promised I'd drive her.'

Marie gave her a sloppy kiss on the cheek and breathed in Nina's scent. 'What is that, tea tree and argan shampoo? You're such a yummy mummy, you know that?'

'Hardly,' Nina replied, smiling. She picked up her handbag.

'I mean it, though,' Marie said, her voice warm. 'You're a great mum, really.'

'And you're a great sister,' Nina said, slinging her bag over her shoulder, hoping it wouldn't take too long to hail a taxi on the street below, 'but this mum says it's time for bed. I'll call you tomorrow.'

34

Sometimes the horizon frightens her.

When the weather is nice, when – despite the freezing December air – the sky is clear and full of the white, early winter sun, the beach becomes an outdoor sanatorium: wicker *Strandkörbe* and striped deckchairs and thick blankets and nylon windbreakers litter the beach, covering the sections of grey sand that haven't been appropriated by the grassy mounds of washed-up seaweed. Asthmatic children and rheumatic geriatrics and stick-thin teenagers and the occasional, apparently affliction-free middle-aged couple; they all burst forth from the indoor confines of their respective rehabilitation clinics, and the beach becomes a wheezing, scratching, coughing, deep-breathing version of its yelping, frolicking, skinny-dipping summer counterpart. And Nina joins them, more often than not, because the salty, silty air gives her an appetite, and she needs as much of that as she can get.

But she prefers the beach on days like today, when the clouds are solid and black and menacing, and the pewter sea doesn't pretend to be your friend, but instead jumps and lunges towards the shore, baring its teeth and showing off its savage potential – *don't mess with me*. On days like these, she feels comforted that she is here, not out there. But when she looks far out to the line of darker grey that marks the horizon, where, from a distance, everything seems calm and peaceful although, in reality, it's just as savage and threatening as the sea close up, she understands that it is just a matter of perspective. And this frightens her.

Nina is by far the oldest patient at the eating disorder clinic – older, in fact, than many of the nurses – but this doesn't bother her. Indeed, joint meals and group therapy sessions with some of the girls whose teeth are rotten with hydrochloric acid, girls with jaundiced, translucent skin and unnaturally large eyes, provide her with a sense of unspoken privilege, that she will be well and home a long time before most of them. She will have survived.

She speaks on the telephone with her mother every day for news of the children. Apparently – and she's not sure of the details – her mother and Sebastian have reached some kind of agreement, whereby Antonia picks up the children from school, takes them to her house, feeds them, helps with homework, and then drives them (reluctantly, Nina imagines) to Sebastian for an hour before bedtime. Their conversations are tentative, but tender. Her mother doesn't ask for any information that Nina doesn't offer voluntarily, which, however, increases in detail every time they talk.

Sara emailed: 'Darling Nina, I'll cut to the chase – I'm back in Berlin for Christmas and will force-feed you goose and dumplings if that's what it takes!!! But seriously, I love you dearly and wouldn't know what to do without you. Talk to you very soon, Sx.'

Sebastian has been forwarding her mail: every four or five days, Nina receives an envelope containing letters, bills, pictures drawn by Kai, even junk mail – all of which she consumes hungrily. Each time she gets such an envelope, she opens it with a sense of apprehension, anxious that Sebastian might have included a letter of his own. It is not a path she is ready to travel yet. But so far, he hasn't.

This morning, she received a letter from Jan Steinmacher; a generous, characteristically enthusiastic letter that made Nina smile, informing her that he was in the process of wrapping up her practice, that thankfully, she would be left debt-free (though with no capital to speak of), and that his sister-in-law, a secretary at the personnel department of the Martin Luther Hospital had told him that a position as deputy head of the ob-gyn department was opening up in a few months. He's also fairly confident, although Nina treats this with caution, that given her condition, she might be able to file a claim for occupational disability insurance.

Last week, when she opened her mail she found a post-card from Turkey, picturing a beach that looked a thousand miles away from the one here: white sand, turquoise water, an artificially blue sky with a smear of cloud. On the back, in somewhat untidy handwriting, the words: 'With my kindest wishes, Alex.'

The wind darts and dips, tugging at her coat and sending hisses of sea spray in her direction. She's nervous. She has put on weight – according to the scales, she's back up to 50.1 kilos. A small, but vociferous part of her is worried by this, but if she makes it to 51 in the next two weeks, they will let her spend Christmas at home.

She turns and spots them in the distance. Two tall figures, one smaller one, looking around. Then they see her and the smaller figure lifts his hands and waves, arms outstretched, like a semaphore without the flags. Without intending to, wrapped up in her thoughts, Nina has walked several hundred metres away from the arranged meeting point, the car park situated behind two large dunes at the entrance to the beach, close to the narrow wooden pier that stretches out for what seems like miles, making you feel as though you are strolling out to sea when you venture a walk along it.

She heads in the direction of the figures, stumbling now and again as her feet attempt to get proper purchase on the sand. Kai has started running, too; head down and arms pumping as he sprints towards her, kicking up sprays of sand with every step. Behind him, Rebekka is walking at a more hesitant pace. Nina's mother remains standing between the dunes. When Kai reaches her, the force of his speed almost knocks her over, but she is strong, she keeps her balance and scoops him up, kissing his cool pink cheeks and sandy hair as though her life depends on it. She looks up and sees her daughter picking up her pace; soon, she is flying directly towards Nina, long blonde hair a wind-blown mess, crying and laughing, running with the unselfconsciousness of a much younger child. Nina lets Kai slide off her hip onto the sand and opens her arms wide for Rebekka.

Acknowledgements

Writing a novel means spending much of my time inside my own head, experiencing the joy and satisfaction of creation, but also terrible feelings of inadequacy and despair. It can be a very lonely place, so I'd like to thank everyone who has accompanied me along the way, providing generous support and encouragement. I would not be a writer without you. *Sisters of Berlin* is book number four, and contrary to (my) expectations, it doesn't get any easier!

Special thanks go to:

Super-agent Jenny Brown, to whom this novel is dedicated, for her untiring support, kindness and friendship,

Gill Tasker, for such useful feedback on a very early draft,

The entire team at Black & White Publishing, especially Emma Hargrave for her unflinching eye and judicious and insightful editing,

And to my family: Jake, Fay, Amy, June, and of course Chrissi – much love.

Juliet Conlin was born in London and grew up in England and Germany. She has an MA in Creative Writing from Lancaster University and a PhD in Psychology from the University of Durham. She works as a writer and translator and lives with her husband and four children in Berlin. Her novels include *The Fractured Man* (Cargo, 2013), *The Uncommon Life of Alfred Warner in Six Days* (Black & White Publishing, 2017) and *The Lives Before Us* (2019).

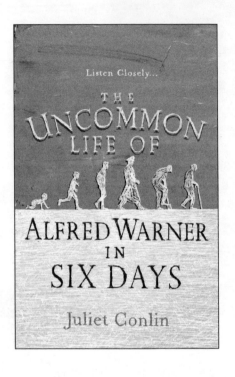

The Uncommon Life of Alfred Warner in Six Days

A tour de force of evocative storytelling set
against the backdrop of pre-Second World War
Germany and post-war Britain.

blackandwhitepublishing.com

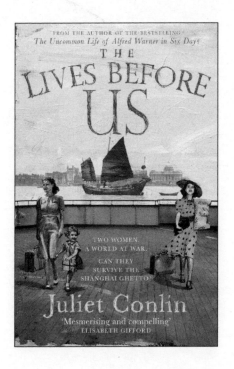

The Lives Before Us

A sweeping story of survival, community and
friendship in defiance of the worst threat to
humanity the world has ever faced.

blackandwhitepublishing.com